UNSCHOOLED

ALSO BY ALLAN WOODROW

Class Dismissed

The Pet War

UNSCHOOLED

ALLAN WOODROW

SCHOLASTIC PRESS | NEW YORK

Text copyright © 2017 by Allan Woodrow

Illustrations by Lissy Marlin

Library of Congress Cataloging-in-Publication Data

Names: Woodrow, Allan, author.
Title: Unschooled / Allan Woodrow.
Description: First edition. | New York : Scholastic Press, 2017. | Summary: Fifth graders George and Lilly are best friends, but when they end up leading separate teams competing for the Spirit Week prize, it puts a strain on their friendship, especially when the competition generates a host of nasty pranks designed to sabotage their teams—and if Principal Klein finds out what is going on Spirit Week will be canceled and everybody concerned will spend the rest of the year in detention.
Identifiers: LCCN 2016059056 | ISBN 9781338116885
Subjects: LCSH: Best friends—Juvenile fiction. | Friendship—Juvenile fiction. | Competition (Psychology)—Juvenile fiction. | Practical jokes—Juvenile fiction. | Schools—Juvenile fiction. | CYAC: Best friends—Fiction. | Friendship—Fiction. | Competition (Psychology)—Fiction. | Practical jokes—Fiction. | Schools—Fiction.
Classification: LCC PZ7.W86047 Un 2017 | DDC 813.6 [Fic]—dc23

10 9 8 7 6 5 4 3 2 1   17 18 19 20 21

Printed in the U.S.A.   23
First edition, September 2017

Book design by Yaffa Jaskoll

TO LAUREN—
YOU MAKE ME A BETTER ME . . .
BECAUSE INSTEAD OF JUST A "ME"
THERE'S A "YOU AND ME"

1
GEORGE

As we enter the school gym, the heat hits me like a steam train. I scrunch my nose to keep sweat stink from entering my nostrils. The gym is always hot, but today it feels hotter.

"Please take a seat," Mr. Foley, my teacher, instructs my class, his forehead dotted with beads of sweat. "And no running."

To my left, I see my best friend, Lilly, already sprinting past a few slower kids. I lose sight of her for a moment, but it's easy to spot her red hair and flapping ponytails.

"Lilly! Hold up!" I call out.

"You're as slow as Elvis," she teases, waiting. Elvis is her class's pet turtle, and he's so slow I bet he couldn't outrace a snail. "I am just super excited for the assembly to begin."

"As long as we're on the same team."

"Of course we'll be on the same team. Stop always being a worrywart."

"I would hate not being together . . ."

"We'll be on the same team," she insists.

We walk up the middle bleacher aisle, and Lilly sits next to Sarah and Grace. They are in Lilly's class. They both have curly hair, are dressed in identical skirts, and grumble when they need to slide over to make room for us.

"Do you think Principal Klein will announce the prize?" Lilly asks me. She wiggles on the wooden bleacher bench. She's wiry and springy and bouncy.

I blink and scratch my head. "Prize?"

Lilly looks at me like I'm an alien from another planet. "The prize! Don't tell me you forgot. The school is giving away a prize to whichever team wins Spirit Week."

I've heard about the prize, of course. Everyone has. "I think we should just play for fun," I say.

Lilly shakes her head. "Are you crazy? Playing for fun isn't fun at all."

Luke sits right above me, and he wiggles and fidgets on his seat almost as much as Lilly. "I heard the prize is ice-cream cones. All you can eat ice-cream cones forever and ever. A truck a week." Luke's leg dances up and down and his body wriggles. "Or maybe popcorn balls."

Sarah leans closer to us and shakes her head. "I heard the winning team gets to be on the front cover of *Tween Beat* magazine." She fluffs her hair. "Perfect for me."

"With a pullout poster, too," says Grace, also fluffing her hair.

"That would be awesomesauce," says Lilly, still bouncing. "But we'll hear what the prize will be soon." With her and Luke springing up and down, I'm getting seasick.

Principal Klein walks to the microphone in the center of the gym. The fifth-grade teachers stand behind him. Principal Klein clears his throat. I pull out my notebook.

"Why do you have a notebook?" asks Sarah, rolling her eyes.

"I don't think we're going to be tested on an assembly," adds Grace, also with an eye roll.

Lilly pats me on the shoulder. "George always brings a notebook." She flashes me a smile and whispers in my ear, "It's a little weird. But I like you anyway." She gives my arm a playful squeeze.

Our principal taps the microphone to make sure it's working. A big BOOM, like a thunderclap, bursts forth from the speakers and echoes through the gym.

Lilly's green eyes light up and shift back and forth, which they sometimes do when her mind is racing all over the place. "Maybe we can choose our own snacks if we win. Or maybe we'll all win jelly beans. Or phones. Or electric scooters."

"Good morning, students," says Principal Klein. A hush falls over the bleachers.

"Maybe everyone will win a puppy!" exclaims Lilly. "I've always wanted a puppy."

"I don't like puppies," says Sarah, wrinkling her nose. Grace nods in agreement.

"Please be quiet," says Principal Klein. He has a loud and commanding voice. I uncap my pen. Our principal raises his hand, motioning us to silence.

"Maybe we will win a moon rock," suggests Lilly. She is the only one speaking, but I'm not sure she notices. "I don't know what you would do with a moon rock, but that would be, like, the best prize ever."

"I need everyone quiet," says Principal Klein. He's a big man, and even though he always wears an orange cardigan sweater, he reminds me of an army general, if army generals wore orange sweaters.

The bleachers are silent. Lilly opens her mouth to speak, but then changes her mind and closes her lips. But she still bounces, and so does Luke behind me.

Principal Klein smiles and says, "I'm delighted to be here with you, fifth graders. I have some exciting news."

"I bet it's about the prize," says Lilly between bounces.

"Ssshhh," I urge with some exasperation, my finger over my mouth.

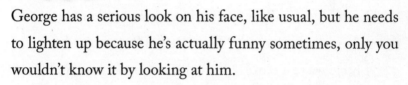

2
LILLY

George has a serious look on his face, like usual, but he needs to lighten up because he's actually funny sometimes, only you wouldn't know it by looking at him.

He furiously scribbles notes while Principal Klein speaks.

"As you know, on Monday we continue a long Liberty Falls Elementary School tradition," our principal says. "Monday marks the beginning of Spirit Week, and it's only for our fifth graders."

I let out a loud "Woo-hoo!" and a bunch of other kids yell, too. I've looked forward to this week all year, but the absolutely most amazing part of Spirit Week is Field Day. Field Day is filled with events like balloon fights and egg tosses.

Last year I snuck out of class to watch Field Day. My teacher yelled at me for sneaking out of class, and so did my parents, and so did Principal Klein.

But it was worth every yell. Field Day was awesomesauce.

"Spirit Week is about fair play," continues our principal. "It's about teamwork and friendship. It's a reward for your hard work the last five years. A celebration of sorts before you go on to Liberty Falls Middle School."

A whole bunch of cheers erupt around us. I can't wait until we start middle school next year, and I turn to George, but he's still taking notes, so I turn to high-five Sarah instead. She looks at my palm, shrugs, and then slaps my hand.

"Each of you will be assigned to participate on one of two teams," says our principal. "Team Red or Team Blue."

"I hope we're Team Red," I whisper to George. Red is my favorite color, and not just because my hair is red. Well, maybe because my hair is red, but I'm glad my hair is red, because some people have boring-colored hair and that wouldn't suit me at all.

George finally looks up from his notebook. "As long as we're on the same team, I don't care what color I am." His teacher is Mr. Foley and mine is Mrs. Crawford. Every year their classes are on the same team.

This school year is the first time George and I have not had the same teacher. Last summer, when I found out we were going to be in different classes, I was so mad I almost made a giant sign that read UNFAIR CLASS ASSIGNMENTS!

I was going to march in front of the school with it, but Mom wouldn't let me.

I was also going to make a giant frown-y face out of clay. I'm pretty good at making things out of clay. It calms me. I can also hold my breath for forty-two seconds, which is a pretty long time.

But it's been a long year without George sitting next to me in class. At least we'll be together during Spirit Week.

Principal Klein continues. "As most of you know, each team wins points based on a different contest every day, culminating with Friday's Field Day. Field Day is worth half your team's points. In the past, we've played just for fun. But we're doing something new this year. At the end of the week, the team with the most points will win a special prize."

Almost everyone in the bleachers starts talking at once. I begin bouncing in my seat again because sometimes my legs just have to bounce. Behind me, Luke says, "I bet everyone wins an ant farm."

"A kitten!" shouts Jessie, who sits in front of me. "Wouldn't that just be incredible if everyone won a kitten?"

"No," says Sarah, while rolling her eyes. "I don't like kittens."

"Me neither," adds Grace.

Maggie, who sits in front of George, turns around and grins and straightens her glasses. "Maybe we'll win a trip to the new science center that opened up downtown."

"If the prize is a trip to the science center, I don't want to win," says Sarah.

"I don't like science centers," says Grace.

"Well, if I want to get into Harvard someday, I have to really know my science," says Maggie, ignoring Sarah and Grace's frowns. "Going to Harvard is sort of a family tradition. My great-great-great-uncle was one of the first African Americans to ever graduate from there."

Maggie is the smartest kid in our school. I bet she'd make a great teacher someday. She'd probably make a great teacher now! She's in Mrs. Rosenbloom's class, and even though she's new, I hear she's pretty nice.

Everyone talks and argues about the mystery prize, and Principal Klein has to say "Please settle down" and raise his hands a bunch of times before we quiet.

"What's the prize?" yells someone from across the bleachers.

"It's a surprise," answers Principal Klein. "The prize will be revealed at the end of the competition."

Probably half the kids in the bleachers groan. I do.

Our principal continues. "This year, Mrs. Crawford's and Mrs. Greeley's classes will be on Team Red, while the students from Mr. Foley's and Mrs. Rosenbloom's classes will be on Team Blue."

My mouth falls open and all bouncing leaves my legs. George and I are on different teams? Every time I've ever thought about Spirit Week—and I've thought about it a zillion times—I've always pictured George and me side by side, passing eggs or tossing water balloons together.

George's smile falls, too. "It'll still be fun," he says, but he doesn't sound like he means it.

"We need a volunteer from each team to lead their team to victory," announces Principal Klein. "Who wants to lead Team Red?"

Despite my disappointment, both my hands immediately shoot up as if pulled by invisible strings. Being a team leader wasn't something I had planned, but planning is overrated. Sometimes you just have to do what you have to do, and I do want to win the mystery prize, whatever it is.

Principal Klein looks right at me. "Okay, then. The Team Red captain will be Lilly Bloch."

"Yes!" I exclaim, and George looks up quickly enough to exchange my hand slap.

I just know I'll be the most fantastic team captain ever, because I hardly ever lose at anything. I was only in Adventure Scouts for one year, but I sold more cookies than anyone, and

I've won 228 straight games of tic-tac-toe against George. That has to be some sort of world record.

My team will win by so many points that the school will probably build a statue of me, or name the gym after me, or something like that.

"Congratulations," says George.

I grin and grin and my cheeks hurt, I grin so hard. "I wonder if the team captain gets an extra prize? Like, if everyone got a puppy, maybe I'd get two puppies. Or two lifetime supplies of ice-cream cones."

"I doubt it. But being a team captain is a lot of work," George cautions, wearing his Mr. Serious look. It's a look he sometimes has when he thinks I'm not thinking, and I know he means well, but I can think perfectly well without his help. Most of the time anyway. "It takes organization to lead a team. And note taking. And arranging things."

I laugh and look at his notebook. "Maybe you should be team leader, then. You've got the note-taking thing down."

Then Principal Klein asks, "And who wants to be the Team Blue captain?"

George actually looks like he's thinking about it, but Maggie's hand quickly pops up.

"Thank you, Maggie Cranberry," says Principal Klein. "Why don't our two team captains come down and get their team leader pins?"

I jump out of my seat as if my legs are on springs. I practically leap into the aisle, ready to head down the bleachers.

I don't know what that special prize is, but I know it will be extra, extra awesomesauce and that no one is going to stop me from winning.

3

GEORGE

As Lilly leaps from her seat, I wonder if she knows what she's getting herself into. Leading a team takes a lot of responsibility and planning. Lilly's not very good at that sort of thing. She never has a number two pencil for tests, and she hardly ever brings an umbrella on rainy days. Last year she lost her math textbook twice.

But I'm excited for her as she hops into the aisle.

"We'll crush Team Blue!" Grace yells. She has this low, gravelly voice that sounds as if it should come out of a bigger person.

"Of course we will. Losing is for losers," Sarah says, and she and Grace wrap their pinkies together and exchange a firm pinkie shake.

Lilly looks back at Sarah and Grace, grinning. She isn't watching where she is going.

Maggie slips past the final person in her row, stepping into the aisle just as Lilly steps down.

Lilly's foot hits Maggie's leg. Maggie cries out and starts to fall. So does Lilly.

Lilly's arms wave as she tries to keep her balance. One of those arms smacks into Maggie's head. Lilly's other foot steps on Maggie's foot. Lilly's shoulder slams into Maggie's chest.

Both of their arms wave up and down, but unless they can flap and fly away like birds, none of that arm waving is going to do them any good. They both tumble backward. Maggie squeaks, "Help!"

Lilly screams, "Oh no!"

I yell, "Someone catch them!"

But it's too late. As Maggie topples over, her glasses fly off her face and her body teeters toward the ground. Lilly's legs twist around Maggie's legs. Maggie hits the wooden floor of the bleachers first. Lilly lands directly on top of Maggie.

Everyone gasps.

"Ow, my arm," cries Maggie.

"Ow, my everything," groans Lilly.

Lilly slowly eases herself off Maggie and stretches her arms and legs. She seems to be unhurt, but Maggie lingers on the ground, moaning.

"Sorry," says Lilly. "I'm so, so sorry," she repeats. She looks horrified as Maggie sits up, cradling her arm and yelping. The yelps remind me of a dog, like the ones I've seen in cages at the pet store hoping to be noticed and let out.

Mrs. Bigelow, our school nurse, marches up the stairs with a determined look of purpose. She kneels down next to Maggie. The nurse gingerly touches Maggie's arm, and Maggie lets out another yowl.

"I think it's broken, dear," Mrs. Bigelow says to Maggie.

Maggie yelps even louder, over and over again. She most definitely sounds like a caged dog.

Lilly stands frozen to her spot, a look of guilt across her face.

Mrs. Bigelow helps Maggie to her feet, and they walk slowly down the aisle, picking up Maggie's glasses as they go. Tears drip down Maggie's cheeks, although her yelping has stopped. Soon, both she and our nurse are out of the gym, but everyone remains silent.

"Winning Spirit Week just got easier," says Sarah, breaking the quiet. She has a small, cruel smile on her lips.

Grace smiles, too.

Lilly still stands in the aisle. "That was an accident, I swear." She bites her lip and tugs on her ponytail.

Sarah and Grace shake their heads as if they don't quite believe her.

"I hope Maggie is okay," our principal says worriedly. He

speaks so loudly that his voice booms across the gym even without the microphone. But then he leans into the mic and his voice grows even louder. "I'm sure we will all keep Maggie in our thoughts." He looks down at his feet as if unsure what to do, but then he clears his throat and continues. "Unfortunately, we will need a new captain to step up and lead Team Blue. Does anyone else want to be Team Blue captain?"

I'm still thinking of Maggie and her yelping, and I feel terrible for her. I raise my hand.

I instantly regret raising it, but Maggie will take over as our team captain when she gets back to school, hopefully on Monday. As Lilly said, I'm good at taking notes. I can fill Maggie in on everything as soon as she's recovered.

"George Martinez. Terrific," says Principal Klein. "Why don't you and Lilly head down the bleachers?" He pauses and then adds, "And, please, please be careful."

I exit the aisle. Lilly waits patiently and even lends me her arm so I don't stumble getting out of my row. She squeezes my arm as she leans into my ear and whispers, "It looks like we're enemies now." She says this with a smile, so it's a joke, I think.

"Yep, that's us—enemies forever." I laugh as we step down the aisle together. "Just remember: Winning is about organization and planning."

Lilly laughs. "It's called Spirit Week, not Organizing and Boring Week. And no one can out-spirit me."

A few kids cheer as we step onto the gym floor and approach Principal Klein. I'm not sure if they cheer because we are captains, or because we walked down the bleachers without falling. I hate standing here, with everyone's eyes on me, but I focus on our principal and try to ignore the bleachers. He holds two shiny badges. They look sort of like police badges, except made of cheap bronze-colored plastic.

"These were the only pins they had at the store," Principal Klein mumbles to us as an apology of sorts. My team leader pin features a picture of a goldfish with the words I LOVE GOLDFISH! underneath it.

"Congratulations, George," says Mr. Foley.

I throw him a smile and a thumbs-up. "I'm sure it'll be fun."

"That's the spirit!" says Mr. Foley.

After we pin our badges to our chests, Principal Klein steps up to the microphone again. "Spirit Week begins on Monday with our first official contest: Twin Day. Everyone should pick a teammate and dress in identical clothing. The team with the most and best matches will get five points. I'll personally judge Twin Day on Monday morning right here in the gym." He clears his throat, smiles at Lilly and me, and adds, "Just remember, the week is about spirit and teamwork. Let's compete with good sportsmanship. I'm sure you'll make Liberty Falls Elementary proud."

Nearly every kid in the bleachers applauds, but I notice Sarah and Grace do not. They whisper to each other, quietly huddling, as if they are passing secrets.

"Good luck," I say to Lilly.

She grins back to me. "You bet."

But I notice that she doesn't wish me good luck back.

As we join the rest of our grade in exiting the gym, Lilly hurries ahead of me and reaches Sarah and Grace. The three of them walk off with their arms around one another's shoulders, and I get an uneasy feeling about them.

I don't want to compete against Lilly and secretive Sarah and Grace. I regret volunteering to be team captain even more.

4
LILLY

Mrs. Martinez pats her lips with her napkin, which she does after every bite. George does the exact same thing, even when eating in the lunchroom, which used to drive me batty, but now I just giggle.

We have dinner with the Martinez family every Friday and sometimes we eat at my house and sometimes we eat at George's house and sometimes we meet at a restaurant. Restaurant nights are my favorite Friday night dinners, especially if they let George and me pick where we go, because George always lets me pick.

But tonight dinner is at my house, and I hate that because Mom makes me clean up my stuff first, and it's not easy picking up an entire week's worth of clothes and junk from every room. I usually cram everything into my closet.

We host more dinners than the Martinezes host dinners,

and I'm pretty sure it's because Mom likes me cleaning up stuff. Thankfully, she never looks in my closet.

"I hear you are both Spirit Week captains," George's dad says. Mr. Martinez always wears a tie because he works in an office, unlike my dad who works out of our house. George looks a lot like his dad. They both have the same dark eyebrows and tan skin and they both look serious all the time. I think George will wear a tie every day when he's older.

"Hard to believe." George beams. "I didn't really want to be captain. But someone needed to step up, at least until Maggie is back."

"We're proud of you," says his mom. "It's not easy being a team captain, even for only a day or two. It's a lot of responsibility."

"And we're proud of you, Lilly," says my mom. When I got home from school and told her the news, she gushed and hugged me and acted like it was a really big deal.

She flashes me a smaller smile now. Mom isn't the sort to fuss over me in front of other people.

To George I say, "You guys don't have a chance."

"We'll see," says George in his serious tone. "It's all about organization, you know."

I shake my head. "It's all about winning."

"Well, I hope it's a tie," interrupts Mr. Martinez.

"Amen to that," says my dad. "I'm sure you'll both be great leaders, and you'll have a lot of fun no matter who wins."

"Just remember you two are best friends," adds my mom.

Moms say the weirdest things sometimes. "Why would we forget that?" I ask.

"Competition can bring out the ugliness in people," says Mr. Martinez, frowning.

All the parents nod their heads, and my mom looks right at me. She keeps her stare fixed on me.

"What now?" I ask.

"Remember Adventure Scouts a few years ago, and your cookie sales?" Mom takes a bite of her lasagna, but she continues to watch me.

"Sure, I sold more cookies . . ."

"You stole Francine Pepper's list of cookie sales," says Mom. "That's how you sold so many cookies."

"I didn't steal it!" I insist. "She gave it to me."

"Because you promised you'd be her best friend."

"I was her best friend for a whole week, so I kept my promise," I retort with a frown. So I like to win? Who doesn't? "I even earned enough points for a free sleeping bag."

"I just know how you can be sometimes," Mom says.

"It would take a lot more than Spirit Week to break this

team." I motion to George and me. "Team George and Lilly is way more important than Team Red or Team Blue."

"I'm glad to hear that," says Dad.

"Just remember that friendship is forever and the silly Spirit Week is only a week," adds Mom.

"It's not silly," I say. "There's a giant prize this year for the winning team, and it's probably better than an Adventure Scouts sleeping bag. Principal Klein won't say what the prize is, but I hear it's something like a trip to Hawaii. And don't you want me to win a trip to Hawaii?"

Dad laughs. "I don't think the school could afford to send half the grade to Hawaii."

"Well, I'm sure it will still be a great prize," I say. I wish Spirit Week started right then. I'd prove to everyone that my team is unbeatable and show my parents what a fantastic prize we all get. "My team is going to win, and win big." I glare at George.

"Stop it, Lilly," says Mom.

I break my stare and remind myself that the week is just for fun. I laugh at myself. Maybe I can be a little competitive, but like Sarah said, losing is for losers. I dig into my lasagna again. Mom still watches me as if she's worried I'm going to do something terrible, but a little competition won't get in the way of my friendship with George. We've been best friends since before I can remember anything. My parents even have pictures of us sleeping next to each other as babies.

In each photo, I'm lying in the middle with all the stuffed animals while George is curled off to the side. If we ever fought over the stuffed animals, then I won every time.

5
GEORGE

Lilly's bedspread is a confusing maze of pink diamonds and green swirls. Her walls are bright blue and her carpet is orange. I always get a headache if I stare at the carpet too long. But I can't see that much of it anyway, because her floor is usually covered with clothes and books and random things like a stuffed bear and a shoebox. I grit my teeth as I look at everything that's out of place. I want to walk around and clean it all up.

This is why I never spend much time in Lilly's bedroom. I always feel like screaming at the mess. Once I made the mistake of opening her closet. It's all empty hangers and balled-up clothes on the floor. I offered to help her organize all her clothes, and even started to diagram a special area for sweaters, but she wasn't interested.

Her dresser and shelves are lined with small clay figurines of all sorts, including a guitar without a neck, a ballet dancer with only one leg, a soccer player with no arms, and a unicorn without legs. Lilly isn't great at finishing things, although she loves making things out of clay.

I have a miniature U.S. Capitol building in my bedroom that she made for me last year. The bottom half looks just like the real U.S. Capitol. It doesn't have a top half though, and that's sort of the most important half.

On the floor by my feet is a deck of cards. Lilly and I used to play all the time, but we played Go Fish a few weeks ago and I won by accident, because I usually let her win, and she hasn't wanted to play since.

She's not a good loser. One time she bought two Hula-Hoops, and it turned out I was really good and Lilly wasn't. She threw the Hula-Hoops away the next day.

"It's right here," Lilly says, digging through her sock drawer. "At least I think it's here." She tosses socks around the room, which just adds more mess. I wonder how she can find anything in such a disorganized disaster of a room.

"Oh, I've got them," she says at last. I think the drawer is now empty of all socks. She holds out two bracelets made of interwoven green, red, and blue string. She hands one to me. "A friendship bracelet."

"What's that?"

"We each wear one. It means we're best friends. Forever."

"I don't need a bracelet to know that." But I tie it on my wrist. Lilly does the same. I throw her a big grin. "Thanks. It's pretty great."

"Just like me," says Lilly, but with a playful smile. "Mom bought me a kit, and I started them a few weeks ago, but then I think we had dinner and I put them away and sort of forgot. But anyway, here they are." She beams.

As I look at the bracelet hugging my wrist, I forget all about Lilly's glare at dinner. I just hope Maggie is feeling better. Our parents might have been excited that we are both captains, but I'm not. I think it's more fun to take notes than to give them. I've been taking plenty of notes for Maggie. I'll pass them to her when she's back at school, hopefully on Monday.

"And don't worry about the stupid Spirit Week and us being captains," Lilly says, as if reading my mind. "It would take more than a contest to break us apart." She throws me a smile, and it's a warm smile, one that I can feel deep down in my stomach all the way up my chest and down my arm where my new bracelet is wrapped snugly. "But that doesn't mean I don't want to win."

"I think we'll give your team a run for your money," I say with a smile.

"You can try, but we're not going to lose," Lilly adds, but she is not smiling. "And I'll do anything to win." She glares at me, the same glare from dinner. But then she breaks the glare and giggles. "I'm just goofing around."

But I honestly can't tell if she's totally goofing around or not.

6
LILLY

I don't know why George feels his team has a chance to beat my team this week. He seems to think I can't even organize my lunch.

Which, by the way, I did today all by myself—a cheese sandwich and some cookies and a bag of chips. I forgot the fruit, but so what? Fruit is overrated.

On Friday, Principal Klein gave George and me a list of the events planned for the week so we could prepare, and I read it over during the weekend, or at least I read most of it because I was busy doing other stuff. Mom bought me some new clay and I made a totally incredible penguin, except I didn't finish its beak or feet. But otherwise it looks exactly like a penguin, sort of.

Today, Monday, is Twin Day, and Team Red has this contest wrapped up like a cozy blanket. Because it turns out that

I'm an organizing queen, even if George doesn't think I am. Saturday morning I called Sarah, and she was going to text Grace, who was going to text a few other people, and then Aisha volunteered to call a few kids from class, and so I'm sure someone reminded everyone, somehow.

There is no way Team Blue can match our matches.

Aisha and I are twins today. It wasn't easy figuring out what clothes made sense, since she wears sweat pants and team jerseys almost every day and I don't play sports like she does. But we both have red sweaters, so we wore those and that's perfect because we're Team Red. I own two of the same scarves, because I thought I lost mine last year but I found it under my bed after Mom had already bought me a new one, so we're wearing those, too. Aisha also bought two silly straw hats at the party store yesterday.

I haven't seen Aisha yet this morning, but she came over to my house last night and we swapped clothes. We will look fantastic together.

It feels a little weird being Aisha's twin, since I always thought George and I would be twins today. He has these goofy orange beanies, and I figured we could wear those, and we were going to buy matching shirts, but you can't be twins with some-one from the other team, obviously.

Mom dropped me off early at school today. Every Monday morning I eat breakfast at school because she has to leave early for work, and George comes early, too, because his mom and my mom work together. As soon as I enter the cafeteria, I look for George.

I can't wait to see his face when he realizes Twin Day is Team Red day, but I don't feel quite as confident after I look around.

It's like I'm seeing double, and not just Team Red double, because every fifth grader I see has a twin. Two lunch ladies are dressed alike, too. They wear pirate hats and eye patches.

My stomach sinks. I should have known Team Blue would be ready. If I'm an organizing queen, George is like the note-taking and organizing king of the universe.

Noah says the special prize is a road trip to the Grand Canyon. Aisha says that's not true, that the winning team gets to go to a soccer game, or a baseball game, or a track meet, or some sort of sporting event but she can't remember what.

Either way, we would miss school, so we have to win. If we go to the Grand Canyon, I'll spend my entire time writing postcards to George, bragging about how great our team was and that I'm having the best time ever.

Well, maybe that would be a little mean. I'll end every postcard with a big *I miss you!* and a smiley face because I would miss having my best friend with me.

I pay for my orange juice, oatmeal, milk, and a banana. I thank the lunch lady, who says, "Arrrr you sure that's all you want?" in a pirate growl. I tell her that I'm sure, and then I look around for George.

He's sitting with Luke at a table in the middle of the room. They both wear extra-large yellow shirts with George's goofy orange beanies.

I feel a twinge of hurt. That was supposed to be me in the orange beanie and not Luke. Part of me wants to ignore George because the beanies were my idea in the first place. But I look down at my wrist and see my friendship bracelet. Friendship is way more important than beanies, and Team George and Lilly is more important than anything.

Of course I know that already, but the bracelet is a nice reminder.

I'll walk over to George, wish him good luck, congratulate him on his great organizing skills—and of course mention how mine are just as good—and then we'll eat breakfast together. There's no reason today shouldn't be like every other Monday. Just thinking of sitting with George makes me feel good.

Grace waves to me, walking over. She wears giant plastic glasses and a red T-shirt that says TEAM RED IS FABULICIOUS! and in smaller letters TEAM BLUE STINKS! "Sarah and I made these last night."

"Awesomesauce," I say.

She points to a table in the far corner of the lunchroom, which is where she usually eats. "Let's sit over there and have breakfast. Sarah and I were talking while we made these shirts last night. We have some ideas on how we can win."

"Like what?" I ask.

"I can't tell you here." She looks right and left, and then left and right, and then she whispers, "Someone might be listening."

"Listening to what?"

"Secrets." She fluffs her hair and smirks.

George sees me and waves, and I smile back. Grace has never asked me to eat breakfast with her before. She and Sarah usually eat by themselves, and it would be nice to eat with her and hear about her secret plans. But I guess they can wait until later. "I'm going to sit with George. I always do."

"But he's on Team Blue," Grace says with a look of horror spreading across her face.

"He's just George." I weave past a group of third graders to join my best friend. "Hey, George," I call out. "Nice out—"

I never say *fit* as in *outfit*, which is what I wanted to say. George stands up as I approach him, and I guess I'm not expecting him to stand up, so I stutter-step, and I don't know where that leg came from, but my foot hits someone's leg.

My lunch tray flies up. I reach for it, but instead I knock the tray and make it flip completely over.

I see the tray turn and spin and flip like it's in slow motion, but like a slow-motion horror movie.

My orange juice soars into the air as if spouting from a water fountain. My oatmeal forms a gray, flying, lumpy cloud. My milk spins from its cup like a sort of mini-tornado.

I can see where everything is going to land before it does.

Everything is going to land on George.

SPLAT!

The oatmeal bowl ends up oatmeal-side down, right on George's head, on top of his orange beanie.

SPLASH!

The juice completely drenches his shirt.

SPLOOSH!

The milk sprays his shoulders.

Oatmeal skids down his face and liquid drips from his shirt.

"Oh no!" I say. The entire cafeteria stares at us in silence. I know how George hates messes, and he's just a giant mess. He stands there, in shock. "I'm so sorry!"

Then I hear someone clap and Grace call out, "That's the way to do it, Lilly!"

7
GEORGE

"Now where is that box? Oh, there it is." After a moment of thinking, Mrs. Frank, our school secretary, drags a large cardboard box from the corner of the walk-in storage closet. The shelves of the room are filled with envelopes and pencils and binders and lots and lots of paper. I've never seen so much paper. Mrs. Frank breathes heavily as she pulls the box to the middle of the floor. Her gray-hair bun sways back and forth. "Take what you need. You can change in the bathroom."

My shirt and pants stick to me with wet, cold orange juice. Big clods of half-dried oatmeal fall in flakes from my head to the floor. I smell like someone's stale and rotten breakfast. My orange beanie is ruined, too.

I washed some of the mess off in the bathroom, but a lot of Lilly's breakfast still clings to me. The small bottle of hand sanitizer I keep in my pocket wasn't helpful, either. You can't hand-sanitize your clothes and your hair and your entire body.

Mrs. Frank called my mom, but she's at work and can't get away yet. So I'm forced to change into clothes from the dreaded Lost and Found box.

I sift through clothing that has probably been here for decades. The box is filled with single sneakers, unmatched and random socks, an assortment of old jeans, a purple bathing suit, seven flannel shirts, and lots and lots of winter hats and mittens.

There is one boot, three pairs of underwear, and a belt. Who loses underwear? The even bigger question: Who loses their pants?

I picture someone walking home without pants. I hope it wasn't cold that day. I shiver thinking about it, although the cold orange juice in my underwear isn't keeping me warm, either.

The only shirt that sort of fits me is a green T-shirt that reads PANDA-MONIUM! It has a picture of a smiling panda bear on it. Most of the pants are too small. I guess younger kids lose more clothes. The only pants that fit me are a pair of old jeans with big rainbow patches on the pockets and glitter down the legs. I think about keeping the pants I'm currently wearing, even though they are messy and wet.

In the end, dry clothes with rainbow patches and glitter win. But I wouldn't be surprised if the person who wore these pants lost them on purpose.

I stuff my wet clothes into a garbage bag to bring home later and then exit the bathroom.

Luke looks bummed out when he sees me walk out into the hall. He taps his feet and wiggles his body like usual. It's like he's always listening to music in his head. But there is no happiness in his wiggles today.

"Sorry," I say. "This stinks."

"If there is another panda shirt in the Lost and Found box, I can wear the other one. We can still match." We spent half the morning on Saturday finding just the right shirts.

"No such luck."

"Great!" he replies. I throw him a frown. "I mean, it's not great that we don't match, and I have nothing against pandas, but that shirt . . ." Then he adds in a quiet, apologetic tone, "But on you it looks good." He looks me up and down. "And I sort of like the pants."

I frown. "They have rainbow patches and glitter on them."

"I like rainbows." I'm not sure if he's kidding or not.

"Let's just get to the gym," I say with a grumble. "I hope I haven't let Maggie down. But at least she can take over as team captain." I've had enough of leading a team. Being drenched in breakfast is about all I can handle.

"Didn't you hear? Maggie broke her arm in two places. She might be out all week." Suddenly, my borrowed clothes feel ten times heavier. "You're our team captain for keeps."

I groan. I don't think today could get worse. School hasn't even started yet, and not only am I wearing the world's most embarrassing clothes, but I have to march into the gym wearing them as our team captain.

I knew I never should have raised my hand in the auditorium. I could make a list of everything I know about leading a team, but I can't think of anything to put on it.

I'm glad we don't see anyone as we walk down the hall and toward the gym. I glance at my reflection in the glass trophy case that hangs on the wall.

I still have some oatmeal crusties clinging to my hair. I swat them off.

We turn the corner and the gymnasium is straight ahead. A few kids laugh when they see me. I want to hide. Hiding would really be the best thing to do, but I'm team captain now and I need to stay and support us. Team captains don't hide.

Brian and Seth stand against the wall. They are both in Mrs. Rosenbloom's class, which means they are on my team. When they see me, Seth giggles. "Nice pants."

Brian doesn't laugh. He sneers. He looks angry. Brian and Seth are the two biggest kids in our school. They are the meanest kids, too.

They are dressed in shoulder pads, football pants, and jerseys with the name of our local sports team: the Fighting Bells. They are football twins.

"We heard what Lilly did," growls Brian.

"I can't believe she would sink so low," agrees Seth, no longer giggling at my pants. His angry frown now matches Brian's. Seth makes a fist and pounds it against his open palm. "We need to teach her a lesson."

"It was just an accident," I say.

"That's not what I heard," replies Brian.

"Team Red is planning all sorts of stuff," says Seth, frowning. He bares his teeth, which reminds me of an angry bear.

He and Brian are two guys you don't want to mess with. Even Luke has stopped his usual wiggling and toe-tapping, and instead slowly walks away, keeping his distance from them.

"Uh, what sort of stuff do they have planned?" I ask, slowly inching away, too.

"Stuff," says Brian. "I don't know what, but we can't let them get away with this."

There is no way Lilly would deliberately spill her breakfast on me to win Twin Day, and I doubt she would be planning something. But didn't Lilly tell me she'd do anything to win?

Lilly then said she was only kidding, but maybe she was kidding when she said she was kidding. And didn't I hear Grace clap after I was drenched?

I look down at my wrist and at the friendship bracelet that avoided the milk and orange juice spill. Best friends forever. That's what Lilly said the bracelet meant.

"We're going to get even," says Brian, frowning.

"Team Red will be sorry they messed with Team Blue," adds Seth.

I open my mouth to argue, but as Brian and Seth glare down at me, I remember that they are kids you don't want to argue against. So I just smile and nod. "Whatever you say, guys." But I'm team captain, so I add, quieter, "As long as we play fair, right?"

"If they cheat, we'll cheat," says Brian.

Seth nods. "That seems pretty fair to me. I hear everyone on the winning team gets a free bike."

"I need a new bike," says Brian, sneering with a steely, hard look.

"Bikes are nice," I agree. The two of them are whispering to each other, I can't hear what, but they are probably planning horrible things. I should say something to them. I should argue that we need to exhibit good sportsmanship. Instead, I just repeat, "Bikes are nice."

Brian ignores my comment. "Do you like slime?"

"I guess," I say, confused. "Slime is nice, and so are bikes." I don't know what I'm saying. Just talking to Brian and Seth makes me nervous.

"My older brother can make slime," Brian says.

"Good for him," I say, grinning awkwardly.

Then the school bell rings.

"Come on," says Luke. "We have to get inside the gym for the Twin Day judging. Everyone else is already sitting." As he nudges me forward he asks me, "What were those guys saying, anyway?"

"Nothing important." I follow Luke into the gym. Meanwhile, Brian and Seth's quiet but disturbing chuckles continue ringing in my ears. I look back at them, and I know I should tell them to forget whatever they are thinking of doing, but all I say is, "Bikes are really nice, aren't they?"

"I guess," agrees Luke.

I hate myself for not saying anything more. I should make a list of everything Brian and Seth could do with slime. But I don't think I want to know what they plan to do. Some lists are better left unwritten.

8
LILLY

The gym bleachers are split in half, with my team on the side closest to the front doors. That's the better side, because sometimes you can feel a slight breeze from the hallway, but not always and not today. It's as hot as ever in here.

I look for George, but I don't see him. He ran out of the cafeteria all covered in food. Poor George. I hope he's not mad at me.

Aisha is my twin, and I have to say, we look pretty great. Sarah sits on the other side of me, and her face is one giant grin. "Nicely done, Captain."

"Great job," adds Grace, nodding. Both she and Sarah fluff their hair, although I think their hair already looks pretty fluffy.

"Thanks," I say with pride. "We got the word out, didn't we? I think everyone on our team is dressed as someone's twin today."

"Sure, that too, I guess," Sarah says with a shrug.

I look at her, confused.

From the bleacher row above me, Amelia pats my back. She removes her glasses and winks. "Nice going."

"Anything to win, right?" says Grace.

"Sure, but I don't know what you guys are talking about." I cross my arms and try to ignore them.

But suddenly I know exactly what she's talking about and why everyone is congratulating me, and it has nothing to do with my planning talents. I overhear Ruby, sitting in front of me, telling Koko that Grace told her I spilled my breakfast on George on purpose.

I want to stand up to tell her and everyone that George is my best friend and I would never, ever, ever spill my breakfast on him on purpose and I told him I was sorry.

But am I the really, truly, sorry-to-my-toes kind of sorry?

Because part of me is a little glad about it. I want to win, and if accidents happen, then that is one fantastic accident for Team Red.

Principal Klein walks up and down the aisles holding a clipboard and a marker, counting twins. He looks right at me and at Aisha, and writes a big check mark.

A peal of laughter rings out from the bleachers that are closest to the front doors. George and Luke walk in, and everyone around me bursts into giggles, especially Sarah, but

I'm not sure if I should laugh or cry. George wears glittery jeans with rainbow patches on them and a weird panda shirt. Sarah elbows me in the ribs. "Best captain ever."

I don't say anything, but a big guilty ball forms in my stomach.

George refuses to look at anyone as he trudges past our side of the bleachers, his head down and his shoulders slumped. Team Red's laughter continues, louder.

Finally, George reaches the far end of the bleachers, where he sits with his team and stares at his feet.

But while my entire team laughs, I don't hear any laughter from the members of Team Blue. They throw us dirty, hostile looks. Meanwhile, Principal Klein is checking Team Blue for twins. He writes: check, check, check, check . . . He sees George and makes a mark on his clipboard that is definitely not a check, but an *X*.

Amelia pats me on the back again. "I hear the winning team gets a free milkshake machine. Wouldn't that be great?"

"Um, no," says Sarah. She glances at Amelia and shakes her head. "I don't like milkshakes."

"Me neither," agrees Grace, and Amelia's face turns red and she doesn't say anything else. "But I like smoothies. Maybe they'll give out smoothie machines."

Sarah nods. "That's a much better prize. But whatever it is, we can't lose. Not with Lilly as our captain." Sarah and

Grace exchange pinkie shakes and then flash me wide, toothy grins.

Aisha, my twin, looks at me with her eyes wide and asks, "Did you really spill your food—"

"Of course not," I insist before she even finishes her sentence. "It was an accident."

"Good," says Aisha. "Because I'd hate to win by cheating." I feel a little better knowing that at least one person believes I'm telling the truth, but I don't feel a whole lot better, because I peek another look at sad, frowning George.

Our principal finishes his count, walks down the bleachers, and makes his way toward the middle of the gym. The other fifth-grade teachers wait for him.

Principal Klein clears his throat, stares at his clipboard, and then looks up and speaks into the microphone.

"Congratulations to both teams," he announces. "I am greatly impressed by the school spirit shown here today. I have never seen so many twins. In fact, one team has everyone dressed as a twin today! That's simply incredible. Five points to Team Red."

Everyone around me jumps up and hoots. It feels good to win. No, it feels *great* to win, and I can't keep myself from bouncing up and down. But then I glance at the end of the bleachers, where George hangs his head in his ridiculous rainbow-patched pants and panda outfit. I whoop, "We won!"

but winning just doesn't feel as great as it should, and I stop bouncing.

Winning should always feel good. We're one step closer to free smoothie machines, or whatever super surprise Principal Klein will spring on us.

But.

Part of my joy floats away like a helium balloon and circles my best friend who sits alone, dejected. I've never felt bad about winning before. It's a strange feeling. I sit down while the rest of my team continues to celebrate. Meanwhile, I can feel stares from Team Blue aimed at me. They all think I'm a cheat.

Sarah leans close and whispers into my ear as if we're exchanging a big secret. "So what are you planning tomorrow? Maybe our entire team can spill food on Team Blue?"

"It was an accident," I insist.

Sarah rolls her eyes. "Fine. Don't tell me. It's probably best to keep it quiet, anyway. You never know who might blab."

She and Grace grin.

At the end of the bleachers, George no longer looks at his feet. Instead, he looks up directly at me, and his mouth is curled into an angry sneer, just like the rest of his team. Luke says something to George, and then they both glare at me.

"High five!" cries Sarah, holding her palm out for me.

I ignore it.

9
GEORGE

Mom sits on a folding chair against the wall, waiting for me at the school office with a new, clean set of clothes. I know she hates being called away from work. She frowns with an impatient fidget as I enter through the doors.

I'm sorry that she had to come to school. But I feel worse looking in the office mirror at my outfit.

When Mom sees me her expression changes from annoyance to horror. "Oh no. What did they do to you?"

"It's just clothes, Mom," I say, grabbing the plastic bag from her outstretched hand.

"But you're a glittery rainbow panda." Then she adds, "Maybe I should take a picture to show Dad?" She hunts in her handbag for her cell phone.

"Please don't," I say. "I would rather forget I ever wore this."

Mom stops her handbag poking. She puts her arm around me as if to give me a hug, but I step back. Parent hugs are fine at home but sort of weird in public, especially at school, even if it's just in front of the office staff. "Mrs. Frank told me you picked the outfit out yourself?"

"I didn't have a lot to choose from," I say. "I guess people don't lose good clothes. I think most Lost and Found clothes stay lost for a reason." I look in the plastic bag Mom handed me. Inside are stuffed normal blue jeans and a plain striped shirt. I can't wait to get them on.

Mom kisses me on the forehead, and I let her. A kiss is faster than a hug. "Well, I hope you have a better rest of your day. I suppose it's been a difficult morning."

"It can't get worse. Unless Lilly decides to ruin something else of mine."

"It was just an accident," says Mom with a warm smile. "You know that Lilly's always been a little clumsy."

Last month Lilly helped clear the dishes after dinner at my house and tripped. A spaghetti-sauce stain still splotches the ceiling of our kitchen. "I don't know, Mom. She says she'll do anything to win. And everyone says she did it on purpose."

"You can't believe that. She's your best friend."

"I don't know what to believe."

"Well, I believe in Lilly. And you should, too."

She's right, though. I shouldn't be thinking the thoughts I'm thinking. I feel awful for thinking badly of Lilly. It makes me feel dirty, and I suddenly have an urge to spurt more hand sanitizer on my palms.

A few minutes later, after I've thanked Mom and I'm in the bathroom changing out of the panda shirt and borrowed jeans, I make a decision. Next time I see Lilly, I will apologize for even imagining mean things about her.

Everyone else might think Lilly intentionally spoiled my outfit, but I know better.

Dressed in normal clothes, with the Lost and Found outfit folded neatly and put back into its cardboard box, I feel like a new person. I hurry down the hallway to the cafeteria. I've already missed the start of the fifth-grade lunch period, so I'll need to eat quickly.

I hate eating quickly. I think the ideal number of bites is fourteen for every mouthful, and you can't chew your food fourteen times, every time, if you are in a rush.

I once experimented with twelve bites for every mouthful, and it just wasn't the same.

As soon as I walk through the glass cafeteria doors, I look for my best friend. We always sit together at lunch, and I need to show her that I don't blame her for being clumsy.

But when I see her, I don't approach her.

She sits with Grace and Sarah in the far corner. Lilly never ate with them before, but now it seems like the three of them are always together. It's almost like she has two new best friends.

Lilly laughs and Sarah laughs, and maybe it's my imagination, but they seem to laugh a little too loudly, and they look like they are plotting.

I stare at them. Lilly must sense my stare, because it's easy to sense stares like that. She looks up and sees me. She smiles, but I don't smile back. I'll just stand right here, in the middle of the lunchroom, until she gets up and apologizes.

Then, maybe, we'll pretend the accident never happened, and we can have lunch together like usual.

The sooner I forget about my rainbow pants and panda shirt, the better, anyway.

Lilly starts to rise from her seat. She's about halfway up when Sarah tugs on Lilly's arm. I can't hear what Sarah says, but Lilly sits back down. I don't move, waiting. But Lilly isn't coming. She's not even looking at me anymore. She and Grace and Sarah huddle, talking. It's pretty obvious no apology is coming.

"Over here," says Luke. He waves me to his table, where he sits with Toby and a few other Team Blue kids. I sneak one last glance at Lilly, but she's forgotten me. So I join Luke and the others from my team.

Luke scoots over to make room for me on the lunch table bench. He wiggles as always, and it makes the entire table shake a little.

"Sorry about losing Twin Day," I say.

"It's not your fault," says Toby. Toby is one of the nicest kids in the fifth grade. He's always smiling—and he's got such a big smile that you can't help but smile back. Today he frowns. It's a very large frown. "We have to get even," says Toby, frowning even deeper.

"What do you mean?" I ask.

"You know. Stand up for ourselves, do something back," Toby insists. "An eye for an eye. They did something horrible to us, so we should do something horrible to them."

"If it was done on purpose, then sure," I say. "But accidents happen."

"I hear Brian and Seth like slime," says Bjorn, who is an exchange student from Sweden and has the blondest hair I've ever seen. He looks down at his phone and starts punching buttons. You're not supposed to bring phones to school, but every time I see Bjorn, he's on one or on a computer in class or the library.

"What about slime?" I ask. I think back to my conversation in the hall with Brian and Seth that morning. I get a little worried.

But Bjorn is back playing on his phone and doesn't hear me.

"What did you hear about slime?" I repeat, but Bjorn is in his own world. Someone told me he has four computers at home.

The bell rings, signaling the end of lunchtime. I haven't even started my sandwich yet, let alone had time for my fourteen chews a bite. The rest of the group stands up to leave, and I stuff a cookie into my mouth, but it's too large of a piece and I choke.

I need to know what Brian and Seth have planned, but I'm choking so I can't say a word. Everyone walks away as I spit half of the cookie into a napkin.

I take a deep breath before I stand to go. Maybe I'm worried for no reason. What's the worst thing that can happen with slime?

But Lilly spilled her breakfast on me, possibly on purpose to win Twin Day, so even if the worst thing that can happen does happen, then maybe Team Red has it coming to them. It's not like I can do anything to stop their plan from happening, anyway. I'm only team captain because Maggie broke her arm. I'm not a leader.

As everyone walks down the hall, I stop in the bathroom to wash my hands like I always do after lunch. I wonder, if I just stayed in the bathroom all day, would someone else be named team captain? Probably not, unfortunately.

10

LILLY

Everyone leaves the cafeteria to head to class, but I stay behind because I want to say something to George. My best friend! But before I can get his attention, he walks away, surrounded by members of Team Blue, who I think all hate me.

So I wait until he's completely out of the cafeteria before I leave.

At least he's no longer wearing that silly outfit. A lot of kids in our grade dressed funny for Twin Day, including me, but his outfit was the worst, and it didn't even match a twin, and that made it even worse than worst, and it was my fault. I should have apologized to him when he walked into the lunchroom, but he looked so angry, and Sarah convinced me to stay put.

He's the enemy now, and Sarah says you don't apologize to the enemy. But George and I could never be enemies in a million, billion years. Not real enemies at least, just sort of pretend ones.

As my teammates pass me, a few say "Congrats" or throw me a thumbs-up. I flash them smiles, but behind those smiles, I feel guilty because maybe I did spill my breakfast on George on purpose just like everyone says. I mean, I didn't, but deep down maybe I wanted to spill on him. Which makes me feel terrible.

That's called the subconscious, which is what makes you do or say things you don't want to do or say but you really do deep down, and then they sort of bubble up when you don't want them to.

I trudge out of the cafeteria, and the hallways are emptying as fifth graders rush to class. I pass Principal Klein and Mrs. Rosenbloom, who both stare at a glass display case filled with trophies. Kyle Anderson won a regional poetry competition last month and his trophy is inside. Our school also won some spelling bees and a robotics fair a few years ago.

I think our trophy case should be more full of stuff. They should give Team Red a trophy after we win Spirit Week and put that in the case. I can even make the trophy out of clay for them. That would be awesomesauce.

Principal Klein's loud voice is sort of hard to miss as I walk by. "Do you know I have never won a trophy?" he says to Mrs. Rosenbloom.

"No! You must have won at least one," she says.

Principal Klein shakes his head. "Sadly, no. Not even as a child. Times have changed, haven't they? Every child wins a trophy now just for participating, but back in my day they were harder to come by. It's a regret."

"You've accomplished a lot. You're principal of an entire school."

"True. But they don't make trophies for that."

"Well, they should," says Mrs. Rosenbloom, patting him on the back.

Their voices trail off as I hurry past them, but even before I push through the large swinging glass doors that separate the fifth-grade hall from the rest of the school, I hear moaning and angry shouts.

I walk into our hall and enter a scene of total horror.

Every kid stands in front of his or her locker, grimacing and wincing. Puddles of green slime surround their feet.

My locker is near the front of the hallway. I step over a puddle of murky slime and turn my locker combination. Right. Left. Right. I open my locker.

Greenish blobby liquid pours out and onto my tennis shoes.

Inside my locker is a whole bunch of green goop. My backpack is unzipped and sitting on the bottom, and I can see that it is filled with slime.

The inside of my locker door is covered with the stuff. It appears that someone poured the slime through the open grates near the top of the door, and also hit every single locker in our hallway.

Tara, whose locker is only five down from mine, cries out: "My report on cumulus clouds! Ruined! Destroyed!"

"Who did this?" demands Finn, who is the biggest kid in my class. He's probably half a foot taller than me, and I'm not short. He slams his locker in anger. He has a wide nose that reminds me of a slightly squished potato. His potato nose twitches.

We're all wondering the exact same thing: Who would pour slime into every fifth-grade locker? And why?

But then I realize that someone didn't pour slime into *every* fifth-grade locker, because the lockers at one end of the hall haven't been slimed at all.

Those are the lockers near Mrs. Rosenbloom's and Mr. Foley's classes. Those are the Team Blue lockers.

A few of the Team Blue kids wander to our side of the hallway. Some gasp, covering their mouths. Most look as horrified as I feel. But not everyone on Team Blue gasps and groans and looks wide-eyed at the catastrophe all around my feet.

Brian and Seth, two bullies I've never liked very much, stand at the end of the hallway, laughing.

"They ruined my cat posters!" howls Jessie. Jessie always talks about her cats.

"I just earned my blue belt in karate, but now it's a green belt," wails Jai, holding up a white karate outfit tinged with green splotches.

George pushes through the doors into our hall. I don't know where he's been, but he takes one look at the horror show that is our hallway and his mouth drops open.

But I'm not buying his act. This is a Team Blue act of sabotage, and he's the Team Blue captain, so there is no way he didn't know about this plan. I slam my locker and stride toward him. "You think this is funny?" I demand.

"Why . . . what . . . when . . ." His eyes roam the hall-way, back and forth, in a look of total shock. "Who did this?"

But my eyes just narrow, and I poke him in the shoulder as hard as I can. "As if you don't know who slimed us."

"Hey!" He steps back and rubs his shoulder, but his eyes remain gazing on the puddles of green muck and the shocked faces of my teammates. "Someone did this to every locker?"

"No," I hiss. "Just every Team Red locker." I can feel the anger building inside me. "If you want to play dirty, we can play dirty," I warn.

Finn marches toward us. His face is bright red. Sarah and Grace approach, too, their faces twisted in rage.

Other kids are approaching us as well. Sarah stomps closer. Grace looks furious. Even Aisha, who is normally so calm, looks like she wants to scream.

"B-But I didn't . . ." George sees everyone approaching, the same as I do. He doesn't finish the sentence. He sprints down the hallway toward the safety of the Team Blue locker side.

When he reaches the end of the hallway, a few members of his team let out a loud, "Hooray, George!"

I hear it, and so do Sarah and Grace and Finn and the rest of my team.

While Team Blue clasps George on the shoulder, welcoming their hero, I look into the angry eyes of my team members.

"If they want war, we'll give them one," says Sarah.

"We need to do something," agrees Grace. "Something terrible."

I feel a shiver up my back. "The best revenge will be winning Spirit Week, and winning the prize."

"I hear the prize is a free helicopter ride," says Finn.

"I don't like helicopters," says Sarah.

"Me neither," says Grace.

Finn frowns. "I don't like them, either, I guess."

"Whatever it is, I want to win it," says Sarah. "And if winning Spirit Week is the best revenge, then I know just the way to do it. You guys with me?"

"I am," I say, and I wrap my pinkie around Sarah's and Grace's. We all squeeze.

11
GEORGE

I hope today is a better day than yesterday, because yesterday was the worst day of my life. I don't know why I raised my hand to be team captain in the first place.

I wish I could take it back, but you can't take back things like that.

When I volunteered I never thought I would have to hide in my classroom until school was over. But that's exactly what I did yesterday. Everyone on Team Red looked so angry in the hallway, glaring at me and thinking all sorts of terrible thoughts. I know they blame me for locker sliming, even though I didn't do a thing.

Mr. Foley was nice to let me linger in the classroom after the bell rang. I told him I wanted to finish some schoolwork.

I didn't walk home with Lilly, which was strange. We always walk home together.

I hate being team captain.

I haven't even talked to Lilly since she yelled at me in the hallway yesterday. I still can't believe that she thought I had anything to do with the locker incident. How could she imagine I had something to do with that awful prank?

I push open the doors to the fifth-grade hallway and am surrounded by red shirts. At the end of the hallway, everyone wears blue shirts.

Last night I texted half my team to remind them of Color Wars Day, and instructed each person to call another person. I created a spreadsheet on my mom's computer to make sure not one kid was forgotten. I even brought two blue shirts to school today, just in case someone forgot to wear one.

I might hate being team captain, but I still have to try my hardest to be a good one.

I don't think I needed to do so much planning, though. All the breakfast spilling and locker sliming seems to have made everyone determined to win. No one wants to be the team member that costs us victory.

The hallway floor is still slightly stained with green. It might be that way for a while. Lilly stands by her locker, her bright red shirt almost matching her bright red hair. I smile and raise my hand to greet her, and even start walking toward her until I remember that we aren't speaking.

I suppose when you do something every day, like talk to your best friend, it's hard to remember not to do it. I lower my hand, turn my smile to a frown, and veer away at the last moment. She sees me though. I grunt at her. It's not a friendly grunt but just a grunt. She grunts back and then takes a step away from her locker and trips. Her shoelaces are untied.

Lilly sprawls forward, her arms waving like she's doing the dog paddle before regaining her balance. As my mom said, Lilly's always been a bit clumsy. Is she clumsy enough to spill her breakfast on me, or clumsy like a fox, using her clumsiness to get away with ruining my Twin Day clothes on purpose?

I guess I can't be completely sure of anything, except it figures Lilly would walk around with her shoelaces untied.

I always double knot my shoelaces so they can't come untied. I have a list of things I need to do in the morning, like floss. Double knotting my shoelaces is the eighth thing on my list.

I hurry down the hall to my locker. I don't feel safe surrounded by so many red shirts, and feel relieved when I blend in with a sea of blue. The exchange student, Bjorn, looks up from his phone and smiles at me. "Nice job yesterday. Or as we say in Sweden, *Snyggt gjort.*"

"But I really didn't do anything . . ."

Before I can get more words out, Adam, who is in Mrs. Rosenbloom's class, steps between us. He hands me a small yellow lollipop. "I stole this from the office," he says. "Well, not stole. They are free. I was going to give it to Lizzie, but I forgot she doesn't like lemon."

"Um, thanks," I say, accepting his gift.

Kyle, who is also in Mrs. Rosenbloom's class, slaps me on the back. Kyle is a big guy, so his slap sort of hurts and takes away my breath for a moment. His hair is almost as red as Lilly's and he's almost as big as Brian and Seth. He smiles, and when he speaks it's in sort of a half rap: "Great thinking, pouring that sticky slime. But make it extra goopy next time."

A bunch of other kids slap me on the back or just shout stuff like, "You're the man, George!"

Luke rushes over when he sees me. "Did you really do that? I mean, those guys on Team Red were so mad." He jumps up and down with excitement, like he's on a pogo stick or has springs in his shoes.

"I had nothing to do with that," I insist.

"Everyone says you did."

"I didn't."

"Well, okay. That's good, then. It was sort of a rotten thing to do, I guess. As long as you didn't do it." But he says it in a sort of *I don't believe you* way, before dancing off to his locker.

I want to shout at the top of my lungs after him: "It wasn't me! I didn't do a thing! It was Brian and Seth!"

But I don't say that. Because I see Brian and Seth huddled by Seth's locker, laughing. Brian looks at me and puts his finger to his lips, like we plotted the sliming together and it's our secret to keep.

I know what I should do. I should run to Principal Klein and explain what happened. It's my responsibility as team captain to keep my team under control.

Did I mention that I hate being team captain?

But Brian is big, and Seth is big, and I'm not so big, and I guess I don't have any proof they did anything. You sort of need proof to accuse people of really bad things like locker sliming.

A lump forms in my throat, and my feet feel cemented to the ground. Brian and Seth walk by me and I say, "I like bikes." I don't know why I say that, but I just do, with a goofy smile on my face that I wish I could erase.

Maybe I'll talk to them later about things.

As they brush by me and I simply stand there without moving, Samantha slinks up to me. She wears a royal-blue cashmere sweater with matching blue shoes and a blue headband. They are all the exact same shade. She flips her blond hair over her shoulder. "That sliming was pure genius," she says. "Let me know if you need any help with anything. I'd be happy to give you some free fashion advice sometime. You just have to ask." She looks at me, starting at my feet and going up to my head. "Like, you could use new shoes and a different haircut." She leans over closely. "I hear the special prize for winning Spirit Week is matching handbags for everyone. Wouldn't that be the best?"

I don't know what I would do with a matching handbag.

Before I can say anything about it, Samantha has already turned away to go to class.

My thoughts are interrupted by the squawk of the PA system. Principal Klein's voice is always loud, but over the loudspeaker it sounds like the voice of doom soaring through the school corridors. "This is Principal Klein. Will George Martinez report to my office? Immediately."

I hope he just wants a meeting with the Team Blue captain to congratulate me for my wonderful organizing talents. Maybe he wants to see my Color Wars spreadsheet. Or maybe he will declare yesterday a tie, because he knows Lilly spilled her breakfast on me, on purpose.

But he sounds angry, even over the PA, and my heart quickly sinks as I plod down the hall toward the office.

My teammates watch me, shaking their heads. "Go, Team Blue!" shouts Toby in encouragement, raising his fist in some sort of military salute.

A few people clap. "Stay strong, George!" Luke calls.

But as I walk past the Team Red lockers, the Team Blue claps are replaced by icy Team Red stares. This is how criminals must feel when they march into court, or maybe to jail. Every step takes me closer to the judge. It's a long walk.

As I exit the fifth-grade hall, a group of second graders point at me, whispering to one another. Even they think I'm guilty. Word spreads fast.

When I arrive at the school office, I'm relieved a police officer isn't standing there, waiting to arrest me. Mrs. Frank frowns at me from behind the front desk. She lowers her eyeglasses and shakes her head. Without a word she merely points to Principal Klein's door, which is slightly ajar behind her. I nod, approach the door, and knock before stepping inside. Only bad kids are sent to the principal's office, so does this mean I'm one of the bad kids?

The office is smaller than I thought it would be. I've always imagined a lush, giant room with expensive paintings and fancy statues. But the room is cramped, and our principal sits on a large leather chair behind a wooden desk that takes up half the floor space. He clears his throat, clasps his hands atop his desk, and nods toward the chair facing his desk. "Sit." I do.

We lock eyes, and it takes all my willpower to stay seated rather than run away in terror. He has a mess of pens on his desk, and in the silence I pick some up and put them inside a jar that holds even more pens.

"Don't touch the pens," orders Principal Klein.

"Sorry," I mumble. "They were, um, messy."

"That's not the mess you need to clean up." His eyes peer into mine as he drums his fingers on his desk.

"My room at home is clean," I mutter. "So I don't have a mess to clean up, at home I mean." I smile, as if I made a joke, but this isn't the kind of situation where a joke is appropriate, and it wasn't even really a joke, so I just bite my lip and say nothing else.

"Do you think putting slime into lockers is funny?" He asks this in a tone that implies he definitely does not think that is funny.

"No, sir," I answer. It feels appropriate to call him sir rather than Principal Klein.

"Do you think it's okay to destroy homework and lunches and other things that people keep in their lockers . . ." He pauses and I wait for him to continue. "Like jars."

"What kind of jars?" I ask. I wonder if I'm strange for not having any jars in my locker.

"Well, okay, not jars," says Principal Klein, coughing. "Never mind that. But the homework and lunches, those are in lockers." Principal Klein stares at me, his face a stone of sternness. "Fortunately, the slime washed off most of the clothing and backpacks. But some personal property was still ruined."

"It's awful, sir."

"Beyond awful. I wonder what sort of student would do something so horrible."

I sit up straight. "I had nothing to do with it, sir. I promise you."

He raises an eyebrow. "Didn't you?"

"No, sir. Absolutely not, sir."

"Because it seems odd that only Team Red lockers were slimed. It appears someone on Team Blue did this."

"I guess it would seem that way."

"And you're the team captain."

"Well, only because Maggie broke her arm. I mean, I was just the second team captain, not the first one, right? So it doesn't count as much?"

Our principal frowns. "It still counts."

I look down at my team captain badge, pinned to my chest. Even though it reads I LOVE GOLDFISH!, it represents a lot more than fish. It represents fair play and leadership. It means I made a commitment. "I know it does, sir. You're right, of course, sir," I say, keeping my head bowed. "And I'm sickened by what was done. Really."

"I see." I look up to see him staring at me, deeply staring, as if trying to peer into my brain and pluck the truth from inside my head. He sniffs, as if he's smelled innocence. "But you know who did it?"

I do, at least I'm almost positive I do, but almost positive isn't the same as completely positive. And even if I were completely positive, I know I wouldn't say anything. You don't rat on teammates who can beat you up with one hand tied behind their backs. So I shake my head. "No, sir. I have no idea, sir."

I immediately feel guilty for saying that, but then I think of Brian and Seth and their hugeness.

Principal Klein removes the pens from his pen cup, the ones I placed inside, and lays them on the table, so they are messy again. It seems to make him happy. I really, really want to stuff them back in the cup. I sit on my hands to keep them from cleaning. "Spirit Week is not about slime. Or even about competition."

"It's not about competition, sir?" I ask, blinking.

"Well, a little about competition, yes," he admits. He stands up and begins to pace. There are only a few feet of space behind his desk, so he can only take one or two steps before turning around and taking two more steps. I get a little dizzy watching him. "Competition, sure. But it's called Spirit Week because it's about spirit. Teamwork. About banding together for a common goal."

"Then why do you have two teams compete against each other?" I ask. "If it's not about competition, I mean."

"Because games bring out the spirit in you!" exclaims Principal Klein, stopping his pacing and jutting his fist in the air. He points at me. "I don't want any more hijinks, you understand me? Even if it wasn't you, it was someone on your team. This week is about fun. Have fun, and make sure the rest of your team has fun. Got it?" But there is no fun in Principal Klein's voice.

"We will have fun, sir. Good fun," I squeak.

"If there are any further problems, there will be consequences. Severe consequences. For your team and for you."

"Yes, sir. Thank you, sir. I won't let you down, sir."

"Then we'll see you and your team out on the field after lunchtime for Color Wars."

"Thank you, sir."

As I excuse myself from his office, my hands shake. Because I know he is right. Spirit Week is about fun competition, not mean-spirited competition. I need to keep my team in line. It's my job. I'm our team captain, even if I wish I weren't, and I have my goldfish-lover badge to prove it.

Sure, Lilly might be up to some tricks. I wouldn't put it past her to be planning something with Sarah and Grace right now. But the only way to show her, and everyone, that clean competition is the best competition is by winning Spirit Week. And Team Blue is going to win, and win fairly.

At least I hope everyone on my team plays fairly, because I just don't know if they will, and I really don't know how I can stop it.

12
LILLY

When you're the leader of a team you need to get everyone motivated. Last night I was going to make small clay frogs for all of Team Red. There's an animal called the red poison dart frog that's bright red and poisonous. I thought it could be our mascot, which would be awesomesauce.

But by the time I finished my research, it was sort of late and it would take a long time to make that many frogs and I only had so much clay, so I only made three of them, and I never got around to giving them legs or painting them red, so I left them at home. Maybe I'll finish them tonight. I asked Mom to buy a lot more clay, just in case.

But we don't really need motivation to win, anyway. Not today. Sarah had a great idea that should guarantee us another victory.

It's after lunch, and both teams stand outside in the large field behind the school. Hardly anyone ever comes out here, although there's a whole crew who waters and mows it at least once a week. That seems like a waste of time, just like cleaning my room is a waste of time, since it's just going to be dirty again, probably within minutes. But the field is great for Spirit Week. White lines have been laid down with chalk on the grass, forming a large rectangular court. There are two sides, separated by a line in the middle. My team is on one side, and Team Blue is on the other.

A large bucket of balloons sits near our back line. Our balloons are red and filled with chocolate pudding, and another bucket of balloons lies on the opposite side of the field. Those blue balloons are supposed to be filled with vanilla pudding.

Everyone wears a garbage bag, with holes for our head and arms. Still, this will get wonderfully messy. I know how George hates to get messy, and I feel bad for him, but then I remember the sliming and I don't feel so bad for him anymore. I remind myself that losing is for losers.

On the opposite side of the field, behind Team Blue's back line, Principal Klein stands with Ms. Bryce. They both wear garbage bags, too. Ms. Bryce used to teach fifth grade, but that's a whole other story.

She and our principal will decide who wins today's event by determining which team is least covered with pudding, so if there is more chocolate pudding splattered, we win.

There is no way we're going to lose.

But this day is going to be fantastic for another reason, too. I love pudding! If a few pudding drops fly into my mouth, it will be like an extra bonus treat. I start to bounce on my toes just thinking of winning and eating pudding.

Aisha approaches me. "What's the plan, Captain?"

I blink and stop my toe bouncing. "The plan?"

"Right," says Aisha. "The strategy. How are we going to beat them? Do we all throw balloons at the same time? Do we scatter? Do we form a giant wall?"

"Don't worry," I assure her. "Just throw your balloons as fast as you can. I can guarantee you we're going to win."

Aisha frowns. "What do you mean?"

"Trust me."

I look at the other side of the field, where George stands with his team. He walks up and down, arranging kids this way and that way. Knowing George, he probably spent hours mapping out a strategy for today. That would be just like him.

Well, it was a waste of time.

"I'm ready," says Finn, his mouth frowning with grim determination. "They slimed us yesterday, and we're going to pudding them today."

"We're going to *extra* pudding them," says Pete. He looks like a shorter version of Finn. They both wear angry scowls.

"I'll be like a cat. Fierce and quick and mean," says Jessie. "Well, not mean. Cuddly. Cats are cuddly. But I'll be quick and catlike."

Many of my teammates stand near us now, watching me. I guess they expect me to announce some big strategy.

I do have a strategy. Revenge. "We've got this won, easy. No worries."

"It's fabulicious," Sarah agrees, and holds out her pinkie for me to shake it. I do.

Sarah and Grace say playing fair is for losers. That's true. If I had played fair and hadn't been Francine Pepper's best friend for a week, I would never have won a free Adventure Scouts sleeping bag.

Mom says I should feel bad about winning that sleeping bag, but it was really Francine's fault for giving me all her cookie sales so she could be my best friend. Well, that and maybe because I told her that if she was my best friend, I would let her ride my pet unicorn.

My entire team is listening. George might have better organizing talents than me, but being a team captain is about a lot more than organizing. "Guys, just go out there and throw those balloons as hard and straight as you can. I promise that at the end of the day, we'll show those Team Blue slimers they can't mess with Team Red. We will win. We will be victorious." I smile because *victorious* is a pretty great word to use. "We are Team Red!"

Everyone starts shouting, "We are Team Red! We are Team Red!" I join the cry. "We are Team Red!"

Tara lets loose a howl.

But Aisha lingers a second and glares at me. I ignore it. Glares don't win free trips to the moon, or whatever prize we're winning. I just hope we don't win Adventure Scouts sleeping bags. Mine broke the first time I used it, so it wasn't even worth all that fuss with Francine Pepper.

As we break up the huddle to grab our balloons, my stomach feels a little queasy. Because as much as I want to win and as much as I want to hate George and blame him for the sliming incident, I know deep down, as far deep as anything can go, that George didn't do anything. Not him.

On the other side of the field, Team Blue is ready. George stands stiffly in the very back corner of his square. He has no idea what's about to happen.

My team shouts, "We are Team Red!"

I echo their shout, but not as loudly as I should. "We are Team Red."

Sarah and Grace laugh.

I just wish I didn't feel so guilty for what's about to happen.

13

GEORGE

Each member of our team holds a balloon. So does every member of Team Red. I studied battle formations from great wars in history, and I think I have my team ready. Those who can throw farthest are in the back, like archers. My fastest members are up front, where they can dodge and dart.

Team Red kids just stand around, clumped randomly. It's obvious they have no organization.

I'm happy with my strategy, and I'm even happier about what I'm wearing. I put on some old jeans and a T-shirt and a pair of swimming goggles. I don't want to ruin good clothes with pudding stains or get any food in my eyes. Even though I'm wearing a garbage bag, it won't keep all the pudding off me.

I'll need to keep my mouth closed, too. There is no way I want to get pudding in my mouth.

I brought a brand-new bottle of hand sanitizer for today.

Last year's fifth graders were covered head to toe in pudding after Color Wars. I once heard a rumor that a kid was so covered in chocolate pudding that his teammates accidentally ate him. I don't think it really happened, but you can never be too sure about that sort of thing.

While I'm dressed for pudding, not everyone is as prepared as me. Samantha stands only a few feet away in her cashmere sweater. I don't think she'll be very happy if pudding gets under her garbage bag.

"Remember," shouts Principal Klein. "No stepping out of bounds or over the midline. After all the balloons are thrown, Ms. Bryce and I will determine which team is more pudding-drenched. If we see more chocolate pudding covering fifth graders, then Team Red wins, and if there is more vanilla pudding, then Team Blue will be declared the winner. You will start and stop on her whistle. And remember, there is absolutely no throwing at anyone's head."

Brian and Seth stand next to me. They are in the back, because they can throw far, and I'm in the back so I can study the field and make last-second adjustments, and so I don't get dirty. Brian and Seth each cradle three balloons. They wear extra-wide smiles on their faces.

"Remember the plan," I instruct them. "Aim at their best throwers first. Once we hit them, the rest of the group will be easier targets."

"I'm just aiming for heads," says Brian.

"Most definitely heads," agrees Seth.

I should probably demand they drop their balloons and refuse to let them play if they don't play by the rules, but instead I just smile and nod. "Heads. Right. Great," I mumble.

Before I can say anything else stupid, Ms. Bryce blows her whistle. And the balloons fly.

Dozens of red and blue globes fill the sky. The sounds of splattering rubber surround me.

"Hey!" yells Lacey as a giant lake of chocolate pudding smothers her chest.

"Yuck!" yells Avery, another pudding victim.

A balloon lands right by my feet and another narrowly misses my face. Red balloons crash all over the field, covering the ground and my teammates, and at least one hits Principal Klein, standing behind me.

I hear him yell, "Oh no! There go my slacks."

Chocolate is everywhere. I toss my balloon, not aiming at anyone in particular and just hoping it hits something red. I don't see it land.

I had a plan, but it is obvious no one is following it. Kids in the back run to the front, and those in the front cower in the back. My teammates toss their balloons as randomly as I did. Seth and Brian seem oblivious to the destruction, hurling balloons as fast and as hard as they can, each wearing large grins.

But although we're drenched in chocolate pudding, the Team Red side is in much worse shape. I watch one of Brian's balloons as it sails toward Lilly on the other side. The balloon is on target, down, down, down. She doesn't see it, but I watch the entire arc.

It smashes into her stomach and douses her with a big stain of chocolate pudding, some flying onto her face. She smiles as she licks chocolate pudding off her lips.

Wait. She's licking chocolate pudding?

But our balloons are supposed to be filled with vanilla pudding.

That's when I realize what I should have realized immediately. Not only is my team covered with splotches of chocolate pudding. All the garbage bags worn by Team Red drip with chocolate pudding, too.

A balloon flies over my head and toward Principal Klein. He sidesteps but crashes into Ms. Bryce. The balloon explodes onto their garbage bags.

Below me, the field is a wet, sticky marsh of brown pudding. Principal Klein shouts, "Stop! Wait!" but I can barely hear him over the yells of my teammates. Seth and Brian continue to hurl balloons in groups of three or four each.

A balloon smashes into my shoulder. It stings for a split second, but then the pain is gone and all that lingers is a puddle of chocolate pudding dripping down my chest and onto the bottom of my old jeans.

"Stop!" yells Principal Klein again. "I said stop!" Ms. Bryce blows her whistle, and a few more balloons soar into the air. They fall harmlessly except for one balloon, one final heave from Seth that rises and then falls and splatters on Lilly's head.

Lilly is already so full of pudding that she looks more like a swamp pudding monster than my best friend. At least I think we're still best friends.

Ms. Bryce's whistle shrieks again. Everyone stares at her and our principal. No more balloons fly.

I can barely see the grass at my feet. It's as if we are all in some shallow chocolate-pudding lake. The ground is muddy and brown and sort of disgusting.

I want nothing more than to take a bath and change my clothes. I fish my hand sanitizer from my back pocket and give my hands a great big squirt. But I would need a few gallons of sanitizer to wash all the muck off me.

By now, I think everyone has noticed there is no vanilla pudding anywhere. I hear Luke say, "Does this mean we lose?"

I suspect sabotage.

Principal Klein and Ms. Bryce huddle together. They are close enough that I can hear their conversation. But then, Principal Klein never speaks softly. They both seem to be as confused as I am.

"I thought half the balloons were supposed to be filled with vanilla pudding," says Ms. Bryce.

"Yes, of course," agrees Principal Klein. "That was the plan. There appears to have been a mistake."

"Do you think so? I mean, technically Team Red wins. More chocolate pudding covers kids than vanilla pudding."

"Yes, I guess Team Red wins," answers Principal Klein. But then he shakes his head. "Well, no. We can hardly call it a fair victory, can we? I believe Grace and Sarah were supposed to fill the balloons. Maybe they just lost track of the pudding."

"Yes, it was an accident," agrees Ms. Bryce.

"It has to be," says our principal.

But I don't buy it. Not for a moment. Sarah and Grace are no accidents, and I wouldn't be surprised if Lilly was in on the whole thing from the start.

Our principal walks into the Color Wars court. He trudges carefully, but he's a big guy and his feet sink into the murk with every step. Pudding splashes onto his pant cuffs. His voice booms across the pudding-pond field. "It seems there has been a dreadful pudding error today. Obviously, we cannot declare a winner. We will call today a tie."

A dozen moans fly from our side, but even more moans echo from Team Red.

"That's not fair!" yells Sarah from the other side of the field. She practically growls, and both Grace and Lilly's faces appear just as angry.

Principal Klein ignores the comment. "Please file into the school where clean towels await. We will resume Spirit Week with our next contest tomorrow."

"A tie?" grumbles Brian. "We had this thing won."

"By a mile," agrees Seth.

On the other side of the field, Lilly shouts, "Since today doesn't count, does that mean Team Red is still ahead?"

Principal Klein frowns but calls back, "I suppose it does."

A few Team Red members let out a cheer, as if their cheating victory yesterday is all that matters.

I can't help but notice Lilly exchanging high fives with Sarah and Grace. I stare at Lilly's broad smile gleaming from within her chocolate-smeared head. She runs her finger across her pudding-caked cheek and then plunges her finger into her mouth.

Sarah and Grace grin madly.

"They're a bunch of cheats," says Brian. "They knew we

would win. That's why they messed around with our balloons."

"Of course they did," agrees Seth.

"We need to get revenge," says Brian. "Spread the word. Lilly's a cheater. That whole team is filled with cheaters."

I want to argue that playing fairly is the only way to play, but it's hard to think about that when it's obvious Team Red will do anything to win. So I just smile and nod and bite my lip. Team Red is filled with cheaters, and the proof is in the pudding.

Maybe I should just let Brian and Seth do what they need to do. Brian probably should have been team captain and not me.

14
LILLY

George stands at the edge of the sidewalk that leads from the entrance of our school. I think he's waiting for me, but I decide to walk past him without saying a word, because I know if I say anything, it will probably be something mean.

We've walked home together every day since first grade, not including yesterday, because I think he was hiding after the sliming-locker trouble.

I haven't said a word to him all day today, and I've never gone a whole day without speaking to George, at least none that I can remember, except when I went off to camp, and even then I wrote to him.

Still, I march past him. Maybe I feel a little guilty for agreeing to the pudding plot. I didn't actually fill the puddings, but I knew about it and I agreed to it. I know losing is for losers and everything, like Sarah says, but maybe winning is not only for winners, not always.

"Nice way to cheat today," says George.

I can feel my face go red. I turn to him, and I can't keep the words in my mouth. I know they are mean, and I know they are unfair, but I think it's my subconscious acting up again, or my guilt, or both.

"Only one team can lose, and it won't be us," I reply. George opens his mouth to say something back, but I don't let him. "And you're the one who poured slime into our lockers. You told everyone I spilled food on you on purpose. So don't you dare say anything about our pudding."

George holds his hands up as if he's surrendering, while stepping back. "I didn't do any of that. I didn't slime. And I didn't tell anyone you spilled food on me on purpose."

"You are such a liar!" I exclaim.

George stops retreating and stands up straight. Now he's the one who looks angry. "I am not a liar!" he shouts back at me. I don't think I've ever seen George yell. He looks sort of mean when he raises his voice. "You're the one that ruined my Twin Day outfit. You started everything."

"And I'm glad I did!"

"So you admit it? You admit you ruined my outfit on purpose?"

"I don't admit anything except knowing your team deserves whatever is coming to it."

I'm not sure I believe what I'm saying. I don't really want

to say any of these things, and I feel guilty for cheating, but I'm so worked up I can't stop what I'm saying from flying out of my mouth. It feels good to see George shocked. If we're going to have an argument, then I want to win it.

"It stinks you were slimed, but at least we haven't cheated," says George. "You need to start playing fairly or . . ."

I cut him off. "Or what? We both know what you and your team did. And we both know what you're doing and what you're thinking of doing, and none of it's any good, and you pretending you're not doing anything just makes it all worse."

"You're the one who says you'll do anything to win."

"At least I'm not the one crying about fair play." I continue to stare and fume. I think about the mystery prize for the week, which may mean being mayor for the day, or we get to be in a movie, or something else just as great, and I want to win whatever it is more than anything. "I don't even know why we were friends to begin with."

George's face falls. He takes a small step back. "You don't know why we're friends?" he asks, sputtering. "But—we've been best friends forever."

"Maybe I don't need a best friend anymore."

I hate those words. I don't feel them, and it's as if someone else is saying them, and it's someone I don't like, and it's the same person who agreed that all the balloons should be filled with chocolate pudding today.

But the words come from me, even if they don't feel like they are, and even if I can't stop them from reaching George's ears.

"Fine, maybe you're right," he grumbles.

I want to take back what I said, but I want even more for him to take back what he said. Only it's too late, and now he's puffed out his chest and mine is puffed out and we're staring at each other, our faces only inches apart.

I could hug him. I could put my arms around him and apologize. That's all it would take, really. A hug and an *I'm sorry.*

But I don't do any of that, because all I can hear are the words *losing is for losers* over and over again in my head.

George rips something off his wrist. It's the friendship bracelet I gave him. He holds it in his left hand, the threads torn, the strands waving in the wind. "I guess I don't need this anymore, then." He throws the bracelet to the ground.

A gust of wind blows the ripped bracelet into a bush next to us, wrapping around small brown thorns, half hidden in the greenery. I look up at George.

This whole argument is my fault. I have said too much. I'm clumsy and I ruined his outfit and never apologized, and then it's all gone downhill from there. But I can't even see straight, because my eyes are watery and my anger is steaming and my guilt is swimming and, well, I feel about a million different things tugging me this way and that way.

So I turn away, not saying a thing, leaving George behind me, and I walk home alone for the second straight day.

George doesn't follow me.

I grip the friendship bracelet I'm wearing on my wrist and try to rip it off like George did, but I can't. Mine is knotted tighter and the anger has seeped from my body. I barely have the strength to walk. I untie the bracelet strands, which isn't easy to do while walking, and it takes the better part of two blocks to untangle the knot, and by then I'm already near the street that leads to my neighborhood. I chuck my bracelet into a sewer grate on the side of the curb.

My wrist feels bare, but maybe it's for the best. I told George I didn't need a best friend.

I hope I was right.

15
GEORGE

I get home and hand Mom a note from Principal Klein. It tells her how I was called into his office today and that lockers were slimed and balloons were messed up and as team captain I'm expected to set an example. It doesn't actually accuse me of anything, though.

I've never brought home a note from school before. My hand sort of trembles when I give it to Mom.

She reads it and looks at me and reads it again and looks at me again. "Did you have anything to do with this?" she asks me.

I shake my head. "No."

"Did you know about it?"

I'm about to say I didn't, but I also know that's not entirely the truth. I knew something was going to happen, I just didn't know what. I know who probably did the sliming and pretended I didn't know. But I can't lie to Mom, because I've never lied to her, just like I've never lied to Lilly, although maybe I sort of did today.

Is silence the same as telling a lie?

"I *think* I know who did some of that." I look down at my feet. "But." Mom raises her eyebrows. "But they're really big kids," I blurt out.

"So?" asks Mom, and it's obvious she doesn't understand how school works and that you don't blab on really big kids. It's not easy to say that, because I'm basically admitting that I'm a wimp.

I wish, wish, wish I had never raised my hand to be team captain.

"Have these big kids threatened you?"

I shake my head.

"Do you want me to talk to the principal?"

I shake my head again, even harder. That would be the worst thing she could do.

"Then what do you think you need to do?"

"I don't know," I admit.

"If you know someone did something wrong, is it your responsibility to speak up about it?"

I just stare at my feet and think about her question. I don't know what to say.

"And you are the team captain," she continues. "It's up to you to set an example for your classmates."

I continue to stare at the floor, feeling all squirmy inside.

"Just remember," Mom says, "that it's always best to be honest and open."

"I know that, Mom."

"Are you sure?"

I nod. "But it's not that simple."

"Well, I have faith in you. And I have faith that you'll do the right thing." She kisses me on the forehead and then gives me a hug, and I let her hug me because we're not in a school office, so there's no one to see.

I just wish I felt as confident about me as she does about me.

16
LILLY

After dinner, I'm on the phone with Sarah. She's excited, gloating about our plan today and how it is so unfair we weren't declared winners.

I say "Uh-huh" and "Right," but mostly she talks, and I think it's easier to gloat about cheating when you didn't lose your best friend a few hours earlier like I did.

"So what's the plan tomorrow?" she asks me.

"Maybe we just win by winning?" I suggest.

She laughs a short, nasty laugh. "Good one," she says, as if I told a great joke. "Did you see the look on Team Blue's faces when they saw all the balloons were filled with the same pudding? It was the best look ever."

"They looked angry."

"Losers always look angry," she says. "That's because . . ."

"Losing is for losers," I say before she says it, because I know that's exactly what she is going to say.

When I got my sleeping bag from Adventure Scouts, and Francine Pepper discovered I didn't actually own a unicorn, she never spoke to me again. Francine moved away that next year, so I never apologized or thanked her or anything.

I wonder if George will never speak to me again.

Does that make Francine Pepper a loser? Or George? Or maybe me?

Sarah says that she hates talking on the phone because phone talking is stupid, and I need to get a cell phone because everyone texts, and I can't continue to be friends with her and Grace if I can't text. She says that she might have a sleepover and if she does, maybe I'll be invited, but I'll need a phone. Mom and Dad say I can't get one until seventh grade, and that's a long way away, so I guess I'm not invited to her sleepover and maybe I won't have any friends at all after this week.

We end our phone call without any plans to cheat tomorrow, which is a good thing, I guess.

Maybe if we don't cheat, George and I can be friends again. Or maybe we'll be friends again if I give him a ride on a unicorn.

I think about making a clay unicorn, because making things with clay sometimes makes me feel better about things, but instead I lie on my bed and bury my head in my pillow.

17
GEORGE

I pass Abraham Lincoln on the sidewalk near school. He tips his tall black top hat to me. "Four score and seven years ago," he bellows in an odd western voice, but I don't think Abraham Lincoln was from the West. Walking with him is Amelia Earhart, or maybe it's Bessie Coleman. At least I think it's one of them, because Giovanna wears a flight suit and goggles, and I can't think of any other famous women who wore a flight suit and goggles.

Today's Spirit Week contest is Historical Figure Day. We're all dressed as historical figures. I'm Albert Einstein. My costume was easy to put together, because Mom had this old wig that she no longer wears, so I cut the hair shorter and made it all messy and stand up straight. Albert Einstein had goofy hair. I also carry a test tube and wear a lab coat, since Einstein was a scientist, and I drew a fake bushy mustache under my nose. I hope the marker won't be hard to wash off, since I'd hate to walk around with a fake marker mustache for a few days.

I tried washing a little off with my hand sanitizer, and it didn't work at all. I doubt marker chemicals are good for your skin, either.

I spy Cleopatra. She walks on the sidewalk on the other side of the street. It's Lilly. Her outfit impresses me. She obviously spent some effort finding a long white gown and an Egyptian headdress. She even wears a black wig. "Great costume," I shout, but I don't think she heard me. I'm glad she didn't hear me, because I remembered too late that we're not friends anymore, so I shouldn't compliment her.

It feels strange not walking with Lilly when there she is, striding along the opposite side of the street.

I cross the street at the crosswalk. Mr. Whipple, the crossing guard, waves me across. "Hi, Al," he says.

"It's me, George," I say, but then I realize Al is short for Albert, as in Albert Einstein. "I mean, hello," I mumble.

In front of the school, the entire walkway is filled with fifth graders in costumes. Luke waves to me, a saxophone strapped around his shoulders. He puts his lips to his mouthpiece and plays a few notes. He's pretty good.

"I'm Charlie Parker," he explains. "The all-time greatest saxophone player. I've taken sax lessons since I was little." He plays a few more notes.

I had no idea Luke played music. Maybe that's why he's bouncing all the time.

As we walk toward the school entrance, I wave to Eric. He is dressed as George Washington. "Hi, Mr. President," I say.

"Nncllzqk," Eric grunts. I can't understand a word he says through his oversized wooden teeth. He grimaces. The teeth look painful to wear. I wonder if George's Washington's teeth really looked so weird.

Everyone on Team Blue is in costume, at least everyone I see standing in front of the school. That brings a big grin to my face. I'm sure we'll win today's contest, and we need the victory to even things up with Team Red. I called half the team last night and sent a text to the other half, and many kids texted back which costume they planned to wear today. Some sent selfies.

Not every outfit is great, though. Samantha walks by, insisting she is dressed as Annie Oakley, the famous western sharpshooter. But she wears a fancy dress, sparkly shoes, and a matching purse. She says she dressed how Annie Oakley would have dressed for a fancy dinner party. I'm not sure if the judges will agree.

But I still have a smile on my face because I see a whole Team Red group walk past us, and none of them wear costumes. That's probably because Lilly forgot to remind everyone on her team.

"I think we're going to win this," Luke whispers to me, his legs bouncing with excitement. He toots a few notes on his sax.

"We're winning today, that much is plain. Any other idea is simply insane," rhymes Kyle. He's dressed as William Shakespeare with a fake beard and a fancy frock with a big collar. He continues rhyming, "On the stage I'm not going solo. I'll have Soda, dressed as Marco Polo."

"Great!" I say. Soda is Mrs. Rosenbloom's class hamster. Having her in a costume is a terrific idea.

"Kwwllkc quwlzk," says Eric through his wooden teeth. He spits them out and massages his gums. "Sorry. I mean, I cannot tell a lie, since I'm George Washington. We're going to win."

I just need to make sure Lilly doesn't spill her breakfast on me or on my teammates and ruin our costumes. That's just the sort of devious scheme she would pull.

"I hear the winner gets a year's supply of comic books," says Eric.

"I hear we win season tickets to an amusement park," says Luke.

"Which one?" I ask.

"Every one!" exclaims Luke.

Brian approaches us. He walks with big angry strides, but he always walks that way. He wears a mask and an orange shirt and giant red claws on his hands. On his feet are big black boots.

"Uh, we're supposed to be dressed up as historical figures," says Eric.

"I'm Lobster Man," he says. "That's a historical figure."

"You're who?" asks Eric.

"Lobster Man," Brian declares. He holds out his claws and yells, "Lobster Power!"

"Actually, Eric is right about . . . ," I begin.

"Right about what?" Brian demands, curling his lobster claws into fists.

"Nothing, it's a great costume," I quickly say with an awkward smile. Then I add, "I like bikes." I grimace when I say that last part.

As we walk into school, Brian turns to me. "Don't worry, I have a plan. You're with us, right?"

I remember my discussion with Mom last night, and I know I should speak up and say I'm not with him and whatever he's planning. But I look at Brian, who seems even bigger in his lobster costume, and instead I wither like a dead weed. "Of course. One hundred percent with you," I mumble.

"Because we need to teach Team Red a lesson."

"You bet," I say as we walk into the school, hoping his plan is as half-baked as his costume. I think we're going to win, fair and square. We don't need to cheat.

18
LILLY

While I put my stuff into my locker, Finn laughs a single "Ha!" He's not standing next to me, but it's a loud "Ha" that's hard to miss. It's the sort of laugh you have when you're bigger than almost anyone else so you don't care if anyone knows you're laughing. It's not a funny laugh, but a sort of nasty one, and I don't like it very much. He and Grace are huddled next to her locker, so I suspect the laugh is definitely nasty. Grace sees me. "Hey!" She waves me to join them.

Finn is dressed as a pirate, and Grace is dressed like a nun. Finn seems like the pirate type, but Grace does not seem nun-like.

"I'm Mother Teresa," explains Grace, twirling around. "She was famous for doing good deeds. She did lots of them."

No, Grace's costume does not seem right for her at all.

"What's up?" I ask.

"Just talking about what needs to be done to Team Blue," says Grace.

"I heard the winner of Spirit Week gets an entire truck of french fries. And a second truck of ketchup," adds Finn. He sounds excited.

Grace shakes her head. "I don't like ketchup."

Finn frowns and looks down at his toes.

Personally, I would love my own french-fry truck with extra ketchup, and just thinking about it makes my legs want to bounce and jump, but I'm not sure if I believe that will be the prize. I'm also less interested in imaginary french-fry trucks than I am in what the two of them are planning. "What are you guys thinking of doing?"

"We're not sure," admits Grace.

"Maybe I can get them to walk the plank," says Finn the pirate.

"Where would you get a plank?" I ask.

Finn shrugs. "That's part of the problem."

"But Finn's going to help us," adds Grace.

Finn nods. "Grace says I get to ride her horse if I help you guys cheat."

I scrunch my nose and shake my head. I'm positive Grace doesn't own a horse, and memories of my unicorn promise to Francine Pepper flood my brain. I should say something, but Grace winks at me and I keep quiet.

I hate myself for saying nothing, but I still want to win, and Finn could help us win, and at least I'm not the one doing the lying. Also, maybe this means I can still sleep over at Sarah's house even without owning a phone.

I look around the hallway. Every kid on Team Blue wears a costume of some sort. Some outfits I recognize, like pilgrims and American Revolution heroes. But some kids wear dress shirts and ties or fancy dresses, and they could be almost anyone who was rich or famous from whenever or wherever.

Koko sticks her head into our small circle. I didn't see her approach us. She's dressed in old-timey clothes with an old-timey camera hanging around her neck. I must look confused, because she says, "I'm Dorothea Lange, the photographer. But why doesn't Lilly just spill milk and oatmeal on everyone? That worked last time."

"It was an accident," I insist.

Mother Teresa, or rather Grace, pats me on the back. "Sure it was." She winks.

Aisha pops her head into our growing circle. She wears a track outfit. She called me last night and told me she was dressing as Jackie Joyner-Kersee, a famous Olympic athlete. "What are you guys doing?"

"Plotting," says Grace.

Aisha frowns, shakes her head, and walks away.

"I can make them all disappear," says Pete, who is dressed in a top hat and a cape. "I'm Harry Houdini, a famous magician."

"I can make them all sick," says Amelia. She's dressed in rags. "I'm Typhoid Mary. She was sort of famous for making people sick."

"Um, great costume," I say but thinking the opposite and suddenly wishing George was next to me so I could borrow his hand sanitizer.

Thinking of George makes my stomach sink, and I push his face out of my brain. "Good ideas, guys. But I'm not sure any of those things will work."

Our circle of plotters is now four people deep.

"Let's hypnotize the judges into voting for us," says Pete. "I've been reading about hypnosis. I hypnotized my dog once."

"How could you tell?" I ask.

Pete shrugs. "Well, I think I hypnotized my dog once."

"Let's build a time machine and go back into history and change stuff so there aren't any more historical figures and Team Blue won't be dressed as anyone," says Zachary. I can't tell if he's joking or serious. He seems serious. He's dressed as a mobster from the 1920s with a fake scar down his cheek.

"What if we tell Team Blue the judging has moved to a different building?" says Noah. He's holding a dictionary, and

I heard he's dressed as Noah Webster, who I think wrote the very first dictionary in America. "Or two buildings. Or just tell them the event is canceled. Or change the clocks so they are late, or something different than those ideas."

"Let's steal their shoes," suggests Grace. "And their socks! And put thumbtacks on the ground so they can't walk on the stage."

"Or we can steal the stage!" Koko says excitedly.

Our circle is still growing and people are shouting out ideas that make no sense at all. It's like everyone wants to cheat, but is not sure how. I wonder if, maybe, we should try to win without cheating.

Ugh, I sound like George. I really need to get his head out of my head.

I remove my black Cleopatra wig. It's itchy, and I hope that's how my George thoughts keep popping in, through the itchiness.

As I take off my wig, I look down at my wrist. I only wore the friendship bracelet for a few days, but my wrist looks weird without it. I had been so excited when I made them. I know George and I ended our friendship just yesterday, but I miss having a best friend, and it already seems like forever since we talked. I remember what our parents said right before this whole week started. They said that no contest is more important than friendship.

I will find George and tell him I'm sorry for everything. I'll tell him I knew about the pudding plot, and I'm sorry and I miss him and ask him to forgive me. We'll walk home together today, and everything will be just like it used to be.

I'll tell him that I'm sorry right after we win the costume contest, though. Sure, we don't have a scheme to guarantee victory, but I still want to win that free french-fry truck, or whatever prize will be handed out, and it's easier to apologize when you're a winner.

19
GEORGE

As I push through the doors of the fifth-grade hallway, I don't spot Lilly. Her locker is near the front of the hall, so I usually see her right away. I'm feeling guilty for the way I've been acting and the things that I've been thinking. Sure, she started this whole mess by ruining my Twin Day outfit. Still, just because someone does something mean to you, that doesn't mean you need to do something mean back. How you act is up to you. I can choose to act nicer.

I do choose to act nicer.

But then I notice Lilly. A giant circle of Team Red kids huddle together, and Lilly is right in the middle of them. I can see the top of her bright red head peeking out. She must have taken off her wig.

Lilly and I will talk later, when less people are around. I'll ask her to look me in the eye and be honest with me. Is she behind any of this?

And if she says no, I'll believe her.

And if she says yes, maybe I'll forgive her anyway.

From the corner of my eye, I see someone waving to me from the hallway behind me. I need to get to my locker because class starts soon. But it's hard to ignore a waving hand. So I walk out the doors of the fifth-grade hall.

But I'm anxious to turn around and get to class.

Brian still wears his Lobster Man outfit. "Come here! Quick! Quietly!" he shouts, which sort of ruins the whole idea of being quiet. But no one else is near to hear. Everyone is already filing into his or her room.

"Follow me," orders Brian. He walks briskly ahead, down the hall that leads to the cafeteria. There are no classrooms in this corridor, just closets and maintenance rooms. It's empty except for us.

"We need to get back," I say. "Or we'll be late."

"No time," he says, and I have to jog to keep up with him. We approach the cafeteria door. Brian looks both ways to make sure we're alone.

The hairs on the back of my neck stand up.

"I don't think we're allowed in here," I warn, but Brian has already removed a key from his pocket and inserted it into the lock on the door. He twists the key and pushes the door open.

"My older brother Simon works in the cafeteria," says Brian.

"Does he know you have his key?"

Brian smiles. "He's on our side, don't worry."

The cafeteria is empty. It's already been cleaned from breakfast, but I guess it is too early to serve lunch. It smells like eggs.

Brian walks past the lunch tables. I hurry to keep up. "Where are we going?"

Brian doesn't answer. He marches across the lunchroom and through the swinging door that leads to the kitchen.

I have never been inside the kitchen. I don't think kids are allowed here, and I expect to see the angry face of Principal Klein hiding behind a counter, ready to drag me to his office.

I don't want to go back to his office. I don't want to be team captain. I don't want to be here. I want to go to class.

The kitchen looks clean, crammed with stainless-steel counters and shiny white floors that look recently mopped. But the smell of eggs hits my nose like a soccer ball. I scrunch up my nostrils to keep as much stink out as I can. I want to wipe my nose with hand sanitizer.

"Howdy," Seth says in a southern drawl. He sits on the kitchen floor wearing a cowboy hat and vest. "James is the name. Jesse James. Most ruthless gunslinger in the West."

Next to Seth is an older kid that I can only assume is Brian's brother. He looks like Brian, but with a goatee.

"This is your captain?" Brian's brother asks, looking at me with a sneer. "Doesn't look like much."

Brian nods. "He's okay, and he's no snitch." He points to his brother. "Simon was on Team Blue back when he was in fifth grade."

"We lost," says Simon. His voice has the same tinge of anger that I often hear in Brian's voice. "But we're not losing this year. No way I'm letting my little bro lose to Team Red."

Large woolen blankets lie in heaps around them, and next to those is a giant drum of what looks to be yellowish slime. I peer closer into the drum and the strong egg odor makes my eyes water.

"Egg salad," says Brian with glee. I have no idea why egg salad would make anyone so happy. "Isn't this stuff awful?"

I nod my head.

"We have forty pounds of it," says Simon. "There are three more containers in back. But don't worry, no one will notice anything is missing." He points to himself and says proudly, "I keep track of the inventory and everything. It's an important job."

Brian peers into the egg-salad bucket with a grin.

I'm struggling to breathe, and I wonder how Brian can stand the odor, but it doesn't seem to bother him. "So, um, what are you guys doing with forty pounds of egg salad? Making lunch? Planning a picnic?"

Simon laughs as if I've made a joke. "We're doing what needs to be done." To Seth, he barks, "Stir it so it's nice and goopy, Jesse James."

Seth stirs the drum with a long spatula. "I hear the winner of Spirit Week gets a year without homework." Seth takes a big whiff of the barrel. I think he actually enjoys the stink.

"I heard it's two years without homework," says Brian, who also inhales the egg smell with a happy smile. Meanwhile, I have to hide my nose in my arm to keep the odor away.

"All I know is that Team Red is about to get what's coming to them," says Simon.

"They have egg salad coming to them?" I ask, holding my breath.

Simon laughs again and puts out his palm. "Hit me, little bro." Brian meets it with a loud hand slap. "There's no way you guys lose today."

"What are you guys up to?" I ask, my voice rising along with my worry. "You're not going to pour this inside lockers, are you? Principal Klein said . . ."

"We've been there, done that," says Brian. "This plan is way better."

"Do we have enough blankets?" Simon asks. Seth unfolds two of the blankets. They are large and unfold and unfold. They must fit on some giant bed.

Maybe they plan on making a bed filled with egg salad.

No, that makes no sense.

"I think we have more than enough blankets," says Seth.

Then the school bell rings.

"I should get to class," I say. I take a few steps toward the door, eager to get away from the smell and the stink of whatever rotten thing they are planning. But then I stop.

I'm the team captain. I think of my conversation with Mom. I think of how I promised everyone I would play fair. I don't know what's going on here, but whatever it is, it is not good.

Keeping silent is just as bad as doing bad things.

I turn around. I take a deep breath, which is not easy with the horrible smell of egg salad. I face Seth, Brian, and Simon. "Guys?"

"What?" asks Simon, glaring at me.

They are so much bigger than me that I gulp twice before I continue. "Well, you know, Principal Klein says we're supposed to display good sports . . ." My voice catches in my throat. Speaking out is not easy.

"Good sports?" asks Brian, confused.

I cough. ". . . manship. Principal Klein says we're supposed to, you know, display good sportsmanship. That's what I meant."

They all frown, Simon deepest of all. "I thought you said he was okay," he says to Brian, eyeing me warily.

"I thought he was," growls Brian.

Neither of them looks happy with me, but this is where I put my foot down. This is where I earn my I LOVE GOLDFISH! badge. "Right, good sportsmanship. So, you know, whatever you're going to do with that egg salad, maybe you shouldn't?" I gulp and cough and smile. If I smile really, really wide, maybe they won't do anything terrible to me.

They are all so very, very big.

Why did I volunteer for team captain?

"He's going to ruin everything," says Simon, with a scowl.

"I just wanted to remind you guys of the sportsmanship thing," I say. "And you know I like bikes." I hate myself for saying that last part, since it makes no sense. I smile again.

"If he tells anyone, I could get sacked," says Simon, who is not returning my smile. "And I have an important job."

"He won't tell anyone," says Brian. He stares at me. "Right? You said you were with us."

"Right. Of course. One hundred percent," I say. "But I'm the team captain, and I don't know if—"

Simon interrupts me. "We shouldn't talk about it here." I look around the room. There is no one here but the four of us. "Over there," says Simon, waving me across the room.

I shrug and follow him across the kitchen.

We walk past sinks and a large cooler to what I think might be a closet. Simon puts his hand on the doorknob. "In here."

I guess Simon wants our conversation to be extra private. Maybe he wants to admit he's wrong but is embarrassed to say it in front of Brian and Seth. He opens the door.

"I'm glad you agree that . . . ," I begin, as I take a step forward.

I don't even finish the words. Simon pushes me forward. I stumble, and Simon slams the door shut.

I hear him yell, "He can stay there until we're done!"

I race forward and reach for the knob. The door is locked. "Hey! Let me out!"

No one answers.

I bang on the door.

Nothing.

Thankfully, there is an overhead fluorescent light so I can see where I am. If it was completely dark, I think I would start screaming. The closet is filled with tall shelves that house boxes of ketchup and mustard, and plastic bags filled with sandwich breads, and jars of sauces. At least I won't starve. But I'm helpless to stop whatever those guys have planned.

I so hate being team captain.

20
LILLY

The entire grade files into the school auditorium at lunch-time. Food isn't usually allowed in here, but it's a special week and they ordered pizza, although we're supposed to be extra careful. The usual cafeteria pizza tastes like cardboard with fake cheese, but the school brought in Rosa's Pizza for us. Rosa's is the pizza we order at home, so this is the best school lunch ever.

I sit near the middle of the auditorium, one hand holding my paper plate filled with pizza goodness, and my other hand holding a cup of apple juice. Everything tastes so good I can't help but bounce on my seat, although I splash a little apple juice on my pants, so I try to keep my legs from moving so much.

I sit between Aisha and Sarah. Grace sits next to Sarah.

Sarah has three pieces of pizza on her plate. We were only supposed to grab two pieces each. "I'm a queen, so I can eat whatever I want," she says. Sarah wears a plain blue dress with glitter glued on it, and a cheap tinfoil tiara.

"Whatever you say, Queen," I reply.

"Please address me as 'Your Royal Highness,'" Sarah says with a snooty and dirty look, as if she's royalty and I'm most definitely not. She fluffs her hair. "I'm Queen Mary." Sarah throws a mischievous glance. "As Queen of England, she's considered one of the most ruthless queens in history. She did all sorts of horrible things. Just like we're going to do horrible things to Team Blue."

"Well, maybe not so horrible, right?" I say with a small laugh, but my small laugh is met with stone-cold silence.

I feel something wet and slimy smack against the back of my neck. I quickly reach around and remove a piece of pepperoni that has stuck to my skin like tape.

I turn to see Brian and Seth, five rows in back of me, chucking pepperoni slices at our team while laughing. We were supposed to be careful when eating here, but they don't seem to care. One slice hits Pete in the head. Pete turns around and glares. He is in his Harry Houdini outfit, and I bet he wishes he could perform some sort of disappearing magic on them right now. Seth and Brian both hold a stack of pepperonis that they probably swiped from half the kids on their team.

But before they can launch another volley of meat at us, Principal Klein's bellowing voice reverberates through the room. "Seth and Brian, put down the pepperoni and step into the hallway. Now."

The bullies' smiles vanish as Principal Klein marches down the aisle. They scoot out from their seats to follow, and I want to shout out, "It serves you right!" but I just think it really loudly instead.

Seth wears a cowboy outfit, but Brian is dressed as a weird lobster superhero.

"We should win this contest because we didn't throw pepperoni," says Sarah.

"They're just a couple of idiots," I say.

Sarah shakes her head. "It's a whole team of idiots and cheaters. Brian and Seth just do most of the dirty work."

On the stage in front of us, three judges sit behind a long table waiting for our principal to return. One of the judges is my teacher, Mrs. Crawford, and I hope that she'll want us to win and give us extra judging points. She is dressed as a pilgrim.

Next to her is Mr. Foley, who is George's teacher, and I worry that he might give Team Blue extra points. I guess he and Mrs. Crawford sort of even themselves out. Mr. Foley is dressed in a business suit and has large white sideburns curled almost to his mouth. Someone told me he is supposed to be John Quincy Adams, who was our sixth president, but I don't know why someone would dress as John Quincy Adams when there are so many more famous presidents to choose. The only thing I know about John Quincy Adams is that he was related to John Adams, who was a more famous president, and that he's in our school history book with three names, while most of our other presidents only have two names.

The last judge on stage is older and wears a three-piece suit and a long fake nose. I'm not sure who he is, although he looks sort of familiar, and he talks with the other teachers with big arm flourishes. The other teachers seem sort of annoyed that he talks so much. They nod and smile, but the smiles are obviously pretend.

Aisha takes a big sniff and scrunches her nose. "Do you smell eggs?"

I take a big whiff, too. "Maybe. Gross."

"It seems strange to be smelling eggs, doesn't it?"

Principal Klein returns through the auditorium doors. They slam shut behind him, and he briskly stomps down the aisle. He walks alone, with purpose, his hands swinging. Seth and Brian must be in big trouble, ordered to wait in the principal's office or in prison or somewhere. They are not with him.

As I look around the room, I notice an entire row of Team Red kids who forgot to dress up. They wear what they always wear to school. I suddenly worry that we might not win this contest. Sarah follows my eyes and frowns at me. "Nice planning," she says, dripping with sarcasm. "Maybe you should have texted someone. Oh, right. You don't have a phone."

I know I didn't tell anyone to wear costumes today, but kids should have been able to remember that today is Historical Figure Day without my reminding them. The schedule is posted in every classroom.

"If we lose, do I still get to ride your horse?" Finn asks Grace. He sits behind us.

"Never," says Grace, coldly.

Finn pouts.

Principal Klein walks up the stage steps and to the microphone. "Sorry for the delay, but we are ready to begin." He takes a deep breath, as if trying to exhale any anger that lingers from the pepperoni throwing. "I'm thrilled to announce a special guest to help judge our costumes. Some of you might already know Mr. Wolcott. He was just named the new head of drama at Liberty Falls Community College."

The old guy with the fake nose waves, and a large cheer goes up from the kids in Mrs. Rosenbloom's class. They must know him. He says, "Remember, as the bard himself says, 'All the world's a stage, and all the men and women merely players.'"

I have no idea what he's talking about. The other judges clap politely, although I don't think they know what he's talking about, either.

"Team Blue, please approach the stage," orders Principal Klein.

Half the kids—all of Team Blue—stand up and make their way to the aisle. They march up the stage steps, where they will walk past the judges for scoring. Each judge has a pad of paper to make notes.

I look for George. I still can't get his face out of my brain, but I don't see him.

Where is he?

Up on stage, kids file past the judges in a wide variety of costumes. Some of the getups were obviously put on at the last minute, like a few kids in baseball caps and team jerseys, a couple of which have names taped to the back for famous ball players. But other costumes are pretty great, and either took a lot of time to create or to find in a costume store. Gavin's Abraham Lincoln is almost perfect, from the fake beard to the black suit and hat. Jamaal wears a long black judge's robe. I hear he's dressed as Thurgood Marshall, who was the first African American Supreme Court justice.

Kyle, dressed in some silly outfit with a big white collar, walks past the judges. He holds Soda, their class hamster, who he's dressed in a fake beard, a small furry hat, and a red robe.

It's a nice touch. I wish I had thought of dressing up our class turtle, Elvis, as someone historic.

When the last member of Team Blue leaves the stage, Principal Klein announces, "Wonderful costumes. All the judges are quite impressed. Team Red, please come up."

I leap out of my seat, my fingers crossed, but still wondering: Where is George?

21
GEORGE

I'm not sure how long I've been in this closet. It feels like hours. I almost opened a jar of pickles to eat, but that would be like stealing, so I didn't.

I spent some time reorganizing the shelves. There were some garbanzo beans mixed in with jars of roasted red peppers by accident, and I really thought the condiments should be in alphabetical order.

I put ketchup under *K* even though the jars say *catsup*. The inconsistency bothers me, but I think my filing system makes the most sense.

The doorknob turns. I crouch, expecting to see Simon and Brian, and who knows what they have planned. I'm not a fighter, and I'm not fast, so my best chance of escape is to throw a handful of flour at them. Then, while the white cloud blinds them, I can make a break for it.

I hold a sack of flour, top open, ready.

The door opens.

"Oh!" exclaims one of the lunch ladies, standing in the doorway. But I have already thrown a fistful of flour at her before I realize she's not Simon or Brian.

As she coughs and swipes the air and rubs her eyes, I make my move, dashing past her and through the flour cloud. "Sorry, sorry, sorry," I call out as I run. "And I filed catsup under *K*!"

Then I'm off, racing across the room and banging the kitchen door open.

As I dash across the cafeteria, I look up at the clock. It's lunchtime. The costume judging has already begun and is probably going on right now. Whatever Brian and Seth and Simon have planned may have already happened.

But maybe not; maybe I can still stop it if I hurry.

I sprint down the hall. My sneakers squeak. The auditorium is just two hallways away. Still, when I arrive and push open the auditorium doors, I'm breathing heavily from running.

I am not too late. Team Red is on stage, walking in front of the judges. Lilly leads her group, and nothing terrible seems to have happened. It is calm in here. Too calm. I scan the room, but I'm not sure what I'm looking to find.

Then I see them. Blankets. Big woolen blankets hang from the rafters, stretched wide above the stage, tied in place with ropes. The middles of the blankets sag, as if weighted with something heavy.

A foot peeks out from behind a curtain, way in the back of the stage where no one should be standing. It's a black boot, like something a lobster superhero might wear.

Then, like a lightbulb brightening over my head, suddenly I know exactly what's going to happen.

I yell as loudly as I can, "Run! Egg salad!"

But it's too late, because the moment I scream it, and just as everyone in the entire room turns to me and wonders what I'm talking about and why I'm standing near the front doors and where I've been this whole time, the overhead ropes are loosened and the blankets fall from above. With them, forty pounds of egg salad drench the stage and nearly every member of Team Red.

22
LILLY

I am soaked in eggs.

No. I am soaked in egg salad. This is most definitely egg salad.

To make things even worse, not that anything could be much worse, I hate egg salad.

My hair stinks with eggs and mayo. My arms stink with eggs and mayo. My everything and everywhere stinks with eggs and mayo.

Tara stands next to me, shivering. She wore a toga, dressed as a famous Greek philosopher, which means she's basically just wearing a fancy bedsheet and a leotard under it, so she was probably cold anyway, but now huge clumps of cold egg salad cling to her hair and shoulders. I think she got the worst of it.

Or maybe Sarah got the worst of it. Or maybe Alex got it worse. Or Noah. Or me.

Wet egg-puddle muck surrounds our feet. I step forward,

and my shoes plop in the goop. But the smell is the worst part of it.

The egg salad avoided the judges, though. They are clean. Whoever planned this mess, planned it well. But there is no questioning who planned it.

"Someone is going to pay for this!" yells Finn. For a moment, I'm scared because he looks crazy, like a wild beast. His pirate outfit, covered in egg salad as if he lost some sort of egg-salad pirate battle, just adds to his scariness.

"Oh yeah, they'll pay," echoes Zane. He tries to look fierce, but he can't because his eyes are too kind to ever look fierce, and because he's dressed as Bozo the Clown. (Some clowns are scary, but Zane's Bozo outfit is not.) I'm not even sure if Bozo the Clown really counts as a historical figure, not that it matters anymore.

Jessie, who is dressed as Marie Antoinette, sobs and asks, "Do they hate cats?" She told me earlier that Marie Antoinette loved cats.

"If Team Blue wants war, we'll give them war," growls Mother Teresa, I mean Grace, wiping egg slop from her nun habit. She hisses, but I don't think the real Mother Teresa would have ever hissed.

I heard something right before we were drenched with egg mess. Someone yelled something from the audience, and I think it was George.

Yes, it was George. He yelled, "Egg salad!" He knew this was going to happen. He was in on the plan. Maybe it was even his idea.

I'm so mad at him. I can't believe he'd do something so terrible. Especially when he knows how much I hate egg salad.

And to think I wanted to be friends with him again! I can't believe I've been feeling guilty about cheating and fighting with him, and even thought about apologizing to him.

Pete grunts. Grace snarls. Jessie roars like a big cat.

"Who did this?" Principal Klein cries. He stands near me. His suit pants have a clop of egg salad on the bottom. He bends down and brushes it off with a flick of his finger, the chunk of salad flying a few feet and landing next to me. "I said, who did this?" He stares at me, and then across our entire team. But he can't think one of us did this to ourselves.

"As the great bard William Shakespeare himself once wrote, 'That one may smile, and smile, and be a villain,'" says Mr. Wolcott from the judges' table. The other judges ignore him.

Principal Klein's face is red and his large hands shake as he scans the audience. Team Blue watches us, their jaws hanging open. I think they are too stunned to speak.

But one kid stands out. One kid, standing in the way back of the auditorium, has *guilty* plastered on his face.

"This can't continue and it won't!" yells Principal Klein, his voice exploding in anger. "Shame on you all!"

Someone starts sobbing, the crying spreading through the now otherwise silent auditorium. The only other sound in the room is a plop, plop, plop of egg salad from a clump high up on the rafters continuing to drop on the floor.

"Someone will answer for this," says Principal Klein, now in an eerie and calm voice that's even scarier than when he yelled. His hands are clenched into claws as if he wants to strangle something. Then his arm shoots out and points to the only kid standing in the room. "George Martinez. You!"

George, who stood straight a moment ago, appears to be suddenly made of gelatin. His legs quake and he leans against the auditorium door as if he can't stand on his own.

"Come to my office right now, George Martinez," says Principal Klein, the veins in his neck nearly popping out. He stomps across the stage and down the stairs.

George peels himself off the door when Principal Klein approaches him and stands at attention, ready to follow him out of the room.

I snort, and that's not something I meant to do or do very often, but it is a snort of satisfaction. George deserves whatever punishment he gets, the bigger the better.

Before they walk out the door our principal wheels around, as if suddenly yanked by a string. He looks up to the stage and his eyes rest on me, Cleopatra, Queen of the Nile, Queen of Egg Salad. His eyes are large and wide. His expression is menacing.

"And Lilly Bloch. You come with us, too."

"But . . . ," I say.

"Now!" our principal bellows.

I trudge across the stage, down the steps, and march down the aisle. All eyes watch me.

"Please get these kids cleaned up," Principal Klein calls back to the judges. "Hopefully most kids brought a change of clothes." Then I hear a big clop of egg salad fall from high above the stage and land on the floor. It's the last sound I hear before the auditorium doors swing shut behind us.

23
GEORGE

So here I am, again, in Principal Klein's tiny office. This time, Lilly sits next to me. Mrs. Frank brought in a folding chair for Lilly to sit on, and there is barely room for us across from our principal's desk. Our knees bump each other. Principal Klein's face is as red as a fire engine, and I wouldn't be all that surprised to hear a fire alarm ring out from his nose. He does not sit, but paces in the small space behind his deck, two steps one way and then two steps back, back and forth, back and forth. As he talks, his hands, his incredibly large hands, ball into fists and continually punch the air.

"I have never, in all my years as principal, seen such horrible, terrible, and irresponsible behavior!" he rants. "Poor sportsmanship! A total disregard for decency and rules! I am ashamed, yes, ashamed to be your principal."

"My team had nothing to do with this," says Lilly. "It was all George . . ."

"Quiet!" bellows Principal Klein. "Not a word from either one of you."

"Yes, sir," I say, and I guess that counts as a word from one of us because Principal Klein glares at me and holds his finger up, as if warning me that *one more time* and I will be in even more boatloads of trouble than I am already. I keep quiet.

Our principal continues his small-step pacing. "Spirit Week is about teamwork and caring and doing our best." Fist punch. "This is an embarrassment to me, to the fifth grade, and to the entire school." Two more fist punches. "You've left me no choice. None. Spirit Week is over." Three more fist punches, followed by a sort of karate chop. "No more contests. No more events. No more fun. Instead, the entire fifth grade will serve detention after school today. Mrs. Frank will be calling all of your parents." He juts his fist straight up in the air and then points directly at me. "And, George, I am especially disappointed in you."

I open my mouth to proclaim my innocence, but I've already been warned to keep quiet, so I close my mouth and say nothing as our principal continues.

"George, I warned you there would be consequences. It seems obvious that Team Blue committed this horrendous act. I am suspending you from school, effective immediately."

My jaw drops open. Even though we are forbidden from speaking, my voice flows out of my throat before I can stop it.

"But, sir, I had nothing to do with it. Honestly, sir. Please. You can't suspend me."

Principal Klein—who looks even angrier than Lilly did when I beat her at tic-tac-toe the other week, ruining her streak of 228 wins in a row (although I lost a lot of them on purpose to keep her streak going)—stops pacing and stares at me, and stares and stares, and after about twenty seconds of staring, the veins in his neck ebb just ever so slightly. His face turns a less vibrant shade of red.

"I swear I didn't know," I gulp.

"I hear you were missing from class this morning. And you weren't on stage during Team Blue's costume presentation. And then you appeared and yelled something right before it happened, didn't you?" he asks, his voice still tinged with anger. "It sounded like *egg salad*. It seems strange, in fact it seems impossible, that you would just yell out the words *egg salad* for no reason."

He has a point, but I have a witness. Except I can't tell him that because then Principal Klein will want to know how I got trapped in the closet. I gulp and instead say, "Well, uh, I left part of my costume at home. So then I had to run home, and then run back, and then I went the wrong way, so I was late." I feel my face turn red, but I keep talking. "When I got to the auditorium, I saw blankets with egg salad up on the rafters. I noticed they were about to fall. I wanted to warn everyone."

"You could see blankets from all the way in the back of the auditorium?"

I nod.

He leans over his desk and stares at me, as if willing my thoughts to jump out of my head and land on his table, which is cluttered with pens.

I really, really want to put the pens in his pen jar.

"And you could see these blankets were filled with egg salad?" he asks. "How is that possible?"

I take a deep breath. If I tell him the truth, then I'm a snitch, and I'll have to hide in the halls every time I see Brian or Seth. But if I don't say anything, then I might be expelled. I bite my lip. I fidget.

I told my mom I could handle this. No one is going to help me.

I should just tattle.

I hate being team captain.

But it's not all Brian and Seth's fault. Not entirely. I told Brian I was with him, 100 percent. What did I think he was planning to do? Did I think he was going to bake smiley face cookies for everyone to eat? Of course he wasn't. He was going to do something terrible, and I told him to go ahead and do it.

Even if I spoke up in the end, I didn't speak up soon enough. That makes me sort of guilty, but not really guilty, and not guilty enough to be suspended, I think.

I should get extra bonus points for organizing their food storage closet, at the very least.

I look down at my goldfish pin. I didn't want to be our team captain, but I volunteered, and here I am, and I have to handle this. I take a deep breath. I wonder if I should ask for a lawyer. I put my knees together to stop them from knocking.

"I had nothing to do with it, sir," I mumble. It's all I can think of saying.

"Then who did?" asks Principal Klein.

I bow my head in shame and worry. I keep quiet.

Principal Klein turns to Lilly. I'm sure she's been enjoying every moment watching me squirm. "What do you think, Lilly? Did George have anything to do with the incident?"

Lilly opens her mouth to speak, and I can tell from the slight curl in her mouth that she's going to tell our principal that I'm the sort of person who enjoys hiding egg salad in blankets. But then she looks at me, and her small mouth curl uncurls. Her eyes dash back and forth, so I can tell she's thinking. Her expression turns serious and she shakes her head. "No, sir. I can't imagine George would do that sort of thing. Ever."

My heart, which had been pounding in my chest, quiets a little. I flash her a grateful smile. Of course I would never hatch such a scheme, and of course Lilly would know that.

"So you see, sir, you can't cancel Spirit Week," she continues. "I know a few bad eggs have been ruining things." At the mention of *eggs* our principal's face drops. "Sorry," she mumbles. "But you can't cancel Spirit Week. We've all been trying so hard, and most of us have played by the rules. I mean, you can't punish everyone just because of a few bad eggs, um, I mean apples. Some bad apples." Principal Klein frowns, but he doesn't interrupt her. "And what about the free trip to Disney World we're all going to win? You probably can't get the money back."

Principal Klein looks confused. "Disney World?"

"The prize. The special prize," says Lilly. "I heard it might be Disney World?"

Principal Klein shakes his head. "No, it's not that."

"Please, sir," I add. "Lilly is right. You can't cancel the entire week because of a troublemaker here or there. And I swear I didn't know a thing. I smelled eggs, sir. And I saw the blankets and well, I just figured it out."

"I smelled eggs, too, sir," says Lilly. "And so did Aisha. You can ask her."

"We'll be good," I promise. "I'll make sure of it. And so will Lilly. Both of our teams will play fair, with no more trouble. We swear it."

Lilly nods her head. "We'll all be on our best behavior, sir."

Principal Klein, who had resumed his pacing and is now panting a little from walking back and forth so much, stops and sits down on his leather seat. He spreads his messy pens across his desk so they are even messier.

I grit my teeth and refuse to let myself put the pens back in their jar, even though I really want to.

"I will lift George's suspension," he says, and I breathe a deep sigh of relief. "I can't prove he was responsible, but I suspect he's not being totally honest." He glares at me, but it feels like a giant weight has been lifted from my shoulders. "But I will find out who is responsible for the mess in the auditorium. And that person or persons will be punished." I gulp, and Principal Klein continues. "However, I'm not reversing the rest of it. Spirit Week is canceled and the entire fifth grade will serve detention after school today."

"But . . . ," I begin, and am interrupted by Lilly.

"What about the prize?" she asks.

Our principal responds with a deep frown. "I think there are more important things you should be thinking about right now, like sportsmanship. And responsibility."

We are dismissed from the office and walk past Mrs. Frank's desk. The school secretary frowns at us. Her eyes linger on me. The entire school probably thinks I'm responsible for today's egg-salad incident. I'm relieved that I'm not suspended, but I know I needed to stand up to Brian and Seth. I still need to do something.

I just wish they weren't so much bigger than me.

As we walk out of the office, I hear our principal say to Mrs. Frank behind us: "All this trouble reminds me, did you get me that egg salad recipe? Egg salad is one of my favorite foods, you know."

Lilly shivers. I know how much she dislikes egg salad.

After we open the office door and step into the hallway, I turn to Lilly. "Thanks for sticking up for me." For a moment I think we might be friends again.

But Lilly's face is not friendly. When she speaks, she spits slightly, so I have to step back to avoid spittle. "The only reason I spoke up was to keep him from canceling Spirit Week. I want that prize. But you ruined it. You and your stupid team." She stomps her foot. Egg salad splatters across the floor. "This is not over. Not in the slightest. Spirit Week is continuing as planned. Do you hear me?"

"But Principal Klein said . . ."

"I don't care what he said." She jabs her finger into my chest. "Spirit Week is still on. After what happened today, you owe me. I'm wearing egg salad, George. Egg salad!"

Before I can say anything, she adds, "And we will destroy your team, do you hear me?"

Her eyes lack even a hint of warmth or forgiveness or understanding. I see only dislike and distrust.

But if that's how she wants to be, then I can be that way, too. I meet her glare with one of my own, but it's hard. I don't like glaring. "Beat us? In your dreams."

She jabs me once more in my chest with her finger. "Tomorrow is Pajamas Day. I'll get my team ready, and you get yours. But Team Blue doesn't have a chance."

"But there isn't a Pajamas Day anymore."

"If I say there is Pajamas Day, there's a Pajamas Day." Then, Lilly marches away from me, stomping down the hall. As I stand alone, watching her leave, I wonder why we were best friends in the first place.

But I do know one thing: Team Blue will win Pajamas Day.

24
LILLY

From the cafeteria window, I watch kids leaving school for the day, and I wish I was with them. I stare at a group of second graders racing one another, another group of first graders skipping and holding hands, and a large bunch of fourth graders laughing together as they cross the street to go home.

None of those kids are fifth graders. Our entire grade is stuck serving detention, quietly, which is so unfair because all Team Red did was get doused by egg salad. We should get free laundry, not detention. It's not like we put slime into our lockers and dropped egg salad on ourselves.

At least we get to serve our detention in the cafeteria while Team Blue is stuck in the hot, sock-stinking gym, but they deserve extra heat and extra smelliness.

Fortunately, I wore regular clothes under my costume—a lot of us did, or brought clothes to change into later. Other kids had their parents drop off clean clothes, but a few kids, those who weren't directly under the blankets when they fell, sit on their chairs with a little egg yolk still smeared across their costumes.

While most of us have changed our clothes, our anger hasn't changed at all.

"They got egg in my hair," says Sarah. "My hair!" She fluffs her curly hair, but it doesn't fluff like it usually does. Grace joins her frown, part of her hair as matted down as Sarah's.

"Everyone on Team Blue owes me a horseback ride," says Finn, pouting. He sits across from me at the lunch table, looking at Grace. I shake my head because I still can't believe that he thinks Grace owns a horse. "We need to do something."

"Yes, we do," says Sarah.

I try to think of something terrible, such as sticking lizards inside everyone's pants. I don't know how I will get lizards, or how I can stuff them inside pants, and I don't even like touching lizards since they are wiggly, but I guess that's why pant-stuffing lizards seems so especially mean.

My plan makes no sense.

We could kidnap the entire grade. Or throw paint on them. Or force them to eat the egg salad they poured on us.

All my plans make no sense.

"I think we should . . . ," begins Grace.

"Hush," says Mrs. Greeley. She stands in the middle of the room with her arms folded, looking cross. "Detention means no talking. You are here to learn a lesson, and you will learn that lesson quietly. You will each write a one-page report on the meaning of good sportsmanship. After you are done, you can study or read. But no talking."

I take out a piece of paper and I write, *Good sportsmanship means you'll probably have egg salad dropped on you.*

I push my paper aside. I'm done.

But sitting in the cafeteria for fifty-nine more minutes, without talking, will be almost impossible. I sit still for maybe a minute more, and I'm already fidgeting and bouncing and bored out of my jeans. All I do is think evil thoughts about Team Blue, some involving giant apes and others involving dropping watermelons on them. I wanted to win. I wanted that prize. Team Blue ruined all of it.

I heard Ruby say that the special prize was a guest role on a TV show, which means I could have been discovered, and that would be totally awesomesauce. But now all I get is detention, and detention has no stars.

I think about Pajamas Day and how I told George we would all dress up anyway. That sounded good when I was yelling it in the hallway, but I wasn't really thinking straight. I haven't told any of my teammates what I said to George, but I hope they agree with my plan since it's too late to back out now, not after gloating we would win.

And I won't let George win, prize or no prize.

Mrs. Greeley sits at a table and opens a magazine. I look down at my notebook and draw a flower. I should make a clay flower for my shelf at home. I don't have one of those yet, and a flower seems pretty easy to make, and Mom just bought a whole bunch of clay for me so I could make more frogs, but I have no team to make frogs for anymore. The clock ticks. I draw dogs and cats. I could make some dog and cat figurines, too. With all the clay at home I could make one hundred dogs and cats.

The clock ticks a few million more times.

Mrs. Greeley leans back on her chair. I draw more dogs and more flowers. I don't draw dogs or flowers very well, though. It is easier to make things out of clay.

The clock ticks and tocks. Mrs. Greeley's mouth falls open.

I elbow Sarah and point to Mrs. Greeley. Her eyes are closed and she might even be snoring, just a little. Sarah and I exchange smiles, and so does Grace when she sees what we see.

We whisper, since we don't want to wake up the teacher. "We need to do something to Team Blue," says Sarah.

Grace nods. "They made egg salad. Why don't we just make something more disgusting?"

"I can have my mom make tuna casserole," says Finn, a bit too loudly. "Nothing is worse than my mom's tuna casserole."

"Ssshhh." I point my thumb at Mrs. Greeley.

Our teacher moves her head and I stiffen, but then she's motionless once again.

"They'll be expecting food," I say. "And I doubt your mom would make enough tuna casserole for us to dump on half our grade."

Finn shrugs. "Maybe not. But my mom loves making tuna casserole."

"I can train my cats to bite everyone on Team Blue. Cats are very smart, you know." Jessie pats her Marie Antoinette costume, which is mostly egg salad–free.

"I don't think we have time to start training a gang of biting cats," I say. "And they won't allow pets in school anyway. We need to beat them at their own game, and I have an idea." Everyone around me leans in closer. "We need to win Spirit Week. We started it. We're ending it as Spirit Week victors. That's how we get even."

"But Spirit Week is canceled," complains Finn, a bit too loudly.

We all put our fingers to our lips. "Ssshhh!"

Mrs. Greeley moves slightly. Her mouth opens a bit wider. A speck of drool falls from her lips and onto the table, which is gross, but she continues to breathe steadily, sleeping.

The group leans in even closer. "It's not canceled unless we say it's canceled," I say. "Tomorrow is Pajamas Day, whether Principal Klein says so or not."

"Will Team Blue dress up, too?" asks Sarah.

"It's all been arranged. Tell everyone. Pajamas Day is tomorrow, and we will win."

Everyone nods, and then the doors to the cafeteria bang open. We turn and stare at Aisha, who hurries into the room. I hadn't noticed her missing. Her lips tremble. "Elvis!" she shrieks.

"Keep your voice down," Sarah orders in an urgent whisper. Somehow, Mrs. Greeley doesn't awaken. She still breathes soundly as I turn back to Aisha. "What's going on with our class turtle?"

"I went to feed him," she says. "B-But h-he's missing," she stammers.

"How could he be missing?" I ask. Elvis doesn't do very much. You could watch him in his terrarium for hours, and he won't move more than an inch. Still, he's our class pet, and class pets are important. I even fed him once, and I think he smiled at me.

"I don't know what happened," says Aisha, her lips quivering. "Maybe he escaped? He could have dashed out of his home when no one was looking or something." She sniffs. "He's probably really scared, too." Her voice trembles with worry.

"That turtle is way too slow to escape," says Sarah. "He isn't some magic disappearing turtle."

"I don't like turtles," says Grace. Sarah nods in agreement.

"Elvis is really sweet and would never hurt anyone," says Aisha, frowning. Her eyes water up.

"He's the nicest turtle I know," I say. Of course, he's the only turtle I know. "And our class pet. The Team Red pet. He's important."

There's only one thing that could have happened. Sarah and Grace and Finn and I all say the same thing at the exact same time: "Team Blue."

I knew Team Blue would stop at nothing, but I never imagined they could sink as low as swiping Elvis. I think of George. He's good at organizing stuff, and he probably organized stealing our turtle.

Organized crime, that's what this is.

"But Elvis would never hurt anyone. Why steal him?" asks Aisha, wiping her nose and sniffling.

"Because everyone on Team Blue is mean and horrible," says Sarah.

"And stinky and vicious," agrees Grace.

"We have to hurt them where it hurts the most," whispers Sarah. Our entire table, about a dozen kids, has gathered around us to listen. Meanwhile, Mrs. Greeley snores away. "We need to fight fire with fire."

"We win Spirit Week," I insist. "And Pajamas Day."

Sarah shakes her head. "We'll do that, sure. But they snatch our pet, we'll snatch theirs, too."

"You mean Soda?" asks Grace. "The guinea pig?"

"Actually, she's a hamster," says Aisha. "We'll do a class pet hostage exchange."

Everyone seems to like the plan, because we all nod our heads and smile, even Sarah and Grace, and they hardly ever smile, although their smiles look more evil than happy.

"We need a small team," I say. "A super spy team to nab it." I look around my group and pick the sneakiest people to go. "Sarah, Grace, and me. We'll go." I glance at our teacher. She is breathing heavy and her eyelids twitch as if she's in some deep slumber. "We should leave now, before Mrs. Greeley wakes up. If she discovers us gone, we'll all be in even bigger trouble than we are already."

"I'm going, too," insists Aisha, her face a firm wall of determination. She still wears her Jackie Joyner-Kersee track outfit, so she looks fast. "If we find Elvis, he'll be scared if I'm not there."

"He's a turtle," says Sarah, rolling her eyes. "He has a brain the size of a grain of rice."

"You can come," I say. Grace and Sarah throw me a dirty look, but Aisha is good with animals, and she could be helpful.

I grab my backpack and sling it over my shoulder. "We can keep Soda in here. She just better not poop." I don't know how big hamster poop is, but I don't want it in my backpack.

We slowly creep toward the door. We only take about five steps, and I know we're supposed to be quiet but sometimes I can't help but bounce when I'm excited, and I bump into a table. The legs screech and someone's book falls over. We freeze.

Mrs. Greeley fidgets. Her mouth closes and we stay motionless, not daring to move a muscle. But then her sleepy breathing begins again. We wait a few seconds, and when our teacher remains motionless, we continue sneaking out. A few moments later, after no more table bumps, we're in the hallway and ready to steal a hamster.

25
GEORGE

Brian has Elvis in a shoebox.

I don't know how and when he and Seth managed to sneak out of detention to grab him. I don't know what they're going to do with him, but I don't like it one bit.

Sliming was bad enough. Egg salad was even worse. But they've gone way, way over the line. I gave Principal Klein my word that we wouldn't do anything else wrong.

We all sit on the gym floor. It stinks in here and I'm sweating, and I rub my hands with hand sanitizer. Then I stand up and take a deep breath.

I avoided Brian and Seth all afternoon. I don't know what they are planning to do with Elvis, and I don't want to be locked in a closet again, but I need to speak up. I'll tell Brian and Seth they have to return Elvis immediately. It's my job as team captain, even if I don't have a team anymore to captain.

"Sit down, George!" orders my teacher, Mr. Foley. He sits in a chair he brought into the gym, and is facing all of us. "You're supposed to be writing an essay on good sportsmanship."

I sit back down, secretly relieved. I'll talk to Brian and Seth later.

I start to write, but I don't just write one page about good sportsmanship, I write four pages. I write about how winning doesn't mean anything if you don't win honestly, but playing honestly isn't enough. You also have to make sure everyone else plays honestly, too. I feel guilty the entire time I write.

I wasn't expelled today, but maybe I should have been.

Brian and Seth smirk. They don't even attempt to write an essay, and instead spend their time passing notes. I hear faint sounds from Brian's shoebox.

I will say something to them right after detention, I promise myself.

26
LILLY

We move quietly in the hallway, staying close to the walls as we walk. You can never be too careful when you're sneaking into school, because Principal Klein or any other teacher could be lurking anywhere.

As we walk, Aisha's gym sneakers squeak. She removes her shoes.

Grace's shoes squawk. She also removes her shoes.

We approach the fifth-grade hallway. We haven't seen anyone, but I peer around the corner just to make sure. It looks clear, so I wave the group to hurry along with me, and I open the hallway doors.

Aisha rushes ahead of us and straight to Mrs. Rosenbloom's room, where she throws the door open and it hits against the wall with a loud BANG!

She turns back around. "Sorry, guys." Fortunately, I don't think anyone heard the bang except us. We all follow her inside the room.

The lights in the room are turned off, but sunlight streams in through the cracks of the blinds covering the windows. The only sound is a slight chattering from Soda's cage, which sits on a table next to the window.

Soda licks from a water bottle that's almost empty.

"Let me do it," says Aisha. She gently lifts the top of the cage, places it quietly on the table, and then scoops up the hamster. Soda squeaks and sort of chirps. I'm glad Aisha is with us, because I know she'll be extra gentle with Soda.

As Aisha nestles Soda in her hands, the hamster looks around, eyeing all of us, and then fixes her stare on me, just me, as if she knows I'm the team captain.

I stare back. "Blame Team Blue," I tell Soda. "This isn't my fault."

I unzip my backpack, which is empty except for my pencil bag, and Aisha places Soda gently inside. She keeps part of my bag unzipped so Soda can breathe.

Soda immediately begins scratching the sides of my pack as if trying to crawl out. I don't think she likes being inside my dark bag. Meanwhile, the wall clock ticks above the door. We've been gone too long, and I feel panic gurgling in my stomach. "We should head back before Mrs. Greeley wakes up." The others nod.

I open the door, look both ways down the hall, and we file out. Soon we are tiptoeing back down the hall to the cafeteria.

Sarah grabs my backpack. "I'll take that. I want to bring the rodent home tonight and make some improvements to it."

"What are you talking about?" I gasp. "I thought we were going to exchange Soda for Elvis."

"Tomorrow," says Sarah. "I have plans for Soda."

"What sort of plans?" I ask. My insides start to hurt with worry. What if we're thrown in jail for hamster stealing? Maybe Sarah likes to eat hamsters. Or maybe she wants to sell Soda to a hamster farm somewhere, although I'm not sure if a hamster farm is actually a *thing*.

None of this is Soda's fault. To be honest, I think she's cute. I asked my parents for a hamster a few years ago, but they didn't let me get one.

"Don't worry," says Sarah, who must sense my worrying. "I won't harm it. Our night together will be fabulicious."

As we walk back to the cafeteria, my stomach twists and turns because I don't know what Sarah has planned. Whatever it is, I doubt Soda will like it one bit. I start to reach for my backpack, to grab it from Sarah, but then I think of Team Blue, and how they stole Elvis.

I watch Sarah walk ahead with my backpack. If George can mastermind a little organized crime, then so can we. Soda might be an innocent bystander, but there is nothing innocent about Team Blue.

After detention, I'm standing outside school, near Brian and Seth. They wait for a parent to pick them up. I live close enough to walk, but not everyone does, and buses left an hour ago.

Here is finally my chance to speak up. I walk up to them. I stand in front of them.

"Guys, I wanted to talk about Elvis."

Brian glares at me. "What about him?" He holds the shoebox in front of him.

"I don't think taking a turtle is, well, nice."

Seth laughs. "What does being nice have to do with anything?"

"Maybe Simon needs to lock you in a closet again," says Brian, glaring at me.

I gulp, because I don't want to be locked in a closet, even if I can organize one well. "We just wrote essays on good sportsmanship."

"I didn't," says Brian. "I drew pictures of rocket ships."

"Me too," says Seth.

Team Red files out of school, dozens of kids joining us on the sidewalk. Lilly, Aisha, and Grace stomp up to us. I smile at Lilly, but she doesn't return it. They all stare daggers at us.

"We know you have Elvis," says Lilly.

Brian returns her glare. "Maybe we do, maybe we don't." Lilly stares at the shoebox in Brian's hands, and I can hear the turtle moving inside it, rubbing against the cardboard. "I bought new shoes," says Brian, as if explaining why he might be carefully holding a shoebox that's making noise. "They're running shoes," he adds.

"We have Soda," says Grace.

Kyle, who is standing near us, immediately joins our circle. Kyle usually takes care of Soda, so I think the mention of the class pet's name startles him. "Soda? What about Soda?" he asks loudly.

"We have her," says Lilly.

Kyle's eyes widen. "Where?"

"Somewhere safe, don't worry," says Lilly. "We just need Elvis back first."

Kyle looks at us, puzzled. "Elvis?"

"Don't play dumb with us," Lilly warns, her voice clipped and short. "We'll swap."

"Tomorrow morning, meet us behind the school," says Grace.

"With Elvis," adds Aisha.

"Or you'll never see your precious guinea pig again," says Grace, sneering.

"Actually, she's a hamster," says Kyle.

"Whatever it is, if you want to see it again, you'll meet us tomorrow," Lilly growls.

"You just better hope our turtle is okay," Aisha says.

"You better hope our hamster is okay," Kyle retorts.

All this plotting and stealing makes my head hurt. "Guys, this is all getting out of hand."

Lilly looks at me, eyes narrowed. "You started it."

I put my hands up. "I didn't do anything . . ."

"Save it," she says. "I don't want to hear any more of your excuses."

"I swear . . . ," I begin, but Lilly is already walking away, with Aisha and Grace next to her.

"We have to get Soda back," says Kyle, his voice shaking.

"We will," I assure him. "Um, right, guys?" I ask Brian and Seth.

Brian nods. "Elvis will be there tomorrow. Don't worry. I just might, you know, make him a little more attractive. Turtle green is such a boring color."

I fix them with a steely gaze. I need to stop this, as I promised myself. I open my mouth and start to say, "You can't . . ."

But my voice is drowned out by a loud car honk. A large sedan pulls up to the curb, repeatedly honking. Brian and Seth dash toward it and get in. The car door is only open a moment, but I can hear a loud voice of someone's dad yelling at them before it closes.

I haven't moved, my mouth still open. I spoke up, but not nearly enough. I need to act like our team leader. I'll say something to Brian and Seth tomorrow. Maybe.

28
LILLY

I sit on my bed and stare at the bulletin board next to me. Dad hung the corkboard up on my wall a few years ago, and I've pinned a whole bunch of photos to it. George is in all of them. Some shots are of my family and me and George, and some are George's family and my family, and some are just of me with George.

There's a photo of George and me at a baseball game, and one at the beach house our families rented for a week. I have a photo of George at my birthday party last year. There were about twenty kids at my party, but the only photo I have is with George. There's a photo of me getting on the bus for camp last summer. George didn't go, but instead of shots from camp pinned to the bulletin board I have a single photo of me posing with George near the front of the bus, waving good-bye.

When I was in camp I wrote to George every day. I only

wrote to my parents twice, and that's because the counselors made us write to our parents twice.

I can't believe I wasted so many great times hanging out with a good-for-nothing cheat and turtle stealer like George.

Still, I miss him.

He's too serious much of the time, but not always. He laughs at my jokes, even when they aren't funny. He is always interested in what I'm talking about, even if what I'm talking about isn't very interesting. And he let me win at tic-tac-toe 228 times in a row, even if he pretended he was trying his hardest.

My wrist feels empty without our friendship bracelet on it. I know I only wore it for a few days, but I expected to wear it forever.

I think about Soda, too. I wonder if she's okay. I can't imagine Sarah would hurt her, but I just don't know what to think about anything anymore except that losing is for losers.

And right now, I feel like I'm losing.

I don't feel good about anything I've done this week. I've cheated. I've stolen. The things I've done during Spirit Week have been even worse than promising a unicorn ride for Francine Pepper's cookie sales.

Maybe, sometimes, being a winner or a loser has nothing to do with winning or losing.

"How's it going, champ?" Dad asks. He and Mom stand in my doorway, smiling, holding hands.

They hold hands a lot. I like that about them.

"Everything's fine," I say, but I don't say it with a lot of happiness I guess, because Dad sort of frowns.

"We still need to talk about school today," Mom says. "Your costume was covered in eggs. You stayed after school to serve detention. When you were named team captain we didn't think . . ."

"I know, okay?" I interrupt. Mom looks angry, and I bite my lip. "It's been a bad week. But everything is fine now."

Mom arches her eyebrows.

"Some kids got carried away and some egg salad got spilled, but I didn't do anything," I continue. "It was just some dumb kids. I don't want to talk about it."

"You're going to have to talk about it at some point," says Mom, frowning.

Dad sighs. "We also came up here with some good news. This Friday, instead of eating in, we're going out to a restaurant with George and his family. Any suggestions where we go?"

I always choose the Japanese steakhouse near us. I love how the chefs clang their knives together and make silly jokes while they throw pieces of vegetables at us. We're supposed to catch the veggies in our mouths, but George always misses.

They pour oil in an onion and it steams up like a train. It's awesomesauce.

But today I just shake my head. "I don't care where we eat."

"You always care where we eat," says Dad.

"Well, I don't care now, all right?" I say, trying to keep the irritation from my voice, but I know it's spilling out.

Dad walks into my room and stands next to my bed, looking down at me. "We haven't seen George in a few days. Is everything okay with you guys?"

"You should ask him," I answer, and now I'm even more annoyed and I can hear it in my voice.

"Mrs. Martinez says she hasn't seen you at their house in a few days, either," adds Mom, also walking into my room, and standing next to Dad.

I take a deep breath. So I haven't been seen with George for a few days. You'd think the world was coming to an end. "I'm okay, okay? Everything is great. Everyone is great. I'm just not hanging out with George anymore. Is it against the law not to hang out with George?" My voice gets louder and louder as I talk, and I don't want it to get louder and louder. It just does. When I stop talking the room is eerily silent. Both Mom and Dad's mouths are open.

"Well, all right, then," Mom says, and I know I've totally overreacted to their questions. But she acts as if I'm committing some horrible crime just because George and I aren't doing things together.

I sigh, extra loudly for effect. "I'm sorry. Everything is perfect," I lie. "Can't you guys see I'm busy?"

"When we came in you were just sitting on your bed staring at the wall," says Mom.

"Well, to me that's busy."

"Listen, young lady . . . ," Mom begins, her voice rising, but Dad puts his hand on her shoulder, which calms her.

"We will talk later, when we're all in a better mood," says Dad, and he speaks in this sort of quiet, understanding voice that is more irritating than if he just spoke normally.

He and Mom leave, and they are holding hands again, which I guess is nice since they are best friends. But I don't have a best friend anymore, so looking at their hands suddenly bothers me. I turn away and look at the bulletin board again. It takes all my strength not to jump up and rip all of the photos with George off the board, right then and there.

29
GEORGE

School starts soon but I stand behind it, in my pajamas. I'm with Kyle, Brian, and Seth in a secluded spot hidden from the street, where no one can see us. The only other things that move are the grass and trees from a slow, cool breeze. The school-building shadows cover us.

I hate what I'm wearing. All of my pajamas were in my dirty clothes hamper except for one pair, which I've only worn once before today. Mom apologized. She meant to do the wash last night.

So now I'm stuck wearing these pj's, the ones Grandma Katie bought for me as a birthday present last year. They are pink. Grandma said they're lavender, but they look pink to me. Brian and Seth both already informed me that boys don't wear pink. I didn't bother trying to explain it was lavender.

Still, it's Pajamas Day, even though it's not really, and I'm the team captain, so I need to wear jammies.

Brian, Seth, and Kyle all wear pajamas, too. But they all wear normal-colored ones.

A back door opens. We turn. Lilly exits the building with Soda cradled in her hands. Sarah, Grace, and Aisha walk behind her.

Lilly wears mismatched pajamas. Her shirt is striped and green. Her pants are red and plaid. I've seen her wear the same outfit at her house, when I've come over to watch TV after dinner. I never really thought about it before, but now I think it looks sort of ridiculous.

Those nights seem a lifetime ago.

"Nice outfit," I say, shaking my head because I don't really mean it.

"At least I'm not wearing pink," Lilly answers, rolling her eyes.

Sarah and Grace stand behind her, glaring with huge frowns. But Aisha is all smiles. "Elvis!" she shouts with glee.

The turtle sits in my hands. I have one hand under him and my other hand covers his shell. Egg salad smells worse than turtle, but not a whole lot worse. I can't wait to exchange our pets and wash my hands. I'll need to soak them in water and soap for an hour or I'll never get rid of the turtle germs.

Kyle, standing next to me, tries to get a look at Soda. "She better be okay," he huffs.

"Relax," says Lilly. "She's never been better."

"She even has a new fashion accessory," adds Sarah. Lilly uncuffs her hands to reveal Soda, who has a giant red stripe across her back with the fur propped high like a Mohawk. "Quite an improvement, don't you think?"

I can feel Kyle shaking with anger. "If you've harmed her . . ."

"Oh, relax," says Grace. "It'll wash out."

"Unfortunately," adds Sarah.

I hold up Elvis, who has withdrawn into his shell. I don't think he likes it here, outside his terrarium. I remove my top hand.

"What did you do to Elvis?" asks Aisha, her voice high-pitched, angry.

"Gave him a touch-up," says Brian.

He and Seth wrote *Go, Team Blu* on his shell with blue paint.

"We ran out of room," explains Brian, pointing to the word *Blu*. The letters are pretty large.

"How dare you mess up his shell!" Aisha cries out, taking a step forward.

"It'll wash off. But how dare you give Soda a Mohawk racing stripe!" Kyle retorts, taking a step forward.

Sarah steps forward, too. Her eyes burn, and for a moment I think everyone is going to start fighting.

"Stop it!" I yell, and I surprise myself by yelling. "All of you."

Kyle steps back, as does Aisha. Sarah doesn't move, but she doesn't come closer, either.

"We're here to swap," I say. "Let's just get this over with."

"But her fur . . . ," Kyle blares.

"His shell . . . ," Aisha blurts.

"George is right. Let's just do this," grumbles Lilly. She seems as disinterested in fighting as I do.

I hand Elvis to Aisha, and Lilly hands Soda to Kyle. As we do this, our shoulders slightly graze. "I'm sorry, it wasn't my idea . . . ," I say.

Lilly sniffs. It's a sniff of scorn. "You always have an excuse, don't you?"

I bristle at this and I want to say something back that's just as mean, but I can't think of anything. I just feel guilty for everything.

"We'll see you in the gym for Pajamas Day," says Sarah.

"I hear the winning team gets a new house. A house just for Elvis to live in," Aisha adds. She hugs the turtle like it's her best friend. But I notice Elvis hasn't come out of his shell. I think he just wants to go back into his home.

"You mean, a new house for Soda to live in." Kyle hugs the squirming hamster, but she doesn't seem happy out here, either.

"Whatever that prize is, we're going to win it," says Grace.

I don't say a word, but I know Principal Klein is not giving anyone a prize. I think we'll be lucky if he doesn't expel the entire grade, since he has already canceled Spirit Week and we're all wearing pajamas, anyway.

I sigh. Why did I agree to this?

Kyle, Brian, Seth, and I walk away, Soda cradled safely in Kyle's arms. "Poor girl," he says to her in a soothing voice. "But don't worry, no not today. For you, we'll win Pajamas Day," he says in a sort of rap.

I don't say anything. I just want this week to end. Why did I ever raise my hand to be the team captain?

30
LILLY

Before we enter school, Sarah stops me. Aisha walks ahead to return Elvis to his terrarium. "That was fabulicious," she says. "Did you see the look in their eyes when they saw our racing stripe?"

"Yeah, but Elvis is painted blue," I point out.

Sarah nods. "We'll get revenge for that, too."

I get that sinking feeling in my stomach again. "Do we have to keep getting revenge?" I ask. "I mean, we swiped their pet. We're dressed in pajamas. What else is there?"

Sarah squints. "Losing is for losers. And letting the other team get away with painting our turtle—well, that's for losers."

"I know but . . ."

Sarah keeps her eyes narrowed. "Maybe you don't have what it takes. I thought you could hang out with us after school sometime, but maybe Grace and I were wrong about you. Don't you want to win Spirit Week?"

"Sure, but there is no more Spirit Week. I mean, not really, right?"

Sarah shakes her head in disgust at me. "Grace even said she was going to let you ride her horse."

Sarah marches ahead, joining Grace, who is waiting for her up by the school entrance. I walk slowly by myself thinking of Francine Pepper, pretend horseback riding, and feeling like I've lost already.

31

GEORGE

As I head back into the school, which is now filling up with the rest of the students, I'm amazed at how many fifth graders are wearing pajamas. I guess word spread quickly, and I didn't text anyone about it, either. It's like we're having one big sleepover. Some outfits are sort of funny, like Daisy's bunny pajamas, with ears and everything. I see Maggie, who's back in school with her arm in a cast, and even she wears pj's. I'm not sure how she heard about our plan, but her crimson Harvard sleepwear is exactly what I'd expect the brainiest girl in our grade to wear.

I consider gathering all my notes and handing them to Maggie. She can be our team captain now! Then I remember it's too late. Spirit Week is over, despite our wearing pajamas.

"Hey, Pinky," says Luke with a laugh, and I cringe. He's wiggling around as always, and I'm jealous of his normal, not-strange-at-all green flannel pajamas. They have a thousand wrinkles over them, though, and I wonder if he thrashes around all night, just like he seems to be jittery all day. "Looks like Pajamas Day is actually happening, huh? Do you think we're going to get in trouble? I mean, after the egg-salad disaster and everything?"

I feel a lump in my throat. "I don't know."

Luke hops in place for a moment. "I hope not. I mean, we're just wearing pajamas. There's no school rule about wearing pajamas, right? So, anyway, how are we voting for a winner? Our team better do the counting. Because I don't trust anyone on Team Red to count right."

"I haven't thought about the judging," I admit.

"Well, you better. You're team captain, right?"

I nod, although I hate those words.

As we all walk toward the gym, Harrison, who is in Lilly's class, stumbles in front of me. At first I think it's because of his big fuzzy slippers. But I hear a laugh and realize Brian and Seth are behind me. They shove kids on Team Red, because that's the sort of thing they do.

Brian shoves Pedro, who knocks into Jessie. She's wearing a yellow onesie spotted with pictures of cats. "Watch it," she says. To Brian she adds, "Or I'll sic my cats on you." She almost seems feline herself, with her cat-eye glasses and angry snarl. Brian laughs, but I don't think you want to mess with Jessie and her cats.

"Give it a rest, you guys are being pests," rhymes Kyle, and Brian and Seth stop shoving people. Kyle's the only guy who can ever talk sense into those two. He no longer carries Soda, who is probably resting comfortably back in her cage.

Soon, we enter the sweltering, sock-smelling gym. My lavender pj's are itchy and warm, and I'm already feeling sticky. My team gathers on the far side of the gym. As I join them, kids stick out their palms to exchange high fives with me. "This was a great idea," says Toby.

"It wasn't my idea," I say.

"You know, I can still give you free fashion advice if you want," says Samantha, tapping me on the back and eyeing my pajamas. I blush, and my face probably turns the same shade as my outfit.

The bell rings and that means classes are starting. I wonder what our teachers will think when no one shows up. We're definitely getting expelled. My heart beats faster. I just want to get this over with. I walk to the middle of the gym, and so does Lilly. We meet at the centerline of the basketball court.

"Clearly, Team Red wins Pajamas Day," she says.

I scratch my head, looking at her side and mine again. "What are you talking about?"

"Every kid on Team Red is wearing pajamas."

"So is everyone on Team Blue," I point out.

"Even them?" She points to Danny and Jasmine, twins, who stand near the bleachers wearing blue jeans and T-shirts. I didn't notice them earlier.

"That's what they wear to bed," I say, which I'm guessing isn't true. I point to her side of the court. "And what about them?"

Clearly, Taylor and Olivia are not dressed in pajamas. They both wear dresses and matching green sweaters.

Lilly frowns. "Those are fancy pajamas."

"So here you are." The booming voice of Principal Klein interrupts our meeting. He's hovering in the doorway with Mrs. Rosenbloom by his side. His frown is as long as his face. He stands with his arms crossed, face red. "What is going on here?"

"We're dressed for Pajamas Day," says Adam, who stands near the door. I cringe, because that's not something you should say to a principal who has clearly forbidden Pajamas Day. I think Adam realizes this, because he immediately steps back and hides behind the much-taller Kyle.

"I see," says Principal Klein. The entire gym is quiet. We stare at our principal. I knew we might get in trouble, and I was up half the night worrying about what could happen.

But now, with our principal here, even the worst things I imagined don't seem bad enough.

From the expression on Principal Klein's face, we are in trouble and the trouble is deep, deep, deep. "And who thought this was acceptable?"

No one says a word.

"Spirit Week was canceled because of continued poor sportsmanship, trickery, and tomfoolery," he says, his voice getting louder with each word until it echoes off the walls and bleachers. "It was canceled because, in all my years as principal, I have never seen a fifth grade act with as much malice as all of you." He looks around the room. "And yet here you are, wearing pajamas, skipping class to assemble anyway." His voice rises both in loudness and pitch. "Whose idea was this?"

I look at Lilly, because the answer clearly is *Lilly*. This was all her thinking. She's the one who's created all these problems to begin with, too. I almost shout out, "It was all Lilly's fault," but I hold my tongue, because I don't want to bring attention to myself.

I'll probably be banished from school. And it will all be because of Lilly.

Principal Klein is pacing now. He's not limited to pacing behind his desk in his small office, so he takes long strides back and forth. Kids veer out of his way. "I have never, ever witnessed a more disrespectful group of students. You disrespect the school and me personally. It seems that your serving detention yesterday didn't teach any of you a lesson. So maybe this will—you will all serve detention after school again today."

"But I have baseball practice," complains Seth.

Principal Klein scans the crowd, trying to see who dared speak out, but Seth stands still and seems to shrink just a bit, and our principal doesn't notice him.

There are a few murmurs in the crowd, Seth's outburst seeming to puncture the incredible silence from the kids. Maggie, who stands near me, complains to her friend Lacey that she'll miss her private tutoring classes, and Samantha tells Giovanna she has violin lessons. But most of us are still too nervous to say a word.

I wonder what Lilly is thinking as she stands there, frowning, hitting her fist against her leg. Does she blame herself, like she should? Does she blame me?

Principal Klein talks with Mrs. Rosenbloom now. She nods, and we're all waiting and wondering what they are talking about, but everyone is too nervous to say anything, and after maybe a minute, Principal Klein turns back to us. "Ms. Bryce runs an after-school tutoring program for some of the younger kids. In addition to your detention, you will all attend the program and help instruct the children over the next few weeks. I will create a schedule and share it in a few days. Attendance is mandatory."

Maggie leans over to her friends Lacey and Paige. They all wear the same glasses and look sort of like owls. As Maggie talks she moves her one good hand, since the other is still in a cast. "We're so lucky. I wonder if we can volunteer for multiple tutoring days? I bet we can teach some of those kids a lot."

Paige and Lacey nod their heads in eager agreement. But most of the kids in the gym groan.

"Everyone back to class," says our principal. "Now."

As Lilly and I step forward, our eyes meet. "This is all your fault," she whispers in a nasty tone.

I look at her, and I realize that she is right. "I know." Her eyes widen. I don't think she was expecting me to agree with her. I might not have come up with the idea to wear pajamas today, but I'm wearing them. I am a team captain. That means I'm the leader, only I haven't been doing much leading. I spent time organizing, and that's important, but leading is more than that. It's about doing the right thing, setting an example, and keeping your teammates in check.

I did none of that. I could have spoken up a bunch of times, but I was silent or spoke so softly no one could hear me. And even when I wasn't silent or locked in a closet, did I do everything I could? Did I demand my teammates behave, or was I just afraid?

Doing nothing is sometimes just as bad as doing something. Sometimes it's even worse.

"Lilly, it's your fault, too," I add.

"But I didn't start—"

"Does it really matter who started what?" I can tell she is about to yell at me, so I quickly add, "We both could have stopped this. But I was too scared and you were too competitive." Lilly opens her mouth to argue, but I continue. "You are, Lilly. That's usually okay. But we were both thinking of that stupid prize."

"I heard everyone on the winning team was going to win five thousand dollars," she adds.

"I don't know what we were supposed to win," I said. "But can you put a price on cheating? On doing bad things?" I squeeze her arm. "Or on our friendship?"

With that last word, Lilly's head slumps, and when she looks back up, she smiles. It's a sad sort of smile, but her eyes wrinkle, so I know it's a genuine smile. "Our friendship is worth more than five thousand dollars, or a truck of ice-cream cones, or whatever the prize was. I'm sorry about everything."

"Me too."

Her smile broadens. She no longer looks sad. She looks relieved. "I guess I got carried away, and I know you didn't do any of that stuff, but it made it easier to plot things if I convinced myself you were behind them. And Sarah and Grace said . . . Well, never mind them. But how are we going to make things right?"

"You mean between us?" I ask.

She shakes her head. "That won't be too hard, I think. But we're the team captains. We need to make things right for everyone. But how?"

"I wish I knew." I look down at the ground. I don't think there is any way to fix what we've done, other than serve our punishment.

As we head out of the gym, all our classmates walk with their heads as bowed as mine.

32

LILLY

We stream out of the gym under the watchful glare of Principal Klein. I slink down so he doesn't notice me. I really, really don't want to be noticed right now.

George walks ahead of me, but I can't get his words out of my head because I know he is right, just like I've known every moment of every day that he's not organizing crime or anything. He's not against me. He's my best friend.

Our entire grade walks down the hall without saying much of anything. I think we all feel bad about wearing pajamas today.

While I walk, Seth bumps me on the shoulder. "Sorry," mutters the Team Blue bully. But he's not sorry. That was definitely an on-purpose bump. I guess not everyone feels as bad about things as others.

But Team Blue shouldn't hate me. I didn't force them to wear their pj's. They could have worn whatever they wanted and let us win the contest.

They all chose to be just as guilty as me.

I approach my locker. "I can't believe we get detention and community service and no special prize," moans Grace, her teeth bared like a wolf.

"It's the worst," agrees Sarah as she removes books from her locker. The inside of her door is still tinged with slime stain from the other day, as is mine. "I heard the winner was going on a cruise to the Bahamas."

"And it's all Team Blue's fault," barks Finn.

"We're going to make them sorry," adds Pete. Both Finn and Pete wear dark blue flannel pajamas with our school name across the front: Liberty Falls Elementary.

"We sure are," agrees Sarah.

Anger oozes from all of them, but I no longer share their hatred. I just feel bad for playing any part in the mischief. If I could rewind the week, I would. Too bad life doesn't come with a remote control.

"Guys, relax," I say. I keep my voice calm. "I'm not saying Team Blue isn't guilty, but so are we, okay? We put pudding in half the balloons, you know."

"That was different," says Sarah.

"How?" I ask.

"That was revenge because they filled our lockers with slime," says Grace.

"Which was revenge for Lilly deliberately ruining George's twin outfit," adds Aisha.

"That was an accident," I insist.

"Right, I know," says Aisha, but Sarah and Grace just laugh because they don't believe me at all.

"Look, it doesn't matter," I say, and I'm thinking of George the entire time I talk. "We've all made mistakes. We might as well own up to them. And maybe if we do . . ." My voice trails off, as an idea slowly forms in my head.

George and I talked about making things right. Maybe there's a way. The idea is a bit murky, but something about it feels like it could work.

"Maybe if we do what?" asks Finn.

The idea grows and it forms into a solid block of promise, kind of like when clay hardens in the oven. It's not a great idea, but it's not a terrible one, either. "It starts by taking responsibility for everything we did. It starts with an apology to Principal Klein." I eye my teammates. "And maybe even an apology to Team Blue."

"Never!" yells Sarah, spit flying from her mouth.

"I don't apologize," says Grace. "Apologies are for losers."

"And so is losing," adds Sarah.

"Hear me out," I say. Grace and Sarah seethe, but they wait for me to finish. "Principal Klein is angry because he says we're bad sports."

"Team Blue started it," insists Grace.

"Look," I continue, and I'm nodding my head as I talk because this idea of mine feels more right the more I think it. "It doesn't matter who started what. If we apologize, maybe, just maybe, Principal Klein will change his mind about canceling the week. It's a long shot, sure. But if we show him we can play fair, maybe we can convince him that the best way to learn how to be good sports is to be good sports."

"And then we can destroy Team Blue?" asks Grace, her eyes menacing slits.

"Well, first things first," I say.

Sarah shakes her head. "Apologizing won't change anything."

"I have to agree," says Aisha. "An apology sounds nice and all, but Principal Klein was pretty mad. I don't think an apology is enough for him to change his mind."

"You're right," I say, nodding my head. "That's just the first part. But I know something that might help, a secret something. We're going to need Team Blue's help with this, but if we work together, just maybe . . ."

"Work with Team Blue? Are you nuts?" says Grace.

"I've been looking forward to Field Day for years, and it was supposed to be tomorrow," I say. "Maybe it still can be? I don't know. I'm just saying that it's worth trying. But we need everyone's help if we want to win that prize."

"Do you think the prize could be horseback-riding lessons?" asks Finn.

"You never know," says Grace. Finn grins broadly.

We huddle together as I share my plan. I can tell from the vigorous nods of their heads that they agree it's worth trying, although Sarah grumbles the entire time.

But we have to try something.

33

GEORGE

The entire day is a haze. Our parents were called and we all served detention again. This time we were told to write a one-page report on why it's important to listen to your teachers and follow rules in school. I wrote a five-page report because I couldn't get all I had to say on only one page.

I wrote about how keeping silent is just as wrong as doing bad things. I wrote about how it's not easy to stand up for what you believe in, but if no one ever stood up for things, then good things might never happen. I wrote about how pens should be kept in penholders on desks.

That last part didn't make much sense, but I kept thinking of Principal Klein's desk and it just sort of flowed into the essay. I also wrote about the importance of hand sanitizer.

As soon as I leave detention, I look for Lilly. I'm determined to walk home with her today. I want to forget this week ever happened. Part of me is happy we're not finishing Spirit Week. I hated being team captain.

But I don't have to look for Lilly because she finds me. "George. Good. We need to talk."

"We can talk while we walk home," I say, smiling.

Lilly doesn't return my grin. She speaks with urgency. "Look, I think we can still finish Spirit Week."

I shake my head. "It's over, Lilly. I'm sorry."

"I think we can save it. Well, maybe we can save it."

"You're crazy. You heard Principal Klein," I argue. "You're just going to get us in more trouble."

She takes hold of my arm, and I shake it loose from her grip. She's obviously lost her own grip on reality. "Just hear me out. I need your help."

"You didn't need my help to make a mess of everything." I immediately wish I hadn't said that, and I bite my lip. I thought I had sort of forgiven Lilly, but maybe not entirely. Lilly frowns. "Sorry. I didn't mean that."

"That's okay. Maybe I deserve it." She looks me in the eye, and I know all is forgiven. "But it's in the past. You can organize things better than me. You're better at making lists and stuff."

"I know. So?"

"So we need to act quickly. If we want Field Day tomorrow, we can't mess around. We're going to need a lot of people to help. And both teams will need to work together."

Lilly tells me her plan and when she's done, I have to admit, it's not the worst plan ever. It's a bit scattered and messy, sort of like Lilly, but with some proper planning and organization, it could come together.

I mean, it probably won't work, but maybe it's worth attempting. It would mean I'm still our team captain, at least for tonight, and maybe tomorrow. But I guess I can handle it for one more day.

"Okay, I'm in," I say, and Lilly beams. I haven't seen her smile in days, not a big, broad smile like this one, and it warms me.

I text my mom that I'm going to Lilly's. But instead of leaving, we get too excited, and Lilly and I just plop down on the sidewalk in front of the school. I grab my notebook and we get to work. I have a lot of note taking to do. We'll need to get most of the grade involved. But if we all work together, who knows? Even if it doesn't work, it just feels right to be on the same team as Lilly.

Lilly smiles and bounces next to me as we make plans, and it seems like everything that has come between us just sort of fades away.

I only wish we had been on the same team all week.

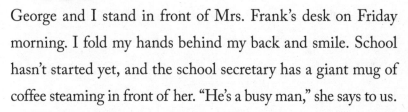

34
LILLY

George and I stand in front of Mrs. Frank's desk on Friday morning. I fold my hands behind my back and smile. School hasn't started yet, and the school secretary has a giant mug of coffee steaming in front of her. "He's a busy man," she says to us.

"We just need to show him something," I say, making my smile more of a friendly grin since it's always a good idea to smile at people if you want them to do things for you.

"Please?" adds George.

Grown-ups love it when you say *please*. You can get them to do just about anything with that word, especially when you throw in the smile. Mrs. Frank sighs, puts down her coffee, and stands up. She turns the knob to Principal Klein's office door and then disappears inside without even knocking.

That's sort of rude, but I guess when you're the school secretary you don't have to knock.

"Do you really think this will work?" George asks.

"I have no idea."

The door opens and Mrs. Frank steps out. Principal Klein walks out with her, still looking angry from the day before. He folds his arms in front of him. "Hello, George and Lilly," he says, his voice clipped. "What can I help you with?"

"We wanted to show you something," I say, my smile plastered on my face.

"In the gym," says George.

"School starts soon," says Principal Klein, his arms still folded, his voice still short and growling a bit. "Shouldn't you be getting to class?"

"Please? It will only take a few minutes," George says. He smiles. I smile.

Principal Klein scrunches his brows. He looks back into his office. A half-eaten bagel sits on his desk.

"It's important," I add.

Principal Klein blows out a heavy sigh. "What is it?"

"We have to show you," I say.

Principal Klein sighs again, and this sigh is louder than the first one.

"Please?" I ask, using the magic word.

"Tell my morning appointment I might be a few minutes late," our principal says to Mrs. Frank.

"That's been canceled. I forgot to update you, sir," says Mrs. Frank.

Our principal frowns and then follows us out of the office.

Kids are rushing down the halls to get to their lockers or to class, but as soon as anyone sees Principal Klein, he or she slows down. It's pretty funny, actually. Four third graders skid to a halt and start walking in slow motion. A large gang of second graders who are sprinting immediately freeze, as if turned to ice. Principal Klein frowns at each and every one of them.

But we don't pass any fifth graders. They are waiting in the gym.

As we walk, with Principal Klein right behind us, I can't believe we did it. George and I share a smile. If they had assigned teams like they were supposed to assign them, with George's class and my class together, maybe none of these problems would have happened. So, in a way, this entire week is our principal's fault.

But I'm not about to tell him *that*.

"We're almost there," George says to Principal Klein.

"Humph," he replies with a frown.

As we near the gym, a loud buzz fills the hallway from the kids inside.

"How many people are in there?" asks Principal Klein.

"The entire fifth grade, I think," I answer.

I push open the doors. The lights are off so we step inside a darkened gym.

35

GEORGE

A light flickers on, a spotlight aimed at the middle of the gym floor. Kyle stands in front of the microphone. Behind him are Finn and Jai, who start to beatbox.

Ryan spins next to them performing some sort of twirling dance. She's a dancer, and she really wanted to do an interpretive spinning dance. I suppose it adds to the spirit of the assembly we've created.

Kyle starts to rap, the beatboxing behind him driving the rhythm.

> *Principal Klein, welcome to the show.*
> *Our grade's got plenty to show you, yo!*
> *No, we haven't gone mad or berserk.*
> *But you can do tons with lots of teamwork.*
> *We got together, Team Red and Team Blue,*
> *To prove what working together can do.*

A switch is flicked and the gym is bathed in dancing green lights. The entire gym has been transformed. Giovanna and Samantha were in charge of the decorations, and they filled the room with streamers and lined the walls with dozens of posters with words like TEAMWORK, SPORTSMANSHIP, and FAIR PLAY. I don't know how they got it all done in one night.

Meanwhile, most of the class sits on the bleachers, clapping along to the rap while Kyle continues.

Like the auditorium—filled with slop.
So some of us came early—with a mop.

He points to a group of fifth graders who hold up their mops. I looked in the auditorium this morning, and I don't think it has ever been so clean.

Kyle continues.

But that's not all, no that's just the start.
Everyone here did a little part.
Like Bjorn, in charge of technology,
And Maggie, who wrote an apology.

Bjorn hits a button on his cell phone, and the room, which had been basked in green light, is now awash in red. He really is good at computer stuff. He rigged all the lights together.

Kyle points to Maggie, who stands off to the side, holding a piece of paper in front of her. She clears her throat. "Dear Principal Klein, we are sorry for acting so poorly. We have learned a valuable lesson about teamwork and fair play. We let our competitive spirit get the best of us, and we realize we were wrong. Please accept our sincere apology. P.S. We can't wait to help out with Ms. Bryce's after-school tutoring program, and can I have some extra sessions, please?"

She runs over to our principal and hands him the note, which has been signed by everyone in our grade.

Our principal accepts the page, his mouth agape. I don't know what he was expecting when he came to the gym, but it wasn't this.

Finn and Jai begin beatboxing again, and Kyle continues his rap.

Great lessons and values, we've learned a ton—
About sportsmanship and playing for fun.
But we've brought you more than my rap ballad.
We've also brought some homemade egg salad.

Toby runs over to our principal with a bowl of egg salad his mom made last night. Toby said his mom makes a really good egg salad. "Here you go. I know it's your favorite," says Toby, and then runs off.

We worked together to bring you this song,
And show you that our grade can get along.
So now we're one team, and those are the facts,
Now let's take a break for Luke on the sax.

Kyle points to Luke, who's dressed in his Charlie Parker costume from Historical Figure Day. He is in front of a microphone, and he starts blowing his horn and moving his fingers at crazy speeds while he taps his toes and wiggles his legs. The entire room fills with the honks and beeps from his instrument.

I find myself tapping my foot and snapping my fingers. Luke ends with a manic flourish and then points back to Kyle.

Thanks for your time—soon the school bell will ring,
But we need to show you one final thing.
It's big and awesome and can't be ignored,
But the world's best principal deserves an award.

Bjorn hits his phone, and the gym fills with a dark purple light, all except for one bright spotlight. It shines on a large trophy, a three-foot statue of Principal Klein made of modeling clay and the words *World's Greatest Principal* etched on the bottom.

Our principal's jaw drops open in surprise. I think that's a good thing.

36
LILLY

Of all the things we did to make this Principal Klein presentation, the trophy was the most impressive. I've always liked making figurines, but I've never made anything this big. Aisha and Giovanna both helped me last night.

I'm not sure if our trophy looks like Principal Klein, but it's a large guy wearing an orange cardigan sweater, so there is no doubt who it's supposed to be.

Principal Klein stares at it, his eyes practically bugging out of his head. He walks toward the clay trophy, slowly at first and then picking up speed. George and I follow him. He stands next to it, staring, as if he's afraid to touch it, as if it might all disappear if he takes even a small step closer.

"I can't believe you were able to make that in one night," George whispers to me.

"It was a very late night, but I heard Principal Klein say that he'd never won a trophy before," I whisper back. "He always wanted one. I hoped to make it taller, but we ran out of modeling clay."

When I look at Principal Klein, I don't know if our plan is going to work or not. He just stares and stares at the trophy. He doesn't seem happy, but he doesn't look angry, either.

The gym is eerily silent except for a couple of coughs.

Finally, Principal Klein reaches his hand out and his fingers gently rub against the clay. They leave a small indent, because the clay isn't completely dry. He pulls his hand back.

He turns to us and sweeps his arms across the room. "You did all of this together?" We nod. "And you made this? For me?"

I nod, beaming.

"This is the . . . ," he begins, his voice starting to rise. "This is the . . ." His voice is louder, and I can't keep from fidgeting I'm so nervous. "This is the nicest thing anyone has ever done for me."

I had been holding my breath for a long time, and I can hold my breath for a very long time, but I let it out in a big sigh of relief. So does George. So do about half the kids in the bleachers. I hear a WOOSH of air around us.

"This will look marvelous in the trophy case," says Principal Klein, his voice choking. "Well, maybe it won't fit in one." He looks disappointed for a moment, but then adds, "But I'll put it somewhere." He circles the sculpture. George and I step back to give him room. He turns to George and me. "How did you guys put this together so quickly?"

"Both of our teams worked together," says George. "It's amazing what you can do with a little teamwork." He flashes me a smile, and I return it.

"I'm sure if you gave us another chance, we could show you we've learned all about teamwork," I say to Principal Klein. "And playing fairly. And for fun."

"Then you've learned a valuable lesson," says Principal Klein. "One that can help you throughout your life, and not just today." He looks at us and then at the rest of the grade. Everyone has now gathered in a big circle with me, George, our principal, and the trophy in the middle. We're all smiles.

Then, in his loud, booming voice, our principal adds, "Yes, you all have learned a great lesson. Good for you. Thank you for this wonderful gift." He wipes his nose. "I'm proud to announce that we will have Field Day this afternoon, as planned."

I bounce on my feet and cheer. The entire gymnasium cheers, and I bet we're so loud that every class in the building can hear us. Principal Klein raises his hands, motioning us to quiet down, but it takes a few moments before we do. A couple of lone yelps of happiness ring out, and then we are silent again. "But you have to show me you've truly learned your lesson. Any hint of shenanigans and Field Day will be canceled immediately. Understand?"

"What about the special prize?" someone yells. I can't see who it is. I think it sounded like Sarah.

"If there's a Field Day, there will be a prize," says Principal Klein, and this gets as loud and long a cheer as did his earlier announcement. "But for now, school is about to start and you all need to get to class."

George and I exchange grins. It's a relief to know that we saved Spirit Week. But I feel even better knowing that we saved it together.

37
GEORGE

Instead of listening to Mr. Foley during class, I spend the morning working on today's schedule. Field Day is full of events, and you need the right people assigned to the right games if you want to win.

Everyone talks about what games we'll play this afternoon. There is a lot of whispering in class and Mr. Foley keeps ordering kids to be quiet, but even he seems excited about Field Day.

Brian and Seth whisper and pass notes constantly, often while giggling. That worries me.

I try to put them out of my mind and concentrate on my schedule.

Most events need somewhere between ten and twelve kids from each team, and every kid is supposed to be assigned to participate in at least two events. It's a little tricky figuring it all out, and knowing where some kids will be great, and where other kids might not do great, but won't be too awful. For example, there's Avery, who is nice and all, but sort of clumsy. She wouldn't be the best person to choose for the Egg Race. And Maggie has her broken arm, so I wouldn't want her balancing cups of water.

But other kids would be perfect for those events. Other games need different skills, like the Tug-of-War, which is all about strength. With guys like Brian, Seth, and Kyle on my team, we should dominate Tug-of-War. That's the final event of the day and worth double points.

"This will be fun," says Luke after the bell rings and we head outside for the start of Field Day. He's changed out of his Charlie Parker costume from this morning, and instead wears a yellow T-shirt and jeans. I blink twice. The jeans are glittery with rainbow patches on the pockets.

"Are those from the Lost and Found?" I ask.

Luke shakes his head. "No, I had my mom make them. I thought they were kind of cool when you wore them the other day." He blushes. "Do I look goofy?"

"You look great," I say.

"Field Day is going to be fantastic," Brian says. He walks with Seth on the other side of me. "I mean, we've been planning stuff for days, you know? I just can't believe it's back on."

"Um, what do you mean 'planning stuff'?" I ask. Brian chuckles. "We have to play fair," I remind him. "We all promised."

"Sure," he answers with a wink. "Fair play. No worries."

I eye him suspiciously. He wears a smirk, and you should never trust a smirk.

"I hear nothing can stop us from winning," adds Toby, behind me. He's grinning, too.

"What's going on?" I demand. "What did you hear?" I cry out to Toby as he rushes past me.

Brian puts his finger to his mouth as a group of Team Red kids near us, also heading outside.

As I walk down the hall, my heart races. I should have known those guys would try to ruin everything. I need to scream at them that we need to play fair. We just performed a whole rap song about it!

But the hall is crowded, and Brian and Seth are now way ahead of me, exiting the school doors.

I also remember being locked in the storage pantry and how big Brian and Seth are, and so I take a deep breath. Maybe I can avoid talking to them. Maybe things aren't as bad as I think.

But then again, they could be even worse.

38

LILLY

Field Day always starts with hot dogs, and hot dogs are awesomesauce. I grab one from the lunch cart and then I stand in the fields behind the school with the rest of my team. It's surprisingly hot today! It almost feels as steamy outside as it usually does inside the gym. There is no breeze, and a breeze can make all the difference. A few portable fans sit on tables, but those are mostly for the parent volunteers, who stand next to the fans at their Field Day stations.

I'm amazed they got so many volunteers with such last-second notice, although Zachary said he heard that Mrs. Frank forgot to call parents to tell them today was canceled.

Everyone on my team wears a bright red Team Red shirt. They were handed out as soon as we walked outside. Big orange cones mark off courses, and ribbons and tape stretch across starting and finish lines for relay races. Spray paint outlines a football field. A lot of time and effort was spent preparing for all of this.

I guess Mrs. Frank forgot to tell the volunteers not to prepare the fields yesterday, either. Mrs. Frank seems to forget stuff sometimes.

There is a lot of equipment and gear, like a stack of Hula-Hoops sitting on a table and a long cord of rope lying on the ground for Tug-of-War. Ms. Bryce stands by a giant table covered in buckets that are filled with old, weird clothes.

I hold a small notepad, where I've scribbled down the participants for our first couple of events. I was supposed to do that this morning, but then I started thinking about what restaurant we should eat at tonight, because Mom and Dad said I could pick and I completely forgot to pick one, so I didn't have time to finish my Field Day assignments.

I squint while I read what I wrote. Is that Aubrey or Amelia? And which Alex did I want to participate in that event? There are two Alexes on my team. I can't read my writing very well. I should have been paying more attention to my writing and less to dinner.

But there is nothing wrong with being spontaneous.

I'll just figure out the rest of it as we go along. I'm sure George has mapped out some complicated schedule for his team, but you don't win by scheduling. You win by doing.

I look up at a giant board that marks each team's total points and will be updated after every event. My team is winning ten points to five for the week. That's not a very big lead. We won

Twin Day, but then both teams were awarded five points for the pudding fight because they called it a tie, Historical Figure Day was ruined, and Pajamas Day didn't count, either. Whoever wins the most events today will win Spirit Week and get the mystery prize.

The last I heard, the special prize is a waffle iron. I guess that prize would be sort of nice, but I don't think that rumor is true because winning a waffle iron would be weird.

George waves at me. He stands with his team, all wearing their royal-blue Team Blue T-shirts. He mouths, "Good luck!"

"You too!" I mouth back, and I mean it. I still want to win more than ever, but I want us both to play well. Winning only really counts when both teams try their hardest. Otherwise, it's not really winning at all.

George starts jogging over to me, and he's holding something in his hand. I meet him halfway across the field, and I can't see exactly what he carries until he's almost next to me.

"New friendship bracelets." He hands me one made from green, yellow, and blue twisted strings. The other bracelet is already around his wrist. "I made them last night. I should never have tossed the old one, but I'll never take this one off."

"Ever?"

His smile vanishes. "If it gets dirty, I might need to take it off to clean it, and I don't want to get hand sanitizer on it, and it could break someday maybe, but otherwise, never."

George keeps his smile off. He stiffens his neck and puts on his Mr. Serious expression. He frowns. "But look, we need to talk. We've got trouble. Kids are planning stuff. There's Brian and Seth, of course. But maybe Toby and other kids, too. I'm not sure, but I think my team has planned all sorts of sabotage today."

"Like what?"

"I don't know. But I think it's bad. Real bad."

"We'll just have to keep an eye out," I say. "We gave our word we would play fair. Maybe you've got it all wrong."

"I don't think so, but I hope you're right. I'll snoop around some more and see if I can figure it out."

"I'll do the same."

I jog back to rejoin my team, but my stomach is already feeling queasy. I smile at Amelia. "Ready to play fair?" I ask. But she just returns my smile with a frown.

"We're going to win," says Sarah to Grace.

Grace nods. "They won't be expecting anything."

"How could they?" asks Sarah. She snickers.

I tap them both on the shoulder. "Expecting what?"

Grace shrugs and Sarah laughs.

"We need to play honestly," I plead. "We gave our word."

Finn walks up to us and says to Grace, "We're all set."

"What's all set?" I ask.

They ignore me.

"You have to stop whatever you're planning!" I urge.

"It's too late now," says Grace.

"Tell me what you've done," I demand.

"So you can blab to your friend George?" asks Sarah, shaking her head and rolling her eyes. "Don't think we haven't noticed. You're either on Team Red or Team Blue. But you look awfully blue to me."

"I'm team captain."

"Not a very good one," says Sarah. "And you can forget about any sleepovers or horseback rides."

I wheel away, my head swimming. Sarah, Grace, and Finn huddle together, whispering. Then Zachary joins their huddle, and then Koko. I don't know how many people are involved or what horrible things have been planned, but it seems like a lot of potential planners and a lot of potential plans.

"What's happening?" I ask Aisha. She stands by herself, stretching her arms and legs.

"As if you don't know," she says.

"I don't!"

Aisha shakes her head and walks away from me. "I thought you were against cheating, too."

"I am!" She continues walking away and I want to scream. I want to pull out my hair, I'm so frustrated, but no one will even look at me.

Across the field, George jogs toward me again, and I run to meet him. I need to warn him about the pranks we're going to pull, even if I have no idea what they are. "What did you learn?" I ask.

"Nothing. No one will say a word to me."

"Same over here," I admit. "We've planned things, things that are maybe even worse than what your team has planned. But no one will tell me what."

"We've got to stop it," says George. "I'm too young to get kicked out of school."

"I don't want to win by cheating. Not anymore. No matter what the prize is."

"Then we've got to be ready for anything," warns George. "Because it's up to you and me to make sure both teams play fair or we're going to be in big, big trouble."

"The biggest," I agree. "As team captains we'll be blamed for everything."

I look down at my new friendship bracelet. I'll keep my word and play fair, but I'm not sure if I can get the rest of the team to do the same, even with George's help.

39
GEORGE

Large fans are positioned near many of the events, but they don't cool you off unless you're standing directly next to one. The teachers and adult volunteers have already taken all the good fan-standing spots. My jeans stick to my legs and sweat covers my forehead.

I squirt hand sanitizer on my palms, using up the final drips of my small bottle. This day will be sweaty and dirty. I groan.

The first event of the day is the Egg Race. One person from each team puts the handle of a spoon in his or her mouth, places an egg on the spoon, and then races across the field while trying to balance the egg.

Then he or she passes the egg to the next member of the team, who has his or her own plastic spoon.

I had to choose ten racers for the event. I didn't pick fast runners, but steady ones. If you drop the egg, you have to go back to the beginning, so you need balanced racers who aren't all twitchy like Luke. Luke would be a horrible egg runner.

Each of my Team Blue egg racers run in a circle, balancing a math book on his or her head. I read that beauty pageant contestants do that, to help with posture. Mario keeps dropping his books, so I replace him with Gavin at the last minute. Gavin seems more balanced, although maybe he just has a flatter head so books don't fall as easily.

My racers jog over to start the event. So do the Team Red racers. The rest of us crowd around the sidelines to cheer them on. Lilly has picked tall, fast kids, but a wobbly fast kid won't win a race for you. I feel good about our chances.

I wish I stood next to one of those portable fans, but I'm sweating from more than the heat. I'm sweating from nerves because I'm worried about what might be planned by my team, and that could be nearly anything. There's a buzz of excitement for the first event to begin, and that makes my nervous butterflies flap harder.

I look down at my notebook, clutched tightly in my grip. I've jotted down all of today's events with my lists of who will be participating in what. But I've also scribbled down ways I think each event can be sabotaged.

Principal Klein smiles broadly while the contestants gather around him and a parent volunteer explains the rules, rules that I'm sure someone will be breaking.

I read the list of potential hazards I wrote in my notebook.

Someone could be planning on:

- Untying everyone's shoelaces (so they trip).
- Digging a giant hole for the racers to fall into.
- Unloading a cage of chickens to attack our team. (Maybe chickens can identify which eggs belonged to them, and they will seek revenge?)
- Throwing erasers at our runners to knock eggs off spoons. (I hear Brian and Seth like to play a game called Eraser Wars.)
- Replacing our eggs with eggs that are about to hatch. We can't carry a live chicken on a spoon!

But honestly, my list doesn't seem particularly helpful.

"Stop staring at that page," orders Lilly. She pushes my notebook away from my face.

"Hey! You could wrinkle the paper." I brush my notepad to smooth it out. "How else are we going to figure out what's happening?"

"Scan the crowd. Use your eyes. Watch everything. Hopefully we'll spot the plan."

"If there is a plan."

Lilly frowns. "Oh, there's a plan. Somewhere."

I nod. I know she's right, and I mentally check the things off my list. Everyone's shoelaces are tied, no one is holding erasers, and I would notice a cage of angry chickens or a giant hole in the ground.

Half the racers line up behind the starting line, which is also the finish line. The other racers jog to the opposite side of the field, for egg swapping. Bella will be the first racer for my team: she's short and a gymnast, and I figure gymnasts have great balance. Team Red's first racer is Wesley. He's a good athlete, but tall. He'll lose time if he needs to bend over and pick up a fallen egg. My racers are all short, so the egg has less distance to drop.

While Principal Klein finishes explaining the rules to the racers, Simon carries two baskets of eggs. He puts one down by Team Red, and the other by our team.

He wipes his hands on his legs, rubbing off some sort of goop—egg yolk, I think.

My stomach is in knots.

Lilly taps me on the shoulder and points to Seth and Brian. They are smiling and whispering, and smiling and whispering is never a great combination when it comes to them.

I can't hear what they are saying from this far away, though. Lilly said I should keep my eyes out. Maybe I should also keep my ears out.

I sneak closer to them, gliding past Maya and Trinity, skipping past Daisy and leaning in behind Kim.

"The yolk's on them," says Brian with a giggle.

Seth nods. "All over them."

"You crack me up."

"Eggs-actly." Then they laugh loudly, too loudly.

I strain to listen to more of their conversation, but other people are talking and I can't hear anything else unless I move even closer, but then my eavesdropping would be way too obvious. At the starting line, Bella and Wesley hold their egg-filled spoons in their hands. They stand, crouched, ready to run. One of the parent volunteers raises her hand.

Lilly wiggles past a few kids and taps me on the shoulder. "What's going on? Did you hear anything?"

Simon stands behind the racers, grinning.

That's when I put it all together. Brian made a confusing yolk joke. Simon carried the eggs and wiped egg-dripping fingers. "Um, the eggs. They are supposed to be hard-boiled, right?"

Lilly nods. "Of course. Otherwise they would break too easily."

"But what if Team Red's eggs weren't hard-boiled? What if they were replaced with regular eggs, or eggs with small cracks in them already? Just think how easily they would break."

"I don't see how they could switch eggs," says Lilly. "You'd need to be the one preparing the eggs."

"Simon, Brian's brother, works in the cafeteria. And he's up to no good."

Lilly's eyes open wide, and she doesn't wait to ask me more questions. Instead, she's all legs and sprinting. She pushes past kids, but there are many in the way. She nudges Avery, nearly trips over Allie, and elbows Elias.

"We'll begin on the count of three," says Principal Klein.

I'm not sure if Lilly is going to make it to the starting line before the event begins, and if she does—I don't know what she plans to do. All I do know is that if our principal discovers that eggs have been switched, Field Day could be canceled before it even begins, and our entire class will probably serve detention for years.

As a team captain, Principal Klein could keep me in detention until high school. Maybe I'll never be allowed into high school, let alone middle school next year.

"One . . . ," says Principal Klein.

The contestants put their spoons in their mouths.

"Two . . . ," says Principal Klein.

Bella and Wesley balance their egg on their spoons.

"Thr . . . ,"

Before Principal Klein can finish even saying *three*, Lilly bludgeons past Derek and Mario.

I see the entire disaster clearly.

Lilly is running too fast.

Her foot hits Mario's left leg.

She topples forward, both of her legs leaving the ground as if she's trying to fly. But she can't fly. Instead, she rams directly into Gerardo, who stands behind Wesley, next in line to race for Team Red.

Gerardo stumbles forward and smacks into Wesley's back. Wesley lurches forward, his mouth opening and the spoon toppling out. Wesley falls to the ground. The egg splatters, cracking into pieces. Wesley falls right next to the shattered egg.

But Lilly is like a freight train that can't stop. She continues falling forward, past the stumbling Gerardo, hitting Pete, and flopping to the ground, where her shoulder collides with the entire basket of Team Red eggs.

The basket falls over. Lilly's entire body continues skidding forward, still moving, and sliding directly on top of the eggs.

". . . ree," continues Principal Klein. But no one moves.

Wesley is on the ground. Gerardo is on the ground. But worst of all is Lilly. She lies, face-first, on top of about two dozen broken eggs.

Lilly rolls over onto her back, eggshells sticking to her hair and yolk smeared across her face. She looks up at

Principal Klein, who stands only a few feet away. "Um, sorry?" she mumbles. "I sort of tripped."

As Lilly stands up, egg dripping from nearly every inch of her, Bella remains at the starting line, standing. She removes her spoon from her mouth. "Should I still run?" she asks Principal Klein.

If she does, we'll win. Team Red doesn't have any eggs left.

But Principal Klein doesn't answer. He looks at Lilly. "Are you okay?"

Lilly nods. "Just a little messy."

"I see." Our principal looks at the ground again and at the egg calamity that covers it. He looks at the parent volunteers. He looks at Lilly. "I thought these were supposed to be hard-boiled." He frowns, scanning the ground and the baskets. "If this was sabotage, we'll have to cancel . . ."

"I was in charge of the eggs, sir," says Simon, stepping up. "But no one told me they were supposed to be hard-boiled." I know he's lying, and the frown he throws at Lilly drips with wickedness and spite.

"Oh my," says our principal. "I'm not sure how things got so confused. Yes, they are always hard-boiled."

"I wish I had known that, sir," says Simon. "Taking care of the eggs is an important job, you know."

"Of course it is," says our principal, nodding vigorously. "No one can blame you. But we don't have enough eggs to go forward with this event, I'm afraid." He looks again at the parents, and then at the egg mess. He shakes his head. "We'll just call this one a tie."

Lilly is a walking egg disaster, but she releases a long sigh of relief. So do I. Lilly looks happy, even with eggshells sticking to her eyebrows.

I think our team would have won this event if we hadn't decided to cheat, but I'd rather tie than win dishonestly.

One event is over, but I know that this is only the beginning. Who knows what other trouble is planned and whether we'll be able to stop it. It will just take one mishap to ruin everything, and I don't think I can plan on Lilly tripping over someone's leg before every event.

"Anyone have a spare towel?" asks Principal Klein, and a parent volunteer hands Lilly a rag to wipe off the yolk. But I have a terrible feeling that things are only going to get messier.

40

LILLY

Mr. Foley stands near the starting line for the second event, which is the Water Cup Relay Race. "Competitors get ready," he cries out. He looks hot in the sweater vest he wears.

Maybe he should call it a sweating vest. His hair, a thick curly ball of black, wilts in the heat.

George's squad gathers around him for instructions. I can't hear what George says to them, but he looks prepared, as if he has a plan all figured out, but of course George would have everything arranged.

My team stands around me. I picked everyone for this event alphabetically by first name. It was the fastest way to choose participants, since I didn't have much time between events, but now I regret not picking my teams more carefully.

"What's the plan?" asks Alex.

"Um, run as fast as you can?" I suggest with a helpless smile. Other than Alex and Aisha, who are both tall and fast,

I think my team might be in trouble during this event. "You'll be okay running?" I ask Charlie. When I assigned him to this race, I forgot he had a broken leg.

"I can hop," Charlie boasts, handing me his crutches and then hopping three times to show me.

His hopping might have been more impressive if his arms didn't fly up every time he moved. I'm not sure how he's going to keep his water cup balanced. But I don't have the heart to take him off the race team. He seems excited to participate.

Each team member has to balance a cup of water on a tray, sort of like a waiter, and then race to a bucket at the far end of the field. Then he or she dumps the water into the bucket, runs back and hands the tray and cup to the next racer, who fills the cup with water and runs back across the field. The race goes back and forth and back.

Whoever fills their bucket with water first, wins. So balancing your water cup is a pretty important part of the race.

"I'm ready, too," says Brianna firmly. Then she hiccups. My eyes widen. That's also going to be a problem. "It's"—hiccup—"fine. I can"—hiccup—"do this," she insists. Then she sucks in a big gulp of air and holds her breath.

Brianna sometimes has hiccupping issues.

"I'll need to walk very slowly," says Colby. "I don't want to twist my ankle. I have a big match tomorrow, and Dad told me to be careful." Colby is a really good golfer, so I guess it makes sense that she needs to be careful, but it will take a miracle for us to win this event.

Finn stands near me. He's not in this race, but he leans over and says, "Don't worry. We can't lose."

"What do you mean?" I ask, but Finn walks away muttering something about Grace and horseback riding.

I start to chase after him, but Mr. Foley is already in position to start the event. I'm just going to have to keep my eyes as wide-open as they can possibly be open. Something's going to happen, and I only wish I knew what.

"Your team looks good," says George, but I know he's just being polite. "Choosing Charlie and his broken leg was an interesting choice."

"He can hop," I say, biting my lip. "But never mind that. Do you see any sabotage planned?" I'm eager to change the subject from Charlie's hopping skills.

"No," admits George, looking this way and that way. "But maybe nothing will happen during this race. At least there aren't any eggs involved."

I shake my head and pick an eggshell out of my hair. "I'm pretty sure Finn did something, or he will do something. Grace has him wrapped around her finger."

The first racers, Bjorn for Team Blue and Aubrey for my team, stand with their trays at the starting line, their water cups full. Two large buckets sit on chairs at the far side of the field.

"Are you ready?" asks Mr. Foley as sweat pours down his face. He stands in front of one of the fans, but it's not blowing enough air to keep water from dripping off his head. "On your mark."

I still don't see anything wrong anywhere. "What's going to happen?" I ask George.

George looks down at his clipboard. "Maybe it will rain and water will fill all the buckets so it'll be a tie?"

I shake my head. There's not a cloud in the sky.

"Get set," Mr. Foley announces.

George looks down at his clipboard. "I thought someone might replace one of the buckets with a thimble so only a tiny amount of water would fill it." George frowns and lowers his list. "And that was my best idea."

"You're not very good at planning trouble." I squeeze his arm. "But that's one of the things I like about you."

"Go!" yells Mr. Foley.

Bjorn and Aubrey are off. Bjorn walks slowly, careful not to spill his water, but Aubrey shoots ahead of him. She's fast and we take a quick lead. "You don't have a chance of winning if your team goes that slow," I warn George.

"Slow and steady wins the race," he replies.

Sure enough, Aubrey stumbles and her water cup flies off her tray. Bjorn from Team Blue walks as slowly as Elvis the turtle, but he's not spilling a drop. As he trudges forward, Aubrey scrambles to her feet and rushes back to the starting line to refill her water cup.

By the time Aubrey finishes filling her cup and dumping it into the bucket, we're behind. Brianna is up next. She's speedy and catching up, but then she hiccups. It's one very, very loud hiccup. Her tray wobbles and the cup teeters.

She swallows some air, smiles, and then runs forward. Her hiccups seem to have hiccupped themselves out after only one. I breathe a deep sigh of relief. She's neck and neck with Lizzie from Team Blue.

"Go, Lizzie!" yells Adam from the sidelines. Lizzie turns her head and smiles. She raises her hand to wave to Adam, forgetting she's holding a tray.

Her cup of water topples over and drenches her pants.

"Pay attention!" cries George, pulling on his hair.

Lizzie rushes back to the starting line to pour water back into her cup while Brianna speeds ahead. My teammates roar their approval.

"All right, Bri!" I shout.

Soon, we're a lap ahead of Team Blue, which is awesome-sauce, but now it is Charlie's turn to run. I can barely watch. He left his crutches on the ground, but his water cup falls every time he hops. Hop, spill. Hop, spill. I really should have replaced him in this race.

After Charlie hops back to refill his cup for the fourth time, he gets down on his knees and crawls forward with his cup and tray. He isn't hopping and spilling all his water out, but he's also creeping like a snail, and our lead vanishes.

Both teams cheer wildly as Charlie finally dumps out his cup and hops back to the start, his arms flailing to keep himself steady. He's actually surprisingly fast when he hops. But we're now two or three cup pours behind.

I don't know how full our water bucket is, but it can't be nearly as full as the Team Blue bucket. I slip past my clapping and hollering teammates and walk to the end of the field for a closer look at the buckets.

I stand on my tiptoes to get a good look. Our bucket is more than half full, but Team Blue's bucket is almost empty.

I blink and stare at it again. I must be seeing things.

Nope. Their bucket is almost empty, but that's impossible.

Or it should be impossible. When I look closely, moving a little farther down the line so I see the back of the buckets, I spy a small but steady stream of water flowing from the bottom of Team Blue's bucket.

A hole. Someone jabbed a hole in the bottom of the blue plastic bucket.

Surprisingly, no one else has seemed to notice. There are no volunteers standing back here to look, probably because there are no fans over here and the volunteers want to keep cool. But one of the parents looks like she's getting ready to check the buckets.

When she gets here, she will see exactly what I see. This will be a disaster. Instead of prizes we'll get lectures, detention, and who knows what else? Nothing good, that's for sure.

Don't my teammates understand they need to play fair?

Finn and Pete whisper to each other near the starting line. Sarah and Grace share a laugh.

No, they don't know how to play fair.

But I gave my word we wouldn't cheat. I need to fill Team Blue's bucket with water before the scheme is discovered.

If only it would rain! As I look around for anything, something, I don't know what, my eyes rest near the supply shed at the back of the school. That's where the ground crew's industrial-strength sprinklers are lined up.

Sprinklers mean water. Industrial-strength sprinklers mean a whole lot of water. That would be even better than rain.

While racers run with trays and water, I sneak over to the sprinklers. The crowds cheer. Even Principal Klein claps.

Then a parent volunteer starts walking down the line, toward the buckets. She is almost at the end.

But I have already reached the sprinklers.

I take a deep breath.

I reach down and twist the sprinkler spigot.

And then I run.

The hose bulges with water.

I'm already back near the pack of kids when the water erupts.

The sprinkler shoots water directly into the line of kids watching the race, a downpour of industrial-strength wetness. The sprinkler clicks and twists, spreading water from left to right, across our entire group. CLICK, CLICK, CLICK, it says. The water soaks me, but since I'm already sort of covered in egg, the water feels good, cleaning me.

But the water spray doesn't stop. The sprinkler head continues to click and rotate. The spray soaks the racers waiting to run, and then the teachers and parents.

The stream of water reaches across the field and cleanly knocks our bucket off its chair, and then the Team Blue bucket gets walloped by water, too.

Then the water stops.

A rainbow forms across the sunny sky from the mist of sprinkler water clinging to the air. Behind it, a red-faced and very angry Principal Klein stands next to the water faucets.

41
GEORGE

I'm convinced Field Day will be canceled. Principal Klein huddles with the fifth-grade teachers, and they each wear deep frowns. All the teachers' clothes are soggy, all the parent volunteers' clothes are soggy, and all the students' clothes are soggy. Only Mrs. Rosenbloom seems to have completely avoided the sprinkler shower, and Principal Klein just has water soaking the bottom of his gray slacks.

Since it's so hot today, many kids seem sort of glad they got doused. Lilly stands next to me, a sparkle in her eyes. The water has washed off most of the egg yolk that still clung to her. She's holding something behind her back, but I can't see what it is. We are close enough to the teachers that we can hear their conversation, or at least we can hear Principal Klein. His loud voice is impossible to miss. We could probably hear him even if we stood clear across the field. "We have to cancel," he says.

Lilly and I scoot a little closer so we're at the very lip of the circle of students all waiting for the conversation to end.

Luke stands next to me. "What do you think they'll do?" he asks, his legs wiggling and his arms twitching.

I put my finger to my lips. I want to listen.

"It's not the students' fault the sprinklers turned on," says Mrs. Crawford.

"Are you sure?" asks Principal Klein, his voice rising.

"Of course I'm sure. Who would do such a thing?" asks Mrs. Rosenbloom.

"I agree," adds Mrs. Greeley. "There has been plenty of poor sportsmanship this week. But those sprinklers ruined both teams' chances to win, not just one."

"But what about the Egg Race?" Principal Klein asks. "That was spoiled, too."

"An accident, plain and simple," says Mrs. Rosenbloom.

Mrs. Greeley nods. "Lilly is a bit of a klutz."

I giggle and Lilly elbows me in the ribs. "Well, you are," I say. "I mean, just a little."

She frowns.

"And you can't blame her for the eggs being made wrong," Mrs. Greeley adds.

"Did any of us see a student turn on the sprinklers?" asks Mrs. Crawford in a clipped, scholarly tone.

All the teachers shake their heads, including our principal.

Lilly lets out a loud sigh and grins. She must have turned on those sprinklers, and I'm sure she must have had a good reason. I assume she stopped some sabotage that I didn't see. I give her arm a gentle squeeze. "Nice job," I whisper.

"Most of those sprinklers are set on timers," adds Mrs. Crawford, as the teachers remain gathered together. "Maybe one just got knocked off its correct time. That sort of thing happens all the time."

This comment gets the other teachers nodding their heads in agreement.

"I can't recall that sort of thing ever happening," counters Principal Klein. "But I suppose it could. And we can't punish the students because someone may have done something. Not if we don't know for sure."

Mrs. Crawford pats the principal's hand, like a parent might do with an upset baby. "I once set the timer for a meat loaf wrong, and it cooked for four hours instead of forty minutes. We had to order a pizza since the meat loaf just wasn't edible."

"A shame," says Mrs. Greeley. "I love meat loaf."

"I think we can all agree that meat loaf is a tasty dinner," says Principal Klein. "But we are not making meat loaf here. Any more suspicious acts will force an immediate cancellation of Field Day."

"Of course," agrees Mrs. Rosenbloom.

"Absolutely," says Mrs. Greeley.

"And worse," says Principal Klein. "A deliberate action to ruin today would result in catastrophic punishments for the kids."

Lilly grips my arm. "What do you think they would do?"

"I don't know and I don't want to find out. There have to be more things planned today, but we can't go around ruining every event. The teachers will be onto us."

"We need to be smarter," agrees Lilly.

I hold up my notebook and tap the page. The water stream soaked my back, but I was able to cradle my notebook so it's mostly dry. "That's why I wrote down all my thoughts. The Hula-Hoop contest is next. What if someone replaced round Hula-Hoops with square ones?"

Lilly laughs. "I think everyone would notice that."

"I guess so." I cross that off my list.

"Besides, I've already figured out what was planned for the Hula-Hoop contest," says Lilly with a grin.

"What? When?"

"When everyone was drying themselves off, Zane dropped this." She shows me what she has been holding behind her back. It's a small and very soggy paper bag. She lifts out a box of pepper from inside it. "The Hula-Hoop contest is right next to one of those big fans. I think Zane, or someone, was going to put the pepper over the fan and make the contestants sneeze. You can't hula-hoop while sneezing."

"But wouldn't that just make everyone sneeze and everyone lose?"

"Not if someone on my team was wearing nose plugs." She holds the bag upside down, and a dozen small spongy plugs fall to the ground.

I bend down and pick one up. "So the entire team was in on it?"

"I don't know. It just takes one person to win. Grace is one of my Hula-Hoopers, and I wouldn't put it past her to be involved."

I'm relieved the Hula-Hoop contest sabotage has been discovered, but there are plenty of events left and plenty of mischief we need to uncover. It will take a miracle to get through the day.

I check my notepad. "I'll run through my notes for the next few events. I have lots of ideas for what might be planned."

"Just keep your eyes and ears open. And your fingers crossed."

42

LILLY

Eight Team Red and eight Team Blue competitors file into a big spray-painted circle to compete in the Hula-Hoop contest.

George and I personally inspected the Hula-Hoops, just in case someone else planned to ruin this event. None of the hoops are wobbly or falling apart or filled with anything weird, like mustard. I don't know why I thought one might be filled with mustard. I guess I'm as rotten a schemer as George. He thought someone might fill the Hula-Hoops with helium so they would fly away.

Zane frantically runs around, yelling out, "Has anyone seen a paper bag? I had a paper bag!"

I put the bag in a trash can, hidden under random garbage. No one will find it.

Samantha, Giovanna, and five other girls from Team Blue grab hoops, and so does George. I think Samantha and

Giovanna are going to be hard to beat. I saw them practicing earlier, and they looked like longtime Hula-Hoopers. George is good, too. He out-hula-hooped me once, and it still annoys me when I think about it.

My team is not awesomesauce. I picked my team alphabetically again because I had to pick them quickly, so I chose Elle, Esmeralda, Finn, Gerardo, Griffin, Grace, Harrison, and Heaven.

Finn glares at me and mumbles something I can't hear, but it's probably best that I don't. I'm sure it wasn't a very nice mumble. I can tell that he does not want to hula-hoop.

But my team is not without hoop hopes. Heaven and Esmeralda both told me they love hoops, but now that I think of it, they may have been talking about earrings. Harrison said he was great at hoops, but I think he meant basketball.

A few members of my team pick up their hoops to practice. Finn, Harrison, and Heaven can't even make their hoops circle their bodies once without falling to their feet. But I only need one great Hula-Hooper to win. The last one standing wins for his or her team.

I spy Grace talking to Zane, probably about the pepper and plugs. Grace stomps away and toward the event. Even without nose plugs, Grace is my secret weapon. She told me she is a two-time Hula-Hoop contest champion. She won those contests in preschool, but she's our best chance to win.

Mrs. Rosenbloom instructs everyone to get ready. Principal Klein watches from the sidelines, as do all of us kids. Our principal glances at the sprinklers but seems satisfied none are about to accidently start spraying.

Mrs. Rosenbloom pushes a button on a laptop computer that has speakers attached to it. Polka music dances out. She cries, "Start hula-hooping, everyone!"

The spinning begins.

Within seconds, nearly half of my team is out of the competition. Finn, Harrison, Heaven, and Gerardo all fail to complete a single twirl. Finn tromps off, glaring at me the entire time.

But that means half of my team still spins, so we still have a chance. Grace swivels her hips calmly and looks like she could spin all day. Griffin hangs in there by wiggling his arms and moving his legs in an awkward and jerking gyrating motion, but it appears to work. Elle and Esmeralda aren't too bad, either.

But there are plenty of good Team Blue spinners, like George, who swivels calmly. Fortunately for us, two Team Blue players get too close to each other. Their hoops collide and then fall.

The accordion polka music continues. Mrs. Rosenbloom orders everyone to take a step closer together.

As Elle moves in, she walks right into a Team Blue player. They both lose their hoops, and their balance. Elle falls and rolls into the legs of Esmeralda, who rolls into another Team Blue Hula-Hooper, who falls into another Team Blue player.

Samantha deftly steps away to avoid the dominos.

Griffin goes out next, tripping over his own feet but also knocking out Samantha from Team Blue.

Grace is now the only Hula-Hooper left for my team. George and Giovanna remain twirling for Team Blue.

They all look really good. This contest could take a long time until someone wins.

Sarah stands behind me. She talks with Zane. "Why is this still going on?"

"I lost the pepper," complains Zane.

I bite my lip and say nothing.

The music swirls, and Mrs. Rosenbloom orders the three contestants to move closer again. Their hoops are only inches apart as they spin round and round. It's sort of mesmerizing. My teammates yell, "Go, Grace!" and Team Blue's spectators scream out, "Go, Team Blue!"

All three spin and spin.

"Take another step closer," orders Mrs. Rosenbloom.

The three of them take a step closer together, but now they are too close. George's and Giovanna's hoops collide. Giovanna's hoop crashes to her feet, but somehow George keeps his going.

Giovanna picks up her hoop and stomps off.

Now it's down to Grace and George, side-by-side, hips circling, hoops barely missing each other as they twirl around and around. One step closer and this will be over for one of them, or maybe both.

I feel a tap on my shoulder. "It's now or never," says Sarah.

"What do you mean?"

"We can't lose," she hisses. "I found a banana peel next to a trash can." She holds up a black and sort of disgusting peel that is dripping with what might be fruit punch. "I can toss it at George's feet."

She steps forward with the banana, but I jump in front of her.

"Get out of the way," she orders.

I stand firm and cross my arms. "No way. We're going to win fair and square. I've had enough of your plotting. Can't you all just give it a rest already?"

Sarah glares at me. "I knew you weren't on our side."

I don't back down. "I'm on our side, but I'm also on the side of playing fairly."

"You're just a Team Blue lover," Sarah says, and spits as if the taste of Team Blue is on her tongue and it's a sour taste.

"This is just a game," I say. "It's about fair play and . . ."

"This isn't just a game," insists Pete, joining us. "It's about winning a special prize, like a lifetime supply of pillows. At least, that's what I heard."

I want to roll my eyes. Instead, I say to everyone, "Don't you want to win fair and square?"

There's a pause and Sarah shakes her head. "Not really."

Others from our team are listening in. Almost half of my team seems to be surrounding us. This is my moment to show my spirit. This is why I am team captain.

"Whether it's tomorrow or next year or years from now, when you look back at today, don't you want to look back knowing you tried your best?" I ask. I point to Team Blue. "Those are our friends. Sure, they might not be in our class this year, but next year they might be. We go to their birthday parties, just like they go to ours. You don't cheat your friends. You don't plot against classmates just to win pillows, or whatever the special prize is."

"Even if that prize is really, really incredible?" asks Amelia.

"Like a litter of kittens?" asks Jessie.

"Or a giant fortress loaded with gold and zebras?" asks Zachary.

"Yes, even then," I say.

"But I love zebras!" exclaims Taylor. "I look good in stripes."

The circle of Team Red members has grown around me. Not too many kids even watch the Hula-Hoop competition. Some nod their heads, agreeing with me. Others seem uncertain. I can see their brows furrowing as my words sink in.

I have a chance to stop the troublemaking right now. I raise my fist. "Let's win fairly," I declare. "Honestly! For fun and spirit! Who's with me?"

No one says a word.

I pump my fist again. "I said, who's with me?" My teammates smile, and I think many of them are going to shout that they agree.

But then Mrs. Rosenbloom yells out, "And the winner is George and Team Blue!"

George won! I think that's great, but no one else does. Every smile on my team is erased. Sarah glowers at me. "If we lose Spirit Week, it's all because of you."

Everyone trudges off.

Aisha, however, throws me a small smile. She puts her arm across my shoulder. "I thought it was a really good speech." She gives me a gentle squeeze. "Even if no one else thinks so."

"We'll take a short break until the next event," announces Mrs. Rosenbloom. "Who wants a snack?"

Everyone runs off to get in line for food, including Aisha.

I can't get my team as excited about playing fairly as they are about eating a snack. I stand by myself as the grass waves gently around me.

I know we need to play fair. But playing fair seems very, very lonely.

43
GEORGE

After standing in line for a frozen Popsicle, I sit on the grass with my treat. It melts quickly in the heat, so I have to lick the dripping orange juice as fast as I can. A few drops land on my jeans. I rub them, but they leave stains and now my hands are sticky. I wish I had brought more hand sanitizer.

Our principal erases the numbers on the scoreboard. With our Hula-Hoop win, the score for the week is now ten to ten.

"We're all tied up," says Brian. He walks past me with a wink.

"I bet we'll win a lot more before this day is through," adds Seth, walking behind Brian.

They wander to one of the tables where Brian's brother Simon stands, waiting for them. They laugh. They chat. Brian hands Simon a paper bag. More smiles. More laughter.

I stare at them and try to read their lips. But I'm not good at reading lips, and Brian's back is to me, anyway.

I should run over there because whatever they are discussing can't be anything good. I need to stand up to them, like I've promised myself I would. They can't lock me in a supply closet out here either. I am team captain, even if I don't want to be.

Simon walks off, and Brian and Seth sit down to lick their Popsicles. I stand up, ball both my fists, and tell myself, *You can do it, George.* But before I take a step, Lilly sits down next to me. "Where are you going?" she asks. "Hey, we match," she adds, pointing at my orange Popsicle. She eats an orange Popsicle, too.

"Of course we do," I say. I'd rather be sitting with Lilly than standing up to bullies, so I sit back down and lick off a big drop clinging to the bottom of my stick.

I sneak glances over to Brian and Seth. I will talk with them later.

"Nice job winning the Hula-Hoop contest," she says.

"Thanks. Remember when we hula-hooped together once?"

Lilly nods. "I was a bad sport, huh?"

"Well . . . ," I say with a shrug.

"Maybe I'm learning to be a better one." Lilly sticks half the Popsicle into her mouth. When she removes it, her lips are orange and her tongue is orange and half the Popsicle is in her stomach. I really want to grab a napkin and wipe her lips, but my napkin is already a mess from my own dripping juice. "Your Hula-Hoop win doesn't matter anyway. Team Red will win the rest of today's contests. We're winning that prize."

Do her eyes narrow when she says this?

"Relax," she says with a giggle when she notices my eyes widening with worry. "We'll win fairly. At least I hope so. Everyone else seems to know more than me about what's planned, and terrible things are definitely planned."

"Brian and Seth keep snickering, so I know they've got things up their sleeves. They were just talking to Brian's older brother Simon. I think he's a bigger sneak than Brian."

"We'll need to watch them. You know, I heard the mystery prize was a week at the White House. As guests of the president and everything."

"I heard the winner gets a trip to the sun."

Lilly laughs. "Wouldn't you sort of, I don't know, melt?" She wipes her forehead. "I can barely stand the sun out here. I don't think I want to get any closer."

I laugh, too. "Everyone has different ideas of what we'll win, but no one has any clue."

"Koko thinks we all win a llama. Really." She giggles and then takes a big chomp from her Popsicle.

Lilly is almost done with her treat, but I'm still licking mine, carefully catching most of the falling orange before it lands on my fingers.

"Too bad there's not a Popsicle-eating contest," Lilly says. "I think I'd win."

"You just might," I agree with a smile.

I look down at my notebook for hints of what might be planned next. A few Popsicle drops have landed on the paper, and when I rub the spots, the liquid spreads more. I frown and wish I could rewrite the page because I hate paper with stains on it. But I don't have time because the Silly Clothes Race will start in a few minutes.

The first competitor dresses up in a bunch of silly clothes, runs across the field, removes the silly clothes, and hands them to the next racer to wear, who then dresses and runs to the next racer. There are twelve kids from each team.

"So what do you think is planned?" asks Lilly.

I peer at my notebook for hints of plots. As usual, my ideas are not helpful.

- Silly clothes could be replaced with suits of armor that would be too heavy and too hard to wear.
- Rockets could be hidden inside the clothes, so a racer zooms away.

- Giant poisonous snakes could be hidden in clothes and bite everyone.

"So? Any thoughts?" asks Lilly.

I shake my head and rip out the page from my notebook. "I'm a horrible troublemaker."

Lilly smiles. "I know." She gnaws a final bite from her Popsicle and jumps to her feet. "I'm going to look around."

She walks away to snoop, and I stand up to scan the crowd. But as I expected, I don't see giant poisonous snakes or jet packs anywhere.

"Everyone please join us for the Silly Clothes Race," announces Principal Klein, his loud voice cutting through the field.

The event is set up near the Hula-Hoop area. But I don't follow the crowd to the event. Instead, I stand and watch, looking for something that's out of place. Seth and Brian have already vanished from where they sat. I regret not watching them more closely. If anyone has put giant snakes inside clothes, it would be them.

Instead of going directly to the Silly Clothes Race, I make a beeline to where they sat. At first, I see nothing, but then I spot a small empty wrapper lying on the ground. I bend down to take a closer look.

It reads UNCLE SCRATCHY'S ITCHING POWDER. MADE FROM ACTUAL ROSE HIPS.

Itching powder. My fingers start to tingle just from touching the wrapper. I have no idea where anyone gets itching powder, but if anyone would know, it would be Brian and Seth.

I quicken my pace to the event.

By the time I arrive, Principal Klein is already talking to the contestants, explaining the rules. Two boxes of clothes sit by the starting line; one box is colored red and one is blue. Odd clothes overflow from the boxes: giant clown shoes, a business suit, a top hat, boas, and more. I don't see any suits of armor, so that's one less thing to worry about.

I spy Brian standing with Seth on the sidelines, snickering. Then I see Simon.

Brian's brother walks briskly toward the boxes of clothes. Since everyone watches Principal Klein and the contestants, no one notices Simon sneaking around, holding a small jar filled with red powder.

It doesn't take a genius to know what's in that jar. As soon as the first Team Red competitor puts on clothes, he or she will be too busy scratching to run.

I cut through the crowd, elbowing past Kyle. "Watch where you're going. Maybe try slowing?" he says, annoyed.

But I'm already past him, ducking around Gavin and Cooper on my way to those silly clothes boxes.

Simon stands next to them, untwisting the cap of his jar.

I break free of the pack, almost colliding into Trevor. "Be careful, you idiot!" shouts Trevor, angrily.

Mr. Foley frowns and turns to Adam, who stands near Trevor. "Watch your language or you'll be sent to the principal's office."

"But I didn't say anything," complains Adam. "It was Trevor."

"No excuses, young man," says a stern Mr. Foley.

I hear Adam spends a lot of time in the principal's office for all sorts of things.

Mr. Foley isn't watching me, and neither is anyone else as I near Simon, who is now tipping the jar over the Team Red box. The first few grains of powder float down, but a slight breeze blows them away, past the clothes and onto the grass.

Simon crouches down, closer to the box.

I hope a tornado might swoop in and blow away the itching powder, but I don't see any tornados. I also don't see the table in front of me.

I smack into it with my leg. The table, which is an unsteady folding table, wobbles. The portable fan that rests on top of it skids and falls off the table.

I grab the fan to keep it from crashing onto the ground. I catch the base, careful not to grab hold of the guard, the part that houses the whirling blade. But I accidentally hit the switch from medium to high.

The fan is powerful and pointing directly at Simon.

WHOOSH!

The itching powder sprinkles out the jar and immediately blows back into Simon, covering his shirt and his face. He's coated in red powder.

Simon's face changes from a mischievous sneer to a horrified grimace. He drops the jar to the ground. He madly scratches his cheeks and chest. "Help! Help!"

Everyone turns to look at him as he itches and jumps around and screams, "Water! I need water!" I return the fan gently atop the table and step slowly back.

Simon is now spinning in crazy circles before finally sprinting off, toward the supply shed and the sprinklers.

As he dashes farther and farther away, the crowd seems to lose interest. Meanwhile, Simon keeps yelling, "Water! Water!" and furiously scratching himself.

"He must be very thirsty," says Mr. Foley.

"Well, it is hot out here." Principal Klein turns to the contestants and claps his hands. "Anyway, let's get dressed," he announces to the racers.

I spot Brian and Seth. Their grins are gone as they watch Simon dashing away.

Meanwhile, the racers take their positions. The first racer will dress at the starting line before dashing to the next racer. Eric is running first for my team, and Tara starts for Team Red. According to Eric's text, he can change out of his clothes in sixteen seconds, which is pretty amazing, I think. He and Tara each slip on fuzzy vests, two weird hats, giant shoes, two business suits, a couple of purple boas, and mittens.

The racers will be hot, but silly.

But at least whoever wins this race will win fairly.

44

LILLY

I exchange high fives with just about everyone on my team, and now my palm hurts after so many slaps. When we won the Silly Clothes Race, our entire team, including me, went crazy with jumping and hollering and celebrating. Even Charlie jumped up and down, although I think he forgot about his broken foot, because after one hop he fell over and knocked down two other kids.

Our win also means we're in the lead again for the week. We're that much closer to winning our own island, or whatever secret prize we get. Zachary says we all get an island, and the island is made of cotton candy, but I think he's just making that up.

I had a lot to do with our winning, too. Instead of just picking kids to compete alphabetically, I spent a few minutes thinking about the event. Fast dressing was important, so I picked kids who like to wear strange clothes to school, like

Koko, who always seems layered in four shirts, and Zane, who wears weird sweaters with many zippers.

I knew they had lots of practice changing and unchanging and zipping and unzipping.

I'll need to be just as clever when choosing the rest of my teams today.

The other kids on Team Red noticed, too. Finn actually smiled at me and said, "Good job, Captain," and while Sarah didn't exactly smile at me (I don't think she can smile in any way other than evilly), she didn't glare, either.

Maybe my team doesn't think I'm working against them anymore, but I am still working against their cheating. I promised George and myself we would play fair, and those are two people I will never break a promise to again.

The next event is Flag Football. Football is a tough sport, so I've chosen kids who seem tough, like Finn and Sarah. They were easy choices.

I'm going to play, even though I'm not that tough, but I can be tough when I need to be. I've never played football, but it seems pretty easy. Someone throws the ball, and you catch it, and you keep on running until someone from the other team grabs your flag.

I join my team on the sidelines. Finn slaps me on the back. "Don't worry. Team Blue won't be able to stop us."

"No they won't," agrees Sarah, grinning. She holds our bag of flags and hands a flag to each of us. The flags are long red ribbons attached to a belt with Velcro, so the other team can easily rip them off. Each belt has two ribbons attached to it.

I buckle my belt around my waist while Sarah continues passing out the rest of the belts. I tug on my flag because I want to see how easily it rips off.

My flag doesn't budge.

I tug on it again, and again it doesn't move, like it's stuck. Then I see Sarah handing a belt to Norm, and pulling out a giant stapler.

That's when I notice that my flags are attached to my belt with about a dozen staples.

"What are you doing?" I ask Sarah, demanding an answer as she hands a stapled belt to Finn.

"What needs to be done," she says with a smirk.

"Both teams come here to begin, please," announces Principal Klein. He waits in the middle of the field.

Sarah tosses the bag and the stapler to the sidelines, and jogs toward our principal.

"I told you to stop it!" I shout. "Come back here!"

"Too late now," Sarah calls over her shoulder as she races away from me.

I join the other football players as our principal asks, "Are you ready to have fun?"

Sarah smirks, and so do other members of my team. I watch the faces of the players on Team Blue and many of them seem to smirk, too. But I don't think they would be smirking if they knew our scheme.

A guilty lump builds in my throat and I can't cough it up.

"General football rules apply," instructs Principal Klein. "To advance the ball you must pass it to another player. If you have the ball and someone removes your flag, the play is down at that spot. Team Red will have the ball first. We'll play for fifteen minutes. Whoever scores the most touchdowns wins."

As my team jogs to the other end of the field, Zachary laughs and tugs one of his unmovable flags. Sarah laughs, too, but I'm so upset that I can't keep my hands from shaking. There's nothing I can do without admitting we're cheaters, and then the entire day will be canceled and we'll all be in deep trouble.

Principal Klein blows his whistle, and Zachary hikes the ball to Finn, who shovels a quick pass back to Zachary. Danny from Team Blue swipes at Zachary's flag. But the flag doesn't budge.

"What's going on?" yells Danny, but Zachary is already racing away from him. Lacey, Pedro, and Kim from Team Blue all converge on Zachary. They surround him, each yanking on Zachary's flag, but it still doesn't move.

"What's going on?" they all cry out.

Zachary is all by himself now, sprinting down the field and easily scoring a touchdown. He spikes the football on the ground and shakes his legs in some sort of weird touchdown celebration. He looks like a wobbly legged flamingo, bobbing his head and zigzagging his skinny legs.

The rest of my team runs down the field to congratulate him, except me.

This is not something worth jumping up and down about, or feeling good about. We scored because we cheated.

Now it's Team Blue's turn with the ball. Cooper hikes the ball to Gavin, who tosses it to Danny. Danny bursts through the line and veers to his left, right at me. I'm ready. I stand my ground and swipe my hand to his belt and grip the flag.

I yank as hard as I can, but the flag doesn't move.

Now it's my turn to yell, "What's going on?"

As Danny runs down the field for an easy score, I find myself standing near the Team Blue sidelines. George calls out to me loudly, but not so loudly that teachers or our principal can hear, "Someone superglued our flags!"

The game continues. We hike the ball and score a touchdown, even though five or six kids grab at our flags. Team Blue hikes the ball and scores a touchdown, despite five or six of my teammates grabbing at the flags.

"What great running!" exclaims Principal Klein. The game is not very long, but I'm betting it's tied at about a zillion to a zillion. Principal Klein says, "You guys are all really good. I've never seen such a great game." I simply nod and force a fake smile. "But we only have time for one last play."

Since Danny on Team Blue has just scored his sixteenth touchdown, we have the ball.

There's only way to keep us from winning. If we don't score, the game will end in a tie. But it won't be easy to stop my team from scoring, unless I stop us myself.

As we huddle for our next play I bark, "Throw me the ball."

Finn eyes me. Sarah frowns. My entire team looks at me. They don't trust me. "Will you catch it?" Finn asks.

I nod.

"Will you score?" he asks.

"Just throw me the ball," I order. I'm our team captain, after all.

We walk to the line. My plan is simple: I'll catch the ball, run a few feet, and then drop the ball. The ball will roll out of bounds, and the game will end in a tie.

"Hike!" yells Finn.

Zachary hikes the ball to Finn, who then tosses it to me. I'm only about two feet away so it's an easy catch. Then I run toward the line where the entire Team Blue is waiting for me.

I run straight into them. I know they can't stop me. But I can stop myself.

Kyle grabs one of my flags. Daisy grabs another. I feel a dozen hands grabbing at my belt.

And then I trip, and I don't even trip over someone's foot but my own foot as I move to my right. As I fall, the ball squirts out of my hands, and not even on purpose.

The ball bounces on the ground once, twice, and then it takes a surprisingly large hop and lands right in Zachary's grasp.

Zachary runs forward, zipping past the outstretched arms of Team Blue as they reach for his flag, but they have no chance of ripping it free. Zachary runs across the open field.

Soon, he's performing his tenth silly touchdown dance of the day, his legs gyrating as if on swivels.

Principal Klein blows his whistle. "What a great game! Team Red wins!"

On the sidelines my teammates jump and whoop. They all pile on top of Zachary in the end zone, celebrating like we just won the Super Bowl.

I watch the fun. Our team has the lead, and I feel simply terrible about it.

Lilly and I run ahead of the pack so we can check out the next event: the Blind Potato Race. Large Idaho potatoes lie spread across a field. One person on each team wears a blindfold while picking up as many potatoes as she or he can. The rest of the team shouts directions such as, "Turn right! Bend down!"

But Lilly heard from Aisha, who heard from Taylor, who heard from Brianna, that Grace made slight alterations to the blindfolds. I remove one from the Team Red box, which sits on the folding table near the event. Running my finger along it, I immediately detect a small slit. That rip would have been impossible for Principal Klein to notice, but if you wrap the blindfold around your eyes, you can see right through it.

Lilly finds an extra blindfold in the Team Blue box, so I put the sabotaged blindfold in my back pocket and replace it with the new, unripped one, just as the rest of the class converges on the area.

I feel good that no one is cheating, but once the contest begins I don't feel so good about the team I picked.

Ten people are on each team, and it is clear my team is in trouble.

I picked players I thought might give good directions, but there are way too many directions.

"Go right!" yells Maggie.

"No, left!" yells Paige.

"No, right and then left!" yells Lacey.

"Do all of those," says Mario.

"No, no, no!" whines Maggie.

Blindfolded Eric keeps spinning randomly, bending down to almost pick up a potato, and then veering off to almost pick up another potato. When time expires, he has only grabbed two spuds, and he only nabbed those because he stepped on them. Meanwhile, Team Red picked up more than a dozen potatoes. I'm disappointed we didn't do better, but at least no one cheated.

I just wish Zachary wouldn't do his weird zigzagging victory dance every time Team Red wins something, though. It's annoying.

Our team is now down a whole bunch of points, too. I do the math in my head. We have to win the rest of today's events, or Team Red will be crowned Spirit Week champion.

Winning fairly is more important than winning, so at least

we'll lose fairly, sort of. But I guess I want to win a little more than I thought I did. I've never thought much about winning things before, but as our team captain, it's my responsibility to help us win. Even if I still really don't want to be our team captain.

Seth and Brian frown at me. All my planning hasn't done us much good. I spent a lot of time picking team members for the events, and we're way behind.

But we still have a chance.

46
LILLY

The next event is the Rubber Chicken Throw, where kids take turns throwing a rubber chicken as far as they can. While Principal Klein explains the rules, George and I inspect the chickens. Sure enough, George spots foul play. Or, as he whispers while holding the chicken, *"Fowl* play." The Team Blue chicken is a lot heavier than ours, which would make it hard for them to throw. George shakes the chicken upside down and a few dozen marbles pour out of its mouth. He cuffs them in his hands and dumps them under a nearby table.

Soon, the event begins, and Ryan from Team Blue is up first. I hear she's the best pitcher on a travel softball team, and while chickens aren't softballs, I figure she might be really good. She grabs a chicken in her hand and starts twirling. I always see her twirling at school, but now she twirls faster and faster, and I hope that maybe it will make her too dizzy to throw straight. But her twirls seem to propel her arm forward, and the chicken soars out of her hand.

Chickens, however, are not softballs. Her chicken flops only fifteen feet away.

I smile, although not too much, because smiling when someone else does poorly isn't nice. But it turns out that no one can throw the chicken very far. It seems that rubber chickens don't fly well, but after a few tosses we have the lead, which is awesomesauce. I think Team Blue is finished, because all we have to do is win one more event and we will win Spirit Week, but then Brian from Team Blue steps up and hurls his chicken ten feet farther than anyone else.

He unleashes a wild yowl of excitement when his team is awarded the victory.

While Brian is being congratulated for his rubber chicken toss, George and I don't waste time watching. We need to hurry to the next event, the Water Balloon Toss.

But when we get to the water balloon station, we find a whole bunch of marbles on the ground and no balloons in sight.

Soon, Principal Klein is talking with one of the parent volunteers. He frowns, nods, frowns, nods, and then finally explains to everyone that they found holes in all of the balloons so the event has been changed. "Faulty balloons. It happens," he says, but I'm pretty sure I know who's at fault.

Sarah and Grace look at each other and frown. Brian and Seth look at each and frown, too. I can only guess that they all had the same idea, but at least they can't sabotage a brand-new competition.

Our principal explains that the event has been changed to Marble Toes, and kids need to pick up as many marbles as they can using only their toes and then drop them into either a red bucket or a blue bucket.

But I can see we're in trouble just by looking at everyone's feet. Team Blue has a whole bunch of players with big feet, like Jamaal. His feet look gigantic and after the event starts he picks up three times more marbles than anyone else.

Sure enough, when Mrs. Rosenbloom blows her whistle to end the game, it's not even close. Team Blue has more than twice as many marbles in their bucket as we do.

We still have a small lead, but Tug-of-War, the final event of the day, is worth double points.

So whoever wins Tug-of-War wins Spirit Week.

47

GEORGE

Both teams gather around Principal Klein, and a rope lies on the ground next to his feet. Our principal clears his throat. "It's been a wonderful day, hasn't it?"

Most of us clap and cheer, but I just let out a sigh. I want the day to be done. It's exhausting uncovering secret plots. Our principal wipes his brow. "Even though it's so very, very hot."

Lilly and I look at each other. I can't read minds, but I can read her mind because she's thinking the same thing as me: *Please, please, please let us just get through this last event without any tricks.*

"You have all displayed great sportsmanship today," says Principal Klein. "I knew you had it in you."

I bite my lip.

"We had some, um, difficulties in the beginning of the day, but that was no fault of yours," Principal Klein continues. I'm standing right next to our principal, and he pats me on the head. "If each captain will send twelve members of their team for our final contest, we'll begin. Whoever wins the Tug-of-War wins the entire Spirit Week. How exciting."

I jog back to my team.

I feel good about our chances. With Brian, Seth, and Kyle all on my team, I don't see how we can lose.

But then I look around. Where are Brian and Seth?

48
LILLY

My team huddles around me, and suddenly I'm bombarded by a flurry of sneers and plotting.

"We need to win, and win that prize," says Grace. "No matter what."

"No matter what," Sarah agrees.

"I love prizes," says Amelia.

"I just love winning," says Sarah.

"Oh, we'll win," says Grace. She chuckles. It's a mean-sounding chuckle.

"Guys, let's just win fairly," I plead. "Please."

That magic word works with adults, but it doesn't always work with kids, unfortunately.

"Do you have the grease?" Grace asks Finn.

Finn nods and removes a tube of some sort of lubricant from his pocket. "We just need to smear it on the Team Blue side of the rope. The rope will slide off their hands. They won't be able to tug at all."

"We'll need to distract everyone while you rub it on," says Sarah. "I'll pretend I see a snake or something and start screaming."

"I don't like snakes," says Grace.

I puff out my chest and walk right into the middle of their small conspiracy circle. Enough is enough, and I've had enough of all of them. "We need to win this event fairly. Stop ruining everything. Let the best team win."

"Everyone knows that winning is everything," says Sarah. "And losing is for losers."

"No, cheating is for losers," I say. "And that's what you and Grace are, and you too, Finn. A bunch of cheating losers."

"But what about the prize?" says Amelia, who stands just outside our circle.

"I'm with Lilly," says Aisha. She shoves past a couple of smaller kids and puts her arm around my shoulders. "We're not cheating."

"I agree," says Colby, and she puts her arms around Aisha's shoulders. "We need to win fairly. That's what we do in golf."

"Me too," says Alex. "I mean, I think we should win fairly. I don't play golf."

"Me three," says Liam. "About the winning fairly part."

We are joined together, our hands on our shoulders, a line of Team Red players vowing to play without cheating. More teammates join us, and soon more than half the team is lined up, all staring at Sarah, Grace, and Finn.

"I just wanted a horseback ride," Finn says in a soft voice and taking a small step back.

"Forget you guys," says Sarah. "I'll spread the grease." She holds her hand out to Finn, demanding he hand over the tube, which he does.

I shake my head. "No way."

"Teams take your positions," orders our principal from the Tug-of-War rope.

Finn, Grace, and Sarah step forward. They were all chosen to participate. But I break our arms-on-shoulders Team Red line and step in front of them. "You guys are sitting this one out."

"What are you talking about?" asks Sarah.

"Sit down," I demand. "All of you."

"I'm the strongest person on the team," argues Finn.

"Maybe," I say. "But you three have been nothing but cheaters from the beginning. I'd rather lose by playing fair than win by playing with cheaters." I turn to the rest of the team. "Noah, Aisha, and Tara—take their places."

"Are you kidding?" demands Sarah. "Do you want to lose?"

"I want to play fair." I turn my back to her.

"Then you're a loser," barks Grace. She stares at me, her stares carving little notches of hate into me.

But I don't care. I'm team captain. I might not be the most organized team captain ever, but I'm an honest one.

I hope I'm a winning one, too.

After I call out the names to compete in Tug-of-War, my stomach sinks. I see Brian and Seth. They are standing near the back of our group, with Simon. I twist my mouth into a frown. They're huddling and laughing. They must be plotting.

This ends now.

"Hey, where are you going?" asks Luke as I march past him. "We need to get everyone on the field!"

I keep going.

"Do you have the egg salad?" Brian asks Simon.

Simon nods. He holds a bucket. "Still had some left from the other day."

Seth cringes. "That egg salad smells worse than wet dog fur."

Simon nods. "Egg salad doesn't stay fresh very long. It's turning a little green, too."

I barge into their group. "Stop it!"

Simon looks at me, and frowns. "You again?" He shakes his head. "Just go away, okay? We're going to win this event. Without your help."

"You guys are going to stop this right now." They glare at me, and their shadows loom over me. I feel very, very small.

They turn their backs to me. Simon barks orders to Brian and Seth. "You guys dump the egg salad on the ground near Team Red. They'll be too busy slipping and sliding to pull their rope." He hands the bucket to his brother.

"Stop!" I shout, as loudly as I can. The three conspirators turn around while I ball my hands into fists and take a deep breath. "You guys are not doing anything anymore. You've helped ruin this entire week with all your plotting. You know, I thought winning was about note taking and organization. But Lilly was right. Spirit Week is about spirit. And you guys have no spirit, and no place on this team. Not anymore. I'm done keeping quiet. This ends now."

I grab the bucket handle, still in Brian's grip.

"Let go!" He yanks his hand away, but I keep my grip tight. He pulls his hand, and I pull toward me, as if we're starting our own game of bucket Tug-of-War. I yank as hard as I can, and the bucket falls from his grip. I drop it, too. The egg salad splatters to the ground next to us.

"Look what you've done," Brian complains.

"Teams take your positions," orders our principal.

Simon steps forward, his eyes fixed on me. "If we lose today it's all because of . . ." He never finishes his sentence. He steps into the egg salad, and as promised, it's slippery. His legs slide. He skids. He reaches out to Brian to keep his balance, but all he does is make Brian teeter, too. Brian's legs hit Seth, who topples over and smashes into Brian.

A moment later they are all on the ground and covered in old, smelly, and slightly green egg salad.

I turn my back to them and pick two new Team Blue players to take their places. I know we'll probably lose now, but I still can't wipe a great big smile from my face.

50
LILLY

The contestants line up next to the ropes. Looking at my team, I know we'll get slaughtered. Finn would have made a big difference for us, especially since Team Blue has some really strong guys on their team.

But when I look at the field, I notice Seth and Brian, who are the biggest Team Blue kids, aren't on the field, either. They stand on the sidelines frowning, arms crossed, and covered in some disgusting-looking yellowish-green stuff, glaring at George.

"Grab your ropes!" shouts Principal Klein.

The teams do.

"On the count of three!" announces Principal Klein.

George smiles at me from across the field. I smile back.

"One . . . ," begins Principal Klein.

"When we lose, it will be all your fault," Grace barks from next to me on the sidelines.

"Two . . . ," continues our principal.

"If the prize is a million dollars, I'll never talk to you again," threatens Sarah.

"Three!" yells Principal Klein.

The teams tug.

The rope inches toward the Team Blue side almost immediately, and I fear the worst. But then our team pulls harder and it inches back to our side.

"Go, Team Red!" I shout. My teammates repeat my cry. "Go, Team Red! Go, Team Red!"

"Go, Team Blue!" shouts the other side. "Go, Team Blue!"

The rope inches one way, and then the other, back and forth and back. The two teams appear to be evenly matched.

"Come on, guys!" I holler.

"Pull for one million dollars!" shouts Amelia. "Or something just as great!"

"Pull! Pull!" I shout, clapping and yelling encouragement. As our team captain, I will urge my team to victory with spirit and fairness.

Both teams tug, the rope inching first one way and then the other.

"C'mon, guys!" I hear George yell from the other side.

"Go, Team Blue!" roars his team behind him.

"Go, Team Red!" I shout, followed by the rest of my team.

The rope moves to our side by a foot, and then two feet to the other.

Kyle, who pulls for Team Blue, grunts loudly. Aisha on my team grunts even louder.

I feel a tap on my shoulder. When I turn, Sarah glowers at me. "You are never sleeping over at my house, you know. Or having lunch with us ever again."

I shrug. "Good. I'd rather eat with George anyway."

"Losers eating together," snarls Sarah.

"I guess that's why you and Grace always eat alone," I answer. I turn my back to her with a smirk just in time to see both teams collapse in a giant heap.

Behind me, I hear our principal cry out. "Team Blue wins!"

51
GEORGE

Everyone on my team meets in the middle of the field, jumping up and down and hugging. A few of us scream. Eric gives me a big squeeze, and so do Luke and Kyle. Kyle squeezes a little too hard, and my bones ache.

Even Brian throws me a thumbs-up. If there are sore feelings lingering from my removing him from the Tug-of-War competition, he doesn't show it. Winning makes everyone happy.

"Do you think we'll get our big-screen televisions immediately?" asks Toby.

"Or maybe we all win saxophones," Luke suggests, fidgeting and clapping.

Now I can see why Lilly is always so competitive. I don't think there is a much greater feeling in the world than winning something, especially when you earn that win with hard work and fair play.

But there is one problem with winning. It means someone else lost. Team Red stands on the sidelines watching us, their faces fixed with sad frowns. I see a tear or two.

But the person who makes me feel worst about winning is Lilly. Her shoulders slump. She stands alone, no one else on the team near her. She's like an island of unhappiness.

Winning isn't worth winning if it means your best friend loses. My victory feels hollow. As my team continues to jump and scream, I trudge across the field to Lilly. She looks up at me, her eyes watery. "Sorry we won," I say.

"Never be sorry for winning. Enjoy it. I'm happy for you."

"You don't look happy."

"I can be sad for me and happy for you at the same time. Now get back there with your team and celebrate."

I want to give her a hug and apologize, but I have nothing to apologize for. I take her advice and rejoin my team. As soon as I enter our circle of joy, I get slapped on the back and congratulated by almost everyone.

"The best team captain ever," exclaims Danny.

"You're not so bad, I guess," says Seth.

Principal Klein walks forward. We all quiet down, controlling our celebration as he clears his throat.

"Team Blue, you won with good sportsmanship and teamwork. I'm proud of each and every one of you today."

I glance at the sidelines. Lilly cracks a grin through her

gloom. If Principal Klein knew the truth about today, I don't think he would be quite so proud.

"As promised, Team Blue will win a special prize." We hold our breath. This is the moment we've worked all week to reach.

"I bet it's our own penguin," says Gavin.

"Or maybe fashion accessories for a year," suggests Samantha.

"Or someone will write a book about us," says Adam, but we all shake our heads because that idea is ridiculous.

"But because you played so fairly today, the prize will go to the entire fifth grade," our principal announces.

Our entire side goes quiet, and our excitement sort of leaks out. No one says a word, until finally Brian yells out, "That's not fair!"

Principal Klein ignores the shout. "Next week, the fifth-grade class will go on a field trip—an exciting field trip. One that I'm sure all of you will love."

I lean in, as does the rest of my team.

"I bet we're going to our own private island," says Luke.

"Sweden!" guesses Bjorn.

"It's a trip to the new science center downtown," announces Principal Klein, raising his large hands in triumph and throwing us all a giant smile. "Isn't that great?"

Maggie yells out, "I knew it! Wow!" But the rest of the grade isn't sure if we should celebrate or frown. A few of us clap. A field trip is better than nothing, but we were all imagining grander things.

"No penguins?" burbles Gavin.

"I hear the science center is terrific," exclaims Principal Klein. We clap, but Lacey, Paige, and Maggie clap loudest and longest.

Principal Klein looks around, puzzled, as he finally seems to realize his announcement hasn't generated the excitement he thought it might. "I think you'll all find it's wonderfully educational." Our principal clears his throat. "But don't forget you will all still need to help with Ms. Bryce's after-school tutoring club, too." This generates even more enthusiastic clapping from Maggie and her friends. I think her arm cast makes her claps louder, although I'm surprised it isn't painful for her.

Our principal continues. "I truly hope this newfound teamwork continues as you finish the year and move on to middle school next year. Now, everyone head to the cafeteria for the special end-of-Spirit-Week dessert."

That gets a shout of enthusiasm from the crowd. Who doesn't like dessert? Our principal marches toward school, and we all follow him like a flock of hungry sheep.

Lilly catches up to me. She reaches out and holds my hand. She gives it a squeeze. "I can't believe we all won that prize. I bet that was the plan all along."

I nod. "Probably. It's the sort of thing adults do."

"At least we get to eat," says Cooper, jogging near us. "It's a Field Day tradition to eat snickerdoodle brownies from the Fireside Bakery. Those are my favorites."

The Fireside Bakery is sort of famous for their snickerdoodle brownies.

The first thing I'm going to do is wash my hands, though. I'm still annoyed I ran out of hand sanitizer. I can't pick up a brownie with such grubby fingers.

I file into the cafeteria along with the rest of my class. But as we enter, a gasp resounds across the room. The cafeteria reeks of eggs.

"I know you'll enjoy this special dessert," says Principal Klein. "Egg salad!"

Lilly practically collapses by my side in disappointment. Everyone was excited for brownies, but that excitement spills out of us like a bucket of water with a hole in it.

"This has to be the worst Field Day victory ever," Luke mumbles, who is so disappointed he's not even wiggling.

As we stare at one another, horrified, a loud laugh booms across the room. Principal Klein slaps his knee. "Oh, I'm just kidding." He shrugs. "It was left over from the faculty lunch today. I'm not sure why everyone doesn't love egg salad as much as I do."

Teachers and parent volunteers stream from the cafeteria doors. They each wheel a cart of snickerdoodle brownies.

Everyone cheers, and then rushes toward the desserts.

I'm near the back, but there's a bunch of commotion and shoving as students elbow one another to reach the carts. I hear Mr. Foley say, "Knock it off, Brian. And you only get one brownie."

After a few minutes, when my hands are washed, we all have our treats, and I'm happily munching on the best brownie on the planet, I sit at my usual cafeteria table with Lilly. We exchange grins. "Too bad we don't have Spirit Week next year," she says. "We'd beat you guys if we had another try." Her smile turns to a frown. "And we'd win at any cost."

I choke on my brownie, but Lilly starts giggling and I know she's only joking.

"If there's a next time, we'll be on the same team," I say.

Lilly squeezes my arm. "Of course. It's only worth winning if you win with the people you care about the most."

I squeeze her arm back. As I take another bite of brownie, I glance at my friendship bracelet. Spirit Week wasn't exactly what I thought it would be, and I'm glad we don't have to go through it again. But the science center will be fun, especially since I'll be going with Lilly.

She looks up at me, bouncing on her seat and with brownie crumbs on her lips. "And George, next time we play tic-tac-toe, don't let me win, okay?"

"Let you win? I would never . . ."

Lilly shakes her head. "No one loses two hundred and twenty-eight times in a row in tic-tac-toe unless they are trying to lose, George. I mean, I think that's sort of impossible."

52
LILLY

I hang up the phone, my ears still buzzing. Aisha said that she heard that after Field Day, Principal Klein found a costume lobster claw in an empty jar of egg salad by the trash cans. She thinks Brian is in super serious trouble—and that his brother might lose his job. She heard Seth got in trouble, too. I guess Seth and Brian admitted everything.

Grace and Sarah didn't get into trouble, but no one would talk to them after Field Day. I don't think anyone likes them much anymore. Finn was especially angry when he heard that Grace doesn't own a horse.

I'm just glad the week is over and I can relax. I lie on my bed, looking first at my clay figurines, and then at my bulletin board, the one filled with pictures of George and me. I'm glad I didn't rip them up the other day. I love looking at them. It seems every time I've had fun, it's been with George.

"Lilly, it's time to go out to eat!" Mom yells up from downstairs.

I almost forgot that it's Friday night, restaurant night, and we're going to a new Mexican restaurant. It was George's idea. He usually lets me pick where we eat, but I insisted that he should choose this time.

I jump off the bed. I put on a clean shirt—I'm still wearing my Team Red shirt from school and it sort of smells like eggs—and I think back on the week. Despite all the problems, I guess everything worked out. I mean, I couldn't ask for a better ending to the week than eating at a restaurant with my best friend.

Or, at least, I couldn't have asked for a better ending to the week that didn't include winning a million dollars or a free penguin. Great friends are much more important than that stuff, anyway.

ACKNOWLEDGMENTS

When I was a kid, if I had been a better athlete, or singer, or artist, I might not have been immediately drawn to writing, so I need to thank my parents for passing me their un-athletic, un-musical, and un-artistic genes. But they also passed on their love and encouragement, which is really all that matters, or at least mostly.

I also need to thank Lauren, Madelyn, and Emmy for putting up with me, because I'm sometimes grumpy or stressed and I work out of the house a lot. And although I work mostly secreted away in my home office, they still have to deal with that grumpiness and anxiousness more than they should, although they do it pretty well, all things considered, and don't make me feel bad about it, most of the time at least.

It goes without saying that I am extremely thankful to the entire Scholastic team, but I'll say it anyway—I am extremely thankful to the entire Scholastic team, and most especially my brilliant editor Jody Corbett who inspires, lifts up, and encourages me every step along the way, and as any writer knows, any book has a whole lot of steps to climb before you reach the end.

Also, thanks to Paper Dog Studio for the fun cover, Lissy Marlin for the awesome chapter illustrations, and to Yaffa Jaskoll for her book design. I am fortunate to have such talent around me.

Lastly, I want to thank the teachers at Districts 73 and 128, who have provided our family and our community with such a wonderful and rich educational experience.

ABOUT THE AUTHOR

Allan Woodrow participated in his school's fifth-grade Field Day many years ago. He was leading the Fast Walking event until he was disqualified for running and not walking. Allan is still bitter about this.

When he wasn't losing Field Day events, Allan was writing. Since then, he has gone on to write the novels *Class Dismissed* (a companion to *Unschooled*) and *The Pet War*, as well as other books for young readers, written under secret names. His writing also appears in the Scholastic anthology *Lucky Dog: Twelve Tales of Rescued Dogs*.

Allan currently lives near Chicago. He regularly visits schools and libraries, and sometimes is even invited to speak in them. For more about Allan and his books, visit his website at www.allanwoodrow.com.

THE CONTACT PARADOX

Also available in the Bloomsbury Sigma series:

THE CONTACT PARADOX

Challenging Our Assumptions in the Search for Extraterrestrial Intelligence

Keith Cooper

BLOOMSBURY SIGMA
LONDON · OXFORD · NEW YORK · NEW DELHI · SYDNEY

BLOOMSBURY SIGMA
Bloomsbury Publishing Plc
50 Bedford Square, London, WC1B 3DP, UK

BLOOMSBURY, BLOOMSBURY SIGMA and the Bloomsbury Sigma logo
are trademarks of Bloomsbury Publishing Plc

First published in the United Kingdom in 2019

A catalogue record for this book is available from the British Library

Library of Congress Cataloguing-in-Publication data has been applied for

ISBN: HB: 978-1-4729-6042-9; eBook: 978-1-4729-6044-3

2 4 6 8 10 9 7 5 3 1

Illustrations by Marc Dando

Typeset by Deanta Global Publishing Services, Chennai, India
Printed and bound in Great Britain by CPI Group (UK) Ltd,
Croydon CR0 4YY

Bloomsbury Sigma, Book Forty-nine

To find out more about our authors and books visit www.bloomsbury.com
and sign up for our newsletters

Contents

Foreword

The modern SETI project – the Search for Extraterrestrial Intelligence, the scientific attempt to detect the alien in the heavens – was initially inspired by an accident of technology. In 1959, not long after the Mark I telescope at Jodrell Bank had been built, two physicist-astronomers called Philip Morrison and Giuseppe Cocconi, writing in a paper for *Nature*, pointed out that the new giant radio telescopes, designed to listen to natural emissions from the stars and planets, happened also to be capable of receiving radio signals from civilisations on the worlds of other stars, and indeed of sending such signals. It was an unexpected opportunity, and since, for all we knew then, the sky might have been awash with the signals of alien cultures, it would have seemed remiss not to at least try to eavesdrop. So the first serious SETI search was made by an American radio astronomer, Frank Drake, in 1960 – with negative results.

Since 2008 I have served on a committee advising the SETI project about the possible cultural implications of contact with ETI (extraterrestrial intelligence), and have met many of the pioneers, including Frank Drake and Jill Tarter – the model for Ellie Arroway in the novel and movie *Contact*. It is my personal impression that they expected to detect ETI with their radio-telescope searches, if not immediately, then soon, perhaps after a few years. But, nearly six decades on from Drake's first attempts as I write, no such unambiguous signal has been detected. Where are they all? In a Galaxy of hundreds of billions of stars, shouldn't at least one host a planet with a civilisation motivated to make contact, as we seem to be?

The mystery deepens when you consider that you don't even need a radio telescope to receive the right kind of signal. Consider 'optical SETI'. I once wrote a story called 'Eagle Song' (in my collection *Obelisk*) about a culture at a nearby star pinging the Solar System with a laser bright enough for

our sunlight-attuned eyes to see. This is technically feasible. A current project by the Breakthrough Starshot group would send a small probe to the stars by using a powerful laser beam to push a light-sail. Such a beam would outshine the brightest star in the sky of a planet of alpha Centauri, say, if aimed that way. The aliens could have made themselves visible to us by means like this even before Galileo turned his first telescope on Jupiter. But, evidently, they haven't.

Something seems wrong. Maybe we are alone in the Universe after all.

But as Keith Cooper argues in this timely, sympathetic but critical survey of the past and future of SETI, our apparently scientific quest for contact with the alien – or at least for evidence of its presence – is actually a deep expression of our humanity: 'the stars are a mirror,' as Cooper eloquently puts it. SETI is perhaps shaped by our deepest impulses, our unconscious prejudices. In which case it may be no surprise that our minds may not be open enough to apprehend the possibilities. Our search is not yet wide or deep enough, our understanding of the null result so far flawed.

So what *do* we expect, hope and fear of the alien?

As a fiction writer, the 'humanity mirror' of most concern to me personally is popular culture: our collective dreaming. In recent years arguably the most pervasive alien figure in our culture (although it may be a close-run thing with *Star Trek*'s Mr Spock) has been DC Comics' Superman, a superhero who first emerged in the American comics in 1938. What can this example tell us about our attitude to SETI?

It is a valid test case, as Superman was created independently of SETI. Indeed, Superman's story had been established and evolving since long before SETI was imagined. The main elements of Superman's story – the flight of baby Kal El from the doomed planet Krypton, his landing in a corn field in Kansas and discovery by adoptive parents Jonathan and Martha Kent – were established quickly after that 1938 debut. Since then, many talented writers have spent decades brainstorming the implications of having an alien like Superman live with us, for good and ill (and it is generally the ill that drives compelling

stories). The elements of the evolving franchise that endure are those that have survived the ruthless Darwinian selection process of success or failure at the bookstands (and latterly in the movies); something in these particular tropes evidently appeals to large numbers of readers.

Superman is not real. But after a decades-long process of storytelling and reader feedback, he may sum up our dream of the alien. So what can he tell us about that dream?

For a start, Superman, though an authentic extraterrestrial alien, is *like* us. In fact he is enough like a human in appearance to pass as one, with the cunning disguise of a pair of glasses. The chances are, though, that the alien will *not* be like us – outside or inside – to the extent that we may not even recognise it as intelligent. Even by 1938 it was a stretch to suppose aliens might be physically indistinguishable from humans; the octopus-like Martians of H.G. Wells' *The War of the Worlds* (1897) were quite unlike us physically (although Wells hinted that they might resemble a future evolution of humanity). That alone may represent a considerable barrier to cultural contact.

And as for their inner nature, as Cooper points out, we have enough trouble assessing the intelligence of the other living things on Earth, even our closest evolutionary cousins such as the chimps and dolphins, to be gung-ho about an easy meeting of minds with creatures from another world entirely.

Meanwhile, Superman is like us, too, in his altruism. Superman uses his powers to help us to survive natural disasters and to defend ourselves against the worst manifestations of our own nature: he fights the bad guys, as he has since 1938. It is of course possible that unambiguous benefits will accrue from contact with the alien. In this regard Superman represents the dream of the purely benevolent alien, which the 'contact optimists' like Carl Sagan prefer. Indeed, as Cooper shows, even an alien culture's remotely signalling to us in the classic SETI scenario would necessarily be an act of altruism towards the stranger; even a simple beacon could incur a significant cost in energy, and much more so a complex signal containing

some kind of helpful *Encyclopaedia Galactica* encoded within, as some SETI proponents hope.

But need an alien be altruistic to us at all? Even if he is altruistic towards other Kryptonians – and one can imagine entirely selfish races – why should Superman care about us? After all *we* are not Superman's kin; we are not even part of his biosphere. Such hypothetical acts of altruism as building SETI beacons become even more puzzling if we imagine worlds beaming out intellectual riches, not just to alien cultures with no hope of reward or even recognition of receipt, but to cultures that *may not even exist*. It is altruism to the hypothetical.

Meanwhile, of course, we fear the non-altruistic invader. The history of contact between human cultures is hardly encouraging – and even an apparently altruistic visitor can be mistrusted. Thus, in the movie *Batman vs Superman: Dawn of Justice* (2016, dir. Z. Snyder), Batman says to his butler Alfred, '[Superman] has the power to wipe out the entire human race. If we believe there's even a 1 per cent chance that he is our enemy, we have to take it as an absolute certainty. And we have to destroy him.' Alfred protests: 'He is not our enemy.' 'Not today,' says Batman grimly.

Batman, a hero himself who is generally an ally of Superman, is actually being supremely rational, if coldly so. He is using language characteristic of modern analyses of existential threats: threats that pose a danger to the continued existence of the human race itself, threats of extinction. Examples include natural disasters such as massive asteroid strikes, or self-induced calamities such as the destabilisation of the vacuum through an unwise high-energy physics experiment. At the minimum, it seems that a consensus is emerging that such threats should be made public and widely debated, before any action is taken that could even potentially bring down a terminal disaster on us.

And perhaps, so some analysts of the SETI project argue, extraterrestrial intelligence represents one such threat. Currently there is much debate about METI (Messaging Extraterrestrial Intelligence – Cooper discusses this more in

Chapter 7), the idea of sending 'loud' signals to the stars to provoke a response. Maybe we are like innocent baby birds 'shouting in the jungle', while the predators wheel in the sky above us, all unseen, and everybody else is keeping quiet – which is why we don't hear them.

Therefore, goes this argument, in case the worst is true, we should not message and thereby incur unnecessary risk. Batman would thoroughly approve.

In this very welcome new survey, Cooper is telling us that SETI has not failed; in fact it has barely begun. The fact that we searched first for radio signals was an accident of history; the first SETI-capable receivers we happened to build were the radio telescopes of the 1950s, as Morrison and Cocconi recognised. But infrared lasers, for example, would actually be a much better means of interstellar communication than radio transmitters. And there are other signs of intelligence that we might detect as well as messages, such as 'technosignatures', evidence of giant technological projects such as the modification of stars. The search is far from over.

And what if SETI succeeds?

The handling of first contact with the alien is absolutely central to the Superman saga. When he lands on Earth as a baby, an evident blank, Kal El can be taught our values, for good or ill. In the canonical story, the Kents find him in rural Kansas, treat him well and encourage him to be kind, loyal and helpful in turn. He is imprinted with altruism towards humanity, that essential quality that is central to much of Cooper's discussion here, and so he uses his powers for good.

But it did not have to be this way. Over the years the creators have enjoyed playing with other versions of Superman's origin story. Kal El's fall to Earth was essentially random. What if he had fallen, in 1938, not in Kansas, but in Nazi Germany, or Stalin's Soviet Union? In the graphic novel *Red Son* by Mark Millar (2003), Kal El grew up, not with the Kents in Smallville, but on a collective farm in the Ukraine. By the 1950s, the 'S' on his chest replaced by a hammer and sickle, he is ready to

wage war to defend the Communist ideals he believes are the highest expression of humanity.

If SETI succeeds, first contact will probably be a moment of crucial importance, our first and best chance to make a lasting impression on the alien. Perhaps all we can do is to be open, altruistic and generous to the visitor in the terms of our own culture – just as the Kents were with baby Kal El – and hope for a similar return.

Stephen Baxter

Little Green Men

It was early August 1967. Strains of The Beatles' 'All You Need is Love' filtered up from a record player downstairs as a young PhD student named Jocelyn Bell shivered and closed the dormer window on the cool summer's evening. Before her were rolls of chart paper, the squiggles etched on them little more than gobbledygook to the untrained eye. To Jocelyn, though, the charts spoke her language. She would come up to the attic with them to avoid getting in the way of the other students with whom she shared the house in Cambridge. Besides, John Lennon aside, it was quiet up here. She could concentrate.

Little did she realise that she was about to make one of the greatest astronomical discoveries of all time. Yet, for a little while, it looked as if it could possibly be something much, much bigger: evidence, at last, that we are not alone in the Universe.

The chart paper was filled with printouts from a telescope that Jocelyn had helped build. It didn't look like a typical telescope; instead it was poles and wires strung across nearly 2 hectares (4½ acres) of muddy Cambridgeshire fields. However, the Interplanetary Scintillation Array, as the contraption was called, was her meal ticket to a PhD. It was designed to detect radio waves from brilliant quasars, which are the blazing cores of distant galaxies. Pen recorders documented any signals that the telescope detected onto paper, 120m (nearly 400ft) of the stuff every four days, which Jocelyn would pick up from the telescope's control room and take home with her to scrutinise. Yet on this particular evening, amid the familiar squiggles of radio waves from cold hydrogen gas in the Milky Way and the occasional active galaxy, something odd caught her eye: a flickering signal, strange and messy compared to typical radio emission from outer space, like a bit of scruff on the chart. Not knowing what to make of it, she made a note and reported it to her supervisor, Antony Hewish, the next day.

The signal was seriously weird. It didn't move, so it couldn't be an aeroplane or a satellite; it was narrowband, meaning that the signal was extremely focused in wavelength and not blaring indiscriminately across the spectrum; and it pulsed exactly once every 1.3 seconds to an accuracy of a millionth of a second each day. Nothing known in nature was so precise. Jocelyn's colleagues initially joked that perhaps the 'scruff' was from 'Little Green Men'. Those jokes quickly turned alarmingly serious. The late geophysicist Teddy Bullard told Hewish quietly over lunch one day that if the signal were narrowband, then it was probably the result of intelligence. 'My God,' thought Hewish. 'It just might be.'

Hewish brought the news that something odd was going on to Sir Martin Ryle, the head of the Mullard Radio Astronomy Observatory at Cambridge University's Cavendish Laboratory. An experienced scientist, yet still a relatively young 49 years old, Ryle was a man who was always very aware of the impact of science on society. He'd seen, for instance, how splitting the atom had led to both new sources of energy and the destruction of Japanese cities; finding aliens would be another scientific discovery of equally Earth-shattering proportions. It wasn't so much the discovery that concerned Ryle, but our reaction to it, followed by the inevitable urge to send a message in reply, and in doing so courting danger by revealing our existence to the Universe. Who knew if the extraterrestrials (ET for short – although not necessarily as nice as the friendly alien from Steven Spielberg's 1982 movie) would be peaceable or belligerent? Even if they weren't looking to invade like their fictional cousins of science-fiction B-movies, they could perhaps deliberately or inadvertently introduce political, religious or cultural memes or revolutionary technology into our society that could prove disruptive. In a biographical interview in 2008, Hewish gave some insight into the machinations of Ryle's mind. 'He was only half-joking, but he said burn the records and forget about this, because if the news gets out that there is intelligence out there, people will want to launch a signal in that direction to talk to them.'

Never mind what it could mean for the fate of the human race; the situation was reaching near-crisis proportions for Jocelyn Bell. She had a PhD thesis to write, damn it, and this talk of aliens was just getting in the way. On 21 December 1967 she stumbled into a high-level meeting between Hewish, Ryle and a few others – the whole affair was being kept hush-hush and, according to Hewish, only half a dozen people knew what was really going on. The reasons for the secrecy were two-fold: to keep the media away for as long as possible, and also to prevent other scientific groups from getting the scoop and beating the Cambridge team to the discovery. Plus, nobody wanted to announce the discovery of Little Green Men until they knew for sure what the signal was. Nevertheless, Bell came away from that meeting severely disheartened, knowing that a discovery of extraterrestrial life, momentous as that might be, would scupper any kind of sensible grasp that she had on her studies.

That evening, after the meeting, she drove back to the observatory on her little Vespa motor-scooter to pick up the latest batch of printouts and run some more observations. It was close to Christmas, and terribly cold, the kind of cold that manages to penetrate through to your bones no matter how many layers you put on, and the recorders on the telescope wouldn't function properly in the deep freeze. After the usual cajoling of the equipment in the form of shouting, swearing and banging it, simply gently breathing on it to warm the electronics proved sufficient and Bell managed to get the thing working for five minutes before it conked out again. Yet, miraculously, it was enough. Perhaps it was fate. She looked at what the telescope had just recorded. There, amid the usual radio emissions of deep space, despite the odds, lay another piece of scruff. A second signal.

She was delighted. To Jocelyn, the odds that two alien civilisations would try signalling Earth at the same time in the same fashion from different parts of the sky seemed highly improbable. Whatever the scruffs were, Jocelyn's mind was made up and soon so was Hewish's. When Bell turned up not only a second source but later a third and fourth, it was clear

that this new phenomenon must be both natural and frequently occurring – we only hadn't seen them before because astronomers had lacked the technology to detect them.

Because they pulsed so rapidly, Hewish realised that whatever they were, they had to be small and powerful. Poring through the literature, he swiftly hit upon a mechanism that could explain Jocelyn's 'scruffs': they were the signals of pulsars, which are the dense, spinning remnants of the cores of destroyed stars. Pulsars rotate so fast that a typical revolution can take place in a second, while beams of energy are channelled away by the magnetic forces at their poles. Every time the beams flash in our direction, we see a pulse, like a lighthouse.* Some pulsars have even been witnessed spinning hundreds of times every second† and, despite being no bigger than a city, their regular pulses of radiation can be detected across large swathes of the Galaxy. Indeed, so regular are they that pulsars are the most efficient timekeepers in the entire Universe, better even than atomic clocks.

The mystery was over. Jocelyn Bell became famous overnight, not as the woman who discovered aliens, but as the young student from Belfast who found one of the most incredible types of astronomical object in the Universe. The media promptly descended on Cambridge following the announcement of the discovery in February 1968 and the publication of the academic report in the journal *Nature*.

---

* When stars eight times the mass of the Sun or greater reach the end of their lives, their cores collapse, the shock wave blowing the star apart in a supernova. What is left behind is the compressed remnant of their core, an object so dense that the electrons and protons of hydrogen nuclei have literally been mushed together into neutrons, hence the term 'neutron star'. The force of the supernova gives birth to a spinning neutron star, which we call a pulsar.

† These whirling dervishes are called millisecond pulsars and they are spun up to such extraordinary rates by the accumulation of matter streaming onto them from a companion star that is a little too close to the pulsar for comfort. The fastest spinning pulsar, known as PSR B1257+12, rotates on its axis 716 times per second.

Today Jocelyn – now Dame Jocelyn Bell Burnell – is a professor and eminent radio astronomer in her own right, and around 2,000 pulsars have been identified in the Milky Way alone. Meanwhile, Antony Hewish and Martin Ryle won the Nobel Prize for Physics in 1974 for their work in the field of radio astronomy, including the discovery of pulsars. For Ryle, however, the questions posed by the possibility of contact didn't end there.

In 1974, American astronomer Frank Drake composed a message that he beamed to the globular star cluster Messier 13 using the transmitter on the newly refurbished Arecibo radio telescope in Puerto Rico. Ryle was aghast, complaining that Drake had no right to try to communicate with any alien intelligences out there on behalf of Earth, lest he inadvertently cause an interstellar diplomatic incident, or reveal our presence to malevolent civilisations. Ryle's warnings fell on deaf ears, but Drake's message proved a one-off, at least until the turn of the millennium. Indeed, the emphasis of the Search for Extraterrestrial Intelligence (SETI) has been on listening for radio signals sent by an alien civilisation, evoking the iconic image of actress Jodie Foster in the film *Contact* listening on her headphones to radio static detected by the upward-turned dishes of radio telescopes.

Drake himself conducted the first search for extraterrestrial radio communication in 1960, and radio searches have dominated SETI ever since. However, since the turn of the millennium, things have been changing. Scientists are increasingly turning towards other ways to look for intelligent extraterrestrial life, such as watching for powerful beams of laser light, or searching for evidence of alien civilisations that have modified their stellar environment in some detectable technological manner. Furthermore, there's a growing impetus from corners of the SETI community to follow in Drake's footsteps and begin transmitting our own messages into space. As our technology to detect and communicate with any alien life that might exist out there grows, SETI is changing, and so too are our ideas about what form alien life might take.

The discovery of pulsars was an important test case for SETI. It wasn't the first false alarm and it won't be the last, but it set the stage to begin asking questions about what communication would mean for humanity. How can we identify a signal of alien origin, or their technology? How can we be sure of ET's intentions? How can we respond and should we even attempt to do so? Who speaks for Earth? What are the dangers of contact? Should we expect there to be life elsewhere in the cosmos? What assumptions are biasing our answers to these questions?

It would be presumptuous to suggest that you will find the definitive answers to these questions in *The Contact Paradox*, but in a way we can actually do better than that because in this case, the journey is at least as important as the destination. Every one of the questions listed above, and many more that we will ask in the following pages, relate just as much to humankind as they do to the search for extraterrestrial life. Maybe there is no one else out there and we are alone, or maybe the Universe is teeming with life of all varieties. In some ways it does not matter, because the journey that takes us to one of these answers can teach us a great deal about ourselves. By pointing our radio telescopes to the sky and patiently waiting for ET to say hello, we are forcing ourselves to explore humanity's own identity.

That, right there, is the crux of the matter, the concept that will play out over the coming pages. The search for extraterrestrial intelligence is at least in part about searching for an echo of ourselves, reflected out there in that starry ocean, a mirror image that we hope will tell us who we are, where we came from and where we are going. Perhaps the answers that we seek are out there, somewhere, hidden in the nuances of that reflection. As Arthur C. Clarke wrote in his 1951 book *The Exploration of Space*, 'The proper study of mankind is not merely man, but intelligence.' Paraphrasing Henry Beston, we are islanded on planet Earth amid a stream of stars, all we can do is gaze out into the ocean of myriad suns and wonder if there is anyone gazing back.

Finding the answers to these questions would be the culmination of a centuries-long quest to discover how we come to find ourselves living on a blue planet around a friendly star in the suburbs of a distinctly average galaxy. That quest has taken us through 13.8 billion years of cosmic history since the Big Bang, across aeons of galactic evolution and generations of stars, to arrive at an understanding of how our planet came to be, and to look at what lies ahead for the Universe in the deep future. SETI is the boldest manifestation of this quest.

Yet all too often SETI concerns itself with just the technical aspects of the search. Vital as these are, they are only one side of the coin. In *The Contact Paradox*, we're going to flip that coin and explore the other side too. We're going to cross the borders between disciplines and embrace the social sciences. What will follow over the next few hundred pages will suitably blow your mind. It will be quite a ride as you embark on a journey through physics and astronomy, chemistry and biology, evolution and neuroscience, history and anthropology, and perhaps we'll visit some new lands too. What role does altruism play? How do we define intelligence, and does being too narrow in our definition mean that our searches will end up missing other, different kinds of intelligence? Are Earth-like planets the only possible abodes for life, and if planets like Earth are rare, does that mean there is unlikely to be life elsewhere? Can life colonise the Galaxy, and how do civilisations end? Which assumptions inherent in our ideas about extraterrestrial life are leading us down the wrong path? And how does all this play into the questions Martin Ryle first asked about the nature of contact between civilisations and what the consequences could be?

The old history of our search for ET has been told ad infinitum. Starting today, with this book, we begin to look to the future. This is not your parents' SETI. Strap in, and get ready for a twenty-first-century SETI.

The Altruism Assumption

William Proxmire knew how to make a name for himself. A Democratic senator, he took his seat in Wisconsin in 1957, replacing the disgraced Joseph McCarthy, who had died months earlier. There Proxmire remained for 32 years, winning re-election five times, yet never spending more than a few hundred dollars during each campaign. It was his tight-fisted attitude towards the use of taxpayers' cash that helped define him as a maverick – each month, from 1975 until 1989, he issued one of his infamous 'Golden Fleece' awards to a government or federally funded agency that had spent cash on what Proxmire believed to be wasteful projects.* The Bureau of Land Management were early 'winners', called to task for spending $11,000 on 'useless' paperwork for a piece of equipment that by itself cost only $4,000. The Environment Protection Agency got it in the neck for spending over a million dollars on preserving a New York sewer as a historical monument. Even the army couldn't escape Proxmire's wrath, criticised for spending $6,000 on a 17-page document explaining 'how to buy a bottle of Worcestershire sauce'.

Scientific projects were frequently awarded Golden Fleeces. The National Science Foundation won the first ever Golden Fleece for spending $84,000 on a study that sought to discover why people fall in love – a job better left to 'poets and mystics', according to Proxmire. The Massachusetts Institute of Technology (MIT) received a Golden Fleece for the Aspen Movie Map, a kind of precursor to Google Map's street-view mode. NASA were also regular award winners, for everything from spending $140,000 on producing books about the

---

* A full list of William Proxmire's 159 Golden Fleece awards, which makes for entertaining reading, can be found at www.wisconsinhistory.org/turningpoints/search.asp?id=1742.

Viking Mars missions, to $2.8 million to build new facilities at Johnson Space Center to house rocks brought back from the Moon, and splashing out up to a billion dollars on a Tracking Data Relay and Satellite System.

And then there was SETI.

In 1978 NASA were awarded the Golden Fleece for planning to spend $15 million over seven years as part of the SETI project, subject to Congressional approval. Those plans were placed in jeopardy thanks to the stigma of the Golden Fleece, which by then had become a regular and popular fixture in Congress (despite Congress itself being on the receiving end of several of the awards). However, as a crucial 1982 Congressional vote on NASA funding neared, Proxmire had reckoned on all but one man: Carl Sagan.

Both men were at the peak of their popularity; the Golden Fleece awards had found favour with the public, while astronomer Sagan's PBS television show *Cosmos* had been a smash hit. Sagan, though, was more than just an astronomer. He was a brilliant polymath with a knack for debating and a keen interest in educating the public about the Universe around us. One suspects Sagan, ever the scientific romantic, would have been fascinated to learn why we fall in love.

So Sagan sought out Proxmire for a showdown in the senator's office. When they met – one tall and wiry and fussy about his appearance (Proxmire was the first senator to receive a facelift and hair transplants to hold back baldness), the other dark and handsome with a winning smile but who didn't take fools gladly – you might have expected sparks to fly, but that's not what happened. Both men were too smart for that. Sagan knew how to speak calmly and rationally, and Proxmire knew how to listen.

Seasoned debater that he was, Sagan knew that getting Proxmire onside was vital and that ridiculing his scientific ignorance wasn't the answer. Sagan realised that the pair had more in common than first met the eye. Despite enlisting as a private in the army after the Pearl Harbor attack, Proxmire was very much a man of peace who campaigned against the Vietnam War and deplored nuclear armament and the threat of mutually

assured destruction. Similarly, Sagan was equally horrified at the potential for nuclear war and became just as well known during the 1980s as a campaigner for nuclear disarmament, twice being arrested at protests outside a Nevada test site. So once they had introduced themselves, Sagan started upon the topic of nuclear war. Indeed, agreed Proxmire, how can we avoid it?

Sagan, having created the opening for himself, now raised the issue of SETI. The Universe is very old – 13.81 billion years. *Homo sapiens* has been around for just 300,000 of those years, and human civilisation far less. The likelihood is that if sentient, intelligent beings exist elsewhere on other planets around other stars, then their civilisations must be much older than us, and Sagan's logic was that they too must have passed through the bottleneck of existential hazards, such as nuclear war, that we face today. Sagan drove his point home: if we can detect a signal from an extraterrestrial civilisation, then it would be proof that intelligent beings do not inevitably wipe themselves out, that there is hope for the future and that we could even learn from ET about how to navigate the problems currently besetting our planet.

Proxmire was sufficiently impressed with Sagan's argument that when the Congressional vote came, he signed off on SETI and even went as far as to apologise publicly for his persecution of the search for extraterrestrial intelligence. Unfortunately, it was a short-lived victory; 10 years later Republican senator Richard Bryan launched a motion that ultimately killed federal funding for SETI in the US. This certainly was not the end for SETI, which has had a rejuvenation of sorts in recent years, as well as being conducted in other parts of the world, but it was still a huge setback from which SETI research took decades to recover.

Amid the Golden Fleeces, Congressional hearings and summit meetings, an unspoken assumption fundamental to how we view SETI had gained ground. Sagan's answer to Proxmire, that finding ET could help us avoid nuking ourselves back to the Stone Age, was a natural progression from an earlier idea he first broached in memorable fashion in *Cosmos*, where he speculated that perhaps aliens would routinely beam into

space a signal containing an *Encyclopaedia Galactica*.* This encyclopaedia would be a collection of knowledge from perhaps a thousand worlds, chronicling the histories, cultures and scientific discoveries of beings far more advanced (in the sense of age and technological prowess) than we, as seen through the (metaphorical) eyes of beings with viewpoints and mindsets maybe much removed from our own. This concept of knowledge being freely available from space would be an enormously altruistic act on the part of the sender, yet the idea has become so entrenched in the mindset of many researchers hunting for ET that it has begun to act as the scaffolding for our subsequent expectations of success in the search.

'I think they will send the *Encyclopaedia Galactica* for two reasons,' Seth Shostak, who is the Senior Astronomer at the SETI Institute in California, nestled deep within Silicon Valley, tells me. 'One, they're not going to send an empty message – what's the point in that? Two, they know it is going to be one-way communication because they are probably pretty far away, at least hundreds of light years away, so two-way communication is going to be pretty tedious. They may as well just send everything at once.'

We will not know for sure what information will be included in a message until we receive one. However, Shostak's second point, which is that the sheer vastness of space is insurmountable to extended conversations between beings of limited lifespans, seems a fair assessment on the face of it, but there's a whiff of circular logic about the reasoning. It assumes that there are just two constraints to transmitting a message across space, namely

---

* Carl Sagan likely developed the idea of the *Encyclopaedia Galactica* from the science-fiction author Isaac Asimov, who first introduced the concept in his 1942 novel *Foundation*, albeit in a slightly different guise as the collection of all knowledge from a great 'Galactic Empire' that is growing stagnant and slowly dying. Ironically, despite his interest in SETI and astrobiology, Asimov himself rarely wrote about aliens in his fiction, reportedly as a result of negative comments about alien characters by his early editor at *Astounding Science Fiction*, John Campbell. One of Asimov's few books about aliens is the award-winning *The Gods Themselves*.

distance and time, and that those practicalities therefore determine what kind of message would be sent.

Let's look at it another way. In the not so distant past, in the days before truly global telecommunications, broadband Internet and Skype, the only way to talk to Aunt Matilda in Sydney from your home in Leeds, or wherever, was via a very expensive long-distance telephone call. As those minutes on the phone totted up, so did the cost. Consequently, perhaps you only called Aunt Matilda on family birthdays and at Christmas, when there was something special to talk about. To call her more frequently without special reason would not have been cost effective.

Similarly, there's a cost, in terms of resources and energy, in transmitting across the stars. Indeed, the vast distances between the stars may be so overwhelming that it could be impractical to embark on a programme of beaming messages into space in any cost-effective manner. The salient point is that it would be incredibly kind of the aliens to do this; maybe too kind, because transmitting across the expanse of space loudly enough to be heard, and maintaining that signal for days, months, years in order to provide the best chance of being heard, would not come cheaply. In terms of the amount of energy required as a percentage of a civilisation's total energy resources, it turns out that a long-term programme of transmission would be rather costly, even for the civilisations that are able to harness the most energy.* SETI generally

---

* So why not just send a spacecraft carrying a message, similar to our Voyager probes and their golden records on which sounds and pictures of Earth are recorded? ET may well have done this, but the huge expanses between the stars mean that unless they have access to some magical faster-than-light star-drive, travelling from one star to another is going to take a long, long time. For example, it would take a spacecraft travelling at the same speed as Voyager 1 – that is, about 17km (11 miles) per second – over 75,000 years to reach the nearest star system to us, which is alpha Centauri, 4.367 light years away. It's quicker to transmit a radio signal instead, which moves at the speed of light and would take just 4.367 years to reach alpha Centauri. That said, we'll tackle interstellar travel further in Chapter 5.

works on the assumption that extraterrestrial civilisations will utilise electromagnetic radiation – be it radio, optical light, *etc.* – as the medium for their signals (we'll challenge this assumption a bit more in Chapter 4), but it's not as simple as making a telephone call. Transmitting across vast distances and timescales requires not only enormous power obtained at great expense, but also a foundation of abundant patience, a deep, burning curiosity about the Universe that never fades, a longevity that makes the time-span of our current civilisation appear as little more than a footnote in cosmic history and, most vitally, it demands that the senders be amazingly altruistic to levels we might regard as saintly.

Understanding altruism may ultimately be the single most significant factor in our quest to make contact with other intelligent life in the Universe. It is at the heart of how and why we think other civilisations would transmit a signal for us to detect. It dominates the discussion of whether a civilisation can survive through its infancy and into the great longevity of maturity, where that civilisation can find itself in the position of having the resources and time to begin beaming messages into space on a persistent basis. And it is crucial in calculating the repercussions of contact, which could leave a lasting legacy on the human race.

An evolutionary trajectory?

The father of SETI, Dr Frank Drake, who pushed the search to prominence in 1960 when he conducted the first ever radio survey for extraterrestrial signals, has said that his rationale for anticipating the detection of a powerful beacon from space – a transmitting device consistently beaming out signals containing messages for us to detect – is that altruism should be ubiquitous in the Universe and can be expected as a Darwinian imperative.

So, if we're talking Darwin, we're talking evolutionary trajectories, the idea that some things in evolution are just inevitable, while others are unique one-offs. Convergent properties versus contingent characteristics. Evoking

'Darwinian imperatives' suggests a well-worn path in the evolutionary journey of intelligent beings, a sense of progression from, in this case, less altruistic to more altruistic. The progression need not be pre-planned by nature or deliberate in any way. Perhaps instead it's natural selection writ large on the scale of civilisations; those societies that are inherently altruistic to a larger degree are more likely to survive and not destroy themselves through violent planetary wars or environmental or cultural breakdown, or through a failure to cooperate in the face of external threats such as doomsday asteroid impacts. Hence, as time progresses, those civilisations that lack altruism will be weeded out, creating the illusion of progression by leaving only those that have the right stuff to survive to the point that they have the wherewithal to build a beacon that can be seen or heard across the Galaxy, despite the great expense to themselves. This is what SETI is looking for, but it is an idea based around what I call the 'altruism assumption'.

Whether you believe in this assumption or not depends on how you view future societies, because the predicted future of human civilisation is often held up as an analogue for advanced extraterrestrial civilisations. Professor Nick Bostrom, Director of the University of Oxford's Future of Humanity Institute and one-time stand-up comedian, doesn't buy into the idea of there being any kind of progression. 'Even if one could detect a pattern of increasing moral enlightenment in human history, it would still be dangerous to extrapolate that into the future,' he tells me in dulcet Swedish tones. 'In fact I think that argument to be extremely weak, but I would imagine that is what underpins some people's optimism about technologically advanced civilisations.'

Professor Steven Pinker, an experimental psychologist and linguist at Harvard University, is one of those to harbour such optimism, disagreeing with Bostrom in a big way. He's investigated the history of violence in human societies, leading up to his best-selling book, *The Better Angels of Our Nature*, wherein he concludes that humanity is steadily growing more peaceable. Sure, violence hasn't been eradicated,

by any stretch of the imagination, and there have been some pretty hefty hiccups along the way, but records of acts of violence, be they murder, rape, beatings or torture, or the decreasing regularity of wars or genocides, do seem to indicate that something is happening to us. Whereas 50,000 years ago you couldn't even step outside your cave to catch a boar and grab a bite to eat without worrying if the caveman next door was going to bonk you over the head with his club and nick your nosh, today we are mostly free to go about our cities without the imminent threat of violence. While wars have continued to be fought, since 1945 there has not been a single skirmish between two major powers (although this is somewhat undermined by the fact that during the Cold War the major powers would fight their battles through the proxies of smaller nations: North Korea and North Vietnam versus the United States, for example, or the Afghan Mujahideen versus the Soviet Union) and, while we stare in horror at the atrocities in Bosnia and Rwanda and Syria that are regularly brought into our homes via news media, the mass murder of innocents, claims Pinker, is now on a downward trend – as a percentage of our total population – compared to the days of Genghis Khan and Richard the Lionheart and An Lushan of the Tang Dynasty. If Pinker's interpretation is correct – and it has to be said that not everybody agrees with his conclusions – then it seems we are growing more peaceful with time, an apparent characteristic of humanity that we can extrapolate into our future, the very thing Bostrom says won't work. Since we're holding up future human civilisation as an analogue for advanced extraterrestrial civilisations, the implications become clear.

In Pinker's eyes, why are people seemingly becoming nicer? He lays it at the feet of a variety of factors: the advent of positive-sum games, the Enlightenment and the rise of human rights and liberalism, an increasing dependence upon rationality over superstition and a civilising process brought about by urbanisation, commerce, industry and secularity under the auspices of Thomas Hobbes' *Leviathan*, all leading to the development of democracies that are inherently more

peaceful. This transformation didn't occur in one fell swoop across the globe, but has been an ongoing process since the Middle Ages, first in Europe and then elsewhere. As such, it could occur at different points in the history of different civilisations, or maybe not at all.

So, can we expect all extraterrestrials to live in liberal utopian democracies, not too dissimilar to The Culture in Iain M. Banks's science-fiction novels, or even The Federation in *Star Trek*? 'I do think the essence of democracy – disinterested, third-party control of violence to inhibit violence among the members of a society, and regulated by its clients so that it does not cause more violence than it prevents – is likely to be the violence-reduction solution that intelligent societies will arrive at,' Pinker tells me.

Democracies operate on a principle of cooperation and this is another altruistic quality, one that we find related to reciprocity. When we cooperate with our family, our friends or our immediate neighbours, social scientists term such acts 'direct reciprocity'. On the other hand, we may come to cooperate with people we are not directly familiar with if they have a good reputation for trustworthiness and acts of reciprocity themselves, which we call 'indirect reciprocity'. It's rather like an elevated sense of enlightened self-interest. Neither mode of reciprocity is particularly dominant within the infrastructure of nations run by dictators or tyrants, because for cooperation to be successful it must result from the freedom to choose to work together.

This willingness to work together has operated at a purely unconscious level and been an important factor in evolution ever since the advent of the first simple biological cells, which reached greater complexity by utilising genes, chromosomes, bacteria and cellular components to combine to become more than the sum of their parts, in the form of complex organisms. Cooperation has sat side-by-side with its opposite force, competition, and managed to prevail while still making use of competition's primary weapon, natural selection, to find a way forward and evolve. Even more stunning is the notion, put forward by Martin Nowak of

Harvard University, that cooperation is most keenly observed in human behaviour and that it has become something special to us that has allowed our species to flourish. Although other animal species on Earth do display cooperation and reciprocity, nowhere in nature do we find it approaching anything like the scale of the cooperative behaviour of humans. Indeed, human society as we know it depends on a high level of voluntary cooperation.

If the intensity of cooperation in humans is something unique in nature on Earth, then all of a sudden reciprocity elevates itself from a convergent facet of evolution that all types of life make use of at one time or another, to a contingent property that instead says something special about humans. Nor can we call it merely biological evolution; the rise of cooperation, fuelling increased altruism and leading to the development of democracies, becomes an aspect of cultural evolution, an emergent property of human nature. Since these characteristics are essential to encourage a civilisation to throw resources at beaming the *Encyclopaedia Galactica* – or indeed any other benevolent message – into space, then we must question how unremarkable our own altruism is. In order to do so, let's take a gander at altruism and cooperation in far more detail.

You've got an itch. Right on the shoulder blades, in that place high up on your back that is agonisingly awkward to reach. Cue endless contortions as you attempt to wrap your arms around your body in unorthodox fashion to reach the burning itch, or comedic shuffling on the floor or against a wall as you seek abrasion against another surface to satisfy that urge to scratch. Why oh why, you may ask, did evolution bless us with body plans that placed parts of our bodies out of easy reach of our limbs?

Natural selection tells us that the answer is a result of the fact that it is more advantageous to have dexterous hands and arms that can reach in front of us; being unable to scratch our

backs is hardly a threat to survival. But by golly, that itch is irritating. So, you get somebody else to scratch it for you. The interesting question is, why should they? What's in it for them? This is why the phrase 'You scratch my back, I'll scratch yours' is more than just a truism, but rather a manifestation of the relationship between actions and rewards, survival instincts and morality and the strength of trade and positive-sum games. As it applies to itchy backs, it equally applies to cosmic altruism and the lighting-up of extraterrestrial beacons because we are forced to ask, what's in it for ET?

The problem is, evolution is not necessarily about altruism, just as it is also not necessarily about intelligence, as we shall see in Chapter 2. Natural selection does not decide which species propagate and which don't simply on the basis of how nice they are to each other. Rather, natural selection works on the basis of genes that are capable of adapting to changing environments and situations and ultimately permitting survival. The ancestors of cheetahs that could run faster were able to catch prey such as gazelles and thus not starve to death. Hence their genes for sprinting were passed onto the next generation, while the slow cheetahs never lived long enough to procreate, and today cheetahs have adapted to become the fastest land animals on the planet. Equally, the gazelle has evolved to run fast to try and escape the cheetah, leading to a kind of genetic arms race between them. Giraffes developed the adaptation of long necks because they found it helped them to reach food on trees that could not be reached by other species competing for the same leafy snacks. And so on – animals that happen to act in ways that improve the probability of their survival, and hence their likelihood of being able to reproduce many times to allow their genes to propagate through the gene pool, would therefore be naturally selected for the traits attached to those genes that allow them to act that way and survive and procreate in the first place. This prompts us to ask whether our sense of morality, our urge to do good, is also an adaptation, like the ability of spiders to weave webs or the long snout of an anteater. To be

an adaptation of evolution and streamlined through natural selection, altruism would therefore be required as an aid to survival.

If altruism were a ubiquitous, biological imperative, then one would figure that there must be an 'altruism gene' that can drive organisms to survive over those that lack the gene, hence allowing the altruistic life-forms to pass their gene on to the next generation. Within a dozen or so generations the gene propagates to the extent that every member of that species has it.

Does such a gene exist? It turns out that it might very well do. A 2010 study by geneticists and psychologists from the University of Bonn in Germany identified two variants of the catechol–O-methyl transferase (COMT) gene, which affects particular couriers in the brain that control social behaviour and positive emotions. These particular couriers seem to increase the willingness of people with the gene variant to behave altruistically, such as by giving more money to charity.

If altruism has a survival advantage, then perhaps a species can evolve with altruism as one of its central tenets, and at first glance it's certainly easy to see how this is possible. Cooperation and mutual support among communities will surely allow for greater potential for survival and a safe and prosperous living environment. However, this does not necessarily tally with how we actually define altruism, which the *Little Oxford Dictionary* that sits on my desk describes as 'regard for others as principle of action', an echo of Immanuel Kant's determination that true morality and goodwill only come from those who seek no reward other than the happiness of those they help. Pure altruism seems light years away from the self-serving 'you scratch my back, I'll scratch yours' philosophy. Rather, our tendencies for cooperation and mutual support, at least in primitive cultures from where we have obtained many of our genetic traits, are more to do with securing one's individual survival and the survival of one's own immediate family. It's the epitome of Richard Dawkins' selfish gene.

Nevertheless, modern human society, at least for the most part, strives to become more altruistic. We're like Pinocchio, wanting to become something better. Because we see extraterrestrial civilisations as being far more advanced than we are, it's easy to project our vision of an advanced human society, wherein Pinocchio has fulfilled his wish to become something better, onto them. This, however, is decidedly anthropocentric – a risky practice for predicting extraterrestrial behaviour. Yet what alternatives to a sense of altruism are there?

Kin selection and heroic squirrels

'It all depends on the scenario of how a species arose and got its intelligence and cultural capacity,' says Jerome Barkow, a sociocultural anthropologist and Professor Emeritus at Dalhousie University in Halifax, Canada, and Honorary Professor at Queens University, Belfast. Barkow studies human evolution, nature and culture and, despite our warnings of anthropocentricity, in lieu of finding someone who studies the evolution, nature and culture of extraterrestrials, researchers like Barkow are the next best bet for learning about the ways that intelligent alien life-forms may have developed.

Barkow concurs that selfless altruism is unlikely to be ubiquitous, but offers up an alternative way that a species could evolve. 'For instance, maybe they [ET] are a fear-filled species, hypersensitive to danger, and they've evolved intelligence that way because that was the only way they could manage to win in competition against other species on their home planet,' he says.[*] In other words, there is nothing to say

---

[*] Interestingly, one of the lead characters in the television series *Star Trek: Discovery* is Commander Saru, a Kelpien, which is a species hypersensitive to danger and death, an ability that manifests itself in the tendrils of their 'threat ganglia' that open whenever danger is near. Because they were bred as prey on their planet, the Kelpiens have evolved to avoid risk and in uncertain situations they would

that they have to be altruistic. What a species needs to be able to amass the technology required to build radio telescopes and beacons, suggests Barkow, is culture and social learning: the ability to accumulate information and cooperate. 'But they don't have to like each other,' he points out. As we've seen, cooperation can be built around self-serving principles, not altruism, and while that may seem strange, it ultimately comes down to genes and an instinct to protect a genetic lineage, which as we see so frequently on our planet, can often manifest itself as ethnocentrism.

If the selfless altruism so hoped for by SETI researchers is not common, perhaps there may be other forms of altruism that favour the selfish gene. Although he didn't invent it, the late evolutionary biologist William Hamilton of Oxford University further developed and publicised the theory of kin selection, also known as nepotistic altruism (coincidentally, Hamilton was educated at Tonbridge School in Kent, about 20m from where I am typing this particular chapter). Kin selection has, at its heart, the propagation of genes. We show kin selection to our children and relatives.* In the theory of

---

assume hostility against them, but when faced with a fight-or-flight choice, they would err on the side of flight rather than fight, somewhat opposite to the scenario Jerome Barkow depicts. This does not mean that either scenario is right or wrong, but it illustrates the power of science fiction to be able to speculate and provide alternative ideas about the behaviour of alien life.

* British-born scientific philosopher Michael Ruse has pointed out how kin selection was a crucial plot-point in one of Hollywood's greatest series of films – *Star Wars*. In the original 1977 movie, Darth Vader would have happily killed Luke Skywalker and vice versa. When Vader realised Luke was his son, he sought to turn him rather than kill him, and when Luke discovered the truth, he tried to save his father rather than kill him. By the finale of *Return of the Jedi* (1983), when it seemed that the Emperor whom Vader served was going to kill Luke, Vader made a choice to save his son at the expense of his own life and the path he had chosen for himself 20 years or so earlier. In this case, kin selection was a far more powerful 'force' than the Dark Side.

kin selection, the more distantly related we are, the less likely we are to be selflessly altruistic. To a stranger, we would demand reciprocation were we to act altruistically on their behalf. To a distant relative we would cut them some slack, while a closer relative would get a lot of slack and our children would not be expected to reciprocate at all – the purpose of kin selection is to ensure our genes are passed on through our offspring or closest relatives.*

Hamilton was a strong believer that cultural evolution is not a self-supporting system, but has to operate in tandem with biological evolution to survive, operating at the lowest levels at which natural selection takes place – *i.e.* at the genetic level – and hence it is genetics that control the path taken by sociocultural development. Thus at the genetic level Hamilton explained altruism through something called 'inclusive fitness'. It is similar to, but not quite the same as, kin selection. In essence, it is the sum of how many offspring a life-form produces and supports, plus the number of equivalents to its offspring (in terms of genes) that it can add to the population by supporting others, usually relatives once or twice removed, such as cousins. An animal may recognise that other members of its close-knit group harbour some of the genes that it also possesses, and supporting them enhances the probability that those shared genes will be passed on to the next generation, including any altruism gene that promulgates through the population as the generations go by. Altruists may even identify the altruistic gene in others through their behaviour, and therefore work to support them. It's why a squirrel will cry out a warning to other squirrels when a predator is lurking, even though in many cases it could prove suicidal for the heroic squirrel. Nevertheless, here the important point is that inclusive fitness is not as limited as kin selection; in human societies inclusive fitness can also extend to close

---

* Although Hamilton developed the theory of kin selection in papers written in 1961 and 1963, it had previously been dabbled with by Ronald Fisher in 1930 and John S. Haldane in 1955. The term 'kin selection' wasn't coined until 1964, by John Maynard Smith.

friends, or people who share the same religion or support the same football team.

Indeed, humans have a 'capacity and proclivity for altruism toward individuals that we're not related to', says Joan Silk, who is an anthropologist from Arizona State University. She spends her time studying the social behaviours of primates and how human behaviour – including cooperation and altruism – evolved. Some aspects of human behaviour have changed since we split from our last common ancestor with primates, and among these new, 'derived' traits is the ability to show altruism beyond kin, even beyond reciprocity. 'It's a really important part of human societies that we don't see in other primates,' Silk tells me.

Of course, understanding why we have evolved that trait and other primates have not would go a long way to answering the altruism assumption. Until then, there are no grounds to expect that an alien civilisation that knows nothing about us will definitely feel sufficient kinship to want to go out of its way to help us. Although I would be remiss not to point out that these factors don't necessarily dictate human behaviour, since we must also factor in our cultural norms based on simple human empathy, biologically speaking altruism decreases the further away we go from our genes and you can't get much further away than an alien species, whose genes (or extraterrestrial equivalents) would be completely unfamiliar and unrelated to us. Thus we can't rely on cosmic kinship to deliver a message to us from smart extraterrestrials.

That means we're back to reciprocal altruism, or quid pro quo – I do something for you, now I expect you to do something for me. We see this in nature, from chimpanzees grooming each other to pilot fish cleaning parasites from sharks' teeth and in return receiving protection from predators. Reciprocity rules in dealings between strangers, or those not considered kin, but it also demands a payback, the more immediate the better. There is surely no better definition of 'stranger' than 'alien' and, by that logic, reciprocal altruism might at first glance be more suited to dealings with extraterrestrials. Bypassing for the moment the tricky question

of whether we have anything to give the aliens in return, the cost-benefit analysis for reciprocal altruism across many light years isn't great and so reciprocity may be an unlikely motivation in such a case. It also leaves the door ajar for betrayal: naive altruists could easily be taken advantage of should the subject of their kindness renege on the unspoken deal and refuse to reciprocate – it would be especially easy to act in an underhand fashion over vast interstellar distances, and this might dissuade the more cynical civilisations out there from bothering to contact us if they hold doubts that we'll return the favour. Things might be different if sender and receiver were reasonably close, maybe a few dozen light years apart, requiring a less powerful and hence less expensive signal (and consequently a lower level of altruism) and close enough to allow hope that a reply could be forthcoming within a lifetime.

If kin selection does not persuade civilisations to build beacons, then what could motivate them to do so? The effect of kin selection across interstellar distances may merely be that extraterrestrial civilisations don't bother constructing great beacons; at worst it could bring out the most fearsome, hateful tendencies of xenophobia that, if coupled with a culture based on fear, could mean that extraterrestrial civilisations are searching the cosmos not for friends, but for potential enemies or threats. We would do best to stay well away from such species.

Jerome Berkow speculates that xenophobia may be deeply linked all the way back to our ancient hominid past when predation against other tool-using species such as the Neanderthals was a way of life. We can still see today how the xenophobic alien hypothesis is aided by the fact that kin selection does not generally extend itself between species. Even our supposedly altruistic human society often fails at this hurdle. For everyone who wants to protect chimps and apes in the wild, there are a dozen pharmaceutical companies queuing up to experiment on them. While we may show unrequited altruism to our pet dogs and cats, not many of us are equally willing to show the same feelings towards

venomous snakes and rats. Indeed, would alien life elicit similar negative feelings in most of us as do snakes or insects?

Maybe things are improving; as science-fiction author David Brin points out, when a whale beaches itself people will often head down to the seashore in herds to try and save it, whereas only a few hundred years ago, and even less in some parts of the world,* we would race down to the beach not to save the whale, but to tuck in. Yet although there are cases of conscious altruism between species – dolphins helping humans stranded in the water by warding off sharks or ferrying them to safety, or dogs protecting their masters – in general altruism between species seems to exist only at the unconscious and reciprocal level. Where is our much-heralded selfless altruism then?

It's a pleasant scene to picture: gentle waves lapping onto a golden sandy beach, white foam crashing between the pebbles, the hot yellow Sun blazing down through a humid haze onto a tropical paradise. This is the island of Tikopia, tossed like a pebble into the South Pacific, a mere 5km² (2 square miles) in area, born of volcanism and sporting a relic of its igneous past in the form of a wide, central lake 80m (260ft) deep that sits in an ancient caldera next to the 380m (1,250ft) peak of Mt Reani.

From Mt Reani, the entire island can be surveyed by the four clans that inhabit Tikopia. Surrounded entirely by the ocean, the view must in some way be akin to when astronauts first punched their way out of our atmosphere on rocket power, to view Earth in all its glory, alone and in its entirety in another sea, the sea of stars. Those photographs of Earth from space, absent of political barriers and racial divisions,

---

* Sadly, whaling continues to be carried out by Canadian Inuits, the Faroe Islands, Greenland, Iceland, Japan, Norway, South Korea, Russia and indigenous peoples in Alaska and Indonesia.

helped to intellectually fund the growing peace movement in the 1960s as war erupted in Vietnam and superpowers stood off over Cuba. From that mountaintop on Tikopia, the Pacific stretches unbroken from horizon to horizon: their island is the world to the Tikopians. As such, when viewing their island in its entirety, they too are experiencing it without the artificial divisions set in place by the four clans. It's a fundamentally transformative experience for the Tikopian mindset, one that has helped them to flourish whereas other islands lying over the horizon that were also colonised by the Polynesians have failed.

From the peak of Mt Reani, the caldera-filling lake – a lagoon the Tikopians call Te Roto – is seen to dominate the island, fed by a small channel into the sea on Tikopia's eastern flank. A towering rainforest lines the steepest cliffs on the seaward side of Mt Reani, while the remainder of the island is intensively farmed to feed the 1,115-strong population. Resource management is crucial to the Tikopians' survival. They've been self-sufficient for 3,000 years, ever since their hardy Polynesian ancestors sailed across the Pacific from the west in canoes constructed from hollowed-out trees. In that time, the Tikopians have made some hard and long-lasting choices. Around AD 1600, for example, the decision was made to cull the entire population of pigs on the island. The swine just weren't efficient to keep, consuming more food than they produced (they had to be fed 10 kilos of vegetables just to get 1 kilo of pork when slaughtered), food that could have fed the islanders instead. The Tikopians therefore returned to fishing to supplement their core diet of fruit (including traditional tropical fare such as coconuts and bananas), vegetables and roots. Rather than chopping down all the trees in a concerted programme of slash and burn, orchards are managed. Agriculture flourishes thanks to the moist, humid climate, the trade winds bringing frequent cloud cover and rain between April and September, while the monsoon period of October to March sees hot, sunny days smashed by occasional downpours and high winds. Indeed, during the monsoon season in December 2002, Cyclone Zoë whirled into Tikopia

and its smaller sister island of Anuta, devastating both. In a
display of pure selfless altruism, friends of the islands, mostly
yachtsmen from the likes of Australia and the UK, raised
funds and resources to repair Tikopia's Gabion Dam, which
separated the freshwater of Te Roto from the sea and which
had been destroyed by Zoë's storm surge. Other altruistic
displays from outsiders have included the donation of canoes,
constructed from traditional means, to assist the islanders in
fishing and transportation to and from the other islands in the
region, just over the horizon.

For the inhabitants of some of those other Polynesian islands
in the Pacific, such as the Pitcairns and Easter Island, life hasn't
worked out too well. On Easter Island, the various clans
competed to build the biggest statues (called *moai*) and their
decorative stone platforms (*ahu*) to show status. The clans had
to compete with themselves, because the other Polynesian
islands were really too distant for frequent contact. Nevertheless,
at first Easter Island proved self-sufficient, being heavily forested
and with several plantations to feed the inhabitants. As statue
building became more intense, more resources were ploughed
into their construction. The islanders thrived, but once they
reached their peak population, things began to collapse around
them. Trees were chopped down to make way for agriculture,
or to assist in the statue building. Without the trees the ecology
of the island fell apart, as did the islanders' civilisation. Their
downfall was the result of both the folly of building bigger and
better statues and overpopulation.

Tikopian society, however, still flourishes to this very day.
Why? On this speck of land poking out of the bobbing tides
of the Pacific, population levels are monitored very carefully.
The island can support around 1,200 people before overpopulation wreaks havoc as it did on Easter Island, although
maintaining population levels is easier said than done; if
couples have too many babies, what do they do? In the past,
methods of population control, besides celibacy, abortion,
delayed marriages and interrupted sexual intercourse to
prevent conception, also included infanticide by burying the
infant alive or smothering it, war between clans, suicide and

'virtual suicide', whereby people headed out into the Pacific, never to return. These fates were not dictated to the populace by a ruling body – these were rules laid down democratically, after discussion, by the people themselves, meeting and debating in the huts of the chiefs of the four clans, chiefs who are only first among equals.*

I distinctly remember discussing this with my mother, who was horrified at the notions of infanticide and suicide and steadfastly refused to believe that any rational society could condone such behaviour. But the acts of the Tikopians were not malicious in their eyes, only what they deemed necessary to protect their society as a whole. To them it was an altruistic act, albeit a sad one, to control population levels, but it had to be done to benefit the majority and the islanders accepted it – the needs of the many outweighed the needs of the few, or the one.† To western society, however, it is considered anathema and the British colonial government eventually declared these methods forbidden, but this only had a negative effect. In 1929, when the Kiwi anthropologist Raymond Firth spent a year living on the island (only the

---

* It should also be noted that during Raymond Firth's stay on Tikopia during the late 1920s, he observed that families had on average 3.5 children, with very few couples lacking children. So regardless of any methods of population control, families were allowed a healthy number of children and there were no rules as strict as China's one-child-per-family rule. Firth reported that the decision to smother an unwanted child was often at the father's discretion.

† You may recognise these as Spock's dying words to Admiral Kirk in the second *Star Trek* movie, *The Wrath of Khan* (1982). There Spock sacrificed himself to save his ship and his crew-mates, but with regard to Tikopia we take the meaning of Spock's words to their ultimate consequence – the sanctioned sacrifice of individuals, including children, to maintain the survival of the population as a whole. As a Vulcan, Spock saw his sacrifice as the logical thing to do and, in the instinct-driven world of biology and natural selection, the Tikopians' actions were also the logical thing to do and, in that sense, perfectly altruistic.

second outsider to do so) the population stood at 1,278. The British governors outlawed suicide and infanticide, and this caused havoc for the islanders' society, resulting in Tikopia's population ballooning up to 1,735 just 24 years later thanks to westernised reforms forced upon the island. This was inevitably unsustainable and, following severe cyclones and starvation during the 1950s, the population fell back to more manageable levels.

Today, of course, population regulation is much simpler without anybody having to actually die; people can simply leave the island, thanks to the reliable technology of boats, helicopters and aeroplanes, with the nearby Russell Islands or Honiara, the capital city of the Solomon Islands, popular destinations for young men in search of work, while immigration into Tikopia is tightly monitored.

Now I know what you're thinking. You've bought this book to read about radio telescopes and advanced civilisations, not the trials and tribulations of the inhabitants of a small island in paradise. What does birth control on Tikopia have to do with aliens? Bear with me. The story of Tikopia throws a spanner into the works of the western philosophy of altruism, showing that even altruism among human societies can be a slippery concept, difficult to define and certainly in the eye of the beholder.

Consider war. One would think that war is hardly an altruistic action. Well, that depends on who wins and who loses, says Joan Silk, who points out that when we're talking about altruism, we forget that actions can have multiple outcomes for different people.

'It depends on whose [inclusive] fitness you're tracking,' she tells me. For example, starting a war with a neighbouring community – and winning – can benefit the inclusive fitness of the triumphant community, even if the people in the community benefiting were not the ones doing the fighting. In particular this is something we see in the animal kingdom, where the winners obtain access to new feeding areas and new mates. The point is, altruism is not necessarily about being nice to one another, or protecting one's family and genes. Altruism

can lead to violence or actions that are not altruistic for those on the receiving end of them. An extraterrestrial civilisation could act in a perfectly altruistic fashion for themselves, but by committing actions that would not benefit us.

Altruism is in the eye of the beholder

It is clear that even human attitudes and ethics are not fixed; our moral compass meanders like a river with time, evolving as our civilisation matures. Harvard's Steven Pinker argues that this is clearly progression. 'Over very long stretches of time, there is a force that would tend to move all intelligent, social species away from the violent competition that marked their origins and toward greater cooperation and peace,' he says, likening it somewhat to the game theory inherent in what Pinker describes as the Pacifist's Dilemma[*], in the sense that violence harms a victim more than it helps an aggressor. 'So to the extent that a species justifies its actions, or accommodates the inevitable historical cycle in which aggressors and victims change places, it will seek ways to incentivise all sides to abjure violence.' However, the example of Tikopia suggests it is not as clear-cut as that – had the Tikopians not murdered their infants or given individuals no choice but to commit suicide,

---

[*] The Pacifist's Dilemma is Steven Pinker's version of the Prisoner's Dilemma. Imagine two bank robbers who are caught by the police and interrogated. If prisoner 1 sells out prisoner 2, prisoner 1 walks free while prisoner 2 ends up in jail for three years. If both confess, they both get a reduced prison sentence, just a few months. If both say nothing, they each go to jail for just one month. While the best result for the pair of them would be to stay silent, both will almost certainly rat on the other with the intention of getting off scot-free, without realising their partner has exactly the same intentions, and both end up serving three years. The dilemma for prisoner 1 is whether to trust the other prisoner will stay silent and be willing to serve just a month, or to try to save his own skin and sell out prisoner 2, although in the end that only serves to harm them both.

then they would have inevitably fallen to the sweeping night of history and doomed themselves just as the Easter Islanders did. Extinction can hardly be described as progression. Let's face it: what we call pure altruism is merely a romanticised, westernised, modern-day view of how we feel we should treat one another. That's not to say it's wrong – as a product of western society I, along with many of you, the readers, buy into it fully, but I also recognise that it's parochial. Globalisation means that western culture and western altruism are gradually becoming worldwide culture and worldwide altruism, but even then they will still seem parochial next to any alien view of altruism. If, in human society, a single action can be seen as altruistic or not depending on your point of view and cultural background, how can we possibly make assumptions about what form altruism in an advanced extraterrestrial civilisation may take? This would then have a bearing on whether altruism motivates members of an extraterrestrial civilisation to invest time, effort and resources in beaming powerful signals into space for years, centuries, perhaps even millennia or longer to increase the chance that someone will detect those signals. SETI is banking on alien altruism, but it's an assumption without foundation.

There's something else that's interesting about Tikopia. It's one of the last holdouts of an egalitarian society. For the past five millennia humans have existed in hierarchical societies, with clear social classes and wealth distributed unevenly, but for much of pre-history our hunter-gatherer ancestors had a far greater say in their own destinies (for what good it did them), relatively speaking, than most of us do today. Tikopia reminds us of a time when decisions that affected the fate of the clan or tribe were made multilaterally. Within the boundaries of such societies a high level of altruism was maintained, with each tribe member, be they man, woman or child, given equal power and respect. To survive they had to share and cooperate, and anyone unwilling to play ball was cast out. Anthropologist Christopher Boehm of the University of Southern California has suggested that a kind of kin selection related to the group was an important evolutionary

adaptation that allowed these egalitarian societies to solve problems and come to decisions fairly, and from this adaptation, the human traits of cooperation and forms of altruism were evolutionary spin-offs.

If we yearn to be altruistic, then would the egalitarian worldview be utopia to our yearning Pinocchio? Would advanced extraterrestrial societies not be democracies as Steven Pinker foresees them, but egalitarian civilisations where every individual shares their wealth and power? With no social inequalities, no class distinction, no racism or sexism, no slavery, many of the motivations for violence would no longer be present. Rather than serving just a few elites, resources could serve everyone and be put to greater use; the foundations of sharing and cooperation behind egalitarian societies might be enough to lead to egalitarian extraterrestrials building a beacon as a natural outcome of their philosophy of life, which looks beyond their own needs and towards helping to raise the standing of others.

So if egalitarian societies worked so well, why did we mostly abandon them? One possibility is that overpopulation got in the way of things, provoking the advent of agriculture to ensure everyone was fed, which resulted in the creation of surplus that needed to be managed by people placed in charge of said surplus, who then went on to exploit that surplus to their own gain, creating inequalities and social classes where before there were none. Agriculture consumed resources, forcing groups to look further afield and expand, which led to conflict with neighbouring groups. When there are winners and losers, there can be no equality.

Ironically, an alternative theory from three anthropologists at Stanford University – Deborah Rogers, Omkar Deshpande and Marcus Feldman – considers that inequality, far from driving the advent of the hierarchical communities in which civilisation lives and by and large prospers today, was actually destabilising and dangerous to the success of the group. They argue that the reduction in egalitarianism initiated by agriculture caused the hunter-gatherer tribes to spread out, as the have-nots suddenly had to look elsewhere for food and

resources to survive, including in the territories of their neighbouring tribes, instigating warfare as the two groups came into conflict. Egalitarian societies were either wiped out or had to transform into unequal, hierarchical societies to fight back successfully. In other words, inequality can drive migration and migration can lead to contact and contact can lead to conflict. Would a migrating extraterrestrial civilisation, moving through star systems like locusts, be motivated to start sending out messages for us to detect, or would they just take what others have?

The fall of egalitarianism is a paradox in light of the idea that human civilisation is progressing towards becoming something better; if the Stanford researchers are correct, the advent of hierarchical, class-driven societies was a step backwards that increased conflict. As we currently survey our shattered environment, with a rising population and depleting resources, some among us look to space and the treasures out there that could assist with our resource and overpopulation problem. Should other civilisations be doing the same, one day in the future we could come into conflict. Expanding civilisations may be unwilling to show altruism to other civilisations that are in their way.

Steven Pinker agrees that expansionist civilisations tend towards being more violent. 'Yes, if colonisation means taking control of territories that are already inhabited,' he says, echoing Joan Silk's comments that violence can be beneficial for the inclusive fitness of the instigators. However, he also points out that if the territories they are moving into are uninhabited, then there is no requirement for violence. Given that the Galaxy is a very big place containing several hundred billion stars across a diameter about 100,000 light years in extent, there could be plenty of space for civilisations to occupy without treading on the toes of others. Perhaps, suggests Pinker, deals could also be reached between civilisations, returning to the practices of reciprocal altruism (but see Chapter 5 for more on this). 'If there were some voluntary agreement between the expanding civilisation and the native one, we would probably not call it colonisation, but something closer to trade.'

So perhaps egalitarianism was doomed from the beginning – even Tikopia is no longer truly an egalitarian society, being under the rule of first the British and, latterly, the Solomon Islands following their independence. We should not expect intelligent extraterrestrials to be egalitarian either, for to have reached an advanced level, a progressive, successful civilisation of individuals may require a degree of inequality to create an environment where excellence and competition are encouraged, in order to push the envelope of technology and culture that little bit further. Without egalitarianism, another motivational driver for lighting up a beacon goes up in smoke and the assumption that pure altruism will be commonplace goes with it.

The exercise of vital powers

There is, as always, a caveat to all this. The psychologist Dennis Krebs, Professor at Simon Fraser University in Canada, has developed the empathy–altruism hypothesis, whereby empathy – the human ability to detect the emotions of others and sympathise with them – encourages altruism. When someone is in pain or in trouble, behaving altruistically towards them – doing a good deed – raises the happiness of the empath, sometimes even when it comes at a cost to them. The ancient Greeks had a saying that happiness was 'the exercise of vital powers, along lines of excellence, in a life affording them scope'.* Perhaps sending an interstellar signal

---

* The origin of this definition of happiness is a little murky. The gist of it definitely came from the ancient Greeks and is frequently attributed to Aristotle and his *Nicomachean Ethics* but, at best, it is paraphrasing him. It seems it was first quoted by Edith Hamilton in her book *The Greek Way*, published in 1930, where the author sums up how the Greeks viewed happiness. Since then it has filtered its way into popular culture via speeches by John F. Kennedy and the title of an episode of *Babylon 5*.

containing the *Encyclopaedia Galactica*, in turn helping those
civilisations that receive it, might make advanced extraterrestrials happy?

Bearing all this in mind, what can we reasonably expect
from SETI? If the trend towards decreasing violence and
greater selfless altruism that we have seen over the last few
centuries on Earth is not unique to our species or even our
time, then it points to the possibility that species do become
more civilised and more altruistic as they grow more mature.
On the one hand, this favours the building of large beacons
as a gift to the other inhabitants of the Galaxy, but on the
other hand, as pointed out by John Smart of the Acceleration
Studies Foundation, this emergent morality with increasing
technological and social evolution could lead to a silent
Universe if extraterrestrial civilisations are cautious about
interfering with another species' development, a bit like *Star
Trek*'s Prime Directive.

Or here is a radical thought: perhaps altruism does not
play a role in beacon-building at all. Other motivations
for transmitting abound. Perhaps they are monuments, like
the Egyptian pyramids or the Eiffel Tower or (in terms
of achievement and ambition) the Apollo Moon landings.
A beacon as a monument would be designed to show the
rest of the Galaxy how fabulous and knowledgeable and
powerful those who constructed it are, with the need for
pride and status certainly derivative of an environment where
competition, be it for mates, resources or money, thrives. Or
perhaps a beacon is a funeral pyre, built by a species on the
verge of being swallowed by the night, one last shout out
into the Universe before they are consumed by war, disease,
environmental damage, misuse of technology, volcanic and
tectonic activity, asteroid impact, the death of their star or
some other threat we haven't even conceived of yet. In such
a scenario, perhaps they would transmit an *Encyclopaedia
Galactica* to pass on all the knowledge of their civilisation
before they perished, the same way that we build seed banks
in the Arctic, or place messages onto the Voyager and Pioneer
space probes.

We should, at this point, note for the record that not all signals have to be deliberate beacons. Unintentional radio leakage could also be detected, and there are other means of detecting extraterrestrials that we will discover in later chapters, but the point remains: to create leakage, or build other means by which they could be detected, a civilisation must be technological, and hence the debate over whether a technological civilisation has to be altruistic or not still holds.

If we cannot even define what pure altruism is on our own planet, among our own species, what chance do we have of understanding alien notions of altruism? Certainly any efforts to equate extraterrestrial civilisations with future human society are fraught with anthropocentricism, so in that sense Oxford philosopher Nick Bostrom is correct: it is dangerous to extrapolate past human experience into the future and to project it onto alien civilisations. Nothing more starkly shows how pure altruism is not a concrete concept than the clash between western values and the actions of the Tikopians to avoid the fate of the Easter Islanders. It's a classic case of cultural relativism, whereby the Tikopians' sense of altruism can only be appreciated when one places it into the context of their culture. You could similarly imagine an intelligent species whose entire grounding in altruistic ethics is dictated by an extreme sense of honour, which could provide further potential paradoxes; witness the example of the rule of honour that saw men stand off at 20 paces with pistols in the pre-twentieth-century United States of America. Ridiculous posturing it may seem to us now, but none of us are very far removed from such actions, as we bristle when insulted or become angry when protecting the integrity of a friend or family member. In *Star Trek* the Klingons famously bang on about honour, but their over-the-top behaviour highlights that it is not very hard to imagine societies where the defence of honour plays as large a role as the quest for justice does in ours. Just as a skewed sense of justice can result in some rather un-altruistic behaviour, so too can a skewed sense of honour.

Now it may well be that intelligent aliens are altruistic and ethically enlightened, a result of some unwritten law of nature and evolution that operates across all sentient species and is responsible for the decrease in violence that Steven Pinker highlights. However, as we've seen here on Earth, it is equally likely that they will have their own ethics based around their own culture, which are very different from, and possibly incompatible with, our own set of values. If what is seen as altruistic can vary among human societies, it can certainly vary among extraterrestrial civilisations that might have evolved with different sets of values based on the selection pressures of their environment. At the unconscious level, kin selection will be focused on their own species, and reciprocal altruism baulks at the insurmountable distances between the stars. Furthermore, the levels of altruism in an extraterrestrial civilisation may vary from individual to individual, from group to group, or from nation to nation, just as they do on our world. Nothing can be taken for granted and the realisation that none of our assumptions regarding SETI are necessarily sacrosanct is a lesson that must be learnt if SETI is to proceed successfully. Consequently, we can't count on selfless altruism being the dominant force among the stars that SETI hopes it to be.

Yet, are we not looking to the stars with a healthy mix of curiosity and wonder? We've even begun beaming our own messages out into space. SETI practitioners aren't in it for fame and fortune, the drive behind the quest isn't some treasure hunt for knowledge or riches beyond our wildest imagination, despite the *Encyclopaedia Galactica* paradigm. A simple signal that confirms that we are not alone in the Universe, even if it remains for ever indecipherable, will be enough to transform how we view ourselves and our place in the heavens.

'Who knows what would be in the message?' remarks Seth Shostak. 'That's alien sociology, we don't know much about that. Really, it almost doesn't matter what they might

be sending. I mean, it would be very interesting to know what they look like, how they are built and the appearance of their world. It's like asking a caveman what he would like to hear from residents of London in the twenty-first century – he'd have a whole bunch of ideas, like how do you build your clubs, what do your caves look like, and there would be a bunch of stuff like that which would be rather puzzling to us. The real information is the fact that they are there – that's why we do the experiment. Some people talk about learning all the secrets of physics; well, that would be nice, but from my point of view the experiment is interesting because we would learn something nifty, which is that they are out there.'

The need to reach out and find others in the Universe comes from deep within ourselves. As a species we feel alone in the cosmos; part of the reason we search is to find someone else like us, whom we can perhaps relate to. Yet extraterrestrial civilisations, if they exist, will not be our kin. Will we share enough characteristic traits to at least be recognisable to one another and allow inclusive fitness to play a role? Perhaps. The altruism assumption would have us believe that this is true, and that although our biological ties will be unrelated, in the grand scheme of things intelligence really does reach out to intelligence. In a cosmic context, the assumption states that that may be all the kin we need, to know there are others out there burning the flame of cognition and intelligence brightly. Yet it's an assumption founded on a parochial understanding of human altruism. Altruism may be a factor in whether we will ever hear from an extraterrestrial civilisation, and it will definitely be a factor in what happens after that, too.

Before we get to that part, though, there's another elephant in the room, one even bigger than altruism and which threatens to derail the entire SETI endeavour. Intelligence is often seen as the pinnacle of evolution on Earth, but is it really as inevitable an evolutionary solution as our human hubris makes it out to be? In the next chapter we will ask

whether intelligence is as ubiquitous among complex life as we hope it to be, because if there is no intelligent life out there, then SETI will never detect a signal. It's just one more uncertainty in our cosmic quest to find someone to share the Universe with.

One thing is for sure: this SETI business? It's gonna be harder than it looks.

Intelligence

Could any grandparent have been more proud than Erasmus Darwin? As his name suggests, one of his grandchildren was Charles Darwin, whose 1859 work *On the Origin of Species* introduced the world to the concept of evolution by natural selection, thereby creating a pathway by which we could come to understand the development of the human species.

Another of his many grandchildren (Erasmus, having married twice, had 14 children) was Francis Galton, and goodness gracious, if you thought Carl Sagan was a polymath genius, he had nothing on Galton. Originally trained in medicine, he turned to mathematics at Trinity College Cambridge, before joining the Royal Geographical Society and embarking on an expedition to what is now Namibia, where he produced a renowned cartographic survey of southwest Africa. From there, he wandered across the scientific disciplines, dipping his hand in wherever he fancied, from sociology to meteorology, and from anthropology to a primitive form of genetics (given that the idea of genes was not even mooted until 1909). Galton was the first scientist to produce weather maps and a theoretical explanation of anti-cyclones. He progressed the science behind criminal fingerprinting, employed his mathematical skill to devise new statistical methods such as correlation and accruing statistical data via surveys, and he even pursued some quintessentially English research in terms of finding the best way to make a cup of tea ('... then, taking as my type of excellence, tea that was full bodied, full tasted, and in no way bitter or flat, I found that this was only produced when the water in the teapot had remained between 180 and 190

degrees Fahrenheit, and had stood eight minutes on the leaves.')[*]

Yet it was his half-cousin's discovery of evolution by natural selection that proved the biggest turning point in Galton's scientific life. It inspired him to study hereditary traits in humans, including whether intellectual ability could be passed down from parents to children (which is still a controversial subject today) and developed psychometrics in order to do so. It was Galton who came up with the phrase 'nature versus nurture'.

The story of human intelligence is certainly one of nature (Darwin's evolution) versus nurture (from environmental and even cultural factors), and whereas evolutionary biologists and anthropologists are still trying to come to terms with the history of the evolution of intelligence in humans and other animals, SETI has already decided where the future of higher intelligence lies. It is an intelligence that we can relate to, one that expresses curiosity about the Universe around it, one that reaches out to the stars. More profoundly, it is an intelligence that is highly technological, with science, engineering and resources far in advance of our own. Intelligence is implicit in SETI and, for SETI, which involves searching for things like radio signals, intelligence equates to technology.

There are unchallenged assumptions in this definition of intelligence, born out of anthropomorphism, coloured by bias, and perpetuated by the arrogance of human hubris. The popularity of such a definition is easy to understand. Humans are the smartest species on Earth by far and our technology appears to be what sets us apart from all the other animals. The connection between intelligence and technology would seem obvious.

---

[*] Francis Galton's tea-making, and many other important tips for adventurers, can be found in his 1855 book *The Art of Travel: or, Shifts and Contrivances Available in Wild Countries*, based on his expedition to Africa, and required reading for Boy and Girl Scouts everywhere!

Our prevalent beliefs about alien civilisations are built on the basis of taking the best parts of our humanity and extrapolating them into the future. It's an easy trap to fall into – it is comforting to project our hopes and dreams for humanity onto a grander canvas of alien shenanigans, because it reassures us that a civilisation like our own can survive and prosper into the deep future and that there is some meaning to the trials and tribulations of our lives, as each generation builds upon the one before, striving for a better future.

Unfortunately the Universe is not obliged to deliver on what we hope or wish it to be. Our mainstream depictions of what we expect extraterrestrial intelligence to be like insidiously introduce bias right under our very noses. Rather than extending the range of possibilities, these depictions narrow it and confine our thinking to extraterrestrials that are just like us, if not in appearance then certainly in behaviour. While there is no question that technology is linked to intelligence – without intelligence we would not have the means to invent new technologies, or use them – can we successfully argue that technology defines intelligence? Or is technology merely a manifestation of intelligence, perhaps one of many? Consider the consequence – if technology is not ubiquitous with intelligence, then there may be myriad minds out there inhabiting the sea of stars that we could never detect from afar. Observations would never meet expectations; although intelligence would be common, technology would be scarce, resulting in a dearth of signals and the incorrect interpretation that we are alone.

SETI, as a community and as a way of thinking about the alien, has to get past this. We need to widen our horizons and demolish our anthropocentric assumptions to find a more fundamental measure of intelligence that allows us to define what we're really searching for. To learn more about what we call intelligence, its relationship with technology and whether we can communicate with other species, we must first learn more about life on Earth and then hope to apply some of what we've learned to the stars. Studying not just human intelligence but levels of intelligence in other species,

such as dolphins, widens our view, puts the origin of our own intelligence into context and, perhaps, tempers our arrogance somewhat. It also utterly smashes through the assumption that we are somehow alone as the sole proprietors of intelligence on Earth. The evolution of intelligence, where it came from and what stimulated it, is a story every bit as wonderful and captivating as the evolution of the stars, planets or large-scale structure of the Universe. Like those astrophysical concepts, it is a story of increasing complexity. Unfortunately, it is also a story that is incomplete, with crucial tracts of relevant plot points missing. In that sense, think of it not just as a historical tale, but as a mystery story in which we are both the detectives and the subjects of the mystery.

When did intelligence begin? It's hard to say, not simply because of our incomplete fossil record (although that certainly doesn't help) but because definitions of intelligence are divergent from researcher to researcher. In 2000 Andrew Knoll of Harvard University and Richard Bambach from Virginia Polytechnic Institute and State University described what they saw as life's six major evolutionary steps, or 'mega-trajectories' as they called them.

The first step was the evolution of life from the last universal common ancestor (LUCA), a species of organism from which all life on Earth subsequently evolved and with which we all share fundamental biochemical traits. If you prefer to think of the tree of life, then LUCA is the base of that tree, the seed from which it all grew, and our best estimates suggest it existed on Earth around 3.8 billion years ago (the age of the Earth is 4.54 billion years). Second is the diversification of the prokaryote organisms, bacteria and archaea, which are single-celled organisms. Third is the evolution of eukaryotic cells – cells that contain complex structures resident within a membrane – and it is with the eukaryotic cells that things start to get interesting. Think about our own body plan, incorporating complex structures,

such as internal organs encased within a membrane, our skin. But one cell on its own is still primitive; for complex life multi-cellularity is required, and this is Knoll and Bambach's fourth mega-trajectory. Multi-cellular life-forms are called eukaryotes and the timing of their arrival on Earth is somewhat up for debate. The oldest eukaryote fossil remnants are 1.7 billion years old, but there are biomarkers that suggest they existed up to 3 billion years ago. Nobody is even sure if the transition from single-celled organisms to multi-cellular life was an easy one or not, but once that transition was made they quickly gained ground, quite literally. The fifth mega-trajectory is life leaving the oceans around half a billion years ago and subsequently conquering the land,* coinciding with what we call the Cambrian explosion – a rapid and not very well understood diversification of life-forms in the sea and on the land. From there on the steady march of evolution has progressed for 500 million years to the present day and the development of technological intelligence in *Homo sapiens* about 50,000 years ago, the sixth (but not necessarily final) mega-trajectory.

Among the mega-trajectories, there are two dates that stand out for different reasons depending upon how you define intelligence. Knoll and Bambach were careful in their description of the mega-trajectories to talk about the onset of technological intelligence, leaving non-technological intelligence aside as a vague notion. If you believe the technocrats, then intelligence can only be technological, manifest in everything from the simple tools and clothing of a caveman to the material goods of smartphones, microwave ovens, television, computers, aeroplanes, rockets and radio

---

* The first known footprints on land date back to approximately 530 million years ago, made by lobster-sized, multi-limbed euthycarcinoids, which are the ancestors of the modern centipede. Twenty-five rows of footprints were found preserved in rocks in south-eastern Canada, along with markings that suggest they had a tail. The euthycarcinoids probably took to land to mate and lay eggs.

telescopes, and everything in between. The great science-fiction author Isaac Asimov defined intelligence not as the possession of technology, but as the ability to develop and improve technology, building on prior inventions and integrating that technology into our civilisation and culture, starting with the taming of fire and the invention of the wheel through to the agricultural and industrial revolutions, the Space Age and our future technological development as a species.

That's how most people see intelligence, both in our dealings with other life on Earth and in SETI. But an astrobiologist's definition can be very different, showing how our anthropic bias is limiting. For Lori Marino, a neuroscientist formerly of Emory University in Atlanta and now founder and Executive Director of the Kimmela Center for Animal Advocacy, intelligence is not rare. Rather, she sees intelligence as being ubiquitous on Earth. In qualitative terms, she reckons, there's little difference between a jellyfish and a human being, despite appearances.

'In my view, once you have multi-cellular life you have everything,' she says, reasoning that multi-cellular life-forms, from the most complex mammals down to the most primitive worms, all have a nervous system, organs and reproductive capabilities, and it's all thanks to those eukaryotic cells. 'It may sound funny, but the difference between an annelid worm and the human brain is just variations on a theme. All multi-cellular animals have pretty much the same brain.'

How so? Favourable mutations in the early cells led to inequalities among them – some performed respiration better, others digested food while others became nerves for transmitting electrical and chemical signals as a form of communication from one cell to another. Some of these cells – the nerves in particular – began to retreat deeper and deeper into the bunch of cells that called itself primitive life. To communicate with the outside world, the nerve cells grew dendrites, which are neural receivers of information. All of a sudden these cellular bundles began to develop

nervous systems and the beginnings of a rudimentary intelligence, even if it was just the instinctive urge to feed and replicate. Some creatures – invertebrates – evolved a network of nerve cells and fibres that spread throughout their body. Others – and these are the ones thought to be prone to evolve higher intelligences – developed centralised neural systems, or in other words a distinct brain and information-processing unit.

It took a billion years to go from that stage of eukaryotic evolution to life on Earth today, including human life. Yet despite the similarities of brain function among vertebrates, *Homo sapiens* still clearly rules over the roost. As Lori Marino says, qualitatively there may not be much difference between a chimpanzee wielding a termite stick or a beaver building a dam, and human engineers constructing an airliner or a radio telescope. Quantitatively, however, there is a huge chasm. A spider may be able to spin webs, a beaver build dams and ants create intricate nests, but this is all instinct, garnered from millions of years of evolution during which the development of their abilities has changed only marginally. Spiders still build the same types of web they've always done and never, ever, do they build anything other than a web. Humans, on the other hand, not only possess and develop technology but use multiple types of technology and are continually inventing new technologies and new avenues for their application. The ability to make use of convergences – where two disparate technologies come together to develop an unheralded new technology, such as the discovery of X-rays and the invention of computers combining to allow medical scans, or splitting the atom and our continual (you could say wasteful) hunger for energy in modern civilisation leading to nuclear power stations – is a uniquely human ability, at least on Earth. We start off by fashioning a tool and then proceed to make it better.

Of course, splitting the atom – nuclear fission – also led to the creation of the nuclear bomb. Sometimes, while our technology becomes more sophisticated, our motivations for

using it do not. Just look at the Internet: a fabulous tool for the gathering, accumulation and dissemination of information and what do we spend most of our time doing with it? Gossiping, just like our ancestors would have done, but instead on social networks and over e-mail. Would a truly intelligent species really build weapons that could wipe out every individual of that species on the planet? Perhaps that's not the question we should be asking; maybe the real mark of an intelligent civilisation is the realisation that they have a choice whether to drop the bomb or not, and the intelligence to ultimately make the right choice.*

This quantitative difference is the factor that continues to elude us. 'We've been trying and looking very hard to find something in the human brain that is unique, but we haven't found it yet and I don't think it is there,' says Marino. The tools to produce our intelligence are therefore to be found in every terrestrial organism's brain. Instead, researchers focus on more obvious variations, namely the size and density of those tools. From there we can begin to make clear demarcations between the primitive intelligence found in the majority of terrestrial organisms and the factors that produce higher intelligence such as self-awareness, problem-solving and communication. Humans have it. Chimps have it.

---

*This also plays into the L-factor – the longevity of a civilisation – in Frank Drake's famous equation for calculating the number of extraterrestrial civilisations in the Galaxy. If long-lived intelligent extraterrestrial civilisations are out there, then they have avoided destroying themselves, and maybe it was the not-so-smart ones that saw their futures evaporate in the shape of a mushroom cloud. However, this is also the logic behind the flawed altruism assumption in Chapter 1, which says that extraterrestrial civilisations that don't blow themselves up must have put all thoughts of violence to bed long ago. However, deciding not to eradicate yourselves is simply in your self-interest and isn't quite the same as having the ability to behave towards other civilisations in a way that human society would like to think is appropriate.

Dolphins and whales have it. Even elephants, dogs, pigs, some cephalopods* and other animals have it to some degree. This is all good news for SETI – if the equipment for eventually becoming intelligent, and technologically intelligent at that, is already hardwired into the brain of all multi-cellular life, it does suggest that higher intelligence could be common throughout the Universe – that's as long as multi-cellular life is common. Yet if Marino's belief that there is nothing truly unique about the human brain is accurate, then how does that explain why, out of all the species ever to have lived on our planet, only we humans have developed technological intelligence, and why did it take 4.54 billion years of Earth's history for it to happen?

The Burgess Shale: contingency versus convergence

Complex, intelligent life was never a fait accompli for the Earth. Instead it arrived here by random mutations and an exceedingly scenic route along the path of evolution. Of course, the situation is more complicated than a single sentence can convey; natural selection opted for the mutations that provided some survival benefit over those that didn't, and genetic drift over generations favoured some characteristics over others. These facts are indisputable, frozen in time in the fossil record. The trick is understanding which properties of life are standard evolutionary solutions that are inevitably arrived at, and which are flukes, one-in-a-million mutations that don't stand a chance of being repeated on another world.

The answers may be found, among other places, in a wall of fossils known as the Burgess Shale. This craggy formation in the Canadian Rockies of British Columbia contains fossils dating back to the Cambrian explosion – 505 million years

---

* Squid intelligence was expertly put to use in one of the most fantastic time-jump sequences ever committed to the page in Stephen Baxter's 1999 science-fiction novel, *Time*.

old, to be precise. It was formed right at the time of the fifth mega-trajectory and it has become a key battleground between two very different ideologies of evolution: contingency versus convergence.

The former, most famously espoused by the late palaeontologist Stephen Jay Gould, suggests that life today is based on contingent characteristics resultant from a random mutation in our genetic heritage that promulgated in response to ecological stimuli and led to a series of unique yet successful solutions that will never be repeated. In other animals different contingent properties were selected by nature because they helped them to survive. Giraffes developed long necks. Elephants developed trunks. Birds developed wings. In such a scenario, higher intelligence is just a parochial adaptation that will never be repeated. In Gould's universe we are alone as the only species with technological intelligence.

An alternative ideology going head to head with Gould's outlook on life is evolutionary convergence, as championed by Simon Conway Morris, a palaeontologist from the University of Cambridge. The idea behind evolutionary convergence is that the laws of nature result in a range of successful evolutionary solutions that are relatively narrow and hence, as a consequence, evolution will inevitably converge on these solutions, given enough time. All biologists agree that convergence plays a role – we see it in the fact that eyes, for example, have evolved from scratch independently many times over – but the degree of importance given to it varies from researcher to researcher.

Conway Morris found academic fame for his work on the Burgess Shale, initiated by his PhD supervisor Harry Whittington in 1972, as he helped to interpret the dazzling array of fossils – some 65,000 types have been catalogued – and identify some wonderfully weird-looking life-forms. Conway Morris, fellow graduate student Derek Briggs, Harry Whittington and their predecessor, Charles Walcott, who discovered the fossil field in 1909, were aided in their task because of what made the Burgess Shale remarkable: a rare

INTELLIGENCE   63

type of protective entombment has preserved the imprints of soft tissue, despite its age, giving a much better look at what kinds of creatures lived back then. And how bizarre they were: to name just two, a sea creature called *Opabinia regalis* with five eyes on stalks and a snout striated like a vacuum-cleaner hose, allowing it to bend in all directions, tipped with a vicious grabbing claw; and a freakish-looking animal with over a dozen legs and multiple hard, spiky spines on top, with a long snout, named *Hallucigenia sparsa* after its almost hallucinogenic appearance.

The body plans of many of the creatures in the Shale are exotic, especially when compared to life-forms today (although we still have some extraordinary creatures on Earth, particularly in the oceans), and Gould argued that the discontinuity between these fossils and life-forms today was evidence that these creatures were evolutionary experiments that died out – random mutations building weird body plans that failed in the competitive environment of the Cambrian explosion. Gould's critique of the Burgess Shale was that life-forms were much more diverse and that their subsequent extinction was evidence for contingency, showing that many things happen in evolution only once as a random mutation, and once they're gone, they're gone. Conway Morris disagrees, saying that almost all the creatures captured in time in fossil fields such as the Burgess Shale (similar fossilised finds have been identified in China and Greenland) can be traced through the past 500 million years to modern-day life-forms. That the appearance of creatures in the Burgess Shale is incredibly diverse cannot be debated, but Conway Morris suggests that their descendants began to converge in biology to the more ordinary body plans we see today.

The crux of the Gould versus Conway Morris, contingency versus convergence, debate is chance versus necessity. For Gould, five-eyed sea creatures with vacuum-hose snouts arise by chance, and if they're not good enough, they disappear. For Conway Morris, the key characteristics of these life-forms evolve because of some ecological imperative that makes them necessary for life to survive, and over the aeons

life will converge towards these necessary characteristics: sense receptors (be they eyes, nose, ears, *etc.*), limbs, feathers, skeletons and the like – all have evolved independently many times across many species and, although they can vary in structure, they all do essentially the same job. This isn't chance, says Conway Morris – eyes evolve because they are, for the most part, needed to fill an evolutionary niche (moles of course can do without, but at least they once had eyesight before they burrowed underground).

'Broadly speaking, convergence is simply the observation that there are particular adaptive solutions and that, as far as I can see, is entirely in line with general neo-Darwinian theory,' says Conway Morris. The inference is that these convergent properties could also evolve on other worlds. The aliens may look outlandish overall, but they would have features that we could recognise as eyes, limbs and so on. 'To the eye of a trained biologist the differences will be skin deep. Once we begin to get to grips with the organisms I think we will find there are just so many limited ways in which things work.'

To illustrate his case, Conway Morris highlights the fact that life on Earth has extended into practically all the ecological niches available, and has done so repeatedly. These organisms, living in volcanic plumes or acidic lakes or bone-dry rocks where no water has flowed for perhaps centuries, are known as extremophiles, and they push the envelope of what amounts to a habitable environment to the limit.

'It seems to me that all the available physical and chemical parameters – temperature, pressure, salinity, you name it – are being fully occupied by terrestrial organisms,' he says. Life has been found filling almost every environment possible (even in space – terrestrial microbes stranded on the Moon for two years on board NASA's Surveyor 3 lander were recovered by the astronauts of Apollo 12 and returned to Earth, where they were reanimated), using and re-using biological solutions that have been converged upon by evolution and invented independently many times over.

Brain power

The biologist's view, described earlier by Lori Marino, is that intelligence is common, but she isn't describing our specific kind of intelligence, which is technological. So the big question is this: is human intelligence a chance by-product of evolution, like the parochial nature of elephant trunks and giraffe necks, fitting in with Gould's contingency theory, or is technological intelligence an eventual occurrence of evolutionary convergence? The answer will impact not only on SETI, but on who we think we are as human beings and our ultimate destiny.

If we are alone, if our technological intelligence is purely a happy accident of evolution never to be repeated, then we have a responsibility to protect that. On the other hand, if we are one of many, our future may well depend on how we interact with those other technological intelligences. Either way, as we encounter other intelligences, whether on Earth or elsewhere in the Galaxy, and learn more about the nature of intelligence, we will be forced to redefine our understanding of who we are. Many of our most cherished assumptions about ourselves could be obliterated. It is for these reasons that the need to investigate and plan for the social and cultural implications of potential contact with extraterrestrial civilisations is of growing importance.

In the absence of any bona fide aliens, we're stuck with studying our own evolutionary history and that of other intelligences on Earth, such as dolphins, to see how we fit in relation to them. There's no risk of us being upstaged by any other life on Earth, so our hubris can remain intact for now, but a better understanding of the intelligence of other species with which we share the planet could bring us closer to them and help us appreciate why we should treat other life better than we currently do.

Intelligence is associated with brain power. The brain is our thinking machine, a biological computer that far outdoes any computer that we can build – so far – in terms of complexity. One of the B-movie stereotypes of science fiction

is aliens with great mental powers thanks to the giant brains they have crammed into their oversized craniums (a more sophisticated example of such fiction can be found in the form of the alien Talosians' ability to create powerful psychic illusions in *The Cage*, the first pilot episode of *Star Trek* in 1966). These stereotypes take things to unlikely extremes and, although a large brain seems important for the development of intelligence, there are questions about how important. Humans have large brains, but certainly not the largest on the planet. Whales and elephants, to name but two, have brains up to six times larger, but they also have bigger bodies. That said, it turns out that relative to body mass the human brain is extremely large. Biologists have observed that the greater an animal's total body mass, the bigger its brain will be. This link between body mass and brain size has been formalised by a mathematical relation, $m^{2/3}$, where 'm' refers to the total body mass.* However, in reality the ratio of an animal's body mass to brain size can differ from that predicted by this relationship, and the degree by which it differs is called the encephalisation quotient (EQ). Anything with an EQ above 1 can be termed big-brained, and below 1 could be thought of, somewhat flippantly, as 'pea-brained'.

Humans have an EQ of 7.4–7.8 above what the law predicts for a typical human body mass, which is the highest EQ on the planet. Bottlenose dolphins come in second at 5.3, capuchin monkeys are in third place at 2.4–4.8, chimpanzees at 2.2–2.5, gibbons at 1.9–2.7, whales at 1.8 and elephants at 1.3. Clearly, despite their large brain mass, elephants and whales are not that impressive in the EQ department.

Though not the whole story. Although capuchin monkeys are considered fairly smart, they're not really as smart as chimps, despite having the higher EQ. Maybe the secret to

---

* Some researchers, including Robert Martin, now at the Field Museum of Natural History in Chicago, argue that the scaling factor should be ¾ rather than ⅔, but the general relationship between body mass and brain size holds either way.

greater intelligence isn't just a large brain, but the density of neurons in the brain. More penetrative studies have examined the number of neurons in the brains of different species and the amount of connections between those neurons that enable processing power. For instance, at the Federal University in Rio, Brazil, Suzana Herculano-Houzel has begun a programme of counting the number of neurons in different brains and has found a significant difference in the way the brains of varying species are wired. In a rodent such as a rat or a hamster, the larger the brain, the more neurons it has. However, the size of the neurons in rodents is upscaled along with the size of their brain, so the extra mass in the brain isn't really utilised effectively. For primates and humans, things work differently. Their brains are bigger, yes, but their neurons are not, meaning they can pack in many more neurons to make their large brains extremely efficient and powerful instruments. An average human brain weighs between 1,250 and 1,450 grams (2¾ and 3¼ ounces) and contains 86 million neurons, but if a human brain could be scaled down to the size of a rat's brain, it would still contain more neurons than the rat's. Vice versa, a human brain is just a scaled-up version of the brains that chimps, gorillas and bonobos possess. If qualitatively they are the same, then perhaps here is the quantitative difference: more neurons, meaning more connections in the brain, equating to greater information processing.

Is the secret of intelligence really just the number of neurons in the brain? Bees and ants have minuscule brains and a severe shortage in the neuron department, but together they can build large and complex hive colonies. Human beings can mimic that style of networked intelligence. A single human cannot build a passenger aircraft or even a modern computer from scratch by themselves – for example, by first mining and refining the necessary materials, and then designing, manufacturing, testing and so on – but groups of humans working together can. Should we therefore measure our intelligence on a singular basis, or as an emergent property of a group or network? Even singular acts of genius

are built on the foundations of previous discoveries. Could the genius of Albert Einstein still have been expressed in quite the same way without the groundwork developed by the likes of Isaac Newton, Christiaan Huygens and Max Planck?

The human brain's neocortex and cerebellum, which respectively are integral to conscious thought and cognitive tasks, follow the EQ trend and are larger than expected for a primate of our size. Yet it has been shown that human brains have shrunk over the past 30,000 years, in which time our species has become truly technological. The average volume of Cro Magnon man's[*] brain was 1,500cm³ (92 cubic inches), but today for *Homo sapiens* it is 1,359cm³ (83 cubic inches). Ultimately, what we are discovering about the human brain is sending mixed messages. Maybe we're looking for something special that isn't really there, as Lori Marino suspects. Or maybe the recipe for intelligence doesn't only include biological ingredients; perhaps we have to factor in ecological influences too.

Let us run the clock backwards, venturing back deep in time to the first stirrings of our own species, our own intelligence. Millions of years ago our tree-dwelling ancestors faced an environmental crisis. In the forests of Africa the climate began to grow colder and drier, the lush tropical rainforests receding to leave large plains of grassland and shrubbery sprouting between the dwindling copses of trees. Our ancestors had a choice: come down from the trees where food was growing scarce, or become extinct. Yet the grasslands were not without their dangers, for big cats prowled there and could make short work of anyone descending from the trees

---

[*] Cro Magnons are more properly referred to as 'European early modern humans', and they existed between 40,000 and 15,000 years ago.

like a fish out of water. To survive, our ancestors had to adapt. Quickly.

Outrunning something like a lion, a tiger or a cheetah has never really been an option, but there were other characteristics that increased our ancestors' chances of survival and which natural selection could favour. For one, standing on our hind legs and becoming bipedal thanks to a backward bend in the spine made our ancestors more mobile, raised their eyes above the grass-line to gain an improved vantage point – all the better for spotting hunting animals in the tall grass – and also freed up the forelimbs that were to become our arms and hands. Australopithecines, who looked like a mixture of human and ape but were no taller than a chimp and still covered in fur, were the first to achieve this, somewhere around 2 to 3 million years ago.*

Freeing up the forelimbs was a boon. Objects could be picked up, investigated and brought closer to the sensory organs in the knowledge that, should danger suddenly pounce, the Australopithecines' legs could still carry them to safety. This closer inspection increased the flow of data into the brain, and chance mutations that provided greater mental capacity for analysing this data and figuring things out meant that those with the slightly sharper brains flourished and passed the mutations down through their genes to their offspring. Sharper brains were more aware of their surroundings, of where to find food and water and where to expect danger. When *Homo habilis* (meaning 'handy man') first started utilising stone tools 2.4 million years ago, their brains were equipped to aid in their survival. Now tool-makers began to be selected for, but to wield them efficiently

---

* The date when the first upright-walking hominids appeared on Earth is slightly controversial, as some highly debated fossil evidence suggests creatures with human-like features were up and about as long ago as 5 million years. But regardless of when they appeared, says Eric Chaisson of the Harvard-Smithsonian Center for Astrophysics, our general picture of human evolution remains broadly the same.

required better hand–eye coordination, which came from bigger brains inside bigger skulls. This, however, wasn't good for the women, who struggled during pregnancy to push children with larger skulls out through their birthing canal. Hence more frequently it was the women who gave birth to premature children with smaller, softer skulls who survived, and natural selection meant that children began to be born earlier in their development. However, the young required more protection and to be reared for longer periods, so their mothers had to stay with them while the men went hunting. This led to tribes remaining in one place for longer periods of time – the beginnings of the notion of 'settlement' that would one day lead to full-blown civilisation. It was perhaps also the birth of modern human altruism and cooperation, as described in Chapter 1.

Temporary at first, but growing permanent with time, these settlements changed everything. No longer were humans merely tribes of hunters and scavengers. They began to build homes and form communities, while social interaction came to play an increasingly important role in survival. As long as you were part of the community where people worked together you stood a better chance of surviving than if you were cast out on your own. From this stage onwards, argues anthropologist and evolutionary psychologist Robin Dunbar of the University of Oxford, the development of intelligence was driven by the sociological problems of learning to live in large, complex groups of people. Suddenly, culture became a factor and we can see this in the relics of *Homo sapiens* from 60,000 years ago, who left behind music (in the form of primitive instruments), art and ornaments. This era coincided with the blossoming of language and grammar and, in turn, syntax and higher intellectual functions. Since then we've been on a fast-track to our modern-day, twenty-first-century technological culture.

Two other things make human intelligence different from other intelligent animals on Earth: our ability to imagine possibilities that are not yet real in our experience; and our continual quest for self-improvement. Two million years ago

Homo habilis was wandering the plains of East Africa, fashioning crude stone implements for hacking at trees or killing animals while hunting. Yet they weren't satisfied with their ill-shaped, blunt and unwieldy instruments, and they could imagine using them for so much more. Those members of our ancestral societies capable of carving sharper stone knives found it easier to kill their prey and have supper each night; when *Homo erectus* discovered how to make fire half a million years ago, those members of society armed with the best wood-cutting tools could provide their tribe with enough firewood to keep warm over chilly winter nights. It's not just the ability to make the technology that is important, but to imagine how it could be utilised and to look for convergences in technology that could lead to better living standards. These developments are not merely evolutionary; they are adaptive, with improvements taking place over a single generation and being passed down to the next, with each successive generation cumulatively adding further improvements so that where once sharpened chunks of flint killed animals and chopped firewood, now guns and power-saws do the same. That's what marks humans out as different and has led us to the point where our evolution may no longer be driven by natural processes but by our own technology.

While we don't necessarily understand the changes in the brain that facilitated the development of our intelligence, we can easily see how the ecological parameters have varied, instigating the need for new adaptations. Climatic conditions are a huge driving force and, while there are variable micro-climates across regions, what matters more is climate on the largest scale. Earth has experienced ice ages and warmer periods, with volcanoes, asteroid impacts, solar variability, atmospheric composition and axial tilt all acting as factors in influencing climate. The implication is that an entirely stable climate would not provide the dramatic environmental changes needed to pile on the evolutionary pressure and force life to adapt. Perhaps in order to develop intelligence, life needs worlds that are a little unstable, but not too unstable.

Earth's axial tilt of 23.5 degrees guarantees regular seasons, whereas Mars' tilt wobbles all over the shop across periods of millions of years, with the potential to vary its tilt relative to the plane of the Solar System from zero degrees to 80 degrees, at which point it would be tipped right over with its poles facing the Sun (see Chapter 3). The resulting climatic variations would probably be too great to allow anything but the hardiest forms of life to gain a foothold.

Dolphins: Earth's second intelligence

So that's the human story; but what about dolphins? They diverged from the evolutionary line of land-based mammals about 60–70 million years ago, when their ancestors (believed to be small, wolf-like creatures) crept back into the oceans, presumably as food was more plentiful there, or possibly to escape predators. We can date when they diverged from land mammals through the differences in their brains: they lack our neocortex, the most recent addition to the mammalian brain, which evolved in us during the time since the dolphins' ancestors became aquatic. As we have seen, the neocortex is important to cognitive thought and, believes Robin Dunbar, crucial to social interactions. Yet dolphins are highly social creatures; they don't have a neocortex, so they just do it some other way. It is the closest thing we know to having contact with an alien intelligence that also possesses a particular human behaviour but achieves it via different means.

Until about 30–35 million years ago, dolphins were just big dumb animals, but remember at this time the ancestors of human beings were equally dumb as they swung through the trees. At this point, something began to change for the dolphins and their brains began to grow, before stabilising in size around 15 million years ago. Dolphins, it turns out, have had big brains for a lot longer than humans. So, why are we the ones to have built technology and civilisations, and not them? Their lack of limbs on a body streamlined for swimming in the ocean has come in for most the blame. While human ancestors developed arms and hands with opposable thumbs,

dolphins developed flippers. It's just the way each species adapted and survived; primitive Australopithecines needed to stand up and free their forelimbs, while dolphins needed to swim better and faster. Regardless, this doesn't seem to have been at the cost of a significant degree of intelligence, and this is where definitions of intelligence that rest solely on the ability to develop technology collapse.

The idea that dolphins could be really intelligent was first brought to prominence in the 1960s by John Lilly, an American psychoanalyst and physician who also contributed to a diverse range of fields, including SETI. In 1961 he joined Frank Drake, Carl Sagan, Philip Morrison, radio-astronomer Otto Struve, businessman Dana Atchley, chemist Melvin Calvin, astronomer Su Shu Huang, inventor Barney Oliver and the conference organiser J. Peter Pearman at the Green Bank Observatory for the first-ever SETI workshop, where Drake defined his famous equation that attempts to estimate the number of communicating extraterrestrial civilisations in the Galaxy.* Because of Lilly's work with dolphins, this small cadre of scientists called themselves the Order of the Dolphin. Although he was a controversial character, Lilly wrote many books on the subject of dolphin intelligence and believed that human beings would be able to speak with dolphins by the end of the twentieth century. However, as Carl Sagan wryly suggested, somewhat tongue-in-cheek, dolphins may understand many human words and concepts, but to this day no human has ever spoken a word of 'Dolphinese'. Nevertheless, the fact that dolphins have communication skills is without doubt and studies are

---

* This is done by multiplying a number of factors considered to be important for the development of intelligent life, starting with meta-properties such as star and planet formation, segueing into evolutionary factors and then cultural and social factors, culminating with 'L', the longevity of a transmitting alien civilisation, to arrive at 'N', an estimate for the number of intelligent, technological civilisations broadcasting messages in the Galaxy that we could detect today.

starting to show that their communicative abilities may be considerably advanced.

Between 1970 and 2004, Louis Herman at the Dolphin Institute and the Kewalo Basin Marine Mammal Laboratory in Hawaii was able to teach dolphins hundreds of words using gestures and symbols. Along with his team of researchers, Herman was able to deduce that dolphins understand symbolism – gestures that might mean 'the blue ball' or 'the red hoop'. They also got syntax – the idea that changing the order of words in a sentence can change the meaning. They understood concepts like 'none' or 'many', and the difference between a statement and a question. If they can do that in communication with humans, then they can do that with each other, indicating sophisticated communication. The question is, does evidence of complex communication stand the test as evidence for higher intelligence? Does one have to be able to speak a language to be considered truly intelligent? There are many examples of complex communication in nature, such as a honeybee's wiggle dance, quorum sensing among bacteria[*] or the chemical signals emitted by plants, but nobody has ever accused a flower of being clever.[†] Nature is a wonderful thing and life-forms of

---

[*] Bacteria, despite being single-celled, in contravention of Lori Marino's suggestion that life needs to be multi-cellular to have a degree of intelligence, are able to communicate in a sense by each secreting a molecule that, once enough have accumulated, triggers bacteria to behave in a certain way en masse. Consequently, populations of bacteria are able to track changes in their environment, and 'vote' on how to behave. Bacteria may be single-celled, but thanks to this 'quorum sensing', many working together can behave as one multi-cellular organism.

[†] Not everybody sees it this way. In conversation with the author for this book, the SETI Institute's Laurance Doyle described how 'trees make their own food and eat it, whereas we just eat. One could argue that if you can make your own food from sunshine and eat it as well, then that is more intelligent than depending on other animals to eat ... you could argue that trees are the dominant species on Earth because they are 90 per cent of the land biomass and they run the show.'

all kinds have arisen on this planet that can do some truly amazing things that humans could never do, but it doesn't mean they are necessarily smart. Something else, it seems, is required for complex communication to rise above the fundamental motivations of survival and begin to push towards true higher intelligence. As we saw in our ancestors, so too we see in dolphins evidence of Robin Dunbar's idea that social interaction, via complex communication, drives the development of higher intelligence. It seems you can't be considered truly intelligent unless you can have some gossip in your life.

CHATting with dolphins

Denise Herzing, who is the Research Director at the Wild Dolphin Project in the somewhat aptly named (at least for our extraterrestrial outlook) Jupiter in Florida, certainly agrees that what Dunbar hit on is the key. 'I think complex social interactions and politics drive intelligence,' she says. 'Everything we know about social species on this planet points to those being the species that seem to have the need for greater intelligence and memory capacity.'

Dolphins are certainly sociable creatures. Just as humans can communicate not only by speech but by hand gestures, body language and eye contact, dolphins can also communicate with each other via several means. They use echo location, which is a sophisticated sonar ability that allows them to 'see' without using their eyes; they produce barks and squawks that sound as if they could come from any mammal; they use a variety of clicks and whistles exclusively for social interaction; and they seem to listen to each other before responding, like having a conversation. In captivity, they seem to enjoy interacting with humans and playing with one another. Out in the wild their behaviour is less certain – one of the stumbling blocks in dolphin research is the difficulty of mounting and maintaining studies in the wild – but the evidence shows that they are quite adept at interacting socially as part of their everyday lives. The famous stories of dolphins

coming to the aid of humans caught adrift in the ocean or threatened by sharks is just a part of it. They take turns to forage and hunt for food. They express concern for other members of their pod who may be injured or dying.* Most telling, however, are the maternal instincts of the females. A nursery group forms within the pod, doting mothers taking it in turns to shepherd the young, who remain with their parents for between three and six years as they grow up. Good parenting is vital, it seems, whether you're a human or a dolphin, and some of the most intimate dolphin communication has been found between mother and child. There is evidence for acquired learning of both communication signals and how to properly interact socially with the other members of the pod. 'Dolphins have at least one word or referential signal,' says Herzing. 'These are signature whistles that are essentially names for each other that a dolphin can call another dolphin by.'

These names – whatever they mean to the dolphins – aren't just plucked at random, but indicate family ties. The signature whistles of young dolphins have similarities to their mother's signature whistle, while at the same time giving it their own personal twist. This alone suggests that dolphins are aware of their own individuality, which is an important step towards both higher intelligence and altruism, because if a being is

---

* A dolphin's reaction to death may depend on how the death occurs. In one case, a dolphin mother was observed by Joan Gonzalvo of the Tethys Research Institute in Milan to spend two days frantically trying to revive her calf that had suddenly died, as if the mother couldn't accept the calf was dead. On the other hand, Gonzalvo has also witnessed a pod of dolphins try and keep a severely wounded infant afloat but, once it died, they allowed it to sink to the sea floor and the pod moved on. Gonzalvo told *New Scientist* how, in his hypothesis, the poorly infant dolphin was kept company and given support by its community, but they expected it to die, and when it did the pod was prepared and able to move on.

not aware of itself and its environment, it cannot then be completely aware of and have empathy for others.

This concept of self-awareness is also called 'theory of mind', and is best displayed in the mirror test, which is where an animal is deemed to be self-aware if it can recognise itself in a mirror. Lori Marino and Diana Reiss were the first to show that dolphins pass the mirror test with flying colours, although the two have since bitterly fallen out over Reiss' use of captive dolphins for research.

Most of the communication experiments with dolphins have been conducted with captive cetaceans, but aside from ethical considerations, experiments in captivity also bring with them limits and biases. To hear the full range of dolphin communication signals, one needs to study pods of dolphins containing dozens or hundreds of members for a substantial length of time, but mounting expeditions to study wild dolphins in the ocean requires patience and money. Denise Herzing and her group in Jupiter have been getting to know the same pod of wild dolphins since 1984, gradually deciphering their communication system, building a catalogue of signals and watching their behaviour and postures over three generations, leading to their latest attempt at striking up a conversation with the cetaceans.

Alongside artificial intelligence expert Thad Starner from the Georgia Institute of Technology, and marine mammal cognitive scientists Adam Pack of the University of Hawaii and Fabienne Delfour of the University of Paris, Herzing has developed a technology that will hopefully revolutionise how we relate to dolphins. The Cetacean Hearing and Telemetry device, or CHAT for short, is a smartphone-sized gizmo that can identify the meaning of a dolphin whistle in real time. It's a fairly hefty contraption that is worn around the neck of a human diver and connected up to a pair of hydrophones and a one-handed keyboard called a 'twiddler', while inside CHAT is a complex algorithm and pattern detector. The idea isn't to translate dolphin whistles, but to agree on specific whistles for things with the dolphins and effectively create an

artificial language with them to open up the door to two-way communication.

'We're saying to the dolphins, let's agree these sounds are the labels for these objects that you like to play with and if you want them you can request them from us, and vice versa,' says Herzing. The subjects talked about may not be the most stimulating topics – things like 'pass me the red hoop' are not the most meaningful conversation, but it would be real-time conversation and that in itself is revolutionary.

In August 2013, while swimming with the pod in the warm waters of the Caribbean, Herzing's CHAT device was triggered by a dolphin whistle. 'Sargassum,' it whispered in English in her ear. Herzing was astonished and delighted, but also cautious. The dolphins had been playing with some sargassum seaweed earlier, but at the moment of the whistle they were not. Nor did Herzing hear any other 'words' during her dives that summer. Yet back on dry land, while reviewing all the whistles recorded from the pod during Herzing's dives, her team discovered that the dolphins had been using the agreed-upon whistles, but at a higher frequency – dolphins sometimes change the pitch of their whistles to counter background noise – which meant that CHAT had not recognised them. After the fact, it was impossible to determine whether the dolphins were using these whistles in proper context, or were just randomly making them without meaning.

It remains to be determined whether CHAT, or a device like it, will ever allow more fluid, two-way real-time conversation between humans and dolphins, but Herzing holds on to the hope that, over extended use, it will bring evidence of the true range of dolphin communication.

Communication and language can be two different things, however. 'In itself, if they have a name for a shark in dolphin whistle communication, you can't then say they have a language, because human words do much more than that,' says Justin Gregg, a senior research associate of the Dolphin Communication Project in Connecticut, who is dubious about the scope of dolphin communication. 'Essentially,

when you look at dolphin behaviour, they do behave in some complicated and interesting ways, but there are no great mysteries in what they do that can only be answered with language. It's something I always get asked about but the onus is on the people making the claims. It's not my job to disprove it; it's their job to prove it.'

Gregg also points out that referential signalling in itself is nothing special − lots of animals including squirrels, chickens and monkeys have the same ability. However, it's the complexity of the grammatical rules − what we call syntax − in dolphin communication that will be the ultimate decider. Human language is not simply made from words that act as labels. Between those words are other words that are there solely to provide the links in the chain of complicated grammatical structures. For example, the word 'the' is not a label referring to anything, but is instead part of the grammatical infrastructure of the English language.

'If dolphins don't have all that complexity then it is not a language in the way that human language is,' says Gregg.

Even if CHAT succeeds, sceptics will point out that the dolphins are essentially mimicking instructions given by Herzing's team, which is not the same as the dolphins having developed a species-specific language, complete with syntax. Now perhaps they do have that complex language and we just haven't studied dolphin communication in the wild long enough to be able to identify the grammatical rules. Recent years have produced some optimistic, or perhaps over-optimistic, results, most notably a 2016 study led by Holli Eskelinen of Dolphins Plus, Inc, in Key Largo of the Florida Keys, in which communication between two dolphins increased significantly when they were cooperating in a task to open a container by pulling two loops of rope attached to two lids. Some researchers have inferred this increase in signalling to be the dolphins 'discussing' how to open the container, with the implied necessary syntax, although this conclusion is disputed by other researchers, including Gregg.

Information theory

Either way, syntax seems to be important for highly intelligent, advanced communication, and as such perhaps it should be applied to SETI more. Over the decades there have been numerous false alarms when signals from space have been detected that caused scientists to think, this is really it, only for the signal to turn out to be terrestrial interference or an orbiting satellite (the European Space Agency's Solar and Heliospheric Orbiter, or SOHO, provided one such false alarm in 1997) or some natural phenomenon (an extraterrestrial explanation was briefly considered for the discovery of pulsars in 1967, as we saw in the introduction). There are still many naturally produced signals in the Universe that remain mysterious, such as Fast Radio Bursts, or FRBs, which are powerful millisecond blasts of radio waves from beyond our Galaxy that currently have a completely unknown origin, but could potentially represent a real alien signal.

In order to distinguish between FRBs and any other unexplained signals, and real signals from extraterrestrial intelligence, Laurance Doyle of the SETI Institute suggests that SETI should be searching for signals that display complex syntax, even if we cannot otherwise decode the signal.

Doyle, a genial and bearded Californian, is someone who is always on the lookout for new ideas, new avenues to explore, new ways to think. An astronomer by training, he has a habit of dipping his toes into the waters of other disciplines to see what they have to offer, admitting that he spends his time 'roaming up and down the factors of Drake's equation'. One particular extra-curricular activity began in 1995 when, with Brenda McCowan and Sean Hanser of the University of California, Davis, and Simon Johnston of the Australian Telescope National Facility, he began applying a concept known as 'information theory' to dolphin whistles.

Information theory was developed by the mathematician and cryptographer Claude Shannon of Bell Laboratories in the 1940s as a means of analysing signal content in the burgeoning telecommunications industry (at that time being

put to use in the Second World War). It can be applied to any system in which information is transmitted, from fibre optics to spoken language. It operates on the knowledge that all information can be broken down into bits and that these bits can either be arranged completely randomly with no order whatsoever, or can be assembled and ordered according to certain rules.

A simple analogy is to consider 100 soldiers marching in random directions across a muddy field. Then, when their drill sergeant blows his whistle, they suddenly come together to stand in 10 rows of 10. Let's think about what is happening here. Prior to the call to attention, there is maximum disorder, maximum complexity, maximum entropy; the possibilities for how to arrange them are great. After the whistle has blown, their distribution becomes ordered and structure is imposed on them. Their entropy decreases, as does their data complexity, but rule structure increases.

In language, rule structure equates to syntax, to grammar and spelling. Write down 100 words on 100 pieces of paper and throw them into the air – upon landing scattered across the carpet or kitchen table, they are disordered and random, and can be arbitrarily arranged in myriad ways. They have maximum entropy. However, if we impose rules on the words, such as sentence structure, our choices narrow. It's similar to the game of Hangman: suppose the player has an unknown five-letter word beginning with the letter 'q'. The rules of English language tell us that the second letter must be 'u'. From there on, there is only a limited number of letters that can follow 'qu', and so you may have 'que' or 'qui' or 'qua', which might lead to you predicting that the word is 'quest' or 'quick' or 'quack'. It is grammatical rules that, for example, lead to predictable pairs of letters such as 'qu' and 'th', or certain combinations of words, which form language's own typo correction facility.*

---

* As my editor points out, it's also the basis for predictive text, so there is a downside to it!

Look at what these rules allow us to do. We do not randomly guess what words with missing letters are; rather we fill in the gaps by predicting what the missing data is, based on the established rules. This has distinct survival advantages for animals smart enough to have the requisite rule structure in their communication. For animals, being able to fill in the gaps in signals they receive relies on their communication system having a structure from which, if some information is missing, the grammatical rules can provide a decent conditional probability of guessing what the missing information is. Cotton plants are preyed on by caterpillars, moths and worms, and so they secrete chemical signals to alert nearby birds to eat the worms and passing wasps to lay their eggs in the caterpillars or tuck into the moths. Each referential signal for 'worm' and 'caterpillar' is comprised of the same nine chemicals but in different ratios. If the plant makes a 'spelling mistake', a wasp might instead fly past while a caterpillar munches on the plant's leaves, unless the wasp is able to understand the meaning despite the typo because of the grammatical rules of the established communication.

'There's so much survival value in being able to recover errors in communication, and error recovery depends on having rule structure in your communication system,' says Doyle. You might not catch all the words being said, but you get the gist of it through syntax. If intelligence and communication complexity, such as syntax, evolved as a survival agent, then perhaps intelligence requires a threatening environment to develop and flourish. However, this error correction facility of language only operates up to a point, depending upon the complexity of the grammatical rule structures – greater complexity allows us to fill in more of the blanks because of the conditional probabilities that certain letters or words follow on from one another. It is like playing Chinese Whispers, when what began as a sensible phrase can begin to mutate into something nonsensical after the fifth or sixth repetition.

'In other words,' says Doyle, 'if you are missing a word in a copy machine you can fill it in. If you're missing two words,

you still have a chance of filling in those two words but you can see that by missing two words in a row you're not as likely to get the missing data.' With each missing word in a row, the likelihood of recovering the missing data spirals downwards. 'It turns out that for humans, if we're missing more than nine words, then any word will pretty much do because they become random, there is no longer a conditional relationship between words. So we say human beings, when it comes to their words, have a complexity of ninth-order Shannon entropy.'

So Shannon entropy (named after Claude Shannon, mentioned above) is a measure of uncertainty or disorder in information. Dolphins, according to Doyle's studies, have at least third- or fourth-order entropy, and maybe more: as we have mentioned, there have been too few detailed studies of dolphins in the wild to accumulate the information required to judge whether they go beyond fourth-order Shannon entropy. But on the basis of what has been gleaned thus far from information theory, dolphin communication is some of the most sophisticated on the planet.

Another way to look at communication complexity through the filter of information theory is something called Zipf's Law, named after George Zipf of Harvard University, who was the first to apply information theory to linguistics. Consider the first paragraph of this chapter. It consists of 56 words (not counting numbers) built from 279 letters. The most common letter is 'e', occurring 37 times and, indeed, it is the most common letter in the English language. Next are 'n' and 'o', each with 23 occurrences, then 'a' and 't' with 21, 'r' with 18 and so on, down to 'k', which occurs only once and 'j', 'q', 'x' and 'z', which don't pop up at all ('q' is the least common letter in the English alphabet, appearing just 0.1 per cent of the time). Placing these numbers on a graph in descending order from left to right results in a slope with a gradient of −1 (see Figure 1). This occurs not only for English, but also for Russian, Chinese, Arabic and pretty much every other language on the planet spoken by adults, showing the innate ability of the human brain to deal with an elaborate

language system.* The slope implies complexity, order and grammatical rules, and that some letters are designed to appear more frequently, or in certain conditions. Dolphin whistles and the sounds of humpback whales also give a -1 slope.† By comparison, consider a baby making babbling noises – on average no sound is more common than any other, and all are completely random, so they would produce a flat line rather than a slope. On the other hand, a toddler learning to talk may focus on certain sounds, like 'mama' or 'dada', so that the most common sounds would occur with a high frequency and other sounds barely at all, leading to a very steep gradient. Infant dolphins share this very same steep gradient with infant humans – both, it seems, are learning to talk.

The power of information theory is the ability to analyse communication systems in a quantitative way and Doyle has applied it to the signals of all manner of life-forms on

---

* As an aside, Doug Vakoch of the METI International organisation (we'll meet them in Chapter 7) is applying Zipf's Law to our own messages to ET. Vakoch initiated a project called Earth Speaks that allowed members of the public from all over the world to post on a website the message that they would like to send to ET. The content of these messages tells us a great deal about our own humanity in general – our hopes, our fears, our views of life on planet Earth. Vakoch found that some of the words posted in Earth Speaks appear far more frequently than they do on average in typical English texts, as compiled by the British National Corpus. The word 'us' is used 22 times more often; 'Earth' 73 times more frequently; 'please' is 55 times more common; and 'help' is used 13 times more often. Posters on the Earth Speaks website often tend to view the world as one, and are either warning aliens that they're best off not contacting us, or asking kindly aliens for help – once more, the notion of altruistic, utopian aliens prevails.

† *Star Trek IV: The Voyage Home* (1986) famously highlighted the ability of humpback whales to communicate. Consequently, the film has become known to those less familiar with the *Star Trek* canon as 'the one with the whales'.

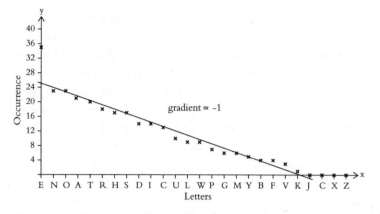

Figure 1: Zipf's Law, as illustrated by the occurrence of each letter in the alphabet in the opening paragraph of this chapter. The line of best fit has a gradient of about −1. The greater the selection of letters, the more accurate this fit becomes.

Earth, from bees and plants and dolphins to the voices of air-traffic control. His eye, though, is really on applying it to any message we may receive from the stars.

'The basic idea is that it is a kind of communication encephalisation quotient,' he says. Although it does not tell us what is being said, it does tell us how complex the signals are. In SETI, it could be quite a useful tool for teasing information out of any possible alien message that we cannot otherwise translate without some kind of Rosetta Stone. Doyle suggests that rather than looking for signals that display artificiality – perhaps by belting out the digits of pi to the umpteenth decimal point in binary code, as some have suggested – SETI should be searching for signals that show -1 slopes in accordance to Zipf's Law.

'SETI is looking for technology, for a transmitter, but we're advocating looking at the message,' says Doyle. If our assumption that communication complexity is related to social complexity is correct, then by measuring the communication complexity of an extraterrestrial signal, we might be able to gain some insight into the cultural or social complexity of the beings that sent the message.

Doyle draws an analogy with astrobiology, which has as one of its avenues of research the study of biology on Earth – especially extreme biology – with the intention of then looking for similar biologies on other worlds. 'I'm trying to convince SETI researchers to study all the communication systems on Earth, especially the extreme ones, with a view to detecting signals in space,' says Doyle. 'It seems pretty straightforward and that's what SETI should be doing, but so far SETI has not been involved much – I'm kind of doing this by myself with my two colleagues from the University of California, Davis.'

Triple entendres

In our pride, our arrogance, our egocentricity, humans have, in general, overlooked that we are not the only intelligence on the planet. Whether other terrestrial life has language or not, whether it has the ability to understand syntax or abstract concepts, whether it has a form of tool-making or not, is immaterial. There's a graded scale of intelligence on Earth, starting with the primitive, automatic functions of multi-cellular life that Lori Marino mentions, all the way up to the likes of ants, bees, chimps, parrots, crows, humpback whales and dolphins, peaking with *Homo sapiens*. These animals are not dumb, but command our respect and instil the awe that we sense in nature around us – the wonder of life.

Yet humans need not be the be-all and end-all of the evolutionary trajectory of life. Ours may not be the superior intellect in the cosmos. There's no reason why human beings have to have the maximum possible Shannon entropy. Imagine alien intelligences with Shannon entropy on the order of 10, or 15, or 20. Their communication would be orders of magnitude beyond that which humans could understand. Should SETI succeed in detecting a message from advanced extraterrestrials, we may not have much hope of understanding it, even if they did send with it some form of decipherment tool.

To imagine how we might feel when confronted by a vastly more complex language exploring concepts we could not even begin to touch, then imagine what it was like to be Koko the gorilla. Koko was a captive gorilla who worked with her trainer, the developmental psychologist Penny Patterson of Stanford University, from the early 1970s. Their relationship was remarkable, crossing the borders between species to establish a four-decade-long friendship, amounting to the longest ongoing inter-species communication ever achieved. Using sign language, Koko learned around 1,000 words and was able to relay her thoughts and feelings, showing that gorillas can understand abstract concepts. If you told Koko that you were going to take her for a walk tomorrow, she understood what tomorrow meant: the future. If you told her that it was raining yesterday, she understood that meant the past. These statements involve single time tenses – yesterday, tomorrow. But if you told her that we would have finished lunch by this time tomorrow, she didn't understand. The combination of two tenses – the idea that the future can have a past – was too complex for her primate brain. Before we scoff at Koko's intellect, let's imagine meeting an extraterrestrial that has a Shannon entropy of, say, 20 in its communication. It may have an even greater mix of past and future tenses: 'Tomorrow I will have to be have been there'. The multiple time jumps make little sense to us at our level of communication complexity and attempts to replicate them as a sentence of English come off as more than a little clunky. Or, perhaps the extraterrestrial will be the star of dinner parties, showing off with triple, quadruple and octuple entendres, putting our double entendres to shame. We'll appear as limited to the extraterrestrials as Koko the gorilla did to us – but are our limits forever binding, or can we uplift ourselves to greater things?*

---

* The concept of 'uplift' – raising our own intelligence or that of other animals to a higher level – has been a common feature in science fiction, from novelist David Brin's *Uplift* saga to Hollywood

Koko died peacefully in her sleep on 19 June 2018, at the age of 46.

🛰

It may not be possible for our brains to grow much more complex – made any more compact, the slender axons that transmit signals from one neuron to the next begin to operate with excessive thermal noise as ion channels that allow chemical signals to pass begin to malfunction. If, biologically, we're hitting the end of the road, perhaps we can jump onto the next road with a little artificial help.

Andrew Knoll and Richard Bambach's mega-trajectories, which we encountered earlier in this chapter, may not be limited to the six that they describe. There may be another evolutionary stage in the development of life whose boundary we might cross one day soon. We've encountered it many times in fiction, from *2001: A Space Odyssey* to the *Terminator* movies and *The Matrix* trilogy. In various fictional guises it has frightened us and it has protected us, and some people are staking their entire reputation, even their lives, on estimating that it will come to pass. This seventh mega-trajectory, as noted by Milan Ćirković of the Astronomical Observatory of Belgrade in Serbia and the late Robert Bradbury, concerns evolution beyond the biological: artificial intelligence twinned with human organics and nanotechnology. In other words, thinking computers fused with the minds of human beings.

The revolution has already begun. If you use a cochlear implant or wear glasses or have a pacemaker, then you are using artificial aids to improve your capabilities. A few people who have lost limbs have gained bionic replacements. In the broadest sense of the word, we are already becoming

---

movies such as *Rise of the Planet of the Apes* (2011). The movement to uplift humanity's own cognitive capabilities with technology has become known as transhumanism.

cyborgs. Admittedly, in all of these cases it is to make up for a deficiency in our health, but it won't be long before artificial aids are designed not just to cover up flaws in our physical well-being, but to improve ourselves beyond the normal human standard, to make us stronger, faster and smarter. Our intelligence will cease to evolve as a reaction to our habitats, social structures or surrounding ecology and instead be forced to evolve through our technology. In essence, the principle is that once a certain level of technology is achieved, intelligence begets intelligence, powering its own evolution at ever-increasing rates.

Have humans reached that level of technology? We're close, but not quite there yet. Computers are able to perform complex calculations for us and their memory storage capabilities can, to an extent, be seen to act as an extension of our own memory, but they are not integrated into us. We can't think and mentally tell our office computer what to do,* or use its processor speed to increase the rate at which we take in information from a book that we are reading. We still have an interface – the keyboard – that separates us, distinguishing 'us' (humans) from 'it' (the computer). To attain true integration and formalise the union between humans and machines, we've got to get to grips with how the human brain works and then be able to back-engineer the brain to make it compatible with computers, which currently are not up to the incredible complexity level of the human brain.

You might not think it, but that blob of grey matter stuck between your ears is the envy of every software engineer and artificial intelligence expert in the world. You might not be

---

* In truth, there are computers that can be controlled merely through brain function, which we call brain–computer interfaces. The most-studied non-invasive technique is electroencephalography (EEG), and there are even commercial applications such as spelling and writing systems. However, the technology is still a long way from hitting the mainstream.

able to beat Garry Kasparov at chess as Deep Thought did in 1997, calculate pi to a trillion digits or simulate billions of years of cosmic evolution in your head as supercomputers can, but computers get to focus solely on those objectives. Your brain, on the other hand, has to worry itself with maintaining and controlling your body, communicating with every nerve, processing a tumultuous cascade of signals from your various sensory organs, making complex leaps of intuition, considering future possibilities and contradictory ideas, contemplating relationships with others, dealing with a whole number of other irrelevant thoughts that may pass through your head, as well as focusing on whatever it is you are doing at any particular moment, and all of that has to be done in milliseconds, because as we have evolved, if we failed to react to stimuli with speed, we would wind up dead.

However, computers have advantages: greater design freedom, the ability to debug, improve, reboot and back-up, the ability to compute tasks without making human mistakes (unless the human-installed programming has a mistake), and they can perform tasks at far greater speeds than humans – computer calculations proceed at a rate of billionths of a second, rather than thousandths of a second for the brain's neurons. As we have seen, computers generally operate only a few separate strands of calculations at a time, whereas the human brain is massively parallel, with many neurons firing simultaneously. Merging computers with biological brains would provide us with the best of both worlds, but to do that we must first be able to model the human brain precisely.

Back-engineering the brain will not be easy. Those 86 million neurons crammed into our craniums are like a tangled net of wires, with the exception that the way they are tangled is very deliberate; self-organised but at the same time chaotic. Various studies have estimated that the computational capacity of the human brain is between 10^{14} (100 trillion) and 10^{16} (10,000 trillion) computations per second. However, to model every sub-neural detail of the brain – all the axons and dendrites and synapses that link neuron to neuron and fire and receive the chemical signals

that pass for computations in the brain – would require something approaching 10^{19} (10,000,000 trillion) calculations per second. By comparison, the most powerful supercomputer in the world as of May 2019, which is called Summit and is based at the Oak Ridge National Laboratory in the United States, can conduct 143.5×10^{15} (1433.5 petaflops, or 143,500 trillion) computations per second,[*] while your desktop Mac or PC can only provide around 10^9 (one billion) calculations per second.

This all fits very nicely into the theory of the coming Technological Singularity, developed by the San Diego State University mathematician, computer scientist and multi-Hugo Award-winning science-fiction novelist Vernor Vinge. In 1993 his essay, 'The Coming Technological Singularity: How to Survive in the Post-Human Era',[†] popularised notions of what could happen when artificial intelligence begins to outstrip human intelligence, building on previous work from Ray Solomonoff, Alan Turing, Stanislaw Ulam and others. The Singularity is a point in time when computing power exceeds anything human biological brains are capable of and, by interfacing with it, we transform our species. Vinge describes it in his essay as 'a point where our models must be discarded and a new reality rules. As we move closer and closer to this point, it will loom vaster and vaster over human affairs till the notion becomes commonplace. Yet when it finally happens it may still be a great surprise and a greater unknown.'

The American inventor and futurist Ray Kurzweil suggests that the Singularity will cause a trillion-fold expansion in human intelligence as we merge with computers. There will no longer be an 'it' and 'us' situation – artificial intelligence and human intelligence will be as one in

---

[*] A petaflop is a computing term to describe 1,000 trillion computations per second. You can keep track of the most powerful computers in the world at the website top500.org.
[†] You can read Vernor Vinge's essay, 'The Coming Technological Singularity', at rohan.sdsu.edu/faculty/vinge/misc/singularity.html

Kurzweil's vision. He cites 2045 as the year he believes the Singularity will take place, based on trends in computational power, studies of the architecture of the human brain and advances in nanotechnology and genetics. Central to these trends is Moore's Law, which describes how the number of transistors that can be squeezed onto a circuit doubles roughly every two years thanks to miniaturisation, and as they become smaller they become far less expensive, leading to the processing speed and memory capacity of computers increasing at a proportional rate.[*] Kurzweil sees this trend continuing exponentially, with ever-increasing returns. Based on this trend, in 2005 he predicted that by 2010 supercomputers would be capable of 10^{15} (1,000 trillion) calculations per second; China's Tianhe-1A and Tianhe-2, the Titan at Oak Ridge National Laboratory, the Lawrence Livermore National Laboratory's Sequoia, the K-computer and the Cray Jaguar among several others all accomplished this in the allotted time. By 2025, reckons Kurzweil, we'll have this level of processing power built into our desktop computers, tablets and gaming machines. As the exponential trend continues, by the early 2030s computers will be operating at up to 10^{29} (100 octillion, or 100 thousand trillion trillion) calculations per second; a single computer would be roughly equivalent to the entire computing capacity of humanity. Artificial intelligence on a giant scale would be achieved, but this isn't a profound enough moment to be the Singularity in Kurzweil's eyes. That will only come when such immense intelligence is cheap, which on his curve of exponential growth arrives in the mid-2040s. Interfacing with these computers, rather than allowing them to dominate us, will transform humanity into a super-intelligence. Where

---

[*] Moore's Law, named after Intel's Gordon Moore, has held since its conception in the 1970s (although the law has its roots in the 1950s). Nobody knows how much longer it will hold up – some predict that it could fall apart within the next decade, while others such as Ray Kurzweil believe progress will accelerate exponentially.

we go from there would be a mystery – the whole point of a singularity, be it technological or in mathematics and physics, is that we can't describe it and we can't see past it. However, Kurzweil imagines us expanding into the Universe, using all its matter as a computational substrate. Immortality beckons.

We're talking about the possible destiny of the human species here. The stakes are immeasurably high. It all sounds quite fantastical and certainly not everybody agrees that the Singularity will ever happen, including Harvard's Steven Pinker (see Chapter 1), who suggests that just because a possible future can be imagined does not mean it will necessarily come to pass. Yet if we are to assume that the Singularity is inevitable, and that intelligent extraterrestrial civilisations are technological, then we have to assume that extraterrestrials will also have gone through their own Singularity. Numerous scientists, including Cambridge's Lord Martin Rees and Seth Shostak of the SETI Institute, have argued that we are more likely to find signals from alien machine life than from biological life. If this is true, it should change many of our assumptions about SETI, about where life will reside (will machine life want to stay planet-bound?), and indeed the idea of robotic envoys is not a new one to SETI (see Chapter 5). Moreover, NASA's former Chief Historian, Steven J. Dick, came up with an 'Intelligence Principle' that states that 'the maintenance, improvement and perpetuation of knowledge and intelligence is the central driving force of cultural evolution, and that to the extent that intelligence can be improved, it will be improved'. If there is intelligence (however you choose to define intelligence), then there will be culture and cultural evolution, says Dick, and one of the possible outcomes of this is artificial intelligence. At a Royal Society discussion meeting in October 2010, Dick described how he believes that 'nothing is more fundamental, or [a] stronger driver of culture, than intelligence and improving the intelligence both of individuals and of our species, and the same can be assumed for any intelligence out there, and that this is a

fundamental fact that would best any other technology or any other thing that culture does.'

Such improvement, while not explicitly mentioning technology (and it would be very interesting one day to apply this to whatever form, if any, dolphin culture takes, for example), does seem to rest on the inherent assumption that technology will be present. Yet ironically it is our adherence to this assumption that leads us to a place where we can no longer predict or claim to know anything about what extraterrestrials will be like – what lies beyond the Singularity is unknowable until we have reached it. It highlights a quintessential fault with our assumptions about SETI, one that has permeated this discussion of the nature of intelligence: that by projecting visions of our own future onto alien civilisations in lieu of any real extraterrestrials to study, we're putting the greasy fingerprints of human bias all over our expectations of alien life.

In this chapter we have journeyed across billions of years of evolution, explored the world of dolphins, met gorillas with a sense of time and looked ahead to when machines might conquer the Universe. In doing so, we have come to a realisation that not only our kind of intelligence, but also our level of communication complexity, may not be the same as that which exists in other intelligent life in the Universe. Human intelligence could be parochial, a fluke of nature, a chance genetic mutation that has benefitted us but is unlikely to occur anywhere ever again. Doug Vakoch, a psychologist working in SETI and founder of METI International (Messaging Extraterrestrial Intelligence – see Chapter 7), has perhaps expressed it best: we're climbing a mountain of technology, of progress, but our route up that mountain is not necessarily the only route – other civilisations could be reaching for the same goals but via different routes, or even climbing different mountains altogether.

It turns out then that SETI isn't looking for purely intelligent life, only technological intelligence. In some ways that is perfectly understandable, in that the only intelligent life that we can detect at this moment in time is life that has technology. The danger is that it introduces anthropomorphic bias into the search – we would do well to remember that our kind of intelligence is not the only possible kind. Much of the intelligent life in the Universe may be more like dolphins than humans (particularly if ocean worlds abound in the cosmos – see Chapter 3). Or there could be a spectrum of intelligence across the Universe, with different species exhibiting different traits and manifestations of intelligence, and to different levels.

Considering this, we must revise our expectations of SETI's chances of success. SETI is only searching for a possible subset of all the different kinds of intelligence, so a null result in the search would not imply that there is no intelligent life out there, only that we could be missing huge swathes of it because of the narrowness of our search parameters, and the limitations of our understanding of what forms intelligence can take.

Denise Herzing recognises this. 'One of the explorations I've done with the SETI scientists is to ask, how do we recognise other intelligence besides a human-biased, primate-biased intelligence?' she says. 'The idea being that we have to open up our definition of what intelligence is.'

In human history, we have seen how environmental factors have driven the evolution of intelligence, when our ancestors came down from the trees and had to be able to think better in order to survive and prosper. Environment, and hence climate, have their part to play in the development of intelligent life. Where would we find such life in the Universe? Astronomers, planetary scientists and geologists are now making huge strides in the discovery and understanding of planets orbiting other stars and their unique environments, as we shall find out in the next chapter.

Homeworld

Once upon a time I visited Iceland, primarily to see the Northern Lights. It's a terrific place; the people are friendly, the food great and the desolate landscape is magnificent. Yet, as I stood on the rim of a shallow pseudo-crater,* looking out onto this igneous land's barren wilderness, with towering table-top mountains sporting crests of snow and hats of billowing cloud, and the craggy peaks and cinder-cones of volcanoes lining the horizon, the immense world-shattering forces that carved this terrain were both obvious and powerful. At our isolated hotel way-station on the shore of frozen Lake Mývatn, in the north-west of the island, we were perched on the eastern edge of the immense Mid-Atlantic Ridge, an open wound in the crust of our planet that is pushing vast continental plates aside while new land (or, for most of the ridge's 19,000km [11,800-mile] extent, new sea floor) spills out from the rupture. At night, as the ephemeral glow of the aurora shimmered over the dark mountains, it was spellbinding.

Being a reluctant traveller, a flight in an airliner is a rare experience for me, so for much of the journey out from Heathrow to Iceland and back again, my face was pressed up to the window, gawping at the vista of the North Atlantic's rolling waves far below. Water stretched from horizon to horizon and yet it was only a small part of a subsection of an enormous ocean in a world of oceans, truly driving home the abundance of water that we have here on our planet.

---

* Pseudo-craters are the product of 'steam explosions' that result from a thin layer of lava passing over water, in this case Lake Mývatn, causing the water in the lake to rapidly boil and expand, blowing downwards in an explosion that gouges out a crater in the lake floor.

This triumvirate of natural phenomena – the ridge, the ghostly auroral lights and the vast oceans – dramatically illustrate some of the primary attributes that help make our planet just right for life, and witnessing them together proved to be a spectacular epiphany. The Mid–Atlantic Ridge is a manifestation of plate tectonics, which are vital for the continued circulation of the carbon that regulates our planet's long-term climate. The Northern Lights are products of the Earth's magnetic envelope that shields our planet from solar storms, while the relevance of water to life is obvious. That Iceland demonstrates all these characteristics is somewhat ironic, considering it can be a harsh country in which to live, but on a worldwide stage over aeons of geological history, nature has found a way for these facets to work in equilibrium with one another, a tangle of feedback cycles and circumstance. If Earth were lacking even one of them, our planet might have ended up as home to no one.

In the previous two chapters, we've asked whether extraterrestrial life will be altruistic, and what degree of intelligence it may have. It also makes sense to ask where it will live, so that when we conduct SETI experiments, we're looking in the right places for ET. The most obvious place to begin the search is on planets that are like Earth and that exhibit the three phenomena I saw during my Iceland trip, plus other factors, such as the right nitrogen-oxygen mix in the atmosphere, the right temperature and maybe a stabilising moon or two. The trouble is, astronomers are yet to identify any worlds around other stars that are definitely like Earth, and the reason for this is that the planets are just too small and too far away for our telescopes to resolve to the required level. This means that we can only make educated guesses as to the character of some of the best candidates for Earth-like planets, which include several of the worlds in the TRAPPIST-1 system 39.5 light years away, the lone known planet orbiting the nearby star Ross 128 almost 11 light years away, and the world accompanying the closest star to the Sun, Proxima Centauri, just 4.2 light years distant. These all exist in what is

termed the 'habitable zone', in which a planet is at just the right distance from its star so that its surface could be at an appropriate temperature to support liquid water, assuming an Earth-like atmosphere that can retain the star's radiant heat. In our Solar System, for example, Venus is closer to the Sun than Earth and has become too hot by far, with a surface simmering at a balmy 460°C (800°F) underneath an oppressive carbon dioxide atmosphere. Meanwhile, Mars is further out than Earth. It's a desert world, but don't think Sahara, think tundra, where the average surface temperature is a chilly -50°C (-58° F) and in the heat of equatorial summer temperatures barely creep above zero degrees Celsius (32° Fahrenheit). Earth, at an average of 149.6 million kilometres (93 million miles) from the Sun, seems to be at just the right distance to fall within the habitable zone.

I'm using the term 'habitable zone' reluctantly. The term has become part of the exoplanetary zeitgeist, but despite the popularity of the phrase, it's really a symptom of over-hyping the possibilities. Being in the habitable zone in no way guarantees that a planet is habitable, or even that it has an atmosphere or water. As we have already suggested, and will discover further, there are other factors involved. Nor does the notion of the habitable zone include all the potentially habitable environments that we can conceive of, such as subterranean oceans beneath the ice of cold worlds, as in the case of the ocean within Jupiter's moon Europa. Still, it's a starting point in our SETI searches.

Rare Earth

Our blue orb, vulnerable in the expanse of space, breathed upon by the incandescent heat of a dull, mid-range star we call the Sun, is thus far the only planetary body we know of that is home to life. Not even so much as the smallest microbe or the most unimpressive amoeba, never mind complex, intelligent life, has been discovered beyond our atmosphere. That doesn't necessarily mean they're not out there, but with no evidence for them, all we currently have to go on is our

own intuition. Many people are optimistic, embracing the Copernican principle that suggests Earth is not special or unique or at the centre of the Universe. However, other scientists point out that the characteristics mentioned above from my trip to Iceland are all very precise on Earth; the more pessimistic (or should that be realistic?) breed of planetary scientist says there's not much leeway for variation, leading such pessimists to suspect that Earth's combination of properties is a lucky accident. They call it the 'Rare Earth' theory, as made famous in the controversial book of the same name written in 2000 by a couple of Seattle-based scientists, palaeontologist Peter Ward and astronomer Donald Brownlee. The central thesis of *Rare Earth* is, essentially, that our planet, with its mix of characteristics and circumstance that lead to its long-term habitability, is a one-in-a-trillion fluke assembly of vital factors, all in the right place at the right time. These factors include plate tectonics, a suitable amount of water, a comfortable amount of warmth, a stable and not too severe planetary tilt, a resident large moon, a none-too-hectic rate of asteroid and comet impacts, and a location in the Galaxy favourable to the presence of elements required to make a star like our Sun, a planet like our Earth and life like human life. Earth is a Goldilocks planet, one that is neither too hot nor too cold and where everything is just right for life as we know it.

If the habitability sceptics are correct, then Earth is alone. We are alone. With no other habitable planets out there, there can be no life, and SETI is an endeavour that is just wasting our time. There would be little point reading the rest of this book.

Before you do anything hasty, such as putting this book back on the shelf, consider this: the Rare Earth theory could be wrong. Over the following pages we will deconstruct its hypothesis, challenge its assumptions and, in doing so, discover that the Universe could be far more benign to life than the sceptics claim. And that's great news for SETI.

Having said that, I encourage you now to put this book down – just for a minute! Take a walk to the front door, step outside and inhale a deep breath of fresh, outdoor air. That's oxygen flooding through your bloodstream right now, produced by photosynthesis in plants and living creatures, but it's really thanks to tiny life-forms called cyanobacteria. Primarily found as gloopy blue-green algae, otherwise known as pond scum, cyanobacteria began producing oxygen on Earth some 2.4 billion years ago, in a chemical reaction that we're all taught about at school: a dose of sunlight, a drop of water and a whiff of carbon dioxide to produce carbohydrates and, as a completely waste product, oxygen. It's not the tree in your garden that is photosynthesising the oxygen, but the cyanobacteria living symbiotically within it that do the job for the tree. It's thanks to these microbial organisms that Earth's atmosphere is today 21 per cent oxygen; before cyanobacteria came along, Earth's residents were anaerobic; oxygen was pure poison to them. Indeed, the full oxygenation of Earth's atmosphere has been nicknamed the 'oxygen catastrophe' because it wiped out vast swaths of prokaryotic (single-celled life-forms), anaerobic species as the cyanobacteria took over. Even then, eukaryotes (multi-cellular life-forms) took a billion years to rise to dominance following their initial appearance on Earth 1.7 billion years ago (the gap being somewhat glibly described as 'the boring billion' by evolutionary biologists).

Eukaryotic life needs to 'fix' atmospheric nitrogen by transforming it into ammonia, which is more palatable to its biochemistry. This is accomplished by bacteria called diazotrophs, which count cyanobacteria among their number. However, diazotrophs need an element called molybdenum to achieve this fixing with any efficiency, but the leading source of molybdenum in the oceans comes from the reactions between molybdenum-bearing rocks and oxygen. Until the oxygen build-up on Earth had reached the levels necessary to produce the required abundances of molybdenum to facilitate nitrogen fixing, around 700 million years ago, eukaryotes were unable to develop to any great extent. Not long after that, relatively speaking, came the Cambrian explosion and

its associated wide diversity of life. Exactly why oxygen levels were so sluggish to begin with is still being debated as an uncertainty of paleontological history, but suffice it to say today we can breathe easily.

Breathe in, breathe out, encouraged Mr Miyagi in *The Karate Kid Part II*. We (that is, aerobic life-forms) breathe in oxygen and breathe out carbon dioxide. It's a cycle – plants take in carbon dioxide and release oxygen, we breathe in the oxygen and produce carbon dioxide – but this organic cycle is only a tiny part of the total circulation of carbon on our planet. The majority originates via inorganic means, a carbon–silicate cycle that regulates long-term global temperatures on Earth, going a long way to deciding when we have ice ages and when we have the inter-glacials, in tandem with the amount of incoming radiation from the Sun. In order for this carbon–silicate cycle to operate we need plate tectonics, which is the shifting of continental plates that causes earthquakes and volcanoes and is the same force behind the upheavals that formed and moulded the sensational scenery that I witnessed first-hand in Iceland.

Carbon dioxide in the atmosphere acts as a 'greenhouse gas'. Greenhouse gases, which also include water vapour, ozone and methane, consist of molecules that are efficient at absorbing infrared heat re-radiated from the surface. With the spectre of the climate emergency looming over all our shoulders, greenhouse gases suffer from a bad rep, but the truth is we need their natural occurrence and without them Earth would freeze at an average temperature of -18°C (0°F). It is the natural greenhouse effect of our atmosphere that warms our planet to the much rosier average of +15°C (59°F). On the other hand, it is the addition of greenhouse gases to the atmosphere as a result of human activity that is proving harmful to the climate.

Carbon dioxide is Earth's primary greenhouse gas, despite amounting to only 0.039 per cent of our atmosphere (yet this meagre contribution is enough to make it Earth's fourth most abundant atmospheric gas, after 78 per cent nitrogen,

21 per cent oxygen and 0.9 per cent argon) and its continued natural presence in the atmosphere is a consequence of geological activity, manifest in plate tectonics. In a way, it forms a blanket that wraps around our planet, keeping us comfortably snug.

'It's like being stood next to a bonfire,' says Lisa Kaltenegger, Director of the Carl Sagan Institute at Cornell University. With a gentle Germanic lilt to her voice, she continues, 'There's one distance where you are comfortable, but if you go further out it gets colder and if you go further in it is too warm. The geologically active carbon–silicate cycle that regulates how much carbon dioxide we have in our atmosphere is like a sweater. You can put a sweater on and you're comfortable further away from the bonfire, while you can take the sweater and most of your clothes off and you're still comfortable closer in to the bonfire.' One can imagine, for example, a planet farther from the Sun than Earth, but with an atmosphere containing more greenhouse gases that are able to trap enough of the Sun's heat to maintain an average surface temperature similar to Earth's, despite its greater distance.

When global temperatures are on average warm, rain washes carbon dioxide out of the atmosphere in the form of a weak carbonic acid rain that interacts with silicate rocks on the ground, dissolving them and producing a solution of calcium, bicarbonate and silica in the runoff water. This solution is eventually transported via streams and rivers into the sea, where single-celled algae such as planktonic coccolithophores and foraminifera incorporate the solution into their shells of calcium carbonate. When they die the calcium carbonate shells sink to the sea floor, coming to rest on the basaltic ocean crust, creating layers of carbonate sediments. Anyone who has walked along the White Cliffs of Dover in southern England has seen such sediments first-hand in the chalky cliff faces.

Often the sediments are subducted back beneath the oceanic crust and into the molten magma of the mantle that

sloshes beneath the crust and continental plates (together termed the lithosphere). Convection currents that have bubbled up from the planet's hot core and hit the rocky ceiling of the less dense (more buoyant) lithosphere transport the magma parallel to the undersides of the plates and towards volcanic vents in locations such as the Mid-Atlantic Ridge, spewing carbon dioxide from the volcanoes and refreshing the carbon dioxide content of the atmosphere.

The removal of carbon dioxide by rain reduces the greenhouse effect, causing the planet to begin to cool, its ability to retain heat diminished. Water begins to freeze, polar white extending deeper into the mid-latitudes from the ice caps as millennia pass, bringing the dawn of a new ice age. Snow is far less efficient at drawing carbon dioxide out of the atmosphere than liquid precipitation, allowing the abundance of carbon dioxide to build up again over time, and the greenhouse effect to rise once more until finally the snow begins to melt and the planet starts to thaw.

This epic saga of the carbon–silicate cycle acts as Earth's thermostat and it now becomes clearer, after understanding this, why a human-made influx of greenhouse gases into the atmosphere can seriously disrupt the operation of that thermostat. It also shows why lithospheric plate tectonics are so crucial; they may be the cause of natural hazards such as earthquakes, volcanoes and tsunamis that result in the deaths of many people, but without the input of tectonic activity in the carbon–silicate cycle, we'd probably have a permanently frozen Earth.

So we can add an addendum to the habitable-zone model: a planet must be at the right distance from its star, but also have an atmosphere where carbon is regulated in a cycle dictated by geological processes. If we take the bowls of porridge from *Goldilocks and the Three Bears* as an analogy to planets inside and outside the so-called habitable zone, it's like saying that Goldilocks only likes Baby Bear's porridge after maple syrup and strawberry jam have been added. The trouble is, some researchers suspect that syrup and jam may run low in the cosmic pantry.

When the Earth moves

Take a look around the Solar System, suggest the Rare Earthers. See any plate tectonics? 'They haven't happened anywhere else in the Solar System,' answers *Rare Earth* author Donald Brownlee. 'Yet plate tectonics have happened on Earth for a long time, so maybe they're not too rare, but if it is just one planet out of four or five, maybe that becomes a factor.'

Until recently, this was certainly the case to the best of our knowledge. However, several new discoveries are forcing planetary scientists to re-think their assumptions about the development of plate tectonics. Computer modelling has indicated that plate tectonics in the icy shell of Jupiter's moon Europa, which covers a deep global ocean, best explain features on the surface that look like subduction zones or regions of salty upwelling. However, Europa does not have a molten mantle, so the upwelling would be from the water ocean below.

Meanwhile, the red planet Mars is an interesting case. It has been assumed to be too small to have retained the internal heat necessary to drive much plate tectonics, despite sporting the largest mountain in the Solar System, the volcanic Olympus Mons. It's colossal; with a base 624km (388 miles) across, Olympus Mons could engulf the entire Hawaiian chain of volcanic islands, while the caldera at its peak is over 24km (15 miles) high, poking out through the pinkish Martian atmosphere, high above the dust storms. It's enormous, a true Mount Olympus. There are other large volcanoes on Mars too, such as the trio of shield volcanoes to the south-east of Olympus Mons – Arsia, Pavonis and Ascraeus Mons, which are 18km, 14km and 18km tall (11 miles, 9 miles and 11 miles) respectively. Whether these behemoths will ever reawaken remains to be seen, but what is for sure is that as time progresses,[*] Mars' volcanic activity

---

[*] There are three different eras of Martian geological time, the Noachian, Hesperian and Amazonian, which have been determined

decreases as the heat leaks out from the planet's core. An Yin, a Professor of Earth and Space Sciences at the University of California, Los Angeles, believes he has detected localised plate tectonics in the Valles Marineris region of the red planet – a huge rift valley that appears to be the boundary between two plates that have slid sideways by 150km (93 miles) since Valles Marineris formed – but there appears to be no subduction and therefore no carbon–silicate cycle. Beyond that, if Mars ever did have plate tectonics on a global scale, then it shuddered to a standstill billions of years ago.

Venus is more enigmatic. As I sit typing this one Saturday evening, I can see it through my window towards the west, a stunning Evening Star set against the golden hues and dark blues of dusk. Venus' brilliance in the sky before sunrise or after sunset is the upshot of its shining carbon-dioxide clouds that wrap thick swathes around the Venusian surface. The clouds reflect as much as 76 per cent of the Sun's light incident on the planet (we call this an 'albedo' of 0.76; albedo is an important property that can aid the control of a planetary climate – Earth's average albedo is about 0.3, although cloudy regions or the brilliant white ice caps tend to have a higher albedo than the continents) and these clouds around Venus

---

based on crater counts (the older the surface, the more impact craters it displays). The Noachian is the oldest era, dating from the dawn of Mars to between 3.8 and 3.5 billion years ago, when the planet may have still had lakes and even an ocean. Then things began to change – fewer craters are recorded – which in this case means that as Mars entered the Hesperian epoch, it saw the rise of Olympus Mons and lava from copious volcanism filling in and removing craters from the red planet's surface, coupled with dramatic floodwaters. Around 1.8 billion years ago things changed once again as Mars entered into the midst of the Amazonian era, which has seen fewer meteorite impacts and rarer outbursts of volcanic resurfacing and liquid water that has gradually faded away into the desert planet of today.

are the lasting legacy of a planet that went to hell and never returned.

The first time I heard of plate tectonics was in the mid-1980s, when I was six years old. My fertile young mind was in awe watching *The Planets*, a British television series presented by Heather Couper, which had the best theme music and managed to bring the worlds of the Solar System to life in a way that no other medium has ever quite done for me since. Through some process of mental osmosis, I soaked up every shred of information from that series. One episode focused on the inner planets, Mercury and Venus, in particular a discussion about what lay below Venus' carbon-dioxide clouds, penetrable only by radar. Svante Arrhenius, the Nobel Prize-winning Swedish physicist/chemist, had postulated in his early twentieth-century book *Destinies of the Stars* that beneath the clouds Venus was a lush swamp-land, but the Soviet Venera probes that landed on Venus put paid to that proposition. Venus is a hell beyond even Dante's imagination, an oppressive world with a surface temperature hot enough to turn a bar of lead into a gooey puddle.

Anyway, radar imagery showed that at least 85 per cent of the sizzling surface is covered in ancient volcanic domes, cones, vents and lava flows, more than any other planet or moon in the Solar System. They are so ancient, in fact, that they all seemed to originate in the same apocalyptic event maybe half a billion years ago. During the episode Heather Couper spoke to a scientist – my memory does not recall who it was – who divulged that this was all down to a lack of plate tectonics. Instead, Venus' seamless crust is like a lid on a pan of simmering water, trapping the heat, but half a billion years ago the pressure told and volcanism burst out all across the planet, the vast lava flows resurfacing large areas.

Suffice it to say, six-year-old me had his mind blown.

Venus was not always this way. Earth and Venus are effectively twins separated at birth. Both are made of rock and are almost identical in size (Venus is 12,104km, 7,500 miles across compared to Earth's 12,742km, 7,900 miles).

Both were formed the same way, coalescing from the same material at the same time, but somewhere along the line, their fates diverged.

Nobody is sure when the two planets went their separate ways. The traditional view is that Venus has always been the way it is, but it is possible that Venus was more Earth-like than Earth itself during the two planets' formative years. Using climate-modelling software, researchers led by Michael Way of NASA's Goddard Space Flight Center have shown that a temperate climate on Venus could have been sustained for billions of years, shielded from the Sun's heat by a thick layer of clouds. Furthermore, Venus could have remained this way until half a billion years ago, when the global volcanic outburst disrupted the planet's climate.

Way's way might have been what happened, or it might not. At present we just don't have enough data to say convincingly one way or another. In many ways, though, it doesn't matter. Because it is 41 million kilometres (25 million miles) closer to the Sun than we are, Venus was always susceptible to the Sun's heat. Whenever it happened, once Venus' climate started to turn, the wet stuff would have been an early casualty. As the atmosphere warmed, perhaps from volcanic greenhouse gases, water molecules in the atmosphere would grow more excited, more energetic and more capable of climbing higher into the ionosphere (the uppermost layer of a planetary atmosphere), where ultraviolet radiation from the Sun could smash the water molecules apart into their constituent hydrogen and oxygen ions. Far below, as the lithosphere and upper mantle experienced a drought that no hosepipe ban could ever hope to alleviate, the water that is essential for lubricating the cogs and gears of plate tectonics at the boundary between the rigid crust and the malleable mantle was severely lacking, meaning that Venus' ability to drive plate tectonics was fatally hampered. Even worse, without water there can be no rain to wash the carbon dioxide from the atmosphere. Venus' volcanoes just continued adding carbon dioxide to the atmosphere to reach the point where, today, we see a

planet with an atmospheric surface pressure approaching 100 times the pressure at sea level on Earth, compressed under the sheer weight of an atmosphere several tens of thousands of times more massive than Earth's breathable envelope. A whopping 96 per cent of that mass is taken up solely by carbon dioxide – a potent greenhouse gas, remember – with just 3 per cent nitrogen and the rest made from trace gases, including sulphur dioxide-laced clouds. That's a serious amount of global warming that Venus has going on – a runaway greenhouse effect that has grown and grown over the aeons.

Venus' story is a compelling one because it highlights the delicate balance of temperature and pressure that exists here on Earth, which permits the evolution of complex life over long stretches of time; it also shows how easy it is for a planet to lose that balance and slip in the direction of Venus. As such, it is inevitable that we're going to find many more worlds around other stars that are hotter and more Venus-like, rather than temperate and Earth-like. When searching for a homeworld for our putative alien cousins, planet-hunters might want to bear this in mind.

Super-earths

Equally common around other stars, it seems, are rocky planets that are more massive than Earth. Our planet is the largest, most massive terrestrial body in the Solar System, but our exoplanet-finding programmes are finding rocky planets out there that are even bigger, with several times the mass of Earth. We call them 'super-earths' and their mass creates higher temperatures within their cores, leading to some interesting complexities.

'There is the caveat in geology that we are trying to figure out whether there could be plate tectonics on super-earths,' says Lisa Kaltenegger. Would a rocky planet five or ten times the mass of Earth be capable of plate tectonics? 'Half of geophysicists say yes, it is going to be easier, and half of them say, "No way."'

Jun Korenaga, who describes himself as a 'freestyle geophysicist' at Yale University, is one of those that says, 'No way.' In fact, he thinks the extra heat might actually cause a big problem. In lieu of any super-earths in our Solar System to study, Korenaga has examined an analogue instead: the early Earth, which was hotter inside in the days following its formation. James Kasting of Penn State University, who acts as a kind of habitable-planet evangelist, an antithesis to the Rare Earthers, picks up the baton from here.

'You'd think that with more heat it would cause everything to move faster, but in Korenaga's model, and in some other models, you get a higher degree of partial melting at the mid-oceanic ridges that makes the very thick oceanic crust,' explains Kasting. 'The hotter mantle beneath dehydrates those thick plates so they become very stiff and then they don't subduct.'

Super-earths are the most common breed of exoplanet found so far; if they really don't have plate tectonics, and if the lack of those shifting continental plates means they are not habitable, then that's a heck of a lot of planets that we can cross off SETI searches. So far, the claim of Rare Earthers that plate tectonics is a sparse phenomenon sounds like it might actually hold some water.

Yet let's not be too hasty. We don't know for sure that super-earths cannot have plate tectonics. Even if they do not, this knowledge helps us set constraints for the existence of plate tectonics in general, meaning the job of planet hunters is now to seek out new worlds in the Galaxy that fit these constraints. In terms of the existence of plate tectonics, we don't want worlds 20 per cent more massive than Earth that are too hot inside, or Mars-sized or smaller planets in which all the heat has leaked out. Given that projections estimate the existence of billions of rocky planets in the Milky Way Galaxy, with perhaps at least a fifth of all Sun-like stars in our Galaxy playing host to Earth-sized worlds in habitable zones, judging by statistical analysis of data from the Kepler Space Telescope, then there should be plenty of worlds that fall within that mass range. As a

percentage, rocky worlds with plate tectonics may not make up the majority of planets; we could just be talking about a few per cent, but a few per cent of a billion still constitutes tens of millions.

There may even be ways around plate tectonics, says Kasting, ever the optimist. 'It's not really clear that you need plate tectonics per se. You need some kind of volcanism to resupply volatiles but you might accomplish the same things with respect to the carbon–silicate cycle without having plate tectonics.' He pauses. 'That said, all in all I'd be much happier if my exoplanet has plate tectonics.'

Venus illustrates that one constraint upon the existence of plate tectonics is the necessity for liquid water, but we also know how vital water is to life as we know it. How many rabid, slathering aliens have invaded Earth in hackneyed science-fiction B-movies to steal both water and women? The implication is that Earth is somehow an oasis in the middle of a desert, a rare world of liquid in a galaxy of baked planets. It's a quaint idea that can be traced back to Percival Lowell's fanciful nineteenth-century notions of Martians building canals in a futile attempt to irrigate a dying red planet, a notion that spurred hundreds of stories about aliens enticed into invading Earth because of our water, starting with H. G. Wells' *The War of the Worlds* and continuing today with Hollywood films such as *Battle: LA*.* It's also hogwash. There's water everywhere, tonnes of the stuff, even where we would least expect to find it, from comets and asteroids to the barren Moon, and in planet-forming discs of gas and dust as well as the most

---

* Other televisual science fiction guilty of the 'water is rare' trope includes the 1980s alien invasion show *V* and a first-season episode of the *Battlestar Galactica* reboot.

distant quasars.* Little surprise – water's constituents, being atoms of hydrogen and oxygen, are among the most plentiful in the Universe.

Water is useful for all kinds of wondrous things. It washes carbon dioxide out of the atmosphere, so without it our planet would have developed into a Venus-like greenhouse long ago. Life needs it, of course, its relevance to us far deeper than quenching our thirst. It's a superb molecular solvent (meaning it's able to dissolve other substances, which comes in handy when transporting them around the body) – the structure of a water molecule (H_2O) is somewhat crooked, with the two hydrogen atoms at an obtuse angle to one another while the oxygen atom between them completes an isosceles triangle if you draw lines joining them. Electrons prefer to gather around the point of the water molecule harbouring the oxygen atom, making the molecule highly polar and hence attractive to other polar molecules such as the complex carbon-bearing molecules that make up us.

'Water has unusual, maybe even unique, properties that make it suitable for life,' explains Chris McKay, an astrobiologist from NASA's Ames Research Center. One of those properties is that water is a very aggressive solvent, he says. 'Life spends a lot of energy protecting itself from dissolution from water, like the Wicked Witch of the West, but life has very cleverly learned to use [water].' For example, a water molecule is described as highly polar, meaning that electrons are not evenly distributed between its chemically-bonded atoms, resulting in slight opposing

---

* A quasar is a galaxy containing a highly active black hole in its centre, surrounded by a bright, hot disc of gas that the black hole is trying to consume. Magnetic fields conspire to eject more charged gas from the centres of quasars than the black hole can ever swallow, driving it away in powerful particle beams that emit large doses of visible light, allowing us to see quasars across the Universe. In the case of water, it has been spotted in the spectrum of light from the quasar APM 08279+5255, the light of which has come from so far away that it has taken 12 billion years to reach us.

electrical charges on opposite sides of the molecule. This powerful polarity is used to create hydrophobic (water-repelling) and hydrophilic (more efficient in water) bonds, by using the very structure of water to help align the molecules. 'If DNA is removed from water, it de-natures and the same with many proteins,' says McKay, 'So water is not just a solvent, it is part of the structural information that life uses in its molecules.'

Suck all the water off the Earth – not just from the oceans and lakes and rivers, but everything in the atmosphere and all the water that has soaked deep underground – and you end up with a sphere of liquid 1,385km (860 miles) wide with a volume of 1,391 million trillion (1.391 × 1021) litres. That's a lot of water, but it's a drop in the ocean compared to what could have been. Computer simulations that recreate the birth of planetary systems within the confines of digital space predict that the delivery of water via comets should commonly lead to worlds that are positively drowning – water-worlds with global oceans hundreds of kilometres deep, leaving little to no land poking out above the waves. Among these worlds is thought to be the small planet TRAPPIST-1d, orbiting a dim red dwarf star 39.5 light years from us. Measurements of its overall density suggest it contains 250 times more water than Earth. Many other worlds are thought to possess similar amounts of water.

Kasting wonders how the carbon–silicate cycle could operate on a world where the ocean is 400km (250 miles) deep. 'It certainly wouldn't operate the same way [as on Earth],' he says. 'Climate regulation wouldn't be the same at all.'

Nevertheless, he thinks that such an ocean world could potentially still be habitable, although one stumbling block would be the development of oxygenic photosynthesis. 'You'd have to think about whether you could build up oxygen on a planet like that because it's not obvious how you would bury the organic carbon [which would otherwise bond to the free oxygen atoms].'

Now, I know what you're thinking. Water may be common, and it's certainly plentiful as both ice and a liquid

on the icy moons of the outer Solar System, such as Jupiter's Europa and Saturn's Enceladus. Yet on the worlds most like Earth – Venus and Mars – it's scarce, to say the least. We know why – the solar wind has stripped those two worlds dry. Earth, however, remains unscathed and habitable. What is happening here?

The answer harks back to the surreal wonderment that I witnessed in the skies above the snowy splendour of northern Iceland. High above the volcanoes and mountain chains, some 80km (50 miles) up, electrons were being accelerated down magnetic field lines that descended onto the magnetic north pole, where they were colliding with molecules of oxygen and nitrogen in the atmosphere, causing the ghostly glow of the Northern Lights. The electrons were being accelerated by the magnetic field carried by the solar wind, which is a high-energy stream of charged particles emanating from the Sun, connecting with Earth's invisible magnetic perimeter. Beyond providing a spectacle for me to gawk at, Earth's magnetic field acts as a buffer between the sanctity of our planet and the harsh environment in space, particularly the strong gusts of the solar wind.

Earth's magnetic field is generated by a powerful dynamo effect in our planet's spinning iron core. The maverick geophysicist Joseph Kirschvink,[*] a professor from Caltech, has indicated in his research that without plate tectonics there would not be a big enough temperature gradient across Earth's core for the convective cells needed to power the dynamo. Contrary to popular belief, Earth's magnetic field is not necessary for blocking harsh space radiation from coming into contact with our fragile organic bodies – Earth's thick atmosphere provides sufficient shielding.

---

[*] Joe Kirschvink was also the first to coin the term 'Snowball Earth' to describe the periods of global ice age that the Earth may have experienced in the distant past, and has performed experiments to see if humans have a sixth 'magnetic' sense, as some animals do.

The magnetic field isn't even necessary to prevent the bulk of our atmosphere from blowing away on the gale-force solar wind, as it appears to have done on Mars – Earth's gravity is strong enough to hold onto the atmosphere, as is Venus' gravity, which is the perfect example because Venus lacks a magnetic field yet still retains a thick gaseous envelope.

Although the atmospheres of Venus and Earth are not alike at all, what they do have in common is that their upper atmospheres – their ionospheres – are dominated by ions of hydrogen and oxygen, which have been split from water molecules by solar ultraviolet radiation. 'This means that water is the easiest [molecule] to escape [into space], so Earth's magnetic field actually protects water,' says Yong Wei of the Max Planck Institute for Solar System Research, who has used the European Space Agency's Mars Express spacecraft to monitor water loss from the ionosphere of Mars, which has low gravity and no magnetic field. 'In other words, without an intrinsic magnetic field, if the planet has high gravity and enough distance from the Sun, it can hold onto a carbon dioxide-enriched atmosphere, but cannot hold onto a water-rich atmosphere.'

Venus' lack of magnetic personality cost it dear, but if Earth and Venus are physically twins, why the magnetic disparity? Planetary magnetic fields require internal dynamos forged from spinning molten iron cores, but it's not the molten core itself that generates the magnetism; rather, it's the convective currents that carry rising bubbles of heat up from the core to the cooler, yet still molten, mantle. As we've seen, these convective currents reach the ceiling of the lithosphere where they begin moving parallel to the crustal plates before breaking through the ocean ridges. Plate tectonics help to cool the mantle, releasing some of this heat and maintaining the temperature differential between core and mantle that drives the convection currents. On Venus, two things may hamper convective currents, one being the lack of plate tectonics – if Venus cannot let off steam on a regular basis, the mantle grows hot and the temperature

differential, upon which the convective currents ride, breaks down. Second is Venus' rather lethargic rotation rate, completing one revolution on its axis in 243 days. This sluggish rate of spin is maintained all the way down to Venus' core, so that convective currents are unable to cause liquid iron in the interior to move in the rotating pattern necessary for a magnetic dynamo.

Venus' rotation on its axis is not only slow, it is backwards (retrograde), which contributes to the angle of its rotation – its axial tilt of 177 degrees – being very stable, for reasons that will shortly become clear. Nobody knows for sure why Venus' rotation has been reversed relative to all the other planets and the Sun, but a leading contender is an ancient, giant impact that violently sent the planet spinning in reverse. The early Earth faced the same catastrophe, the consequences of which have also resulted in axial stability for our planet as they have on Venus, but for a very different reason: the existence of our Moon.

A silvery disc, a friendly face, a constant companion hanging in the sky, our Moon is the first stepping stone to the planets themselves. Twelve brave men have walked boldly on its dusty, cratered and boulder-strewn terrain, while numerous probes have visited it and countless stargazers have cast their eyes on it. Yet many mysteries of the Moon remain unsolved and among them is the question of its origin. Ultimately, the consensus has turned towards one answer: that the Moon coalesced from the molten debris of an impact between the early Earth and a protoplanet named Theia, which was about the size of Mars and was utterly destroyed during the collision 4.45 billion years ago.

Both worlds at the time were still molten from the fires of their birth, allowing them to become differentiated. This means that the heavier elements – iron, nickel – were able to sink through the malleable rock to the core, while the lighter silicate material remained in the outer layers. Hence a picture

emerges, bolstered by computer simulations: Theia, which could have had a mass anywhere between one and five times that of Mars, swung past our young planet, moving at less than 4km (2.5 miles) per second and catching Earth a glancing blow at an angle of 45 degrees. Theia was obliterated, its small iron core absorbed by Earth, which became molten to a depth of 1,000km (620 miles) as a result of the impact. Huge amounts of mantle material were twisted and ripped from the body of Earth, along with the majority of the debris from Theia. The amputated mantle material and chunks of Theia settled into a fiery ring around the battered Earth, dropping globules of lava onto the wounded planet. Within decades the material in the ring was bundled and buffeted and blended into the form of a new body, a phoenix world arising out of the ashes of Theia and tied to Earth: the Moon.

Samples of lunar rocks brought home by the Apollo astronauts, coupled with meteorites that have fallen from the Moon, indicate that the Moon's composition more resembles the lighter material in Earth's mantle, just as is predicted by the collision theory.

At 3,476km (2,160 miles) across, the Moon is large for a natural satellite. Although Ganymede, Io and Callisto around Jupiter, and Titan around Saturn, are larger than the Moon in absolute terms, if comparing the relative sizes of these natural satellites to the planets that they orbit, then the Earth–Moon system has the smallest size difference of them all (although dwarf planet Pluto and its largest moon, Charon, form a similar 'double planet' that has also probably resulted from an ancient collision of bodies). Among the rocky inner planets of our Solar System, the Earth–Moon system is unique, for Mercury and Venus both lack any moons, while the best Mars can offer is two tiny, potato-shaped satellites.

It is the case of Mars that really shows the importance of having a big, sturdy moon; its diminutive natural satellites Phobos and Deimos are no substitute. Mars' rotational axis is currently tilted by 25.2 degrees; very similar in fact to Earth, which is tipped over at an angle of 23.4 degrees. This tilt is the reason we have seasons. However, this similarity between

Earth and Mars is just a coincidence of time. While Earth's tilt remains stable with only small variances, over the course of millions of years Mars wobbles all over the place, with the potential to tip right over onto its side. We can see evidence in the red planet's geological record of this actually happening.* The result is that the wobbles play merry hell with the Martian climate over geological timescales, a situation that is certainly not conducive to the development of complex life, which would face challenges in surviving, or at least developing to any great extent, in a climate so catastrophically unstable.

What's the reason for the wobbles? Born spinning as they accreted material from the primordial protoplanetary disc, Earth and Mars developed equatorial bulges – it's the old analogy of the spinning figure skater feeling her arms moving out in response to a centrifugal force. The bulges are relatively slimline, but they are just wide enough for the gravity of the Sun and other planets to latch onto. The seventeenth-century astronomer Johannes Kepler formulated laws of planetary motion that showed that the orbit of a planet around a star is in the shape of an ellipse, usually with a modest eccentricity (elongation). Think of a planet's elliptical orbit as being slightly squashed, so at certain points in its orbit a planet is closer to its star than at other points. Orbital eccentricities can vary over hundreds of thousands of years, and consequently the gravitational pull from a planet's star also varies with distance. In the Solar System, this variation

---

* This evidence is sedimentary layers in ancient rock faces near the polar regions on Mars. Dark layers were deposited when the atmosphere was dustier, corresponding to periods when Mars was tipped over to a greater extent and the poles received more sunlight, causing the ice caps to melt and vaporise and the atmosphere to thicken by a few per cent. Clearer layers originate from when Mars' obliquity was near zero degrees, the Sun was over the equator and the atmosphere was thinner. The thickness of the clear layers indicates that Mars has rotated at a shallower tilt for greater periods of time than it has at a steep tilt.

leads to gravitational tides that tug on Earth and Mars, causing precession, which is the wandering of a planet's axis of rotation, also known as the polar axis. On Earth this precession makes the identity of the Pole Star switch stars every few thousand years, but on a greater scale it also changes the points in Earth's orbit that dictate when Northern and Southern Hemisphere summers (and winters) take place. Meanwhile, the other planets, in particular giant Jupiter, also exert a torque on Earth and Mars' equatorial bulges, increasing or decreasing the magnitude of each planet's tilt. It's incredible that the planets can exert such influence over each other across such vast distances, but that's what happens.

This trio of factors – eccentricity, the tilt of the axis of rotation (also known as obliquity) and precession – vary

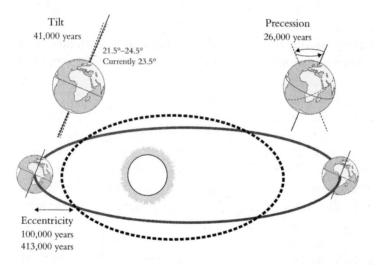

Figure 2: The three major factors that when combined form the Milankovitch cycles that force periodic changes in Earth's climate. These factors are: 1) the change in ellipticity of Earth's orbit as a result of the gravitational influence of the Sun, the Moon and the other planets, resulting in two dominant periods of change in ellipticity approximately every 100,000 and 400,000 years; 2) the change in the angle of Earth's axis of rotation, which varies between 21.5 and 24.5 degrees every 41,000 years; and 3) the precession of Earth's rotation axis, which wobbles much like a spinning top every 26,000 years.

according to their own periodic cycles, which when combined form the Milankovitch cycles that describe Earth's swing in obliquity between 22.1 and 24.5 degrees every 41,000 years. It's a maximum change of only 2.4 degrees in tilt, yet it's sufficient to disrupt the climate enough to force ice ages and inter-glacial periods.

Now, wait. There's a big difference between the periodic variation of Earth's tilt and Mars' chaotic wobbles. Mars' orbit is a bit more eccentric than Earth's, and it's a bit closer to Jupiter, but then again Earth is closer to the Sun. It's not enough to explain why the two planets tip over so differently. Earth's stability has to come from another source.

Countering the torques and tides inflicted on Earth by the Sun and the other planets is the gravitational pull of our Moon, which contains most of the angular momentum[*] in the Earth–Moon system. It stabilises Earth's tilt by speeding up the rate of precession, keeping it different from the oscillation period of Earth's orbit as it's pulled and tugged by the other planets. If they were the same, a resonance would come into play that would see our planet's axial tilt vary by large amounts. Unfortunately, since the red planet does not have a large, sturdy moon to stabilise its rotational axis, it's open season for the Sun and other planets to wreak their worst upon Mars. So, to help maintain a stable planetary climate over millions of years and foster the development of intelligent life on Earth, we needed a big moon. Luckily for us we have ours – and that's not being flippant. It really does seem as though we've fallen into some incredible luck because, by all rights, any random collision between Theia and Earth should not have bequeathed the Moon.

---

[*] All spinning or revolving bodies carry an amount of angular momentum, which is similar to regular momentum that is calculated by the mass of a moving object multiplied by its velocity. Rather than being along a straight line, angular momentum is the momentum around a spinning object's axis of rotation, and is conserved in a system, such as the Earth–Moon system.

The smash that made the Moon

An ancient collision between two planetary mass bodies? That's manna from heaven for theoretical astronomers who love to plug numbers into their complex numerical simulations, powered in many cases by supercomputers. Sure enough, they've done just that with the collision that produced the Moon. What angle could Theia have hit at? At what velocity? How massive was it? How fast were Earth and Theia spinning? They've gleefully tested all the scenarios – it's fun smashing planets together. The trouble is, in most simulated scenarios the debris from the crash is scattered far and wide into space, or it all falls back onto Earth. Only in very precise circumstances – when Theia hits Earth at the right speed relative to our planet (less than 4km or 2.5 miles per second) and at the right angle (45 degrees) – is the debris able to settle into a ring around Earth to form the Moon.

And it gets even more complicated. Today Earth rotates prograde, completing a day every 24 hours, while immediately after the collision a day took just four or five hours to complete. The collision, however, really must have given Earth a dizzying whack because the only rotations prior to the impact that comply with Moon-forming conditions are either a slow prograde rotation, or rotation at any speed in a retrograde direction, like Venus (the opposite direction to Earth's current rotation). Indeed, simulations indicate that the best match is a rapid (say, a few hours) retrograde rotation before the impact – had Earth already been orbiting prograde, it would have flung material too far to have settled into an orbital ring. If we're going to attribute Venus' retrograde rotation to a giant impact, then maybe we have to apply that to early Earth's conceivable retrograde day too, where the young Sun would have risen in the west and set in the east. Earth must have been getting hammered by many collisions in those early days, but the last large impact that formed the Moon wiped away all traces of that early Earth, now a lost world.

Such an exact set of circumstances implies rarity, and we can see why our Moon is unique in the Solar System.

It doesn't bode well for finding large moons around rocky exoplanets either, which is further compounded by the fact that, when we study young planetary systems around other stars, our infrared telescopes have so far failed to detect the telltale signature of dust that would be produced by such Moon-forming collisions. Forget the Rare Earth hypothesis; perhaps it should be renamed 'Rare Moon'.

But – there's always a but – we've wandered into a forest of assumptions and perhaps the situation is not as bleak as it appears. Think of a spinning top; while not an exact comparison, it is a useful analogy. Set the top spinning and it merrily rotates on a point. Soon, though, it starts to flag, its slowing pace permitting it to wobble chaotically, its precession increasing. The message is clear – a rapid rotator remains upright, while a sluggish one wobbles.

Both Earth and Mars are relatively slow rotators, Mars' day lasting 24 hours and 37 minutes. Suppose that instead they rotated in half, or even a third, of that time. French planetary scientist Jacques Laskar has run the numbers and discovered that if Earth had a spin rate of 12 hours or less, it wouldn't even need a Moon to keep its obliquity stable. Yet that's not the whole story, says David Waltham from Royal Holloway, University of London. Waltham is a self-confessed Rare Earther who found himself growing pessimistic for the chances of life beyond Earth after studying the range of possibilities for Earth and her Moon.

'The results I got did seem to show that the Earth–Moon system is quite peculiar,' Waltham explains. He considered all possible rates of rotation and all possible masses of the Moon and found that 99 per cent of scenarios involved a rapidly changing obliquity that can be caused either by the planet spinning too slowly, as Laskar and Kasting describe, or by it spinning too fast and out of control.

'If you look for the conditions that give you the least rapidly changing climate, it is when Earth is precessing not quite slow enough to become chaotic, which is exactly where the Earth–Moon system is, right on the border between chaos and stability, and this is what Jim [Kasting] keeps ignoring,'

says Waltham. 'It's what turned me into a Rare Earther, because it sticks out as being very odd.'

It looks bleak for planets without large moons, but remarkably there are still a few more twists in the tale. Jack Lissauer of NASA's Ames Research Center in northern California has taken simulations of the type run by Laskar and Waltham a stage further, not just by looking at the range of obliquities, but by actually tackling the assumption that a wandering axis is necessarily a 'Bad Thing'. He's discovered that the obliquity of a Moon-less Earth might vary by 15–35 degrees over a million-year period, which admittedly is a lot, but on billion-year timescales the obliquity variation is just 12–40 degrees, which is far smaller than that experienced by diminutive Mars. Researchers at the University of Washington, led by Russell Deitrick, have modelled how the tilts of planets can affect their climates and have found that obliquity variations greater than 35 degrees have the potential to bring about new ice ages – a so-called 'snowball state'. However, Lissauer's simulations suggest that the variations in obliquity of a moon-less planet might not be that large, certainly not on timescales relevant to the development of advanced life, which on Earth has been the 500 million years or so since the Cambrian explosion. Furthermore, Lissauer discovered that if the Earth was rotating in a retrograde fashion just like Venus, then the torques forced by the resonances of the other planets would have little effect.[*] In other words, a retrograde planet does not need a large moon for stability, and some models of planetary formation suggest that at least half of exoplanets could be born spinning backwards. If so many are retrograde, the problem vanishes altogether. So much for Rare Earth!

Even Don Brownlee's concerns are conservative. 'Although it is a factor, if you don't have a massive moon it doesn't necessarily mean that you have a dead planet,' he says. 'It just

---

[*]You can watch a presentation by Jack Lissaur on his research in this area at www.youtube.com/watch?v=cfikWDfJFRM.

means that you would have a different kind of place.' It would be an alien world for alien life – very fitting.

We're almost, but not quite, at the end of the Moon saga. We've assumed that the hypothesis that the Moon was forged from a violent and fiery collision between infant worlds is unassailable, but until recently there has been a niggling worry. A good chunk of the Moon should be made from the wreckage of Theia, but new analysis of titanium and oxygen isotope ratios in Earth and Moon rocks shows they are the same – an impossibility were the Moon constructed largely from Theia, which would have formed in a different location around the Sun, where isotope ratios would have been slightly different. Solutions have been forthcoming – Sarah Stewart-Mukhopadhyay of the Unversity of California, Davis, and the SETI Institute's Matija Cuk have shown that if the young Earth was spinning so fast that a full day lasted a mere two to three hours, as a result of momentum imparted by impacts as our world accreted from the protoplanetary rubble, then the Moon-forming impact would have seen Theia almost completely absorbed by the Earth. However, Theia's angular momentum would have been transferred to Earth, pushing it over the edge so that our planet would be spinning fast enough to actually fling molten material from its equator into orbit, where it would form the Moon. This neatly explains the identical isotopes, but the real twist in the tale is that the Moon has been slowing Earth down all these years through the magic of gravitational tidal resonances; Earth's spin-rate would be vastly different had the collision with Theia never occurred.

'It is possible that, if the Moon-forming impact had not occurred and led to de-spinning the Earth through [tidal] resonances, Earth would be a fast-spinning planet,' Stewart tells me. A fast rotation would mean a stable obliquity, ergo the presence of the Moon was never needed to stabilise our planet; if anything, its existence put Earth's stability at risk. If Stewart and Cuk's model is correct, it changes the game completely, because moon-forming impacts could become more dangerous than the absence of a large moon. It may be a very good thing that we see little evidence of Moon-like

impacts in other burgeoning planetary systems – perhaps it means there are enough stable habitats out there for life to evolve. It's not necessarily a knock-out blow for Rare Earthers, but it is a substantial hit.

Regardless of whether the impact of Theia was required for Earth's habitability or not, we know that impacts of other objects into planets have occurred and will continue to occur, including here on Earth. It turns out that impacts have played a major role in the evolution of not only a habitable environment, but of life itself on our planet. Water was probably delivered here through impacts; debate rages as to whether the water carriers were comets or asteroids. On the other side of the coin, impactors can bring a rain of death rather than water to our world – although there is plenty of evidence that giant reptiles were already on the way out 65 million years ago,[*] the untimely arrival of a 10-kilometre (6-mile) mountain of rock that fell from space and gouged a 180-kilometre (112-mile) hole in what is today Central America certainly didn't help their cause.

Although an asteroid large enough could cause a mass extinction when it slams into planet Earth, it could be doing life a favour in the long run. Any inhabitants incinerated by the impact or who starve to death in the induced artificial winter that follows, as clouds of ash billow threateningly into

---

[*] Principally, mega volcanic flows in the Deccan Traps in India could have been most to blame for the fall of the dinosaurs, releasing noxious greenhouse gases and dust into the atmosphere while piling up volcanic deposits over 3km (almost 2 miles) deep and covering 500,000km^2 (almost 200,000 square miles). Whether the volcanic eruptions or the asteroid impact were the chief instigator is still hotly debated, but Princeton University's Gerta Keller argues that they operated in unison, a one-two killer punch that brought about the mass extinction at the end of the Cretaceous Period.

the sky and block the Sun, probably won't see it that way. However, there is some evidence that every so often a catastrophic event that comes along and kicks over the anthills actually does some good, forcing evolution to find new solutions to challenging environments and move things along, stopping the biosphere from getting stuck in a rut. With the dinosaurs out of the way, little mammals that had burrowed deep underground and taken their food stores with them were able to wait out the harshest of the impact's effects on the planet. When they eventually reclaimed the surface, they happily faced less competition for resources, mates and shelter and were able to thrive, their increased breeding propagating their genes down through the generations where natural selection removed those traits not fit enough to survive in the challenging environment left behind by the catastrophe. Hence *Homo sapiens* eventually rose to dominance. While we've seen in the previous chapter that intelligence does not necessarily have to be a destination for evolution, wiping large parts of the slate clean with extinctions nevertheless gives evolution the opportunity to try new things, with each extinction event affecting the rate of evolution, sometimes speeding it up, other times slowing it down, until the next mass extinction.

So impacts, super-volcanoes and ice ages, while threatening the presence of life itself on Earth, can lead to increased biodiversity in the long run, with the survivors stronger than they were going into the apocalyptic event. Too many of these hazards, however, and nature runs the risk of not even giving life a chance to cope with perilous conditions. The geological record suggests that Earth needs a cooling-off period of some 5 to 10 million years after a cataclysm to get its metaphorical breath back and allow the biosphere time to recover. If sizeable asteroid or comet impacts occur more frequently than that, then the devastated biosphere would not have the opportunity to revive itself.

So what regulates the impact rate and prevents Earth from being constantly battered and bruised? The giant gas planet Jupiter has long been hailed as our saviour, its enormous

gravitational field able to pounce upon and sweep up any interlopers zipping around the Solar System before they get close to Earth. We have felt safer knowing that Jupiter is acting as our guardian with nary an impactor sneaking through. That safety has, however, proved illusory; fate finds Earth in far more danger than we had realised.

Armageddon

Since the 1960s, the major impact hazard to Earth has been considered to be the long-period comets – the dirty snowballs that swoop in from somewhere in the distant Oort Cloud, which is a halo of icy bodies numbering in their trillions, lurking at the outer edge of our Solar System. The long-period comets are on centuries-long treks, or possibly longer, around the Sun. Their large orbital periods mean that many generations can pass on Earth before a given long-period comet will return this way again. We can go about our lives and forget about them, only for our ancestors to rediscover them anew. Until one day – smash! They crash into Earth. Or, at least, that's the fear.

This was backed up in 1994 when the late George Wetherill, a scientist at the Carnegie Institution of Washington, ran computer models that showed Jupiter dictating things in the Solar System. Some comets would be deflected away from us by Jupiter's intervening gravitational field, while others would be swept up by the giant planet itself, plunging deep into its atmosphere and removed from the cosmic shooting gallery that had the inner planets, including Earth, as targets. The most dramatic display of this in action came the same year: a comet, Shoemaker-Levy 9 (the ninth comet discovered jointly by Eugene and Carolyn Shoemaker, and David Levy), had been pulled to pieces by Jupiter's gravitational tides, 21 fragments in all that were on a collision course with the planet that July. The eyes of Earth turned towards Jupiter, the Hubble Space Telescope among others watching as each piece of the comet plunged to its doom in Jupiter's swirling, dense atmosphere, before erupting in brilliant flashes of light,

creating debris clouds rising as plumes into space that left black scars the size of Earth. For many, the pummelling of Jupiter by the cometary fragments represented Wetherill's simulations being acted out in reality – positive proof that Jupiter is the guardian of the inner planets, sweeping up comets and asteroids so they do not strike Earth. Even today Jupiter is seen to gobble up random chunks of space debris – flashes witnessed on Jupiter by amateur astronomers Anthony Wesley and Christopher Go in 2009 and 2010, and by John McKeon and Gerrit Kernbauer in 2016, were the result of asteroids colliding with the planet and being incinerated.

Yet there's always been a discontinuity between that neat picture of Jupiter shielding us from comets and the growing concern about Earth-crossing asteroids so vividly brought to life on the silver screen in the likes of *Deep Impact* and *Armageddon* (although Arthur C. Clarke got there first when depicting an asteroid slamming into Italy at the beginning of his classic 1973 Hugo Award-winning novel *Rendezvous With Rama*, before revisiting the subject 20 years later in his 1993 novel *The Hammer of God*). George Wetherill's simulations don't account for the NEO (Near Earth Object) population, of which we have only recently begun to scrape the surface in terms of a census of potentially dangerous objects. We needed new simulations that fairly reflected our current state of knowledge about the flotsam and jetsam that wander the space lanes.

Enter Jonti Horner and Barrie Jones. Horner, sporting a strong Yorkshire accent from his home town of Wakefield in the West Riding, is one of a new breed of planetary scientists whose career has taken him from Switzerland to Milton Keynes to Queensland. Jones, meanwhile, was a distinguished Professor Emeritus of Astronomy at Milton Keynes' Open University who spent time at Cornell University during the early 1970s, working with the likes of Carl Sagan, before Jones sadly died in 2014. In a series of research papers published between 2008 and 2010, the duo redefined the threat posed by impactors and indeed by Jupiter itself and, in doing so,

they removed one of the barriers to habitability as proclaimed by Rare Earthers.

The secret behind their work was the extra computing power that Wetherill didn't have access to back in 1994. 'The level of detail that Wetherill could go into was limited and that lack of computing power meant he had to make some fairly big approximations and simplifications,' says Horner. 'It was a ground-breaking study, but at the same time it was limited by what he had available.'

Horner and Jones' own simulations hooked up a forest of computers in parallel to vastly increase their processing power, obtaining a degree of accuracy far beyond what Wetherill could achieve. They also fixed that discontinuity, accounting for both NEOs and short-period comets that shadow Earth's orbit and return every five or six years, and the long-period comets that were the sole focus of Wetherill's work. The broader focus brought about the surprising conclusion that, rather than protecting us, Jupiter's gravitational field spends a lot of its time scattering things all over the place, sending many objects our way.

'The main thing that is driving material from the Asteroid Belt into the inner Solar System is something called a secular resonance,' says Horner. Resonances occur when things fall in time with one another – think about pushing your child on a swing at just the right moment in the swing's curving arc to amplify their motion, forcing its curve to be larger and faster. The same thing happens in planetary orbits. The orbits of comets, asteroids, even planets are not entirely steady and, in a secular resonance, the 'wobble' of the orbital plane of two bodies becomes synchronised – similar to the resonant tugs that the other planets have on the obliquities of Earth and Mars' rotational axes. When this happens, the smaller body's wobble, or precession, matches that of the larger body's, in this case Jupiter's. The synched-up asteroid's orbital eccentricity and inclination become vastly amplified, eventually jerking it free from its regular orbit and throwing it through space. In the Solar System this particular resonance falls right on the inner edge of the Asteroid Belt for objects with low orbital

eccentricity, while the location of the resonance moves outwards from the Sun, deeper into the Asteroid Belt, for the more elliptical orbits.

Jupiter is a real Jekyll and Hyde planet. We've witnessed it sucking up its fair share of potential impactors, but equally this resonance allows the giant planet to take pot shots at the inner worlds – Earth among them – with asteroids. So much for being our saviour; but things could have been much worse. To drive home their point, Horner and Jones played god in their various simulations, altering the mass of Jupiter in each one to see what would happen. It turns out that were Jupiter a fifth of its real mass, the resonance would migrate deep into the Belt, smack bang in the middle of all those asteroids, disrupting thousands of them. So while as things stand Jupiter is no saint when it comes to sending asteroids our way, had it been much less massive, things could have been much, much worse – a sobering thought to consider when studying the architectures of exoplanetary systems.

Things don't get much better when considering the short-period comets either. 'It's a balance between Jupiter's ability to put comets, on Earth-crossing orbits from orbits that were initially no danger to Earth, and the ability of Jupiter to remove things from Earth-crossing orbits and throw them out of the Solar System,' says Horner. Jupiter is able to remove short-period comets from the Solar System, but it doesn't do it straight away – its gravitational reach is big, but not that big. A classic example is Lexell's Comet of 1770, which failed to materialise in the sky when it was next predicted to have been visible in 1782 because a close encounter with Jupiter modified its orbit and flung it out of the Solar System. The fact that it did appear in 1770 and perhaps during even earlier, undetected, close encounters illustrates that Jupiter allowed it to have at least one close encounter with our planet. For the short-period comets, Horner and Jones also once again varied the mass of Jupiter and again, at a fifth of its real mass, Jupiter is most dangerous, with the gravitational influence to direct comets towards us, but not strong enough to safely fling them out of the Solar System.

Their simulations did confirm Wetherill's earlier work that Jupiter is efficient at playing goalkeeper against the long-period comets but, even bearing that in mind along with the knowledge that Jupiter will eventually get around to ejecting short-period comets, we shouldn't feel safe. Over 90 per cent of all objects crossing Earth's orbit in a given year are asteroids – the very things Jupiter enjoys scattering in all directions.

So why is this good news for habitability? The Rare Earth argument is that habitable planets require a Jupiter-type world to shield them, but that such worlds might be relatively rare, at least in locations exterior to habitable planets (most of the gaseous exoplanets discovered thus far orbit extremely close to their stars). Furthermore, the most common type of star – the diminutive red dwarfs – are not thought to be capable of forming gas giants like Jupiter. Yet it seems having a Jupiter is no help at all in protecting from impacts, so perhaps those planetary systems that don't have their own Jupiter-like planet aren't missing out. As Dave Waltham says, 'In *Rare Earth* Ward and Brownlee set Jupiter up as a shield, but they didn't really demonstrate it. Horner and Jones put a huge question mark over the idea that Jupiter is essential for habitability. It was almost taken as a given by a lot of people and they've been able to show that actually it's not that simple.'

Let's take another look at Earth. A world of rock with a veneer of water, of which there's plenty to go around but relatively speaking we're not drowning in it. It is oxygenated and comfortably warm, regulated by the shifting masses of plate tectonics. A baleful Moon holds our wobbling hand as we proceed around the Sun under the umbrella of our magnetic field, yet we are always at prey from stalking asteroids. Overall we live on an idyllic world that avoids extremes, so perfect that you couldn't imagine us living anywhere else.

Maybe that's the problem.

Roving through the assorted assertions of the Rare Earth hypothesis, it becomes clear that we're Earth chauvinists: we assume that complex life can only arise on worlds that share Earth's qualities precisely. If SETI adheres to this philosophy then our chances of finding intelligent life in the cosmos automatically narrow. The Rare Earth hypothesis is exactly what it says it is, describing planets exactly like ours and potentially home to life only as we know it. Yet the very definition of 'alien' is 'life as we don't know it' and, if that's the case, perhaps their homeworlds are also habitable planets, just not as we know them. If we accept this scenario as feasible, then suddenly our scope of expectation for habitability blossoms, opening a gamut of possible alien homeworlds. Earth may be rare; habitability may be commonplace.

Jonti Horner perhaps explains it best. 'I don't think there is an absolute "this planet will be habitable, this planet won't be habitable",' he says. 'It's not that clear cut. What I think will be more likely will be a situation where "this planet is a bit more habitable, this one is a bit less habitable".'

For example, Horner points out that a 'water-world' probably wouldn't be affected too much by impacts, while an initially near-airless body may be able to 'grow' an atmosphere thanks to gases released by an increased impact rate that would be devastating to an already habitable planet like Earth. With so many pieces of the jigsaw that can be arranged in a multitude of ways, it becomes clear that planets unlike Earth need not be uninhabitable – they'll just be excitingly different.

This is one of Chris McKay's favourite topics. 'I like to look at what environments we've discovered and ask, are they suitable for life?' says the NASA scientist. Those environments include Titan, which is the icy, methane-drenched largest moon of the gorgeous ringed planet Saturn, as well as the subterranean oceans of Jupiter's satellites Europa and Ganymede, and another of Saturn's moons, Enceladus. Further afield we've discovered searingly hot planets incredibly close to their suns and worlds that always show the same face to their stars as they revolve around dim red dwarfs, including the planetary systems belonging to the stars Proxima Centauri,

Ross 128, LHS 1140, Barnard's Star, Teegarden's Star and
TRAPPIST-1, all of which are a veritable stone's throw away
in cosmic terms. How does McKay set about determining
which alien habitats could be suitable for alien life?

The trick is to challenge our assumptions about what life
needs to work. Water? A methane-based life-form would
scoff at the idea. Oxygen? Life on Earth quite happily got
by without it for over a billion years before the oxygen
catastrophe. A cosy temperature? Extremophiles such as the
Himalayan midge survive down to -18°C (0°F), while on the
flipside the microorganism *Methanopyrus kandleri*, living inside
hot black-smoker fluid at the tectonic boundary of the Central
Indian Ridge beneath the Indian Ocean, continues to exhibit
growth at 122°C, 252°F (such temperatures within water can
be maintained under the high pressures on the sea floor).
Another microbe, known only as 'Strain 121' (*Methanopyrus
kandleri* is Strain 116, referring to the temperature it was
initially discovered at), exists and reproduces happily at
121°C (250°F) and can even survive at 130°C (266°F) – this
truly extreme single-celled archaean also takes in iron oxide
the way we breathe in oxygen. Other extremophiles, which
is what we call those organisms that exist in conditions we
humans would deem extreme, include microbes that thrive
in radioactive environments, or for whom highly acidic or
alkaline habitats are home sweet home. The point being that
what we consider 'habitable' would be like death for these
fantastic creatures, so who are we to judge what is and isn't
habitable?

The world of methane seas

One of the environments that has got McKay particularly
excited is Titan. Here, the Sun is a shallow source of heat
caressing a gelid surface, struggling to permeate a muddy
haze of fine hydrocarbon particles that are gently falling
to the ground like exceedingly small snowflakes, hurried
on their way by flurries of rain as liquid drops of black
oily methane and ethane, in temperatures plumbing depths

beyond a frigid -179°C (-290°F). In such chilly conditions water is inhibited, frozen as hard as rock and yet, even without this thirst-quenching elixir of life, could an alien biochemistry find a way to thrive in this frigid wasteland? Intriguingly, perhaps it could. The depletion of ethane and acetylene (which are both 'hydrocarbon' molecules made only from hydrogen and carbon atoms) on the surface of Titan, compared to the amount of each predicted to be produced from the deconstruction of methane in the upper atmosphere by solar ultraviolet light, is one clue. The other clue is from tentative predictions of the rate of transfer of hydrogen from the atmosphere to the surface, where it appears to vanish, based on assessments of the abundance of hydrogen at different altitudes in Titan's atmosphere. The idea is that these methanogens – as life-forms that produce methane are known – ingest molecular hydrogen, ethane and acetylene, and the chemical reactions between them produce energy, while the methanogens 'breathe' out both methane and carbon dioxide as waste. Back in 2005, McKay actually predicted that life on Titan would operate under these measures, with methane doing the job that water does for life on Earth. Indeed, there are copious lakes filled with methane that NASA's Cassini spacecraft, which toured the Saturnian system between 2004 and 2017, discovered on Titan.

If true it would be an astounding discovery, but McKay himself is cautious about what the results may mean. Perhaps a non-biological agent is reacting with the hydrogen and removing it, or unknown geological activity is present, or somehow the theoretical models are wrong. As the great Carl Sagan was fond of quoting, 'Extraordinary claims require extraordinary evidence.' It's going to take a renewed mission to explore Titan from the surface to determine whether any creatures live there.

Perhaps there are Titan-like worlds around other stars existing in 'methane habitable zones' where temperatures are ripe for liquid methane to flow on the surface, rather than liquid water. Like Venus-type worlds at the other extreme, cold Titan-like planets could be more prevalent than

Earth-like worlds since both forms of planetary climate have no need for the delicate balance of conditions that we have on our own world. In particular, Titan-like exoplanets could find favour in orbit around red dwarf stars, which are effectively the runts of the stellar litter. They may be redder and cooler, smaller and lighter on the cosmic weighing scales, but these meagre stars come packed with some super advantages. First, they are plentiful, so common in fact that there are more red dwarf stars than all the other stars put together in the Universe. Three-quarters of all the stars in the Sun's immediate neighbourhood are red dwarfs and there is no reason why that fraction shouldn't hold up for the full extent of our Milky Way Galaxy. Further afield, ancient elliptical galaxies have been shown to contain 20 times more red dwarfs than our Milky Way. It seems the Universe is adept at forging red dwarf stars from the interstellar elements.

Since they are small and cool stars, red dwarfs have suitably scaled down planetary systems. For instance, the red dwarf Gliese 581, which is located 20.5 light years away and is home to at least three and possibly five planets, has a traditional water-based habitable zone around 19 million kilometres (12 million miles) from the star, and a methane habitable zone between 99 and 248 million kilometres (62 and 154 million miles) – by comparison Earth is 149.6 million kilometres (93 million miles) from our Sun on average, and Titan and Saturn are 1.4 billion kilometres (870 million miles) distant. The red light from a red dwarf is also a factor; Titan's thick, smoggy haze is more transparent at longer, redder wavelengths, and thus more red light can pass through the atmosphere and reach the surface than blue light. The excess light from a red dwarf star would warm the surface of a world in the methane habitable zone, sparking more energetic biochemical processes – the development of hydrocarbons into viable biological products such as proteins, amino acids and possibly even DNA and RNA. However, red dwarf stars are notorious for their violent activity. Studies show that the smallest red dwarfs in particular unleash a frightful torrent of ultraviolet radiation from stellar flares, which could interact with a

planet's upper atmosphere, disassociating hydrocarbon molecules like methane and producing a haze of aerosols that render the atmosphere more opaque to light, cooling the planet. Of course, this might end up being irrelevant – the radiation could potentially sterilise a planet anyway.

To escape the radiation, one option for life would be to go underground. Look at Mars: the red planet contains as much water in its mantle as Earth, and possibly more, enough to fill a global ocean up to a kilometre (3,280ft) deep. This creates hope that a 'deep biosphere' exists underground where temperatures and pressures are suitable for water to be a liquid. This water, rather than being brought by comets or asteroids, probably became trapped inside Mars as it formed and exists not as a subterranean ocean as on Europa or Ganymede, but in pockets, aquifers and hydrated minerals hundreds of kilometres deep. Eriita Jones of the University of South Australia and Charles Lineweaver of the Australian National University in Canberra, along with Jonathan Clarke of the Mars Society Australia, have calculated that the interior of Mars gets hotter with depth at a slower rate than Earth does, an extra five degrees Celsius slower per kilometre (14° Fahrenheit per mile). Consequently, water could remain liquid 310km (193 miles) down beneath the Martian crust, compared to 75km (47 miles) inside Earth.

One could only imagine microbial life existing deep underground on a planet like Mars, which isn't very conducive for SETI. Better prospects lie beneath the surfaces of the icy moons of Jupiter, Saturn and beyond in the outer Solar System, far from the Sun. Europa, one of Jupiter's icy marble-like moons, contains an ocean that extends up to 170km (106 miles) deep with a volume two to three times that of all Earth's oceans combined. Despite Europa being beyond the 'snow line' in the Solar System – the division in the Solar System beyond which water-ice dominates – Europa's interior is kept warm enough for liquid water thanks to gravitational tides from Jupiter flexing Europa's innards, heating the interior. In addition, heat from the radioactive decay of elements such as potassium can keep the interiors of such

moons snug even while the surface remains frozen solid. Europa is certainly not the only moon with an ocean – at least eight others and possibly more have seas beneath a ceiling of ice.[*]

Biosignatures

We're able to send probes to observe these moons close-up and discern the existence of their oceans, but what of planets beyond our Solar System? Detecting a subterranean ocean or biosphere, or hydrogen and acetylene depletion on Titan-like worlds at distances of many light years is practically impossible, at least with our level of telescopic technology. A more reasonable expectation is the ability to detect more prominent biosignatures, such as the presence of oxygen or ozone, large bodies of water or vegetation, sulphur from huge volcanic eruptions, industrial pollution of artificial city lights (technically city lights would be a 'technosignature', a phrase that we will touch upon more in Chapter 8).

Biosignatures tend to fall into one of three categories: changes in how a planet reflects light (albedo), changes that vary with time (suggesting seasonal changes) and the presence of particular atmospheric gases. These gases can be sniffed out with the help of transmission spectroscopy, which splits the light like a prism to reveal all its intrinsic wavelengths. Molecules in the atmospheres of exoplanets absorb particular wavelengths of light from their star, which

---

[*] Dwarf planets Pluto and Eris may also possess subterranean oceans, as may an impressive multitude of outer Solar System moons: Ganymede, Europa and Callisto around Jupiter; Titan, Rhea and Enceladus (which, like Europa, also features explosive geysers of water vapour that erupt into space through fractures in the crust known as 'tiger stripes') around Saturn; Uranus' moons Titania and Oberon; and Neptune's large moon Triton. There could also potentially be dozens or even hundreds of distant denizens of the Kuiper Belt with their own oceans.

causes dark lines to appear in the star's spectra. These lines are at wavelengths characteristic to certain atoms and molecules, allowing scientists to infer the presence of different molecules. Already astronomers have detected the likes of hydrogen, methane, oxygen, water molecules, carbon dioxide, carbon monoxide and sodium in the atmospheres of hot jupiters – gas giants that have migrated ridiculously close in to their parent stars, to within a few million kilometres – while in 2017 an atmosphere was detected around the rocky planet GJ 1132b, which orbits a star 39 light years away and is 1.4 times bigger than Earth. Wind speeds and hot-spots have also been measured on hot jupiters – the weather forecast on exoplanet HD 209458b, which is a gas giant some 150 light years from our Solar System, predicts winds in excess of 10,000km (6,200 miles) per hour.

We can expect discoveries in this field to ramp up during the 2020s. NASA's James Webb Space Telescope will be able to probe the atmospheres of some of the nearest habitable-zone rocky worlds, while the European Space Agency are planning the ARIEL (Atmospheric Remote-sensing Exoplanet Large-survey) mission, which will launch in 2028 specifically to study the atmospheres belonging to a range of different types of world. We're on the edge of a transitional stage in exoplanet research, in which we will move from simply finding these planets to learning more about what they are like.

If we want to determine whether a planet has oceans or continents and whether those continents are barren or teeming with vegetation, we need to push into the realm of direct imaging. This isn't such a new concept any more, with almost two dozen exoplanets imaged as points of light orbiting a star whose glare has been masked to allow the comparatively dim planet to be seen. All of the worlds imaged so far, however, are huge gas giants located at long distances from their stars, mostly very young and still glowing warm from the fires of their birth – hence thermal infrared light is often the chosen wavelength in which to image them, particularly as many stars appear dim at

those wavelengths, reducing the contrast between the two. These exoplanetary snapshots have required the resolving and light-gathering powers of some of the largest observatories in the world, including the 8m (26ft) Very Large Telescope in Chile, the similarly-sized Gemini telescopes in both Chile and Hawaii, and the 10m (33ft) Keck telescopes, which are also in Hawaii. To directly photograph Earth-sized planets in the habitable zone, though, we're going to need bigger telescopes – much bigger. The glare of their stars, the small angular distance between the star and the planet, and the tiny angle that the planet extends to on the sky all make directly imaging an Earth-like world impossible for our current suite of instruments, but next-generation telescopes like the European Southern Observatory's 39m Extremely Large Telescope, or the Thirty Meter Telescope, which is being built in Hawaii, should be capable of doing so. Once such a photograph is taken, it could dramatically alter our perception of Earth's place in the cosmos, just as the first pictures of our planet from space did in the 1960s. We may not be able to see seas or land or forests or deserts, each of which will be too small to resolve, but albedo changes as the planet rotates will inform us indirectly about its surface. Oceans show a change in colour compared to land, while water polarises light and can also act as a mirror to the nearby star, creating bright glints or reflections. Photosynthesising vegetation exhibits sudden rises in reflected light at red wavelengths above 0.7 micrometres, known as the 'red edge', while our first conclusive evidence of a biosphere on an exoplanet could come from forests of large, tree-like plants creating shadows on the ground that would reflect light differently from flat, clear ground. Thus, even if we could only resolve a distant Earth-like world as a 'pale blue dot', potentially we may still be able to determine whether it is home to life of some sort, or not.

The galactic habitable zone

The Kepler Space Telescope has confirmed the discovery of over 2,650 worlds, while NASA's Transiting Exoplanet Survey Satellite (TESS) and the European Space Agency's

PLATO (PLAnetary Transits and Oscillations of stars) mission will find tens of thousands more. Of these, a few hundred may be in the habitable zone of their stars, but there's a larger habitable zone that we must also consider.

It turns out that galaxies also have habitable zones where conditions are more permissive to life. The only trouble is, we can't seem to decide where these galactic habitable zones are. Believe it or not, Earth might not even be in the galactic habitable zone, depending upon whom you talk to. It is still a relatively new concept, first put forward by Ward and Brownlee in *Rare Earth*, along with Guillermo Gonzalez of the University of Washington. They reckoned that the centre of the Galaxy was pretty much a no-go area for life as we know it. The density of stars in the centre means that close encounters, gravitational perturbations and torrents of hard, ionising radiation from conflagrations of exploding supernovae occur far more frequently than in the languid galactic suburbs in which the Sun and planets meander, far from the centre.* However, the galactic centre does sport a wealth of raw materials for planet-building. These 'metals' (astronomer-speak for any elements heavier than hydrogen and helium, ranging from nitrogen, oxygen and carbon to tin, iron and gold) are forged inside stars themselves – true alchemy, scientifically termed 'nucleosynthesis' – by the ferocious fires of nuclear fusion reactions deep within each star's core. These metals are released into space at the end of a star's life. The more stars that are born, live and die in a region of space, the higher that region's metallicity. Consequently, the galactic centre is fertile with these elements,

---

* The nearest star to our Solar System likely to explode as a supernova in the future is red supergiant Betelgeuse, on the shoulder of Orion. Nearing the end of its life, Betelgeuse could explode at any time, be it tomorrow or in the next million years – we just don't know. However, when it does go bang, we'll be safe; Betelgeuse is 640 light years away, placing its harmful radiation out of range of Earth (current estimates suggest that a supernova would have to be up to 300 light years away to threaten mass extinctions).

but abundances decrease with radius from the centre. By the time you reach the galactic rim, it's a metal desert; planets are going to be difficult to build and life is unlikely to form without its raw ingredients. The principle is bolstered by observations of another galaxy, the great grand spiral M101, nicknamed the Pinwheel Galaxy and lying some 27 million light years distant. Observations of the galaxy's cool dust at infrared wavelengths (the preferred radiative output of cool objects) with NASA's Spitzer Space Telescope have discovered that while its centre contains plenty of metals, the metallicity gradient with radius quickly drops off, with the outer regions of the galaxy bereft of organic molecules – a dead zone.

Since the concept was initially mooted, Charles Lineweaver has developed the idea, placing the Milky Way's habitable zone in a narrow ring with an inner radius of 22,800 light years from the centre of the Galaxy, where lies a monstrous, supermassive black hole, and 29,400 light years from the centre on the outer radius. Earth, some 26,000 light years from the black hole, falls nicely into this habitable ring where there are just the right amount of metals and too few supernovae to really spoil things.

What about all those stars in the centre, though? We're talking tens of billions of stars. SETI searches are routinely pointed in the direction of the galactic centre, defying Lineweaver's galactic habitable zone, simply because the presence of more stars is seen to imply greater possibilities for life. There are so many stars, and therefore so many planets, that even though the regular supernovae explosions will sterilise a large proportion of them, many more will be left unscathed on timescales similar to that required on Earth for the evolution of complex life. So here we have the counterpoint to Lineweaver's habitable ring; developed by Michael Gowanlock of Northern Arizona University, and David Patton and Sabine McConnell of Trent University in Ontario, Canada, this alternative view places the optimum location for habitability in a zone immediately outside the galactic core where stellar density and metallicity are the highest (the core itself is a high-energy environment dominated by the

supermassive black hole lurking there; you wouldn't imagine life evolving there, but there may be reasons for life to one day visit this exotic locale, as we'll discover in Chapter 5).

You'll notice something startling. We assume that Earth is a cosmic Garden of Eden, a shining example of the fundamental qualities for planetary habitability that all other worlds must emulate. Instead, in the Gowanlock model, we find that Earth may be far from being located in an ideal piece of galactic real estate. Gowanlock's habitable zone states that the opportunities for terrestrial planets containing the right stuff for complex life diminish as one moves away from the galactic centre. There may be other habitable worlds – even inhabited ones – near us and even further from the centre, but there will be plenty more the closer one moves inwards. If that's right, SETI is doing the correct thing in pointing its telescopes that way.

There are further complications. For example, observations indicate that different supernovae can produce differing amounts of phosphorus, possibly dependent on the mass of the star that is exploding. Phosphorus is an element vital to life, playing an important role in, for example, building the ATP molecule that transports energy between biological cells. Certain areas of the Milky Way Galaxy could be left harbouring greater abundances of phosphorus than other regions, and this too could have a big say in the location of the galactic habitable zone.

Lineweaver's habitable zone narrows the options for SETI; it says, here is a region where life can be found while the rest of the Galaxy is a barren wasteland. In the Gowanlock model, Earth's existence on the periphery of the preferred habitable zone automatically broadens the range of possibilities for SETI, since life could exist not only in our neighbourhood, but among the countless stars closer to the galactic centre. The conflicting arguments are a microcosm of the Rare Earth debate, in which the Rare Earth hypothesis narrows the options for SETI, while the other, more optimistic mindset seeks the potential for life in every nook and cranny of the Galaxy, not just on Earth-like worlds but on alien worlds

far different from the green and blue of Earth. Some of these worlds may be hot, some may be cold; others may be practically within touching distance of their stars, whereas more still could be wandering the depths of space alone, dark but warm underneath a blanket of thick cloud, kept cosy by heat produced from copious amounts of radioactive elements. Dan Hooper and Jason Steffen of the Fermi National Accelerator Laboratory and the University of Nevada, Las Vegas respectively have even proposed that planets in denser regions of invisible dark matter could act as dark matter-particle sinks, accruing large amounts of this mysterious material within them. The dark matter particles, in such close proximity, could start to collide and annihilate each other, releasing heat and keeping the planet snug and potentially habitable.

Fictional worlds

Science fiction also offers a multitude of plausible habitats. Forget planets – what about moons? Both *Return of the Jedi* and *Avatar* featured habitable moons (Endor and Pandora), and David Kipping of the Harvard–Smithsonian Center for Astrophysics has embarked upon a search for 'exomoons' in the data collected by the planet-finding Kepler space telescope. His search has not identified any moons yet, but it has turned up an unusual double planet, wherein a Neptune-sized object orbits around a giant world 10 times more massive than Jupiter. Robert Forward's 1984 novel *The Flight of the Dragonfly* also depicts a binary planet, named Rocheworld, where the atmospheres are actually touching, linking the planets together – a scenario drawn from real-life 'Roche lobes' where 'contact binary' stars experience something similar, being so close to one another that their extended atmospheres touch and their mutual gravity causes their equators to bulge. In the case of Rocheworld, one planet has a bulge of rock as a mountain, and the other a bulge of water.

Then there is Arrakis in Frank Herbert's *Dune*, a particular favourite of Jim Kasting. 'Dune [Arrakis] is an example of a planet that is uninhabitable except for near the poles where the

water depositories are,' he says. 'That's actually been followed up in real life – there's a scientific paper by Yutaka Abe, Kevin Zahnle, Ayako Abe-Ouchi and Norm Sleep where they have made a credible case for the existence of Dune-like planets. That's an example right out of science-fiction literature.'

In a way, Arrakis is similar to Mercury, which rotates three times for every two orbits it makes – in other words, over only two 'days' it has three 'years'. The result is that its hemispheres spend a lot of time pointing towards either the burning incandescence of the Sun or the frigid cold of dark space. However, along the terminator between the two there is a narrow strip of twilight where temperatures are actually quite moderate, and author Kim Stanley Robinson's novel *2312* depicts giant cities on treads moving across Mercury to remain in this habitable strip.* However, 'Mercury is not a direct analogy because Mercury has no atmosphere, unlike Dune,' says Kasting. 'Dune has a climate sort of like Earth's where the poles are cold and the equator is hot, so it would need to have a relatively low obliquity – in fact, zero degrees obliquity might be the best case. Then you just cold trap the water at the poles [*i.e.* in a cold region that condenses water vapour into ice more or less permanently, unless some external heat sources come along to sublimate the ice], even though you don't have as much water as you have on Earth.'

The *Dune* novels are a treasure trove of planets, often imagined to exist around a real star (Arrakis, for example, is described as the third planet around the bright star Canopus in the Southern Hemisphere constellation of Carina, the Keel – part of the great ship Argo Navis that took the Argonauts on their mythical quest for the Golden Fleece). Another world from *Dune* that may be common in reality is Buzzell, whose star isn't explicitly named, but is a water-world populated only with tiny islands amid a global ocean, a bit like Ahch-To, where Luke Skywalker sought refuge in *The Last Jedi*.

---

* For a visual depiction of roving cities on Mercury, see the cover of revered SF artist Chris Foss's book, *Diary of a Space Person* (Paper Tiger, 1990).

All along we have assumed that life, certainly of a complex, intelligent nature, needs a planet on which to evolve. Yet perhaps we're being too anthropocentric. Science fiction reminds us once again of the possibilities – think of the intelligent cloud in astrophysicist Fred Hoyle's novel *The Black Cloud*. Modern-day SF author Stephen Baxter wrote in his 2002 short story 'The We Who Sing' of life-forms formed from 'criss-cross standing waves and solitons', existing in the plasma fields of the early Universe, before the decoupling of matter and radiation at the cusp of the release of the cosmic microwave background radiation, just 379,000 years after the Big Bang.

Alien life is, by its very definition, going to be different from life on Earth and so attributing the necessity of Earth-like environments to its existence seems to ignore its inherent alienness. That said, initially searching for Earth-like habitats with plenty of water and land, and oxygen and plate tectonics, as well as a carbon–silicate cycle, is the most sensible course of action, simply because, whereas we can recognise a habitable planet like Earth, the potential habitability of other environments remains merely hypothetical. Perhaps the discovery of life on Titan or Mars, or in the oceans of Europa or Enceladus, will change that.

Exoplanet discoveries are now helping to direct SETI, with astronomers using radio telescopes to listen for the faint whispers of life. This interplay between exoplanet discoveries and SETI shows that the science of searching for extraterrestrial life is maturing, rather than simply striking out randomly at stars in the night sky.

While what qualifies as a good environment to evolve in may be in the eyes of the beholder, that environment will prove key to how that life evolves. In the preceding chapters we witnessed how altruism and intelligence are at least partly influenced by what is happening in the environment in which life exists, manifest in the form of natural dangers that life faces and in the opportunities that are presented to it. It is impossible to say whether the Rare Earthers are right or not, but Earth-like worlds are not necessarily the only habitable environments possible. Even if Earth-like worlds are rare,

different kinds of habitable environments, such as ocean worlds like Europa, might be common. The simple fact is that we do not fully understand why Earth remains habitable, or how its fertile qualities came about. Even Don Brownlee, co-architect of the Rare Earth 'movement', turned out to be far more optimistic than I expected when I spoke to him.

'Peter [Ward] and I don't look at this in a negative way at all,' he says. 'But this is a huge challenge. There's a kind of dirty little secret in exoplanet work and even SETI, that to really learn about these planets is going to be really tough. For instance, in our Solar System we have had over 30 missions to Mars and spent untold tens of billions of dollars studying it and we still don't have much idea about its history, and Mars is in our backyard, you know? If you think about what we can learn from planets that are tens or hundreds of light years away, it's going to be difficult. The concept of Rare Earth is going to be a really hard nut to crack, but the fantastic thing is that we are now in a situation where, other than imagining how many angels are sitting atop of this pin, we can actually make measurements and discoveries and understand exoplanets and even understand Earth. In the near term, the next few decades, hopefully we can crack that nut.'

Prior to 1992, we knew of no planets beyond our own Solar System. Now we know of thousands, yet while the *Enterprise* was boldly going, while Asimov's Galaxy-spanning empires were being founded, while the Robinson family was lost in space, the planets that they visited were the product of nothing more than fertile imaginations and an expectation bred from Copernicanism that the Sun is just an ordinary star and that if it has planets, then so too must the other stars. In comparison, to now be able to write, over 25 years after the first exoplanets were detected, that we stand on the cusp of an era in which we may be able to tell if there are at least planets that look like Earth, is an awe-inspiring thing.

Interstellar Twitter

When the laser was invented in 1960, it was scoffed at by many scientists who saw lasers as little more than trinkets, not useful for anything.* Fast-forward 20 years, though, and the 'age of lasers' was about to take off as they began to be integrated into all kinds of technology. Today, lasers are so intertwined with our modern lives that we often don't realise we're using them.

So the late 1970s and early 1980s were an exciting time for developing laser applications. At the heart of these developments was Stuart Kingsley. His PhD at University College London had seen him pioneer a breakthrough area of fibre-optic sensing – using lasers to replace traditional sensors in electronics – and in 1981 Battelle Columbus Labs in Ohio had recruited him as their new principal research scientist. Wide-eyed and full of youthful exuberance, he jetted off for the United States.

As part of his job, Kingsley gave presentations on this new technology to fellow scientists and engineers, speaking at such famed locations as the Los Alamos National Labs and the Stanford Research Institute (now known as SRI International). Some members of the audience listening to Kingsley's talks picked up on an intriguing point: that optical sensing could potentially be used for a kind of 'optical SETI' designed to detect alien communications beamed our way using lasers.

Kingsley didn't act on it straight away. However, he'd always had an interest in astronomy and, upon arriving in the United States, he'd joined Carl Sagan's then-fledgling

---

* 'Laser' stands for Light Amplification by Stimulated Emission of Radiation.

Planetary Society and subscribed to their monthly magazine, *The Planetary Report*.

'From time to time they had articles about SETI,' Kingsley reminisces. 'But I became increasingly frustrated that there was never a mention of optical SETI, and I wondered why nobody was talking about it.'

So he sat down and started to crunch the numbers. What kind of laser power would be required to successfully transmit a signal to another star system? How much data could a laser signal carry, and at what rate? How difficult would it be to detect such a signal? His conclusion didn't surprise him. 'It proved my inherent feeling that lasers are far superior to radio waves if you want to have any sort of long-distance communication,' he says.

As I write this in 2018, the most powerful laser in the world – the Shanghai Superintense Ultrafast Laser Facility (SULF) in China – produces 5.2 petawatts (a petawatt is 1,000,000,000,000,000 watts) in pulses lasting just a trillionth of a second. By the time you read this, SULF should have been upgraded to produce 10 petawatts, which would be equivalent to the entire power output of all the power grids in the world, all combined, for a fraction of a second. Scientists around the world, including the Chinese team behind SULF, have their eyes set on an even greater prize of 100-petawatt lasers. Like the 2-petawatt LFEX – Laser for Fast-ignition EXperiments – at Osaka University in Japan, or the 1-petawatt laser system at the National Ignition Facility in California, SULF is primarily focused on nuclear fusion experiments, but in each of their scant nanosecond pulses they shine brighter than the Sun. Clearly, our lasers are already bright enough to be seen across interstellar distances, and we even have photometers today that can easily detect pulses lasting just a billionth of a second.

It's not just power that lasers have in their armoury. They can be highly efficient message bearers, with tighter beams than radio waves and far higher data rates – a terrestrial record is 26 terabits per second (equivalent data to about 1,000 Blu-ray discs) on a single laser beam, achieved by

scientists at the Karlsruhe Institute of Technology in Germany.[*]

Back in the 1980s, laser technology was obviously more primitive. Certainly, lasers were late to the party. Radio had been around since Guglielmo Marconi's experiments in the late nineteenth century, and had benefited from research and development spurred on by two world wars. When lasers were invented by Charles Townes – with the first laser built by Theodore Maiman, based on Townes' design, in 1960 – radio was already a mature technology. It's an ironic coincidence that at the same time that the laser was being invented, a young radio astronomer named Frank Drake conducted the first ever SETI search, called Project Ozma, which used the radio telescope at Green Bank Observatory in West Virginia, USA. Radio was going from strength to strength, while in the meantime Townes was frequently being told by other scientists that lasers, which back in the day could barely muster up a few milliwatts, were a 'solution looking for a problem'.

'We didn't really see what Charlie [Townes] saw, which is that lasers could be very powerful,' says Dan Werthimer, who is a physicist at the University of California, Berkeley, where Townes concluded his career, working until his death in 2015 at the age of 99. 'Charlie suggested optical SETI in the 1960s, very soon after he invented the laser. His office was right next to mine and we had been looking for [signals] in radio waves, but he said, "Dan, look for these lasers instead." I kind of ignored him for a while before finally saying, "Okay, well, there may be something to it, you did get a Nobel Prize after all!" Then people like Stuart Kingsley started trying to do stuff with optical SETI.'

---

[*] Transmission rates of 100 terabits per second have actually been achieved, but this is via a technique known as 'orthogonal frequency division multiplexing', which uses up to 370 different lasers all sent down an optical fibre, rather than a single laser that has a 'frequency comb' of discrete colours of light, as used by the Karlsruhe group.

In Kingsley's own words, his experiments at his Columbus Optical SETI Observatory at his home in Ohio, using just a 254mm-aperture (10in) amateur telescope and a photon detector to search for pulsed nanosecond laser bursts, were a token effort designed more to promote optical SETI rather than being conducted with the expectation of detecting an extraterrestrial signal. At conferences he would hand out floppy discs loaded with information about the potential for optical SETI. Yet Kingsley found himself frequently hitting a brick wall, and that wall was the dominating force in the world of SETI at the time: the founder of Hewlett-Packard Laboratories and Deputy Chief of NASA's SETI project (at least until Richard Bryan got it scrapped), Barney Oliver.

Oliver had been with SETI since the very beginning, visiting Frank Drake in 1960 during his historic Project Ozma search and attending the first-ever SETI conference later that year. When Congress cancelled NASA's project, Oliver came to the rescue of the non-profit SETI Institute, donating millions of dollars to keep the search going. He was a hugely positive influence in SETI, but as Kingsley recalls, for some reason Oliver didn't like optical SETI, favouring radio searches instead.

In 1990 Kingsley was invited to speak at NASA's Ames Research Center. Just before he went to the lectern, Oliver came up to him to give a few words of encouragement, before adding, 'Don't say anything about the superior beaming capabilities of a laser!'

'He wanted to gut my presentation from the start, but I completely ignored him,' says Kingsley. Still, it didn't do much good. Even Charles Townes, who was a friend of Oliver and had all the clout of a Nobel Laureate, couldn't convince him. Says Kingsley, 'Barney Oliver was the gatekeeper and I was told that nobody wanted to go against him, so in the end it came down to politics.'

For the best part of a decade Kingsley ploughed a lone furrow in optical SETI. Since then he has retired and returned to the UK, but after Oliver passed away in 1995, more astronomers took up the mantle of optical SETI. Although

radio SETI is still dominant, optical SETI is finally getting the credit it deserves.

Before we can place the advantages of optical SETI into context, let's probe the pros and cons of its competitor, radio SETI. While Townes and his colleagues and rivals were labouring over patent applications for lasers in the latter years of the 1950s, unbeknown to them the story of radio SETI was beginning 250km (150 miles) north-west from Columbia University, at Cornell University in Ithaca, New York State, where another pioneering scientist was working on a rather different problem: gamma rays.

Philip Morrison was a physicist and astronomer who wanted to know whether gamma rays, which are high-energy, high-frequency photons of electromagnetic radiation, could act as a probe into catastrophic cosmic events such as supernovae.* As Morrison discussed the idea, his colleague Giuseppe Cocconi suggested something very different: that gamma rays could act as an excellent medium for interstellar communication.

They teamed up and examined the problem of interstellar communication in more detail, the end result being their seminal 1959 *Nature* paper, 'Searching for Interstellar Communications'. Their conclusion dismissed gamma rays

---

* Philip Morrison was correct in his hypothesis that gamma rays are produced by violent, energetic events in space. Today NASA's Fermi Space Telescope is the latest in a long line of gamma-ray satellites observing high-energy events and objects such as exploding stars, neutron stars, accreting binary stars and accretion discs around active black holes. Gamma-ray bursts (GRBs) were revealed in 1973 to have been discovered by the top secret Vela series of US satellites, whose job it was to look for the high-energy signature of Soviet nuclear weapons tested in space or in remote corners of the Earth. They are a torrent of gamma rays unleashed by the mighty explosions of the most massive stars.

for the time being and optical lasers hadn't yet been invented, so they focused primarily on radio, specifically the 21cm wavelength (corresponding to a frequency of 1,420MHz) spectral line emitted as radiation from neutral atomic hydrogen in the Universe. Radio communication had seen significant developments in the previous decades and the burgeoning science of radio astronomy was the latest boom area in astrophysics. This was exemplified by the world's largest radio telescope of that era, the 76m (250ft) dish of the Mark I telescope (later renamed the Lovell Telescope after its creator, Bernard Lovell) at Jodrell Bank in Cheshire in the UK, on which construction was completed in 1957.*

'We may presume that the [radio] channel used will be one that places a minimum burden of frequency and angular discrimination on the detector,' wrote Cocconi and Morrison in 1959. 'Moreover, the channel must not be highly attenuated in space or in the Earth's atmosphere.'

By this logic, the choice of the 1,420MHz hydrogen line seems a natural one. Neutral hydrogen is the most common atom in the Universe, with vast clouds of the stuff filling the cosmos and lacing the arms of spiral galaxies. Measuring the Doppler shifts of interstellar gas clouds can tell us about their movement around the galactic centre and thus give us information about the rotation of the Milky Way and, on a larger scale, the rotation of other galaxies. The resulting 'rotation curves' allow astronomers to determine the mass of galaxies (rotational velocity is directly related to the gravitational force, and hence mass). Furthermore, and directly

---

* Ironically, Bernard Lovell initially turned down the chance to partake in SETI when Cocconi and Morrison contacted him. It was only later that Lovell changed his mind about SETI, and the giant dish of the Lovell Telescope was used in the 1990s as part of Project Phoenix (the survey funded by Barney Oliver and his philanthropist friends following the cancellation of NASA's SETI project), to check possible detections made by the Arecibo telescope and confirm them if possible.

relevant to SETI, the radio waves produced by neutral hydrogen atoms pass through space and Earth's atmosphere unhindered. Since astronomical equipment at radio observatories around the world is already set up to explore this frequency, it makes sense to begin the search there.

A year later, having independently arrived at the same conclusion as Morrison and Cocconi, Frank Drake conducted his aforementioned Project Ozma, a search for radio signals originating from two stars, tau Ceti and epsilon Eridani.* Ozma was named after the Princess of Oz in L. Frank Baum's tale of Dorothy's journey to a strange and magical land – a neat analogy to the distant, alien worlds to which SETI listens. Despite Ozma not detecting any extraterrestrial signals (there was one false alarm, when Drake picked up a signal that turned out to be a U2 spy plane at 24,400m [80,000ft], a month before Gary Powers was shot down over Soviet territory) the die was cast: radio communication and SETI jumped into bed together and this particular convergence of technology and science has held firm ever since, for better or worse.

Consequently, practically our entire SETI strategy has its roots in Cocconi and Morrison's famous *Nature* paper. We're putting a great deal of weight on the expectation that they were right.

The water hole

Radio SETI certainly has a number of very strong elements to it. Radio technology has come a long way since 1960 and still has a long way to go in the foreseeable future as it continues to follow Moore's Law, whereby the number of

---

* Science-fiction aficionados may recognise epsilon Eridani from all manner of fiction, but perhaps most notably as the star system in which the space station *Babylon 5* resides, as well as the planet Yellowstone in the novels of Alastair Reynolds. In reality, the discovery of a gas-giant world with one and a half times the mass of Jupiter orbiting the star was announced in 2000.

transistors that can be placed inexpensively on a circuit doubles every 18–24 months. This means that computing power is growing exponentially as long as this trend is sustained, and it's this computing power that drives our ability to analyse potential radio signals (or indeed any other kind of signal) from the stars.

Project Ozma, for instance, involved listening to just two stars on a single-channel receiver tuned to the lone frequency band of 1,420–1,420.4MHz that had been favoured by Morrison and Cocconi. Today, SETI surveys have the computing power and the technology to search hundreds or thousands of stars, some specifically targeted because they are known to harbour planets of their own, across billions of narrow-frequency channels. Still, it would help if we could confine the search parameters somewhat. In the previous chapter we explored habitable zones based upon the existence of liquid water. The search for environments that support running water is central to astrobiology and our quest for alien life, and we might assume that intelligent extraterrestrials will recognise life's need for water. How can this be conveyed in radio astronomy? As Barney Oliver once asked rhetorically, 'Where shall we meet our neighbours? At the water hole where species have always gathered.'

The water hole invokes images of dusty deserts where a menagerie of animals gather at rare oases for vital water. In SETI, it is a range of radio frequencies bracketed by neutral hydrogen (H) at 1,420MHz and hydroxyl (OH) molecules at 1,666MHz (the latter corresponding to a wavelength of 18cm (7in) – the higher the frequency, the lower the wavelength). A single water molecule is formed from two atoms of hydrogen and one atom of oxygen bound together (H_2O), or if you want to think about it another way, a hydrogen atom combined with a hydroxyl molecule – hence the water hole between those two frequencies. Oliver's hope was that the 'galactic water hole' would be attractive to all life-forms that are water-based and that understand the importance of water to life. Of course, this could be parochial thinking. Life as we know it, on Earth, requires water – we humans would die after three

or four days with no water. Our bodies are 70 per cent water. It acts as a solvent, allowing molecules to move around in cells and perform the basic functions of life. Yet, as we've seen in Chapter 3, water may not be the be-all and end-all. Methane-based life is a possibility, and Jonathan Lunine of the University of Arizona suspects that methane-rich worlds like Saturn's moon Titan could be more abundant in the Universe than water-based worlds, especially around dim red dwarf stars. The water hole may mean nothing to life based around methane, and there's no methane-hole equivalent at radio wavelengths (although carbon is a feature predominant in both terrestrial life and hypothetical methane-based life – could carbon, radiating at 492.162GHz and 809.350GHz, have greater universal meaning than the water hole?)[*]

Of course, there's no evidence to confirm that methane-based life exists, or that it could develop the complexity required for intelligent life, but the point is, how much is our own experience of life on Earth clouding our judgement about how extraterrestrial life might try to communicate across the sea of stars? Perhaps the best strategy for radio SETI is to incorporate multiple strategies encapsulating a range of disparate frequencies, keeping the water hole in our sights but considering other possibilities and never assuming that life must always be like us.

Things have developed since 1971, when Oliver coined the water-hole idea. Today, SETI astronomers have multi-channel receivers at their disposal, which dramatically widen the range and number of frequencies that can be listened to, making multiple-strategy SETI that much easier. The image of Jodie Foster in the film *Contact*, headphones over her ears, listening for the arrival of an alien signal in her radio telescope, depicts her character, Ellie Arroway, listening to just one channel. Today the Breakthrough Listen SETI initiative, funded to the tune of $100 million over 10 years by Yuri

---

[*] The SETI League has a very handy list of atoms and molecules and their radio-emission frequencies at www.setileague.org/articles/protectd.htm.

Milner's Breakthrough Foundation, uses instrumentation capable of listening to over 100 million channels simultaneously, handling 130 gigabits (130,000,000,000 bits) of data every second. SETI is well beyond the water hole now, and going off the reservation with explorations of other parts of the radio spectrum, such as the hydrogen frequency multiplied by pi (known colloquially among SETI scientists as the 'PiHi' frequency), based on the logic that aliens may be mathematically inclined and unwilling to transmit interference on the 1,420MHz line that is so important to their radio astronomers, just as it is to ours.* In fact, on Earth, 1,420MHz is a protected frequency for astronomers; why would we expect aliens to transmit at that frequency when we ourselves forbid such transmissions?

Radio-ga-ga

Frequency and bandwidth (the amount of data that can be transmitted) are important characteristics of any radio signal, but there are other properties that can have a dramatic effect on how detectable any alien signal might be. For example, is the transmitter based on a planet, or in space? It makes a big difference, because if it is ground-based then it is rotating with its planet, causing the signal to incur an additional Doppler shift. Think of a police car speeding towards you, lights flashing, siren blaring; as it approaches the sound waves from the siren are compressed to higher frequencies and therefore a higher pitch. Then, as the police car passes, the sound waves that you hear become stretched as the vehicle recedes from your standpoint and the frequency drops to a lower pitch. Since light also behaves as a wave, a transmitter on a spinning planet will incur an increase and decrease in frequency, just like the moving police car, as the transmitter rotates into view on one limb of the planet, starts transiting across the face of the planet's disc towards us, then crosses the

---

* Ironically, a signal on the PiHi frequency was detected in Carl Sagan's novel *Contact*, upon which the Jodie Foster film was based.

planet's central meridian and begins moving away before disappearing behind the other limb. For example, Earth's own rotation adds an extra 3.4cm (just over 1¼ inch) per second squared when observing at 1,420MHz, corresponding to a Doppler shift in frequency of 0.16 hertz per second, which if left uncorrected could cause a signal to wander outside of a single hertz channel in six seconds. The problem is, while we know Earth's rotation and can account for it, we don't know the spin-rate of the transmitter's own planet. If a signal is beamed directly at Earth, then the senders could adjust the transmission to account for the rate of their planet's rotation. However, an omnidirectional beacon that is broadcasting indiscriminately to the Universe in all directions (the idea behind an omnidirectional beacon is that the transmitting civilisation does not know where to find life, so it sends its message in every direction) would be unable to account for the rotation along all lines of sight.

Then there's dispersion. As radio waves propagate through the cosmos, they come into contact with the interstellar medium: a sort of mishmash of gas and dust particles. In particular, the gas is mostly ionised, each gaseous atom shorn of an electron or two by impacts from cosmic rays or ultraviolet light from nearby hot stars. The electrons, once liberated, are left to just float around space aimlessly and pretty much get in the way of things, such as radio transmissions. As a radio signal passes an electron, it shakes the electron at the frequency of the radio wave, in the process giving the electron some of the wave's energy. Longer radio wavelengths (the higher the wavelength, the lower the frequency) are able to shake electrons more vigorously, slowing the speed at which the radio wave propagates. If you have a wide, hence broadband, signal containing many wavelengths, some frequencies will be slowed more than others; the signal becomes dispersed across its frequency range, with lower frequencies lagging behind higher frequencies. The signal then arrives at its destination incomplete. We can try to correct for it by estimating the electron density in the direction of the signal, but that's hardly a perfect science. Instead, it's assumed that aliens will transmit narrowband

signals, which have a much narrower range of wavelengths, meaning that dispersion will remain fairly equal across the frequency range.

There is a possible elegant solution to this. The Director of Research at the SETI Institute in California, Gerry Harp, suggests that simply transmitting the signal, and then a copy of the signal, with a short time delay between the two, will solve the problem.

'Sending two signals with a delay does a complete end-run around the dispersion problem,' he says. Dispersion will apply equally to both signals, but those signals will still correlate with one another and their identical patterns will stand out against the background noise. 'The new trick is that by assuming there are two or more copies of the signal, we have the opportunity to apply correction techniques.'

That's great – but there is a problem. For Harp's technique to work, the signal has to be quite strong for us to autocorrelate the original and the copy with confidence. Imagine searching for a signal on a monitor filled with static. The signal, when it emerges, will appear as an image – maybe a sinusoidal wave (a smooth pattern of oscillation). There are all kinds of twitches in the background, little power surges that look like images, but to be sure you've seen the same sinusoidal wave twice you'd need the signal to be fairly strong to clearly stand out from the background. In SETI, strong signals would be the result of either the transmitter being quite nearby in galactic terms – which is possible, but the odds are against it because there are far more stars, and therefore more chances of finding life, a long way away from us than there are nearby – or of the transmitter being extremely powerful.

Harp gives an example of the transmitter power that would be required. The Allen Telescope Array (ATA) is a network of forty-two 6.1m (20ft) radio telescopes in northern California, managed by SRI International and used primarily for SETI. Seth Shostak likes to describe the ATA as 'frequency nimble', because it is capable of hopping across a wide range of frequencies – 500MHz to 10GHz in 100MHz-wide narrowband chunks – at will. Harp reckons that within a

distance of 100 light years the ATA can detect a transmitter 10 times more powerful than that of the 305m-diameter (1,000ft) Arecibo radio telescope and transmitter in Puerto Rico. However, to be capable of confirming the auto-correlation signal – for the signal to be strong enough to be clearly the same signal and allow autocorrelation – the same transmitter must be either just one light year away, or 10,000 times more powerful at 100 light years. In other words, we would be looking for a transmitter with the power of 100,000 Arecibos at a distance of 100 light years, and this value will only increase with distance.

The Arecibo Myth

To generate enough power to transmit loudly across interstellar space comes at a cost, which leads us to another issue. Because our radio telescopes are limited in size, they can only detect signals that are loud enough to be heard by them. Is ET transmitting loud enough for our telescopes to hear?

There's been an unfortunate tendency for SETI scientists to hand-wave this away. After all, if extraterrestrial civilisations are going to be older and more technologically advanced than we are, then building a transmitter loud enough to be detected across the Galaxy should be no problem for them, whatever the cost. Yet if this were true, you'd think that loud radio beacons would be so obvious that they would have been detected a long time ago. Instead, there's just silence.

The vast distances between the stars are unforgiving. Any kind of electromagnetic transmission depletes with the inverse square law, meaning that at any given point on its journey from the transmitter to us, the strength of a signal is inversely proportional to the square of the distance. For example, the strength of a signal two light years from its transmitter is a quarter of what it was when it was transmitted, whereas at four light years its strength has dropped to one-sixteenth. When we're talking about dozens, hundreds or even thousands of light years, what was once a strong signal quickly becomes a feeble whisper. This is why our TV signals

that are leaking into space, and which were never particularly powerful to begin with, are virtually undetectable by the time they reach a distance of a light year or so from Earth, because their signal-to-noise ratio is so low that they're lost in the background.

The expectation has been that the 'heavy lifting' will fall on the shoulders of the aliens, says Seth Shostak, the Senior Astronomer at the SETI Institute, whom we first met in Chapter 1. An extraterrestrial civilisation will be so advanced, Shostak and others argue, that their transmitters will be more than powerful enough to be detected all across the Galaxy. Not only that, but the transmitters will be switched on constantly, beaming in every direction, for decades, centuries, millennia or even longer. The resources required for such a project would be staggering. What would be the motivation to go to such lengths? It's unlikely to be pure, selfless altruism – as we learned in Chapter 1, that kind of altruism is rarely displayed in nature. Kin altruism or reciprocal altruism seem to be the most likely forces, neither of which seem viable in this context. We're not ET's kin, and thanks to the distances involved the time it takes to send a message and then wait for a reply means reciprocity will be a long time coming – it would take 200 years to receive a message back from a star system 100 light years away, for example; 20,000 years for a reply from a star 10,000 light years away; and so on. 'If they want instant gratification then they're probably not broadcasting to us anyway,' quips Shostak.

Instead, lacking a strong altruistic influence, ET will probably have to contend with at least a degree of frugality in order to transmit messages in the most cost-effective fashion. We do not know what would be considered frugal to an advanced extraterrestrial civilisation, but it seems fair to suggest that at minimum they are using a transmitter at least as powerful as Arecibo, which is our largest transmitter. So let's use this as a baseline, a way to put the discussion into some kind of context.

The funny thing is, nobody can agree on how far away one Arecibo telescope could hear another Arecibo. On his course

at the University of California, Santa Cruz, Frank Drake used to teach that our Arecibo could detect another Arecibo at a distance of at least 25,000 light years – virtually all the way to the centre of our Milky Way Galaxy. H. Paul Shuch of the SETI League – a non-profit, independent, grassroots SETI organisation – has called this into question, declaring it the 'Arecibo Myth' and instead calculating the Arecibo-to-Arecibo range to be in the realm of 10,500 light years – still a heck of a way across the Galaxy, but Shuch's calculations leave Seth Shostak cold.

'I know what Paul did but I didn't understand his calculations,' he says. Shostak himself favours an Arecibo-to-Arecibo range of just 400 light years, far shorter than anything Drake or Shuch have suggested. Scientists working at the Parkes radio observatory in Australia, as part of the Breakthrough Listen project, claim that their 64m (210ft) telescope can detect a transmitter with a power of 20 Arecibos all the way from the galactic centre. Meanwhile James Benford, who is a physicist and expert in microwave communication at Microwave Sciences Inc., is dubious about all of them, citing assumptions made about bandwidth, duration, tracking and power.

This highlights why our assumptions are key. From a certain point of view, Drake and Shuch are correct. Arecibo can, in principle, detect another Arecibo at distances of many thousands of light years, but by necessity the bandwidth of the transmission would be required to be very narrow to avoid dispersion and to concentrate the radio power. So if we assume a large bandwidth for communicating, it just isn't going to work.

In his calculation, Shostak used a bandwidth of one hertz, but Benford claims that it would need to be as low as 0.01 hertz, meaning that the bit rate will be glacial, perhaps one solitary bit per hour. Okay, so maybe that doesn't matter too much – an artificial signal with no message would still be sufficient to be hailed as the most fantastic discovery in human history – but it wouldn't really facilitate the conveyance of much information.

Shostak explains how he arrived at his 400 light years. 'I took what we know to be the detection threshold for Project Phoenix when we were using Arecibo, which is about five janskys,* he says. From here, he worked backwards, calculating how far away another Arecibo, with a transmitter power of one to two megawatts, could be and still produce a signal of five janskys at Earth. 'It is a very trivial but unassailable calculation and what I got was 400 light years.'

Unfortunately, there's more to it than just power and bandwidth, a point that Benford implores us to pay attention to. The receiver and transmitter will be required to track each other precisely for many hours in order to integrate what would have become a very weak signal by the time it reached its destination. Quite apart from having to know exactly where to point the receiver, integrating over enough time would prove impossible for ground-based receivers on rotating planets that will move away from the direction of the transmitter as their planet spins on its axis. Perhaps space-based equipment keeping station in the gravitationally neutral Lagrange points, where the gravity of Earth, the Sun and the Moon balance out, would evade such drawbacks as are incurred by planets with day and night cycles, but given that we have no space-based radio receivers it seems a moot point. Theoretically, Shostak's sums show that detection may be possible across 400 light years, although communication – a subtle difference in concept – would not, according to Benford.

Shostak doesn't think it matters what values people come up with because our detectors are growing larger all the time and soon Arecibo will be outdated, as a receiver at least. 'I don't think this [distance] figure is terribly important, certainly not for the people who practise SETI, because as you plot the size of antennas as a function of time, you see that

---

* A jansky, named after the American radio astronomer Karl Guthe Jansky, is the unit of flux density of energy in the form of electromagnetic radiation coming from an astronomical object. The most powerful radio sources have flux densities of about 100 janskys.

it is a very temporary number to begin with,' he says. 'After all, the Chinese Five-hundred-metre Aperture Spherical Telescope [FAST] has ten times Arecibo's collecting area, so that's an extra factor of three right there.'

This viewpoint somewhat misses the point. It's about expectations. Let's suppose that Frank Drake's optimistic estimation of 10,000 communicating civilisations in our Galaxy is correct.[*] There are in the order of several hundred billion stars in our Galaxy, so Drake's estimate means that we can expect one communicating civilisation per 10 million stars, at least. Now, let's suppose they are using an Arecibo-sized transmitter to signal to us and that we are listening with our real Arecibo. If we expect an Arecibo-sized transmitter to be able to make a point-to-point communication from one side of the Milky Way Galaxy to the other, then that encompasses all those hundreds of billions of stars and we should have high expectations of being able to detect a signal. On the other hand, if we expect the range to be 10,500 light years, as Paul Shuch calculates, then that volume of space only encompasses in the order of 100 million stars and we might be lucky to find 10 transmitting societies. If the worst-case scenario – Shostak's calculation of 400 light years – holds true, then that only covers a volume of space containing around 10,000 stars. Our expectation of finding one of the 10,000 civilisations in that sphere of space, assuming they are using an Arecibo-sized transmitter, would be negligible.

Of course, their transmitter could be more powerful, and we have larger radio telescopes, such as FAST or the Square Kilometre Array (SKA) spread across southern Africa and

---

[*] Drake derived his estimate from his famous eponymous equation, which multiplies seven factors to arrive at the number of communicating civilisations in the Galaxy (see Chapter 2). However, the only factors that we know with any degree of accuracy are the first two or three, and the factors that relate directly to life are completely unknown. Therefore, Drake's estimate of 10,000 communicating civilisations in the Milky Way is nothing more than a guess and should be treated as such.

Australia, which will be ready to come online in the early 2020s and will dramatically extend our range and sensitivity. So although we should think of the Arecibo calculation as a minimum constraint, it does give some indication of how difficult it is to detect a signal, and could go some way to explaining why we haven't found a signal yet.

Benford Beacons

The more powerful the transmitter, the greater the cost it incurs, which brings us back to the discussion of altruism and the motivation to transmit. When we talk about the 'cost' of transmitting, we're not talking about the vagaries of alien economies, but rather the amount of energy consumed by transmitting as a percentage of a civilisation's total energy generation.

One way to reduce the cost of transmitting is to keep the signal brief. 'The way I figure it is their broadcasts have to be short, simply because they are pinging large numbers of planetary systems,' says Shostak. 'That means we have to be prepared for a signal that is very short and intermittent rather than a steady signal always aimed at us because that is very expensive for them.'

This echoes the views of James Benford. Surely, he says, if the brilliant beacons that everyone clamours to find really existed, we would have seen them by now. 'Omnidirectional beacons are big-time and expensive, but easily noticed,' he says. 'But we haven't seen any, so the observational test result is that they don't exist.'

The alternative is Shostak's pings, which Benford, along with his son, NASA scientist Dominic Benford, and his twin brother, science-fiction author Gregory Benford, have quantified as a new form of signal that has taken on the name 'Benford Beacon'. The idea is that we'll receive a signal more akin to Twitter than to *Encyclopaedia Galactica*, blasting a short burst towards us before cycling onto another planetary system, and another and another until it cycles back to us after a given period of unknown duration and we manage to catch

two consecutive bursts. This way, extraterrestrial civilisations will be able to transmit to many worlds, but more importantly they'll be able to do it without breaking the bank.

Quantifying the Benford Beacon hypothesis, the Benford trio take the example of a transient radio burst of unknown origin designated as GCRT J17445-3009, which was discovered in 2002 by the Very Large Array of 27 radio telescopes in Socorro, New Mexico. This burst hailed from the direction of the galactic centre, had a frequency of 330MHz and was re-observed in 2003 and 2004. Its characteristics were unusual – a coherent, nearly 10-minute burst of radiation that has been seen to repeat with a period of 77 minutes. It is very unusual, but before we get too excited, note that there is a host of possible natural explanations, from quirky stellar flares to precessing pulsars, and we detect transient signals like this popping up all over the sky all the time. However, its characteristics are somewhat similar to what we would expect were it artificial in nature, making it the perfect testbed on which to model the properties of an extraterrestrial signal. The Benfords imagined how much power GCRT J17445-3009 would consume were it an extraterrestrial beacon 1,000 light years away beaming in just one direction at a time. They calculated a total power of 4.7×10^9 watts (and a diameter of 22km, 13.7 miles for the transmitter), which is about 100-quadrillionths of the maximum power that an interplanetary civilisation could potentially harness from its star (which is around 10^{26} watts).

Let's imagine that GCRT J17445-3009 wasn't seen to pulse, but was a constant source of radiation, not just in our direction but in every direction simultaneously. It's going to require a little more than 50 pence in the meter, that's for sure. According to the Benfords, a transmitter like this would guzzle energy at a frightening rate, with a total power of 1.4×10^{26} watts. An efficient, interplanetary civilisation harnessing the entire power of its star – perhaps with a Dyson sphere (see Chapter 5) – just to send a message. Such a signal would practically bankrupt them, leaving them with no energy to allow their civilisation to function. This is why cost-optimised

Benford Beacons would be far more attractive to the transmitting civilisation. The concept of transmitting on the cheap could even solve one of SETI's most enduring mysteries: the Wow! signal.

On 15 August 1977, the Ohio State University Radio Observatory (affectionately known as the Big Ear radio telescope) picked up a 72-second burst of radio waves at 1,420MHz, originating from the constellation of Sagittarius, close to the direction of the galactic centre. The observatory was unmanned when the detection was made; a technician was tasked with collecting data printouts from the observatory's IBM 1130 computer every few days and delivering them to Ohio radio astronomer Jerry Ehman for examination.

To the uninitiated the printouts, recorded on that old flimsy printer paper with the perforated edges that you could tear off, look like gibberish, just random columns of letters and numbers. To Ehman, though, as he scrolled down to the printout for 15 August, one particular series of numbers and letters – 6EQUJ5 – represented the most powerful narrowband signal (just 10Hz wide) he had ever seen. The signal strength was measured over 12-second intervals, with signal strengths between zero and nine times the background noise represented by numbers and signal strengths of 10 and above represented by letters. So the '6' indicates a level 6 times greater than the background noise, growing to a value 14 times higher ('E' being the fifth letter of the alphabet, therefore 9+5 = 14), then 26 times higher, growing to 30 times higher, before dropping to 19 and then 5 times the background noise. The signal was so stunningly powerful that Ehman was compelled to circle the collection of six numbers and letters and exclaim with red pen in the margin, 'Wow!', and in doing so enter SETI folklore.

The rise and fade of the mysterious signal was telling. The Big Ear telescope, rather than being the more familiar form

of a radio dish, was instead an unusual-looking rectangle of aluminium placed flat on a grassy field surrounded by trees, with a fixed curved reflector of steel mesh standing at one end of the aluminium ground plate, and a tilting flat reflector at the opposite side that allowed movement in declination (altitude above the horizon) but not across-ways (in what is called right ascension). Instead, the heavens would move for it, celestial targets riding across the sky from east to west as Earth rotated. When plotted on a graph of signal strength against right ascension, the signal intensities produced a perfectly symmetrical curve and the rise and fade was caused by the source of the signal moving into view of the Big Ear and then moving out again. This strongly implied the signal originated from space, because a terrestrial source of interference located close by would instead suddenly flood the receiver rather than act as though it were rotating with the celestial sphere.

There was something else about the rotation, something eerie. The Big Ear's unique design had a dual-horn feed. In other words it had two detectors, separated by almost 1.5m (5ft) along an east–west line, into which signals were focused and fed by the curved reflector. The rate of Earth's rotation meant that radio sources on the celestial sphere would first appear in one horn and then a few minutes later in the other but, as Ehman perused the printout, he could find no sign of the signal in the other horn. As it passed in the void between the horns, the signal had effectively switched itself off.

Of course, the nature of transient signals, whether natural or artificial, means they turn on and off, but it does seem rather surprising that such a powerful signal, which was on when the Big Ear first detected it, would shut down so rapidly and absolutely in the space of a minute or two in the period between the horns. Although it is impossible to know how long the signal had been 'on' prior to Big Ear's detection, the odds are that it wasn't a great deal of time, otherwise shutting down between the horns would be an even more suspicious coincidence.

To this day the Wow! signal remains unexplained. Although he cannot prove it, Jerry Ehman is of the opinion that no explanation, be it interference from satellites, spacecraft, aeroplanes or ground-based transmitters, is as good as the extraterrestrial hypothesis. No terrestrial transmitter should have been broadcasting on the protected 1,420MHz band anyway. Subsequent efforts to recover the Wow! signal have proved futile, with follow-up searches conducted perhaps once or twice a year and lasting no more than a few hours at a time. These have been further hampered by the fact that the IBM 1130 at the Big Ear had not been programmed to identify which horn the signal had been detected in, rendering triangulation of the signal's exact location on the sky imprecise[*] (not knowing which feed horn the signal was detected in could also mean that the signal switched on between horns rather than switched off, but either way it constitutes the same problem).

As much as we would like to believe it, there is no surefire evidence that it was an extraterrestrial signal, only what our hearts tell us. Our heads, on the other hand, warn caution. In SETI, the cardinal rule is that for a signal to be confirmed as real and extraterrestrial in origin, it must be seen to repeat, allowing other radio telescopes to hone in on it. Yet the Wow! signal has all the hallmarks of a Benford Beacon. If real, the amount of time it spends aimed at us (known as the 'dwell time') before moving away to point to another planetary system, and then another, and another, and so on before eventually cycling back around to us would be somewhere above 72 seconds, but probably not too much higher given the coincidence of it shutting off between the horns. Its revisit time is the big unknown – without picking it up again we have no idea what its period of recurrence is. So if the Wow! signal is such a strong candidate, why not just stick a radio

---

[*] The origin of the Wow! signal is somewhere to the north-west of the globular star cluster M55 in Sagittarius, but star maps reveal nothing there of obvious note.

telescope on it constantly and wait for it to show up again? I put this question to Frank Drake when I got my one and only opportunity to speak with him for about 30 seconds at a Royal Society meeting in London in January 2010. His one-word response was succinct, simple and damning of the climate that SETI has existed in for most of its history: 'Money.' According to the Benfords, taking the time to return to the sites of the most interesting 'hi and bye' transients and observe them constantly for year-long periods would amount to more work than all the SETI surveys between 1960 and 2015 combined.*

Further problems abound if we want to detect transient beacons of the Benford variety. Although bursts with dwell times of a few minutes are detectable, when faced with the shortest dwell times of just a few microseconds, things become problematic. 'Current SETI surveys can't detect such pulsed signals well, because [the detectors] integrate over time,' says Jim Benford.

The detectors don't collate data over a continuous span of time, but instead aggregate all the data in a given time-frame into one batch. SETI experiments sum all their data together after about, say, 200 seconds, the reason for this being that a longer integration time improves the signal-to-noise ratio. However, should we detect a Benford Beacon-type signal lasting, say, 0.1 seconds, then when it is mixed in with other data across a 200-second duration, its apparent signal strength will be reduced by a factor of 2,000, quite possibly rendering it invisible.

Normal radio astronomy experiments are able to detect short signals such as Fast Radio Bursts because their receivers cover a broader bandwidth of, for example, 100 kHz. This increases their sensitivity to broadband signals especially, but not to narrowband SETI signals with bandwidths of just a hertz.

---

* In 2016 the 10-year Breakthrough Listen project began, signalling an immense jump in SETI capability and coverage.

Shostak agrees that the detection of cost-optimised beacons seems largely off the menu at present. 'To be honest I think that is still a capability that we want but don't have, because if you see something like that it is very much like the Wow! signal from 1977, seen once and then never seen again,' he says. 'When we get something like that we just throw our hands up and say we don't know what it was.'

Unfortunately that is exactly the situation that the Wow! signal and dozens, perhaps even hundreds of similar detections that never received the same publicity, are stuck in.[*] It is ironic that our SETI experiments are set up to detect not the efficient beacons, which many in the SETI community are now beginning to lean towards as being the most likely type of signal, but rather the expensive and unlikely omnidirectional transmitters with their continuous signals.

All this talk of short, rapid signals sounds distinctly similar to searching for optical flashes from lasers. And so, we come

---

[*] For example, Project META (Megachannel ExtraTerrestrial Assay) was a continuous five-year meridian search of the northern sky for narrowband signals at the water-hole frequency. Partly funded by Steven Spielberg, META was run by Paul Horowitz of Harvard University and Carl Sagan of Cornell University and, in a paper published in 1993 in *The Astrophysical Journal*, they announced the discovery of 37 candidate signals, all located in the galactic plane, that defied explanation but were only ever detected once. META's integrating time was three minutes and, on the second integration, all of the signals had vanished, meaning that they were impossible to confirm. Sagan suggested that if they were real ET signals they could have been microlensed, which means an object passing between us and the transmitter, such as a star or planet, was boosting the signal momentarily with its gravity to within detection range – a small-scale gravitational lens. As the alignment between transmitter, foreground body and ourselves is brief, the gravity boost is short and never repeats. Alternatively, they may fit into the Benford Beacon model.

full circle. By pulsing or modulating lasers, as is done in telecommunications, it is possible to have a high data rate that can pack in much more data than radio bursts. A pulsed laser would certainly guzzle less energy than a continuous, modulated laser, although a continuous laser does a much better job at transmitting data. 'You could send the whole Library of Congress in a minute or two with a continuous laser,' says Werthimer.

Lasers don't suffer from frequency dispersion like radio waves do, although their beams do broaden with distance – just take a laser pointer, shine it at a wall and you will see what I mean: the fuzzy red blob of laser light on the wall is wider than the laser's aperture. Across interstellar distances this can add up, even for the best collimated (tightly-focused) lasers, to everyone's advantage. If the beam has dispersed in width to several hundred million kilometres, it could encapsulate several planets orbiting a star, increasing the chances of it being detected if it is unknown which of the planets harbours life.

Lasers' Achilles heel, however, is distance. While the range of radio signals is limited by the economics of both the transmitting and receiving civilisation, optical SETI has a more nefarious enemy: dust.

It's a problem encountered in astronomy. Our Milky Way Galaxy is laden with dust; not the fluffy clumps you find behind the dresser, but tiny grains, no larger than smoke particles. The dust is made by the stars themselves and spewed out into space on stellar winds, or when those stars die. A supernova (1987A) that exploded in a nearby galaxy called the Large Magellanic Cloud produced enough dust to build 230,000 planets with masses equal to Earth. Supernovae explode in the Milky Way Galaxy on average once or twice per century, so over the aeons an extremely dusty environment has built up.

The dust absorbs and scatters blue light more than red light, meaning that the light from astronomical objects beyond the dust becomes faint and reddened. What holds for light from astronomical objects also holds for laser light. That means that extraterrestrial lasers will be limited in range.

'We're not talking about really long stellar distances,' says Stuart Kingsley. 'Certainly [lasers are limited] to under a thousand light years and possibly just a few hundred light years.'

As with the Arecibo Myth, the limited range of lasers operating in visible wavelengths mean we have to constrain our expectations. If extraterrestrial civilisations are not all that common, the chances that they will be close enough to use visible-wavelength lasers are low.

'Really, by the time you get to a thousand light years, you would lose 90 per cent of all your light,' says Shelley Wright, a Professor of Astronomy at the University of California, San Diego. 'If you're trying to communicate, why would you want to lose all your light?'

Way back in 1999, Wright was an undergraduate student at the University of California, Santa Cruz, when she built a photomultiplier detector that was affixed to the 1m (3.3ft) Nickel Telescope at the famous Lick Observatory on Mount Hamilton in California. That search, led by Frank Drake, surveyed over 5,000 stars for flashes of laser light over a 10-year period. Although the search came to naught, Wright had been heavily influenced by Charles Townes – 'I'm a super-fan of his; he was a remarkable individual and a SETI fan from the start,' she says – and, in the years since, Wright has kept her toe dipped in the SETI waters. Now she's back with a new instrument on the Nickel that has the interstellar dust beat.

Some of astronomers' favourite objects – growing planets, star-bursting galaxies and star-forming nebulae – are smothered with dust. Yet they've found that if one looks with infrared eyes, it is possible to lift the dusty veil and see through it. We know that dust absorbs red light less than blue light, and the absorption becomes even less once you move into the longer wavelength parts of the spectrum, including infrared (and radio). Way back in 1961, just after the invention of the laser, Charles Townes realised that infrared light would be needed to make the Universe transparent to lasers.

Yet in all those years, nobody had attempted optical SETI at infrared wavelengths, so Wright decided that she should be the first. The problem had been that for a long time the

detectors available on the market just weren't sensitive enough for infrared work. It was only when the technology matured that Wright felt she could take it on. Her new instrument would be called NIROSETI: Near InfraRed Optical SETI.

'With infrared light we can look at stars that are thousands of light years away,' she enthuses. Alas, the funding bodies in the United States didn't share her enthusiasm; her applications to NASA and the National Science Foundation to provide funding for NIROSETI were turned down, as has been typical for SETI.

'Then one day, a member of our team was giving a public lecture,' she remembers. 'That night I received a call from him, saying that there was someone sat in the audience at his lecture who had offered to be a private donor for the project. So that's how it happened.'

Earth's water-laden atmosphere is notoriously unforgiving when it comes to infrared, absorbing most infrared wavelengths. At an altitude of 1,283m (4,209ft), the Lick Observatory is above much of the atmospheric water, permitting NIROSETI a window between 0.8 and 1.9 microns through which to view some infrared light. Of course that means it is blind to longer wavelengths that are absorbed by the atmosphere – to see them SETI would have to go into space. Nevertheless, Wright is hoping that ET will have tailored their laser system to emit at wavelengths that can pass through interstellar dust, but won't be absorbed by the atmospheres of water-rich habitable worlds where the inhabitants might be watching for a signal.

What's particularly cool about the NIROSETI project is the way the data it collects is digitised for further perusal later on. We talked about the difficulty of integrating over short timescales for radio SETI, but with NIROSETI the digitised data means that Wright's team can look at the data 'at different time resolutions, so if we want to look for signals lasting 20 nanoseconds, or switch to a millisecond, we can do that quickly, whereas before we were stuck to whatever time rhythm we were recording.'

It's tempting to suggest that what optical SETI needs next is an infrared space mission to take in all those wavelengths

that Earth's atmosphere blocks, but Wright admits that the funding is not there for that. Besides, adds Stuart Kingsley, you may not want to go too deep into the infrared. 'The beam becomes less tight, so it might be that you want to keep nearer to the one micron wavelength, or maybe 1.5 microns, which is the wavelength we use for fibre optics,' he says.

Near-infrared lasers may be the best form of interstellar communication. They penetrate interstellar dust, they are more cost-effective for frugal aliens, their range is great and they don't suffer from the kind of dispersion that radio waves do. This is in complete contrast to the assumption that radio is best, based on the conclusions of a paper that was written before lasers were even invented! That's not to say we shouldn't listen for radio signals, or look for visible wavelength lasers, since they are still valid modes of communication. We need to search for them all equally, rather than allowing one to dominate our search parameters.

Neutrino SETI and hyper-dimensional physics

There is an assumption in our thinking, which is that the development of technology in an extraterrestrial civilisation will match our own. There's no reason why technological extraterrestrials will invent the same technology we have; rather, their technological development will depend on many stimuli, including how they have uniquely evolved to adapt to their environment and the needs of their society. For example, if they have the ability to echolocate like bats or dolphins and rely primarily on this to communicate, then maybe they would develop radar, and hence radio communication, but remain ignorant of the usefulness of lasers.

We're potentially also making the same mistake twice. In the 1960s radio was emphasised over lasers because of the relative states of their respective technological development at the time. Are we ignoring some other communication medium because it is not as developed today as radio and lasers?

'We're a little bit parochial, we look at what humans are doing and say that is what ET is going to be doing,' says Dan

Werthimer. 'Two hundred years ago there weren't lasers or radios and people thought that ET would communicate by making large geometric structures on Mars, and there were ideas for making big bonfires, or using mirrors to reflect sunlight to the Martians, or making big squares or triangles of wheat or water on Earth that could be seen from Mars. Now we think lasers or radio or [some other form of] electromagnetic communication is the best thing, but that is an anthropocentric argument. That's what we know works, but perhaps in a few hundred years' time we'll think differently.'

'I think that as our technology develops, we need to continue to develop our search strategies,' adds Shelley Wright. Are there any prospective technologies on the horizon that one day might make excellent modes of interstellar communication?

Every second of every day, trillions of tiny, ghost-like particles called neutrinos pass through your body at almost the speed of light. They're doing so right now, even as you read this. It's a slightly disconcerting thought, but they are perfectly harmless since they barely ever interact with other matter, so much so that if you suspend your disbelief for a moment and imagine a bar of dense material, let's say lead, 9.5 trillion kilometres thick – a light year – then the bar would only interact with and stop half the neutrinos passing through it.

Despite this, we are able to detect neutrinos, mainly because there are so many of them that we can play the law of averages: if enough neutrinos pass through our detectors, then the probability is that a small number will interact and become detectable. When supernova 1987A exploded in the Large Magellanic Cloud in 1987, it emitted a whopping number of neutrinos, 10^{58} (10 billion trillion trillion trillion trillion). As some of those neutrinos raced towards and then through Earth, our detectors only managed to interact with, and therefore catch, 24 of them. Yet even this small number was significantly above the background average, enough to clearly highlight that an unusual event had occurred.

Artificially generating neutrinos is not difficult – nuclear reactors do just that as a by-product of their reactions. If an extraterrestrial civilisation fired an intense neutrino beam

towards Earth, we might detect an increase in neutrinos similar to supernova 1987A, but big deal: a single burst of neutrinos would tell us nothing, not even that it was artificial. How then to encode that information?

Professor John Learned of the University of Hawaii thinks he's figured it out. He reasons that information could be encoded into the timing of neutrino pulses, like a drawn-out version of Morse code. The senders would want to use higher energy neutrinos to make sure they stand out, but this is going to have a dramatic consequence on their energy costs. If aliens are as frugal as logic dictates they should be, they may baulk at an omnidirectional neutrino beacon that is reaching total power levels similar to the Sun itself (which makes sense when you consider that, in one sense, the Sun is just an omnidirectional neutrino transmitter powered by a giant nuclear reactor). Therefore a directed beam is the more likely option, but even the Benford Beacon paradigm fails us here, because a transient neutrino beam will not contain sufficient information by itself: it may take a year's worth of transmitting and receiving to build up enough neutrino detections to make sense of any encoded message. And why use difficult neutrinos when an infrared laser is easier to produce and detect and does the job just as well?

Maybe in the future neutrino technology will develop to the point that these difficulties disappear. We can keep it on the radar for now. What about other modes of communication? The discovery of gravitational waves in 2016 opened up a new field in which to study the Universe, but detectable gravitational waves are produced by the cataclysmic events of weighty objects: colliding black holes, binary neutron stars in a death spiral, the Big Bang itself, that sort of thing. Hypothetically it may be possible to artificially generate gravitational waves and manipulate them to encode a message, but in order to do so, space-time itself has to be manipulated and that would take not only a knowledge of physics that we currently lack, but also a serious amount of energy and, again, it might be a step too far for frugal aliens when they have far cheaper and more efficient means of communication at hand.

That said, some enterprising civilisation might piggyback their optical or radio signals on a natural gravitational wave burst, knowing that there's a good chance our astronomers will be watching it anyway.

Ultimately we can only search for the things that we have the ability to search for. 'I was on a radio show one time where some guy called up and said, "They might be using hyper-dimensional physics", whatever that is,' comments Shostak wryly. 'Of course we don't know what they're using, but you can't do an experiment with physics you don't have. People can always criticise by saying they probably have physics that allows them faster-than-light communication, but we don't know anything about it so what are we supposed to do, sit here on our hands and say there is nothing to be done? You might as well have told Christopher Columbus to wait for jet aircraft!'

Given all that we have learned, infrared lasers appear to be the best option, yet an inflexible adherence to the gospel of the early years of SETI, with Cocconi, Morrison, Drake and the relative ease with which radio SETI can be conducted, has seen our obsession with radio, especially the 21cm hydrogen line, dominate. Although things are now improving as advancements in processing power enable simultaneous searches across billions of narrow wavebands, our approach to SETI in the past has been too rigid. In many ways, our ideas about interstellar communication tend to race ahead of, if not our technology, then our willingness to use our resources to implement those ideas. We have the scientific and technological tools to build an orbiting observatory designed to look for infrared lasers, a project that would completely refocus the attention of SETI, but we lack the resources in an era when SETI is still often considered a pariah of the sciences and is competing against 'mainstream' science projects that themselves are fighting hard for even a thin slice of the pie in a miserly economic climate. The technology is there, all we need is the will.

'The amazing thing is that if we take our modern technology, and we put our resources into it, using our brightest laser, using the largest telescope, we can outshine

our Sun by thousands of times over thousands of light years,'
says Wright. 'That's a phenomenal realisation that we can do
this now, and we're just in our technological infancy.'

Far from letting the aliens do the heavy lifting, we're
discovering that the burden of interstellar communication
may instead fall on us, the receivers, rather than the transmitters.
We must be careful not to start with a false premise based on
our expectation of how advanced other civilisations could be,
for false expectations could play into the cynics' hands, over
time affecting the enthusiasm of the public for SETI as they
are continually told that the discovery of ET is always 10 years
away, but it never comes because we are over-estimating the
power of the signal. The alternative is that ET is going to have
to be extremely generous with its resources to make this work,
and to devote such a large amount of energy into transmitting
is no longer just a technical problem, but also an issue of
motivations and altruism.

In 50 years of searching the skies we've heard or seen
nothing that can be confirmed as extraterrestrial, but in truth
we have searched so little of the sky it is hardly surprising.
Project Phoenix listened carefully to only 800 Sun-like stars,
most of which are less than 240 light years away, nothing but
a footstep into a Galaxy over 100,000 light years across and
filled with hundreds of billions of stars. Until the advent of
the Breakthrough Listen project in 2016, which has given
SETI a much-needed shot in the arm, all the searches
combined had listened closely and carefully for a prolonged
amount of time to just 1,000 stars. Breakthrough Listen will
survey a million stars, but the odds are against even this vast
increase in coverage: even if there are 10,000 technological
civilisations in our Galaxy, we'd have to search 10 million
stars on average to have a reasonable chance of finding just
one communicating civilisation. It's little wonder SETI has
drawn a blank so far: our search is just beginning.

Galactic Empire

To the young boy, the tree seemed impossibly high. Craning his neck upwards, he considered how it towered into the sky. Maybe, he wondered, as high as the Moon and stars. Canopies of branches with umbrellas of verdant green foliage stretched out over him, higher layers visible through gaps. Moving down the gnarled trunk of the old oak tree, his vision came to rest where the tree sprouted out of the ground, an eruption of bark and branches and leaves. Clumps of grass and patches of powder-dry dirt ringed the trunk as tiny ants hurried to and fro about their daily insect business, utterly dwarfed by this vast, woody, monolithic structure to which nature had given birth. There was no way the ants could comprehend the scale of the tree from their ground-level existence, much less understand what the tree was. To the boy, however, what the tree stood for was very clear: a challenge, like Mount Everest or crossing the Alps, and today was the day he was going to meet that challenge head on.

For a boy of eight years old, this was a formidable moment. He had climbed trees before – smaller, perhaps safer, ascents – but they had not provided the satisfaction of achievement that scaling this ancient tree would; the boy felt an urge from deep within to push the boundaries in front of him. A low-hanging branch provided the starting point and he heaved himself up, struggling to wrap his legs around it. Clinging to the trunk he reached for the next branch, then the next, pushing past leaves and twigs, disturbing a sparrow on an adjacent branch. Before he knew it, he looked down and the grassy ground seemed far below. He was already halfway to the stars.

According to his wife, Freeman Dyson only stopped climbing trees when he was well into his eighties, but in truth he never left the parapet afforded him by those trees since his youth. Little did he realise at the age of eight, as he found solace in the trees away from vindictive teachers and boarding-school bullies, that those trees would come to symbolise the ethos of his subsequent 70-year career as a world-renowned mathematician, physicist and space scientist, graduating at Trinity College Cambridge and, for much of his life, associated with Princeton University in the United States, having worked with such great names in science as Hans Bethe, Richard Feynman and Robert Oppenheimer. For Dyson is of a rare breed, not only the last of the great scientific polymaths of the twentieth century, but also a scientist who has been content to spend much of his time looking towards the future and what science and technology have the potential to make possible.

The perspective that the trees afforded him never left his approach to science. Consider that the oldest tree known in the world today is around 5,060 years old, according to studies of its rings.* A twisted, gnarled and ancient thing, this tree sits in the craggy, dry slopes of the White Mountains of California. Let's put its history into context: it was a mere sapling in the days when the great city of Troy was founded around 3,000 BC. Empires have risen and fallen, kings have come and gone, there have been great moments of progress and equally terrible moments of tragedy, but this tree has sat there through all of it. While no other tree is as old, there are numerous others known to have outlived large swathes of recorded history, their persistence and longevity far greater than any human lifetime.

At Trinity College there is an avenue lined with magnificent elm trees. When Dyson was a student there in the 1940s, the college made the decision to chop them all down, despite the trees having been planted in the eighteenth century. The reason was not careless environmental vandalism to pave the

---

* See the Rocky Mountain Tree Ring Research website, www. rmtrr.org/oldlist.htm.

way for new buildings; given that the trees had grown old and were past their best, new trees were planted in their stead so that future students could also have a row of magnificent elms to enjoy, even if the students at Cambridge in the 1940s would not be able to. Sure enough, if you walk down by the River Cam towards Trinity College today, you will see that these trees have blossomed into a beautiful row of elms.

Planning for the future – the real future, not just next week or next year – takes an appreciation of timescales greater than those within which we typically live our everyday lives. What is true for trees is equally true for how science and technology can be used to influence the future of human civilisation. Nothing illustrates this better than a paper Dyson wrote in 1960 that described a possible technological future for humanity and also, for the first time, scientifically addressed a different means by which to conduct the search for extraterrestrial intelligence other than radio communication.

As papers go, this one is probably not high on Dyson's personal list of favourites – he'd probably consider it a mere footnote in his career – but it is perhaps one of the things he will be best remembered for by the public. The year 1960 had already become a pivotal one in the annals of SETI, being the same 12 months in which Frank Drake launched the first radio search for extraterrestrial signals and the year when Charles Townes invented the laser, which would ultimately pave the way for optical SETI. Radio and lasers were about deliberate communication, but Dyson took a different tack. His insight was not to search for messages, but to search for evidence of technology belonging to advanced extraterrestrial civilisations or, more specifically, how this technology was advancing their rate of energy consumption.

The Earth receives 1.7×10^{17} (170,000 trillion, or 170 quadrillion) watts from the Sun, which is a mere fraction of the total amount of power, 3.8×10^{26} (380 trillion trillion) watts, radiated by the Sun in all directions. Dyson imagined that if an advanced civilisation wished to harness the entire power output of its star, then that civilisation could build a

gigantic swarm of solar collectors – nothing more fancy than solar panels – surrounding the star to absorb all the energy that it radiates. Over time the energy collectors and the devices they were powering would grow hot, just as your computer does when it's plugged in, and to avoid melting, the devices or objects drawing that power would have to radiate some of the excess heat away into space, making them appear to glow dimly in infrared light.

This is the key to finding this technology, reckons Dyson. 'If there is a civilisation that has a very large output of energy, then there has to be some kind of infrared radiation that would be highly visible,' he tells me on the telephone from his office in Princeton, where he still goes to work every day, solving mathematical problems using pencil and paper, despite being in his nineties now.

The concept has become universally known as a 'Dyson sphere', but Dyson wasn't the first to postulate their existence and he baulks at the notion that his name should be ubiquitous with the idea. An enthusiastic reader of science fiction, Dyson originally came across the concept of an array of solar collectors in Olaf Stapledon's 1937 science-fiction novel *Star Maker*, an idea that in turn was influenced somewhat by John Desmond Bernal's 1929 proposal of a habitat in space powered by solar energy, which the great Gerard O'Neill, who was also at Princeton alongside Dyson, riffed on in the seventies when he was busy popularising the notion of orbiting space colonies in his bestselling book, *The High Frontier*.

Dyson never intended his sphere to be a single rigid structure encompassing a star, but rather a spherical swarm of countless solar collectors – a single structure would be prone to drifting and colliding with the star inside it whenever the structure received a nudge, maybe from a large asteroid impact on its surface, or the gravitational push of a passing star.* Nevertheless, to build a cloud of solar-collecting stations that encapsulated

---

* Anders Sandberg of Oxford University answers all the questions that you could possibly have about Dyson spheres at www.aleph.se/Nada/dysonFAQ.html.

the Solar System would require an extraordinary amount of raw material; in his original paper Dyson casually suggests 'disassembling and reassembling Jupiter'. Take a deep breath and just think about that idea for a moment. The audacity behind the proposition is breathtaking; does it tell us more about the scale of Dyson's imagination or more about our own lack of imagination that we respond so disbelievingly to such a notion? Clearly, the ability to take apart a planet is beyond us at present, but perhaps not beyond an advanced extraterrestrial civilisation. Standard logic from futurists suggests that what is possible for advanced technological aliens will also be possible for an advanced future human society and vice versa, as though we are all following the same well-trodden path of science and technology. Dyson himself does not necessarily subscribe to this assumption – 'I certainly don't like that way of reasoning and I've always tried to talk about aliens as aliens and not necessarily resembling us in the least,' he tells me – but there is nothing in the physical laws of nature that says dismantling Jupiter is impossible, for us or for extraterrestrials. A more interesting question, perhaps, is not how we dismantle Jupiter to build a Dyson sphere, but rather how we become a civilisation capable of wielding sufficient power to do so, compared to where we currently are in terms of our technology and our ability to wrap our heads around the scale of such mega-projects. Can we bridge the gap between the present day and what we imagine our distant descendants (or for that matter, extraterrestrial societies) will be capable of, no matter how advanced the technology, or is this chasm just too wide to cross? A good way to at least start down the path that might one day lead us to this awesome future would be to take a leaf out of Freeman Dyson's book and go and climb some trees – especially 'trees' of our own making.

Keith Hjelmstad has a problem with wind.

As a structural engineer at Arizona State University, Hjelmstad is used to thinking big: skyscrapers hundreds of

metres high, for example. Then he met Neal Stephenson, an
encounter that prompted him to realise how everything he
had worked on until now was actually rather small.

Stephenson is a science-fiction author with a specialism
in cyberpunk. The literary tales of this bald, bearded and
physically imposing physicist-turned-author have focused on
the virtual worlds within computing and information
technology. So, like other successful SF authors, he has an idea
or two. A 20km-tall (12-mile) idea, actually, born out of a
challenge. Stephenson wants to develop a concept to build a
tower over 24 times taller than the current record holder, the
828m (2,717ft) Burj Khalifa in Dubai, and launch spacecraft
from the top, in response to criticism that science fiction today
is happy to retread the ground of old ideas but often fears to
step into the fertile land of new ideas. His 'Tall Tower' project
is one hell of a tree to climb, springing from this fertile new
land, but in order to set the process in motion Stephenson
needed someone who knew what they were talking about.
So the call went out, to be answered by Hjelmstad.

'My first reaction was doubt that a 20km tower was
physically possible,' remembers Hjelmstad. 'But I eventually
convinced myself that it is theoretically possible.'

The Tall Tower project has an inherently profound significance far beyond the technological and engineering feats
that will be required to construct it. The tower's construction
would make a statement that humanity means business, that
we can handle challenges bigger than the experiences of our
humdrum everyday lives and that we can look further than
just the next three months. It would symbolise hope in the
future and exemplify that we can think big when we want to.
Most pertinently, the Tall Tower is a step towards a future
where we take to the stars, build Dyson spheres and, perhaps,
come face to face with whoever lurks out there.

We'll have to reach that future by a different route if we
cannot overcome Hjelmstad's wind problem. At 20km in
height, the peak of the tower will find itself in pretty rarefied
air, but at somewhere between 6 and 16km (3.7–10 miles) one
of our atmosphere's jet streams is going to slam into the

tower's mid-section,[*] potentially causing the tower to shake and sway to the point of collapse. Hence the tower needs to be reinforced, but that increases the amount of steel required, adding more weight, and even then it does not necessarily stop the wind problem. More imaginative solutions put forward regard the tower more like an aircraft with wind compensators ranging from aerofoils to, believe it or not, rocket engines that would counteract the sway brought on by the powerful winds. These solutions only currently exist as back-of-the-envelope calculations, but engineers and architects are limited – they do not have the option of building prototypes of 20km-high towers. The only way to learn is by doing.

'This is one reason why progress in infrastructure is incremental,' says Hjelmstad. Just look at the history of skyscrapers. Prior to the advent of modern, 'Chicago-style' skyscrapers, large buildings were made from heavy stone that could not take the weight of too many floors, while the few windows they had were narrow, since anything larger would be structurally unsound. Some Roman apartment-style buildings known as 'insulae' achieved 10 floors, as did some Arabian and Egyptian buildings. Then came the age of steel and the first modern-style skyscraper, the Home Insurance Tower in Chicago in 1885. While it too had only 10 floors, it sported larger windows and rooms and a lighter framework. As the decades progressed, so did skyscraper technology, with ever-lighter infrastructures allowing towers to climb higher and higher into the sky. Each advance was incremental, a dozen or so metres (~40ft) in height

---

[*] The impact of the jet stream will depend upon where the Tall Tower is built. Polar jet streams are found between 7 and 12km (4 and 7 miles) above sea level, meandering as far south as the mid-latitudes of Asia, Europe and North America, while sub-tropical jet streams blow between 10 and 16km (6 and 10 miles), all at velocities faster than 100km (62 miles) per hour and reaching as high as 400km (250 miles) per hour. Other, seasonal, jet streams could also provide a hazard for the Tall Tower.

added each time. The Burj Khalifa is so tall that, if you watch the sunset from the ground floor, you can hop into an express elevator, ascend up 163 floors to the top and watch the sunset all over again three minutes later. It is hoped that the Kingdom Tower in Jeddah will be completed by the year 2020 at a height of 1km (3,280ft, or 0.6 miles), while there have been plentiful discussions about mile-high (1.6km) towers that we could see under construction by the 2020s or 2030s.

Nevertheless, skyscrapers have seen no large single jumps in height throughout all of the history of civilisation. 'We don't spend much time doing twenty-times leaps,' says Hjelmstad. Yet the Tall Tower intends to do just that. 'To embark on something really big that has never been done before would have to include figuring stuff out as we create. This is an engineering problem in itself. Engineers manage risk and this would be a huge risk – but so was going to the Moon.'

Building the Tall Tower is going to take a huge amount of commitment, namely of time, resources and effort. There are other ways into space, of course, and the failure to build a Tall Tower, or a space elevator (another grand project to reel giant cables down from space up which cable cars can travel) will in no way impede our progress, or an alien civilisation's progress, into space. The Tall Tower's significance would be to prove that we can think big and that we're serious about becoming a more ambitious civilisation.

Fortunately, even though progress towards the Tall Tower cannot really be done in increments, a Dyson sphere can be built a piece at a time. It doesn't even have to ever be finished, but the beauty of it is that the more of the Dyson sphere you build, the easier it gets. In fact, building a Dyson sphere is so easy that we have already begun and we just haven't realised it.

The International Space Station generates power thanks to eight solar arrays that transform sunlight into electrical energy, producing 110 kilowatts in total power. Some satellites also use solar panels, while space entrepreneurs

envisage a time in the next few decades when they can mine mineral-rich asteroids for metals that could be used to build vast solar arrays that can generate power to be beamed back to Earth in the form of microwaves. These solar arrays are the first step towards harnessing all the Sun's energy – the first pieces of a Dyson sphere.

This is how Jason Wright, an astronomer from Penn State University who has gone out on a limb to look for Dyson spheres, envisages these enormous power stations could be built. 'It's just a matter of saying, "Look, we need energy and energy is coming from the Sun, so let's go up and get it,"' he says.

The energy collected from our solar arrays will allow us to do more and more on ever-increasing scales. The Dyson sphere will be constructed in increments, just like building a tall tower, but the returns will grow exponentially. If we can do it, then we can reasonably expect Dyson spheres to be within reach of extraterrestrials too, but if ET also shares our preponderance for leaving construction jobs half done, we can expect to find plenty of half-built Dyson 'hemispheres' rather than completed spheres.

Energy for the Information Age

The energy that a Dyson sphere provides gives you a leg up the cosmic tree so that you can accomplish whatever grand project it is that you wish to achieve. Maybe it is complete interplanetary colonisation, or advanced computing, or a hundred other things for which we need the energy to drive the technology to help a civilisation grow and realise its potential. This is at least according to one possible prognosis for what the future may hold for a society that reaches for the stars, be they literal or figurative.

Despite our preponderance for electronic gadgetry, energy use per capita hasn't increased much, because our gadgets have developed in efficiency side by side with their sophistication. Energy usage instead increases along with population – the more people there are, the more gadgets there are and the

greater the net energy consumption is[*] – but the population is predicted to plateau at somewhere between 9 and 11 billion people later this century and will possibly even begin to decline, as it has already in many nations across Europe. So all things being equal, we would have more than enough energy to sustain everyone on Earth. All things are not equal, however, because of the data centres.

We're talking about the vast servers that maintain the Internet, banking systems, telecommunications and online entertainment. These servers consume huge amounts of energy, as much as 2 per cent of our total energy output. Every time you make a query into a search engine, it is using energy somewhere as the servers generate heat during the processing and have to be cooled.

'What intrigues me about data centres is that they are a way to use a lot of energy without us really noticing we are doing it,' says Wright. As we march onwards through the information age, data centres have the potential to rack up arbitrarily high energy use per capita, particular as we chase increasing computations at a faster rate, not to mention the dream of artificial intelligence. The solution, says Wright, is to send the data centres into space, where there is even more solar energy available and where all that emitted heat cannot damage the environment. In fact, the colder the environment, the faster the waste heat from the data centres will dissipate, and therefore the faster the centres can compute – since the outskirts of our Galaxy, or deep into intergalactic space, are the coldest environments in the local Universe, would these attract advanced extraterrestrials with powerful computers?

---

[*] According to data from the International Energy Agency, energy usage per person increased by 10 per cent between 1990 and 2008, but this corresponded with a much larger increase in world population of 27 per cent. See the IEA's 'Worldwide Trends in Energy Use and Efficiency' (2008), www.iea.org/publications/freepublications/publication/Indicators_2008.pdf.

Artificial intelligence and extreme super-computers could be used to solve some of humanity's most serious problems, from combating the climate emergency to fighting disease or making sense of fluctuating economics, and even solving problems we may not have recognised yet. Some futurists are even planning for a potential time, a few decades from now, when artificial intelligence outstrips human brain power and consciousness, and we might even merge with our computer cousins in the Technological Singularity (see Chapter 2). Who could tell what things a super-advanced mind would seek to do with the energy available to it from the Sun?*

We're getting ahead of ourselves – and we'll come back to robotic computer minds before the end of the chapter, I assure you – but understanding terrestrial energy use and where we might be going with it in the future is an important first step towards understanding the energy consumption of an advanced extraterrestrial civilisation and why they might utilise Dyson spheres to generate their energy. Now, maybe here on Earth, the above prognosis is wrong and we will eventually level out in our energy usage and choose a different trajectory for our future development, but as long as there is expansion – as long as we are curious enough to look over yonder and explore new horizons – our energy requirements will need to keep pace with our increasing sphere of influence. From Earth to the Solar System and then to the stars beyond, each new level will bring its own new scales of technology and energy, each vastly larger than the preceding levels.

Believe it or not, such expansion has already been quantified, by the Soviet astrophysicist Nikolai Kardashev in 1963. He

---

* Artificial intelligences that could be incorporated into Dyson spheres are known as either 'Jupiter brains' or 'Matrioshka brains', the latter involving two or more Dyson spheres nested inside each other, like a Russian Matrioshka doll. This arrangement, devised by Robert Bradbury, maximises capacity and energy collected, whereas a straightforward 'Jupiter brain' formed from a single Dyson sphere is maximised for computational speed.

realised that our ability to detect radio signals from other civilisations depended in part on the power of the transmitter being used – as we have already seen in Chapter 4 – and that the available power is in turn dependent upon the amount of energy that a civilisation can expend on such a venture. To this end he devised three different levels of expansion and energy consumption that an advanced civilisation could achieve (Carl Sagan later expanded on this, adding sub-levels on a decimal scale). The first, known as a Kardashev Type I civilisation, describes a society able to use all the energy available to it on its home planet. Human civilisation has not yet reached Type I status – we are somewhere around 0.73 on Sagan's extension to the Kardashev scale. The total energy available to us on Earth is approximately 170,000 trillion (10^{17}) watts.* That said, as we enter the Anthropocene (a proposed geological era happening today in which human activity is the driving force influencing the planet's environment) and see the damage that is being done by our urge to use more and more resources, one might perhaps conclude that a true Kardashev Type I civilisation is unattainable.

If a Type I civilisation is a planetary society, the next step up – Type II – is an interplanetary society. A civilisation at this level doesn't just use the energy available on its home planet; instead it makes use of the entire energy output of its star. Type II civilisations are the societies that build Dyson spheres around their sun. Kardashev defined the energy consumption of a Dyson sphere-building civilisation as 400 trillion trillion (4×10^{26}) watts, equivalent to the Sun's total output. Part of the difficulty in defining the energy consumption of a Type II civilisation (or a Type I, for that matter), at least when it comes to extraterrestrials, is that different stars have different energy outputs. For example, a

---

* Kardashev actually defined the energy consumption of a Type I civilisation as somewhat less, around 4×10^{19} ergs per second, which is equivalent to 4×10^{12} watts, but the principle was the same.

civilisation living in a planetary system orbiting a small, dimmer red dwarf star that has a luminosity less than 10 per cent of the Sun will receive far less stellar energy than we do. This means that it is impossible to standardise the Kardashev scale. If you want to simplify matters, then we can say that a Type I civilisation is mostly bound to a single planet, while a Type II civilisation has explored and colonised its planetary system and wields enough power to build a Dyson sphere. Achieving Type II status is certainly where our mid-term aspirations lie. One could imagine human civilisation reaching this level within millennia – of course, this is not a fait accompli, but it is within reach if we can come together and want it badly enough.

Building Dyson spheres is a method of bootstrapping your way across a galaxy. If ET can build one Dyson sphere, they can build many. The energy wielded by a Type II civilisation is more than sufficient to drive interstellar travel. Voyaging across their galaxies, a Type II civilisation might colonise each star system it comes across, and each new colony starts on the path to become its own Type II civilisation that is independent of its parent, building a Dyson sphere around its star. These colonies can then launch more expeditions and so on, creating a wave of colonisation and Dyson sphere-building until the entire galaxy is filled with Dyson spheres, cloaking all of its stars. A civilisation that can achieve such a galaxy-spanning empire is deemed to be a Type III civilisation, consuming the energy of hundreds of billions of stars in a galaxy, plus the energy output of the mighty black hole at its centre. Kardashev defined the energy consumption of a Type III civilisation as 40 trillion trillion trillion (4×10^{37}) watts, which is a truly colossal amount. Galaxies that have been fully colonised in this manner, with 100 per cent of their starlight transformed into infrared emission, should in theory be far easier to spot than a single Dyson sphere nestled among myriad stars. This has been put to the test with a comprehensive search of 100,000 galaxies and the result of this experiment could be deemed to be utterly profound.

Search for the super-civilisations

By taking advantage of the principle that a Dyson sphere absorbs the light of a star and re-emits some of that energy as thermal infrared radiation, a team of scientists led by Jason Wright have bucked the trend of over half a century. There is a truism that haunts SETI: absence of evidence is not evidence of absence. In other words, the fact that we haven't found any evidence for ET does not prove that they are not out there. However, rather than grow frustrated with an absence of evidence, for the first time in any SETI search, Wright's team have provided evidence of absence.

That news isn't as depressing as it sounds. To understand why, we have to understand the project, called Glimpsing Heat from Alien Technologies (G-HAT for short, or Ĝ for even shorter), which is hunting for infrared excesses around stars and even whole galaxies. Its aim is to sift through the huge library of data from NASA's WISE (Wide-field Infrared Survey Explorer) satellite and to look for anything unusual.

G-HAT is not the first time this has been attempted. Richard Carrigan, a physicist at the Fermi National Accelerator Laboratory in the United States, has scoured the database compiled by the Infrared Astronomical Satellite, or IRAS, which was the first dedicated infrared space mission, launched back in 1983 as a joint effort between the United States, the United Kingdom and the Netherlands. Although it operated for only a year, IRAS was a true pioneer and the precursor to WISE, mapping the infrared Universe at four different wavelengths (specifically, IRAS operated at wavelengths of 12, 25, 60 and 100 microns, which is the lower end of the far-infrared waveband) and discovering around 350,000 new natural sources of infrared radiation, including the first ever detection of planetary systems in the making, in the shape of dust discs around the stars Vega and beta Pictoris. All of the data collected by IRAS was archived and for over 30 years it has provided astronomers, among them Carrigan, with a useful library of information to dip into. Out to a

distance of almost a thousand light years he searched the IRAS library for unidentified objects sporting an infrared signature matching what we might expect from the waste heat emitted by a Dyson sphere. The four different wavelengths that IRAS observed were perfect for the search, corresponding to temperatures between -173 and +326 degrees Celsius (-279 and +619 degrees Fahrenheit), typical of what one might expect a Dyson sphere to be radiating at. Carrigan actually turned up a handful of candidates but, alas, he ultimately concluded that none of these were convincing, favouring instead natural explanations.

G-HAT has continued where Carrigan left off and, in spring 2015, Wright's team released their first round of results. The G-HAT group had selected 100,000 galaxies that had been observed and catalogued by WISE, and searched them for Type III civilisations that had colonised all of the stars in their galaxy with Dyson spheres, causing their galaxy to emit a widespread excess of anomalous infrared light. The results were clear: not a single galaxy displayed any evidence for a Type III civilisation.

Should we be disheartened by this finding? 'This search would have only found the most extreme case of advanced civilisation, one that had spread throughout its entire galaxy and was capturing and harnessing 100 per cent of the starlight for its own purpose,' says Wright. 'Kardashev 3.0 is the most extreme possible case, but there could still be a Kardashev 2.9, where on average only 10 per cent of the starlight is being used, or 2.8 where only 1 per cent of the starlight is being used. So we've ruled out 3.0, but we've not even gotten down to 2.9 yet, much less something smaller like 2.5, which could be very hard [to detect].'

A Kardashev 2.9 or 2.8 civilisation could still encompass wide swathes of a galaxy. Most of the starlight comes from luminous giant stars, but these have a habit of going supernova after a few million years. On the other hand, in Chapter 3 we met the red dwarfs, which are the most common type of star, but also the dimmest. Even if they built Dyson spheres around every red dwarf in a galaxy, but ignored the giant stars, a

civilisation might still only be using a few per cent of a galaxy's starlight.

Our telescopes are not powerful enough to be able to photograph an actual honest-to-god Dyson sphere. At best they will only be able to see a faint star-like object that has an excess of fuzzy infrared radiation. Complicating matters even further is the fact that there are an awful lot of natural phenomena that like to mimic the appearance of Dyson spheres. The nebulous wombs around baby stars are filled with warm, infrared-emitting dust that can look very much like the infrared glow of a Dyson sphere, as can elderly stars that have puffed off their dusty outer layers as they expand and die. One variety of these evolved stars is carbon stars, which have shed their stellar skins to reveal carbon-enriched interiors, some of which prominently shine at a wavelength similar to those looked at by IRAS. Nature, it seems, does not want to make things easy for us.

'If we did find an anomalous object, we wouldn't just jump in and say we've found aliens,' points out Wright. 'Instead we have to assume a natural interpretation that it's dust or something like that and try to figure it out. That's very exciting because we would still be doing astronomy and astrophysics. The road to detection is very long.'

Even so, the result is pretty clear: if Type III civilisations exist, then they are rarer than one in 100,000 galaxies. That's massively significant. The G-HAT result did identify 50 galaxies that had between 50 and 85 per cent of their light dominated by infrared wavelengths, but even these did not remain anomalous for long: supplemental measurements by Michael Garrett of the University of Leiden in the Netherlands, using data collected during surveys by the Very Large Array of radio telescopes in New Mexico, USA, have shown that the radio emission from these best-candidate galaxies matches what would be expected if the infrared emission is from interstellar dust warmed by nearby concentrations of star formation. So really, we must always try to adhere to Occam's razor – that the simplest answer is likely to be the real answer – before jumping to extreme conclusions. There

are plenty of natural phenomena out there that even a Type III civilisation could be mistaken for, such as starburst galaxies that are shrouded in a veil of dust produced by frenetic cycles of star-birth and star-death.

Maybe building a Dyson sphere is more difficult than we anticipate, so much so that no civilisation can complete one. The futurist Robert Bradbury calculated that to mechanically disassemble a planet like Jupiter by overcoming its gravitational binding energy would require 169 years-worth of the entire energy output of the Sun. It gets even worse, because solar cells are not 100 per cent efficient, which extends the energy requirements to 563 years-worth of the Sun's total output. And, since you need a Dyson sphere in the first place, how can you ever gather that much energy? It starts to become a chicken-and-egg scenario: you need to disassemble Jupiter to build a Dyson sphere, but you can't disassemble Jupiter without the energy provided by a Dyson sphere.

Bradbury pointed out that there are ways around this, harking back to Jason Wright's insight that we are, in a way, already beginning the building of a Dyson sphere. The process can be bootstrapped: cover the surface of Mercury in solar cells and use the energy collected there to start to tear Jupiter apart, and with that material take small steps in constructing a Dyson sphere. Each small step will result in more energy collected, meaning more energy with which to dig into Jupiter and hence more material to make a Dyson sphere. Maybe the really insurmountable obstacle then is not energy, or technological prowess, or even timescales per se; rather, the real obstacle might be patience, because any civilisation is going to need a lot of it to see through to the end any project as long-term and large-scale as building a Dyson sphere. We're talking many millennia, but all of a sudden it raises the spectre of partially built Dyson spheres littering the galaxy.

Of course, we're inferring human-like impatience driven by human-like lifespans. Maybe if advanced extraterrestrials can live for many centuries, or are even immortal, such projects become relatively simple. But long timescales also

increase the risk factor, providing more time for things to go wrong: war, disease, natural or technological disasters, or some other risk we have never even considered in our naivety. As we shall see in Chapter 6, there are many threats out there that could end civilisation in a jiffy and suddenly call an unscheduled halt to Dyson sphere construction.

When things do go wrong, they only become catastrophic if everyone is in the same place – rather like how rolling a grenade into a room hosting a global SETI convention with all the field's top scientists is quickly going to have a negative effect on future SETI research. The same holds for humanity in a larger context. If something bad happens on Earth – and take your pick of apocalyptic end-of-the-world scenarios – then our colonies on the Moon, Mars and alpha Centauri will be able to carry on in our stead.

Of course, no such colonies currently exist. Humanity, worryingly, has all its eggs in one basket at the moment and, as we shall see in the next chapter, this is when civilisations are at their most vulnerable. Space travel – first interplanetary and then interstellar – will start to move some of those eggs around. Interstellar travel – flying to other stars – is also a key concept that would be implicit in the development of Type III civilisations. You can't colonise a galaxy sitting at home, after all, but is interstellar travel even feasible?

'If you believe that building a Dyson sphere is much easier than interstellar travel, then you might have a Type II civilisation that never spreads to other stars,' says Wright. 'But if you think that interstellar travel is an easier problem and just a trivial addition to a Type II civilisation, then you don't have to imagine a vastly different scale of technology to get to a Type III because a Type III civilisation is just a lot of Type IIs replicated across the Galaxy.'

One fault of science fiction is its habit of making interstellar travel seem too easy. In E. E. 'Doc' Smith's famous pulp classic *Lensman* series, if the heroes needed a new, faster,

more powerful vessel to defeat their enemies, they would simply pull out their slide rule, scribble down a few equations and then six weeks later a whole new breed of starship would roll off the production line.* Meanwhile, from watching *Star Trek*, you might be forgiven for thinking that travelling to nearby stars is no more difficult than taking a drive to the next town along the motorway. Of course, *Star Trek* would be pretty dull if it took the *Enterprise* years to boldly go anywhere.

Obviously these fictional tales are of fantasy and the fantastical. In the real world, even a vessel moving at 10 per cent of the speed of light would take almost half a century to reach alpha Centauri, which is the nearest star system to our Sun, 4.3 light years away (the average distance between stars, at least in our neck of the woods in the Galaxy, is around four light years). Ten per cent of the speed of light is feasible, at least assuming certain criteria, such as the development of efficient nuclear fusion energy to drive a starship. Even so, if a civilisation, whether it be human or alien, goes to the stars, then those space voyagers had better be ready for the long haul. Even travelling at the speed of light it would take 100,000 years without stopping to cross the Milky Way Galaxy.

Colonising the Galaxy is not something we could plan to do tomorrow, yet like Jason Wright's depiction of a ramshackle Dyson sphere, the colonisation of the Galaxy could ultimately happen by default.

Latecomers to the Galaxy we may be, but we are already an interstellar civilisation of sorts. Two robotic emissaries, Voyagers 1 and 2, have so far breached the Sun's outer magnetic

---

* E. E. 'Doc' Smith's *Lensman* stories were written between 1936 and 1960 and had a huge influence on the 'space opera' genre. The unrealistic development of starships isn't a predilection of just 'Doc' Smith's work, either – for a more recent example, Peter F. Hamilton's *Judas Unchained* from 2005 touched on similar ground in the engineering of starships (the story also included a Dyson sphere, of sorts).

boundary,* which is about 18 billion kilometres (11 million miles) away, and they are now travelling at 17 kilometres per second (relative to the Sun) through the interstellar medium, which is the gas and radiation that is to be found in the vast stretches of space between the stars.† Both spacecraft were launched in 1977; Voyager 1 took 35 years to reach the boundary in August 2012, while Voyager 2, which took a more indirect route by visiting more planets, crossed the boundary after 41 years in November 2018. They will continue onwards, unperturbed, with Voyager 1 getting within 1.6 light years of the red dwarf star AC +79 3888 in around 40,000 years' time, and Voyager 2 passing within 1.7 light years of the star Ross 248 in about 42,000 years' time. Afterwards, both spacecraft will settle into long and lonely orbits around the Galaxy.

Granted, the Voyagers will have long since been drained of power by then – they are expected to switch off around the year 2025, just shy of their fiftieth birthdays. Their legacy will remain, however; they have proved that it is possible to launch probes into interstellar space. If we could do that 20 years after the dawn of the Space Age, surely an advanced extraterrestrial civilisation, be it hundreds, thousands, millions or even billions of years older than us, could easily do so too. If it can, and if it does, then the picture this possibility paints for SETI is a complex one, even when it takes many millennia to spread across the stars.

---

* The Sun is surrounded by a vast magnetic bubble, which is its own magnetic field carried away on the solar wind. This field weakens as it gets further from the Sun, until eventually the pressure of magnetic fields and radiation in the interstellar medium becomes too great, limiting the size of the bubble. We call this bubble the heliosphere.

† The Voyagers are in a paradoxical position: they have entered the interstellar medium, but are still in the Solar System, feeling the Sun's gravity and they have not yet passed beyond the distant realm of the Oort Cloud of comets, which extends about a light year from the Sun.

Mountain climbing

There are caveats to this argument, assumptions born, once again, from our human-centric perspective. We assume that curiosity and an urge to explore and colonise are ubiquitous traits that characterise intelligent life, simply because we exhibit them. We assume that our fledgling steps are in lockstep with similar efforts taken by other alien civilisations. We take for granted that the way we think about mathematics and science is universal, when it might not be. Doug Vakoch likens scientific progress to climbing a mountain. More advanced extraterrestrials may have climbed up further than we have, perhaps along the same path, or perhaps they climbed up a different path to reach the same peak, or maybe they are climbing a different mountain altogether, as a result of different factors in their evolution and their environment. For instance, intelligent beings existing in a sea beneath an icy crust, as on Jupiter's moon Europa, where it is always dark, may have no concept of what even lies on the other side of their ice ceiling or that existence is possible out of the water. They may create highly advanced flippers, but starships are not even going to come into their thoughts.

Would they even be climbing up Vakoch's mountains at all? Is science an inevitable outcome of intelligence? Greg Feist, a Professor of Psychology at San José State University, thinks that the answer is both yes and no. He is the founding editor-in-chief of the *Journal of Psychology of Science and Technology*, and spends his research time studying the minds of scientists and understanding scientific thinking. He rules out the idea that we evolved intelligence specifically so that we could become scientific – 'That idea would be kind of silly,' he comments – but rather our brains have evolved to be able to problem-solve, which is what's really at the heart of science.

'Sensory experience is just our way of trying to figure out the world,' he tells me. 'Ultimately the most adaptive elements of that are dealing with survival and reproduction from a purely evolutionary point of view, and one of the things about survival is obviously figuring out how the world works.'

This makes sense. If you want to survive, you need to know around which corner danger lurks and where safety

and shelter can be found. You need to be able to figure out your environment and understand cause and effect, the way that specific actions within that environment can lead to consequences. Challenging environments that test a life-form's ability to survive can often stimulate the greatest innovations, in evolutionary terms but also technologically, points out Yakup Bektas, a historian of science and technology at the Tokyo Institute of Technology. 'Technology is seen as a means of controlling nature, and difficult environments often stimulate technological innovations to make living more convenient,' Bektas tells me. On the other hand, he points out, benign natural environments may stimulate technological innovations too. For example, Britain's numerous rivers, streams, long coastal areas and the availability of coal and ores would have been major factors to the development of the Industrial Revolution.

However, 'the case of Japan presents a contrary example,' says Bektas. 'Being an energy and natural resource-poor nation did not prevent Japan from becoming a major industrial nation and perhaps motivated Japan to innovate technologically to compensate for what it was lacking.' In Bektas's description of how technological innovations come about, it would therefore seem that both rich pickings and hardship can drive technology and the science that underlies that technology. The innate need to understand how the world and the wider Universe work in order to be able to survive and prosper in it is what drives much of our science. 'The brain evolved to figure out the world, so science is just a systematic expression of that,' adds Feist. 'As a species and as individuals, we are always doing science, from the moment we tried to figure out the world as infants.'

Feist calls this 'implicit science', the kind of problem-solving that we all do innately to try and get along with the world around us. It can vary from the practical implementations of engineering or physics to a more philosophical science of developing ideas about how the world works, including religion. Infants and even animals can do very rudimentary forms of implicit science, too – just watch as your pet dog

judges the curve of the flight of a Frisbee in order to catch it in mid-air, or how dragonflies catch their prey by judging their flight path.

At the heart of both implicit science and the 'explicit' science that scientists do is model-building – creating descriptions of the world around us based on our observations, *i.e.* our sensory input – so if we are asking the question whether intelligent extraterrestrial life will have science, then it seems a fair assumption to suggest that if they have senses, they can make observations and build models of the world around them to make sense of their observations. This would be implicit science. Whether they take that model-building as far as doing explicit science, and whether that science is going to be the same as ours, is not a question we can reliably answer. Even within human civilisation, the number of 'proper' scientists is just a small percentage of the overall population. Yet as we have seen in human society, even with that small percentage working in science, we have made giant scientific strides forward.

And it is going to take enormous scientific, technological, engineering and sociological strides to head forth across the stars. The huge distances and timescales are far more daunting than building a 20-km (12-mile) tall tower, and look at how we take a sharp intake of breath at that notion. Yet as the Dyson sphere is built piece by piece, a galactic empire can be built one star system at a time, making voyages in many little steps.

Ad astra

Oh, it would be wonderful if faster-than-light (FTL) travel were possible and, theoretically, it is. Wormholes and warp drives both work on paper, but may ultimately be nothing more than a paper fantasy; the amount of energy required to open a wormhole or to warp space is enormous and quite possibly insurmountable. Furthermore, that energy needs to be of a magical type with a property known as negative density, which sports antigravity properties, repelling instead of attracting.

There are much better slower-than-light possibilities, a whole slew of them in fact. Nuclear fusion is numero uno. Nuclear physicists are aiming to develop nuclear fusion reactors so that by the middle of this century they are contributing large amounts of energy to the National Grid; fusion can be far more efficient than fission, producing no waste and more energy per reaction. It's the Holy Grail of energy production, one that could eradicate the need for fossil fuels (the ingredients for fusion reactions – deuterium and tritium – are just isotopes of hydrogen and are plentiful in sea water) and vastly increase the amount of energy we produce, edging us closer to becoming a true Kardashev Type I society. It is still the technology of tomorrow, for sure, despite the billions that have been pumped into fusion research so far, and no fusion reactor has ever been built that operates efficiently by producing more energy than goes into it, but we are getting closer. It is certainly the go-to energy source of starship designers; the British Interplanetary Society's Project Daedalus, which is a complete design for a starship dating back to the late 1970s, harnesses fusion power, as does its successor, Project Icarus.* Granted, these are still just paper designs, but they certainly imply that sub-light interstellar travel with a speed of around 10 or 12 per cent of the speed of light is possible.

There are other propulsion options, too, such as powerful lasers or masers† that are focused using giant space lenses and aimed at starships heading out of the Solar System. The photons in the beam impart a momentum upon a giant sail deployed by the starship, ever so gradually pushing it up to

---

* There is a burgeoning cottage industry of interstellar organisations, the most important of which are Icarus Interstellar, which was born out of Project Icarus; the Initiative for Interstellar Studies; the Tau Zero Foundation, tied with Paul Gilster's excellent Centauri Dreams website; and the Tennessee Valley Interstellar Workshop.

† Masers are the microwave version of lasers, using microwaves rather than light. 'Maser' stands for Microwave Amplification by Stimulated Emission of Radiation.

velocities of nearly a fifth of the speed of light, depending upon the power of the beam and the design of the sail. Breakthrough Listen's sister project, Breakthrough Starshot, is planning to launch a fleet of nano-probes driven by laser beams pushing them on to their destination, alpha Centauri, at up to 20 per cent of the speed of light, by the middle of this century. At such velocities, the probes would reach alpha Centauri, which is 4.3 light years away, in less than 25 years. Indeed, by using these propulsion methods, we are talking journey times of decades to reach the nearest stars, centuries to reach stars in our immediate neighbourhood and many millennia to get anywhere else. It is an immense task for any civilisation.

Back in Chapter 1 we met the Polynesian islanders of Tikopia in the Pacific. They had developed their own sense of altruism in order to survive on an island of limited resources, but how did they come to be on such a tiny scrap of land amid a vast ocean that stretches from horizon to horizon? If we consider the sea as an analogy to space, and the islands as representing star systems, then perhaps there are lessons to be learned from how the Polynesians conquered the largest ocean on the planet, the Pacific, with just wooden canoes.

The origins of the Polynesians have become lost in the mists of time. There are several sets of theories, some based on genetic evidence of a 'Polynesian motif' in their DNA, others based on linguistics and the evolution of language, or on cultural heritage such as the Lapita archaeological culture, which had its own distinctive pottery, techniques for building boats and agriculture. Did they disperse from Taiwan and the islands of South-east Asia 4,000 years ago, or do they go even further back, 6,000–8,000 years, coming out of the ancient region of Near Oceania that consisted of the Bismarck Archipelago and the Solomon Islands, which in turn had been settled 35,000 years ago? Perhaps interstellar travellers of the future, be they extraterrestrial or of human descent, will also lose sight of their own true origins, much as the people of the Galactic Empire in Isaac Asimov's

Foundation novels had forgotten that Earth was the birthplace of humanity.

Either way, it is how they crossed the Pacific that we are most interested in. Remember, this was thousands of years before Europeans were able to cross the Atlantic, or Ferdinand Magellan and James Cook sailed into the Pacific. Even by the time the Europeans arrived, the Polynesian outrigger canoes could still outpace the likes of the *Endeavour*. The Polynesian colonisation success story was a mixture of carefully applied navigation techniques, a cultural emphasis on the skills required for sailing, a good application of technology and, most crucially, a healthy ethos for exploring, coupled with overpopulation pressures and cultural baggage that actually pushed the Polynesians to expand their frontier.

For example, the Polynesians had a rule: the first-born son inherits everything. When the Chief died, his eldest son would take over. This really didn't leave many options open to the Chief's younger sons, so sometimes they would set sail in search of their own islands to rule over. Leaving everything they knew would have been a huge wrench, tempered by the spirit of exploration that exemplified Polynesian culture. It was something they were born to do.

So leave the island they did, on their outrigger canoes, built from two hulls linked by crossbeams, on top of which was a habitation platform. These 30m (100ft) canoes, racing across the water at 190km (120 miles) per day, could carry up to 50 people, including entire families, animals and supplies – enough to begin a new colony on some distant island over the horizon. The canoes were products of supreme ingenuity, built using local materials: beech hibiscus wood for the forward crossbeam and the hull of the vessel, fibre from coconut shells for lashing the wood together, wood from mango trees to cover the bow and stern, ironwood for the back crossbeam, and so on. The dual hull actually made them more stable than the European galleons that came along in the seventeenth and eighteenth centuries.

Once out at sea, the navigators would come into their own. Most voyages would not have lasted more than 100 days, after

which supplies carried on board the canoes would run out. Perhaps for this reason, the Polynesians did not think in terms of distance travelled, but of time travelled – and we can draw direct analogies here with interstellar travel, where the duration is what concerns us the most. Polynesian navigators were some of the most esteemed members of a society that valued the skills of sailors essential to the continued survival of the colonists. Contrast that attitude with the contempt that science is held in today by some quarters.

It is really quite amazing how they ventured across the ocean and discovered new islands lost among all that water. The Polynesian navigation system essentially considered the canoe to be at rest, with the ocean and the islands dotted within it moving. In an ocean where the water stretched from horizon to horizon for weeks on end, with no ability to measure latitude and longitude, the canoe and the stars were the only reference points to remain constant.

Navigators used a variety of 'wayfinding' techniques. The skill of using the stars to navigate was called *kavenga*, and those navigators who were practised at this were as familiar with the constellations as they were with their children's faces. They knew when particular stars rose and set, and when they would be at their highest in the sky. There were other cues, too. Deep-sea phosphorescence always pointed towards land. Islands could affect the swell of the waves, creating complex patterns that caused the canoe to bob up and down and which the navigators could recognise. The presence of coastal birds in the sky was also an indication that land was near, while the quality of driftwood could give an indication of how long it had been afloat. None of this was an exact science, but through ingenuity the Polynesians were able to cross thousands of kilometres of ocean, with no maps, to find new homes.

After many weeks spent in the ocean with nothing to look at beyond the canoe other than the crests of the waves and the scintillating stars overhead, the colonists would find a new island. Tikopia was one of these safe havens, but there were many others. The new colonists would settle on their

new-found land, families would be born and eventually the second- and third-born sons would depart to venture anew. In this way the Polynesians hopped from island to island, spreading forth as far north as Hawaii, as far south as New Zealand and as far east as Easter Island. Their civilisation spanned an area much larger than the Roman Empire.

When the Europeans wandered into Polynesian waters, the complex interactions during contact between societies did great damage to the Polynesian cultures, which the Europeans arrogantly viewed as primitive. Much of their knowledge about colonising the Pacific was lost. This knowledge was not found in books, but passed down through the generations, from a father to his son. When the Europeans came with their large galleons, which were later superseded by steamships and then aircraft, the Polynesian sons stopped learning from their fathers and adopted the new, European way of doing things. A few kept the spark of their culture alive, however, and today the myths of the Polynesians are made real in the names that astronomers give to objects that orbit the Sun in the distant region of space beyond Neptune and Pluto, where icy comets and dwarf planets lurk in the darkness of the Kuiper Belt and the Oort Cloud. These include Makemake (pronounced Mah-keh-mah-keh), named after the Rapanui Creator of Humanity and the God of Fertility on Easter Island, and Haumea (pronounced How-may-ah), the Hawaiian goddess of childbirth.

It is from this reservoir of frozen bodies at the Solar System's edge that Freeman Dyson has devised a way to spread humanity's seed to the stars. His method harks back to the means by which the Polynesians conquered what must have seemed to them to be the infinite waters of the Pacific Ocean. He has proposed that the first interstellar travellers will use comets to gradually edge further and further away from the Sun, and closer and closer to other stars. There's an added twist, though, because in an ironic way Dyson's story comes full circle here; once a boy who climbed trees to get closer to the stars, he now imagines comets with trees growing on them as one day taking humanity beyond the Solar System.

Comet-hopping

Comets are rich in useful stuff. They are the leftover debris from the planetary construction yard that was our Solar System for the first few tens of millions of years of its life. They're a potpourri of rock, dust and various ices, coming in a variety of shapes, from those that are approximately round to those that are irregular, such as the 'rubber duck'-shaped comet 67P/Churyumov–Gerasimenko, around which the European Space Agency's Rosetta mission orbited between 2014 and 2016. Water in the form of ice is the obvious useful material that comets have to offer, but dig a little deeper and one finds all kinds of organic compounds such as methane, formaldehyde, methanol, even amino acids and more complex hydrocarbon molecules.

So this is how Dyson envisions a civilisation could become a star-faring one. They start out small-scale, visiting nearby planets in their rocket ships, before venturing into the Kuiper Belt. Here they can hop onto objects whose orbits transition between the Kuiper Belt and the 'Scattered Disc', a realm of icy cometary bodies that were pushed outwards when the outer planets, particular Uranus and Neptune, moved away from the Sun in the early days of the Solar System. Members of the Scattered Disc have already been discovered – Sedna, Eris and a mysterious body known as 2012 VP113, which spends its entire life more than 80 times further from the Sun than Earth, and at its greatest distance in its elongated orbit reaches 450 times further away from the Sun than Earth. There's strong evidence, too, in the perturbed orbits of some of these Scattered Disc inhabitants, for a ninth planet – a frozen super-earth – lying undiscovered in these far reaches of the Solar System. Explorers could hop from comet to comet, extending the range of humanity outwards like an extending telescope. To survive out there, imagines Dyson, we would have to engineer life to exist on the surface of a comet, specifically in the shape of the aforementioned giant trees. We would manipulate the genome of an engineered biosphere and seed this genome into the comets. Warm-blooded plants, capable of capturing sunlight and converting

it into energy, would grow, simultaneously also growing a form of greenhouse to insulate them, plus a mirror to focus sunlight onto them. These trees would be enormous, the walls of their trunks thick but their interiors hollow, capable of housing a crew. The roots of the tree would reach deep into the comet, feeding from nutrients extant within the ice. Sails could blossom from the comet, providing a means of gentle propulsion as they catch the breeze of starlight. The Oort Cloud extends perhaps a light year from the Sun, where the Sun's gravity is feeble, and the Oort Cloud around the alpha Centauri system probably covers a similar distance. Between the two of them comets will flock, carrying our deep-space adventurers and a treasure trove of genetic infor-mation.[*] Given enough time, humanity, aboard their comets, will expand from one star system to the next. The discovery of the mysterious interstellar object 'Oumuamua, which was found cruising through our Solar System in October 2017, having hailed from another star system (which one remains unknown), shows that it is eminently possible for cometary bodies to span the distances between stars; estimates suggest that there could be as many as 10,000 'Oumuamuas passing through the Solar System every year.

Self-replicating robots

'For myself, I find the biological route to be very promising and, in a way, much more interesting to me,' Dyson tells me. Yet the biological route is only one possible option for colonising the Galaxy. Others look towards an evolution in the robotic probes that we are sending to the stars right now, machines that are able to think and replicate for themselves. They don't necessarily have to be conscious, just highly intelligent machines reflecting their equally intelligent

---

[*] You can watch Freeman Dyson talk about 'Dyson trees' in a presentation that he gave to the Starship Century conference in June 2013: www.youtube.com/watch?v=_yzgPMwshqE.

programming. Robotic autonomy is fairly rudimentary today, but then the field of robotic intelligence is still in its infancy.

Now consider the convergence of robotic intelligence with 3D printing. The RepRap project, which is short for Replicating Rapid Prototyper, is an open-source initiative to build a 3D printer that can print almost all the components it needs to build a replica of itself. Most 3D printers are designed to work in Earth's gravity, but the challenge of 3D printing in the microgravity of Earth orbit has already been overcome after NASA tested a 3D printer on the International Space Station. Meanwhile, asteroid-prospecting company Deep Space Industries (now part of Bradford Space, Inc) has patented the Microgravity Foundry, a 3D printer designed to be incorporated into robotic mining craft in order to turn asteroidal material into useful things such as solar-power platforms and, yes, more robotic craft. It is becoming increasingly clear that a probe armed with a 3D printer could mine an asteroid, creating offspring replicas of itself to go forth, mine more asteroids and potentially procreate some more. Couple this widespread breeding of probes with some form of onboard artificial intelligence, and we arrive at a fascinating scenario.

A colonising wave of self-replicating robotic probes may precede the biological expansion of people beyond the Solar System. These (currently hypothetical) machines have been termed von Neumann probes, after the American-Hungarian physicist John von Neumann, who first developed the concept of a universal constructor – essentially a self-replicating machine – in 1948. A universal constructor is formed of four primary components: a factory, a duplicator, a controller and an instruction program. The factory is where the replica probes are built according to the blueprint contained within the instruction program stored within the parent probe's memory. Once the daughter probe is built, the instruction program is copied by the duplicator, while the controller links the duplicator with the factory and facilitates the copying of the program into the daughter probe's memory banks. The daughter can then go off and build grandchildren, and they will build great-grandchildren, and so on.

Hang on, though; in order to breed, a von Neumann probe would need a source of spare parts and a workforce to do the assembling. Lucky, then, that everything our robotic creations will need can be found in huge quantities in space, in the chunks of asteroidal debris that litter the void between planets. Like comets, asteroids are awash with useful stuff: common but useful metals such as nickel and iron, precious metals like platinum and iridium, and water-ice, from which can be drawn liquid hydrogen for rocket fuel. Nor are we oblivious to these riches. Several companies are planning to send little probes to prospect near-Earth asteroids with a view to mining them with automated robots. Don't scoff; just one asteroid has the potential to contain more platinum than is found on the entirety of Earth's surface and asteroid mining has the potential to become a multi-trillion-pound industry. Materials mined from the asteroids could be utilised to build solar-power platforms that, as part of a fledgling Dyson sphere, could collect energy from the Sun and beam it down to Earth to be collected by receiving stations. Duncan Forgan of the University of St Andrews and Martin Elvis of Harvard have even suggested that it would be possible to search asteroid belts around other stars for signs of disruption caused by extraterrestrial mining activities. In many ways, such a discovery would be even more significant than receiving a radio or optical signal, because it would tell us that ET is not only technological, but also space-faring.

In any case, it looks as if our first von Neumann probes will be deep-space miners. Yet mining is only the start. Ores must be refined before they can be used for anything useful, and then assembled into that something useful. A single probe could not do all this by itself. Deep Space Industries produced artwork depicting all manner of robotic craft, some that will prospect, others that will dig, still others that will act as refineries. Yet the *coup de grâce* is their microgravity foundry, which could build pretty much anything in the marginal gravitational fields found in near-Earth space. This will be our von Neumann probe's factory.

You might imagine a colony of probes formed of various types of robot. There could be the 'queen' probe, a mothership that is the largest in the colony, capable of building other probes, including replicas of itself, within its cavernous confines. Smaller explorer probes could survey planetary systems, identifying potential resource bases. Forager probes could then head out to these locations to prospect for resources, and miner probes to do the grunt work of digging. Worker probes would do the assembly, buzzing in and out of the mothership, building other motherships that head off for pastures new, armed with their own blueprints to start their own little family of probes when they arrive at their destination. Different families of probes could keep in touch with one another through a network of narrowband transmissions from probes in one planetary system to those in a neighbouring system. These tight beams over relatively short distances of just a few light years would be impossible to stumble upon if you're not the intended recipient, which according to John Mathews of Penn State University, could potentially explain SETI's great silence.

In the 1960s, astronomer Ronald Bracewell of Stanford University added another type of probe to this menagerie of probe types. Perhaps a good moniker for Bracewell's probes would be 'Ambassador probes', though they would also double up as librarians. Bracewell envisaged such probes of alien design visiting planetary systems, making contact and gathering information on the cultures, science and technology of a thousand worlds, forming a repository of knowledge from across the Galaxy. Meanwhile, science-fiction author Fred Saberhagen held up a dark mirror to the Bracewell probes to develop the notion of Berserker probes, designed to eliminate any intelligent life they found that could pose a threat to their creators.

Fermi's paradox

Regardless of the individual probes' responsibilities, if an intelligent extraterrestrial civilisation released a swarm of self-replicating von Neumann-style probes at some point

in galactic history, how quickly could they colonise our entire Galaxy?

The mathematics is easy; it is the assumptions built into the calculations that make the estimates vary wildly. Suppose that a civilisation sends probes to its 100 nearest stars, which then replicate once they arrive at their target systems and immediately move on to more stars at the same rate, travelling at a tenth of the speed of light – the same velocity as proposed fusion-powered starships such as *Daedalus* – then a colonising wavefront could encompass the Galaxy within 650,000 years, assuming that the probes don't spend undue amounts of time in a planetary system before sending their daughter probes on further. Frank Tipler of Tulane University in the US estimated a much longer 300 million years for the colonisation of the Milky Way Galaxy, using just today's rocket technology mixed with self-replicating machines. Ian Crawford, of Birkbeck, University of London, assumed that colonists would follow the probes, setting up new civilisations on new worlds. If we assume that it takes 400 years between the founding of a colony and that colony launching a new daughter colony, and that the typical spacing between colonies is 10 light years, and that starships move at 10 per cent of the speed of light, Crawford calculated that it would take 5 million years to colonise the Galaxy, with the colonising wavefront moving at 0.02 light years per year on average. Even if it took 5,000 years between the founding of a colony and the launching of a new one, it would still take 'only' 50 million years, he says. More extreme is Chris Boyce's calculation, which suggests that, had an intelligent extraterrestrial civilisation existed in our Galaxy a billion years ago and launched their own fleet of self-replicating probes, enough time would have elapsed for them to have ventured 100 million light years at 10 per cent of the speed of light, far beyond the nearest large cluster of galaxies, the Virgo Cluster.

Make no mistake, to our tiny human perspective, these time-spans are mind-bogglingly enormous. However, compared to the age of the Universe, which is 13.81 billion

years old, such time-spans are actually quite small. On the face of it extraterrestrial intelligence, be it robotic or biological, has had more than enough time to colonise our Galaxy, which raises a problem, because if it is that easy, then surely they should be here by now. As Ken Olum of the Tufts Institute of Cosmology wrote in 2004, 'Something must be wrong with our understanding of how civilisations evolve if only one in a billion can colonise its galaxy.'

The most famous version of this problem is called the Fermi Paradox, after the Italian-American physicist Enrico Fermi, who worked at the Los Alamos Laboratory in the 1940s and 1950s on the Manhattan Project and all the top-secret high-level physics that was going on at the time. However, maybe it shouldn't be named after Fermi, since what he originally said has since been flipped upside down by other scientists.

The story behind the Fermi Paradox has been told a thousand times, but it's a good one so it bears rehashing here. As the equivalent of SETI urban legend would have it, Fermi was sitting in the common room one lunchtime in 1950 with his colleagues, one of whom, Emil Konopinski, had read a recent copy of the *New Yorker* (the 2 May issue, to be exact), a satirical news magazine that is still published today. This particular issue reported two puzzling stories from the Big Apple. In one, there were reports of a spate of bizarre thefts of trash cans. The other described the latest craze to hit America, which was flying-saucer sightings. The *New Yorker*'s cartoonist put the two stories together, depicting little green men running off into their flying saucers while gripping rubbish bins with their tentacles.

This got Fermi thinking – not about rubbish bins or flying saucers, but the broader picture. 'Where is everybody?' he asked rhetorically. He presumably assumed the reports of flying saucers were hoaxes or misidentified aircraft and instead wondered whether the reason we had not really been visited by ET was that interstellar travel was impossible.

In the 1970s Fermi's question was adapted by scientists such as Frank Tipler, who turned it into what they described

as a paradox. The seventies were the era of Project Daedalus, while the Voyager spacecraft were on the verge of blasting off for the outer Solar System and then the stars. Humans had set foot on the Moon; interstellar flight did not seem as crazy as it had in 1950. So if interstellar travel was possible, and if there has been enough time for a civilisation to colonise the entire Galaxy, why were they not here? David Stephenson of the University of Saskatchewan in Canada, writing in the *Journal of the British Interplanetary Society* in 1977, phrased this 'paradox' as 'Fermi's Paradox'. The name stuck.

For some in the SETI community, the only outcome that they could see from this was a pessimistic one – that if ETs are not here, then they do not exist, because the assumptions of the paradox say they should be here. Even if there are a hundred or a thousand or a million societies in the Galaxy with no interest at all in the stars, it only takes one to colonise the Galaxy, hopping from star system to star system just as the Polynesians hopped from island to island.

Galactic percolation

As we have seen, interstellar flight is theoretically possible, but should not be considered a fait accompli. We can imagine how the Galaxy could be colonised, but our imagination paints a picture of space flight that is perhaps too romantic, where motivation for space exploration abounds and the technology works perfectly. It doesn't account for things going wrong.

The obvious problem that could beset any robotic colonising effort is that the robotic probes break down. It takes a long time to travel between stars, even at a tenth of the speed of light. Certainly with our current technology we cannot build a probe that will survive the journey. Voyager 1 and 2 will probably drain all their power before they reach their half-century, while NASA's New Horizons probe that encountered Pluto in July 2015 will also inevitably fall silent, probably in the late 2030s. If nuclear-fusion power becomes commonplace that will help solve the energy crisis for space probes, but on

timescales of hundreds of thousands of years it is still hard to see how any energy source can sustain a spacecraft indefinitely. Plus, machines will simply wear out and the more moving parts they have, the faster that will happen. Granted, robots have the advantage of not having to suffer as much from the ravages of time as biological life does – with self-replication, it is possible to build replacement parts for anything that breaks down on the probe. What will increasingly factor into the equation are copy-errors – mistakes in the implementation of the blueprint, just as when DNA replicates incorrectly within the human body, often as a result of radiation exposure, causing cancers. There's plenty of radiation in space. Perhaps a probe's programming can become corrupted – a rogue cosmic-ray strike might be enough to do the trick, so that when the probe replicates, the instruction manual it passes down to its daughter is an incorrect version of the one it was given. Sometimes the mutation will have no great effect, but at other times the mutation could cause a probe to shut down, or corrupt its programming so that, for example, a mining probe under instructions to stay away from inhabited worlds could begin strip-mining planets with indigenous life – a disastrous first-contact scenario.

It's not just the robots that could break down. If crewed missions are sent to colonise planets around other stars, then some of these colonies could also fail and, if and when they do, they will become a dead end on the road to conquering the Galaxy. For Geoffrey Landis, a science-fiction author and scientist working at NASA's John Glenn Research Center, this explains both the Fermi Paradox and even the G-HAT results.

Landis has called his idea the 'percolation model', after percolation theory, which explains how things connect or clump together in clusters as they percolate through a given environment. It works like this: let's say a civilisation launches a handful of colonies into space, each one departing for a different planetary system. They embark on this grand colonising effort using the physics and engineering that we know is possible – so no warp drives – which means they

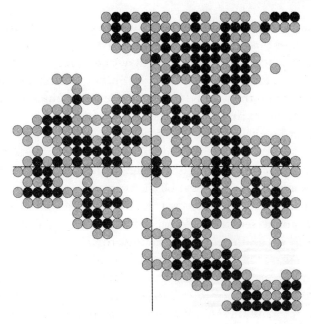

Figure 3: Part of a simulation showing percolation theory at work in galactic colonisation. Black circles indicate worlds that are actively colonising other systems. Shaded circles indicate worlds that have stopped colonising other worlds, for whatever reason. The empty spaces refer to parts of space that have not been visited yet by this colonising wave, but we can see how voids are beginning to form, surrounded by non-colonising worlds. Image credit: Geoffrey Landis.

venture to stars within a reasonable travel time and across a reasonable distance, less than 10 light years. To give some idea of what could be found inside a volume 10 light years in radius, within the same volume around the Sun there are only three Sun-like stars and seven smaller red dwarfs. Of these ten stars, only two so far are known to have planets: Proxima Centauri and Barnard's Star. So a colony may not necessarily have many options in terms of future destinations (although, of course, planets need not be the only destinations – a civilisation that chooses to live entirely in space may just head to where the comets and asteroids are, to use their resources).

Suppose a handful of colonies are successful and, around four centuries later, they are able to develop their own civilisations to the point that they can launch their own colonies. These colonies reach their destinations, become successful and then send out their own colonies, and so on, to continue the expansion into the Galaxy.

What Landis realised is that not all colonising efforts will be equally successful in producing daughter colonies, for a whole variety of reasons, some bad for the colonists, others not so much. Some of the colonies may succumb to warfare. Alternatively, combating the alien biosphere on their new world could see the colonists wiped out by diseases, or starving to death from an inability to grow crops in this foreign land.* Or, colonies could be governed badly and experience societal breakdown or simply lose the skill and knowledge necessary to launch spacecraft and new colonies. They may find themselves trapped in a void where there are no other destinations within reach for them to colonise, perhaps because these places are too far away or have already been colonised. Or, they may simply choose not to launch daughter colonies for cultural reasons, just like the Chinese, who called all their ships back and stopped exploring the world in the fifteenth century.

For each colony, Landis assigns a probability, P, that they will launch daughter colonies, and a probability of 1-P that they will not. A critical percolation threshold value, Pc, controls how far the wave of colonisation continues. If P is much less than Pc, then the colonising wave will stop near its origin. If P is roughly equal to Pc, then although there will be clusters of colonised star systems, these will be surrounded by many

---

* Research by Japanese scientists Norio Narita and Shigeyuki Masaoka has shown that oxygen-rich atmospheres could still be generated on habitable planets by the reaction of ultraviolet light from the Sun on titanium oxide, a common material found in rocky worlds, in the ground. This reaction could create habitable worlds with breathable atmospheres but no indigenous biosphere that colonists would have to adapt to and, in some cases, fight off.

uncolonised voids. If P is much in excess of Pc, then colonisation is widespread, although smaller voids will remain. This model holds for a colonising wave of robotic probes, too: they can break down, or their programming eventually becomes corrupted, bringing a halt to colonisation or exploration. Regardless of the means of colonisation or whatever values we decide to attribute to P and Pc, the end result is always the same: eventually more and more dead ends will appear until the colonising wave slows to a stream, then a trickle, then a dead stop as it struggles to percolate through the Galaxy. The presence of the voids would explain why G-HAT failed to detect any Type III civilisations – under percolation theory, it would be unlikely that a civilisation would completely colonise a galaxy. An even worse outcome might be that the centres of the pockets of the Galaxy that they do conquer could suffer resource depletion under population pressure, similar to the fate of Easter Island, particularly as the colonising wave leaves them behind for fresher pastures. The cores of colonised regions could start to die off, creating new voids.

If all this is true, then we could very well be living in a void, which would explain why we have not seen any evidence of ET nearby yet. The size of the void would depend on the size of the critical-percolation threshold value. We could be surrounded by ancient, dead colony civilisations that failed to colonise any further.

Landis' model has not found favour with everyone. Economist and futurist Robin Hanson, a professor of economics at George Mason University in Virginia, USA, points out that it lacks the element of economic competition, whereby colonies would be competing for resources in a kind of interstellar 'gold rush' and would be swept along in this colonising wave because of the fear of missing out and being invaded or usurped by competing colonies. This way there would always be a leading edge of the colonising wave, although small voids could be overlooked in the rush for richer pickings elsewhere. Hanson makes an analogy with the Wild West, but in Landis' original model there were no invasions because he deemed the distances to be too great.

'I'm of two minds as to whether it would be possible to mount an invasion,' Landis tells me. 'In my original model I was thinking that interstellar war was a little too far-fetched – it's an awful long way to take an army. But if you don't think invasion so much as you think extermination and removing the civilisation entirely, this could conceivably be done with a plague, which isn't so utterly science fictional.'

If Hanson is correct, it would be a body-blow to SETI. We know there are a huge amount of resources that we still see out there in the Milky Way Galaxy. Whether we are in a void or not, we can see that if a colonising wave has plundered its way through the Galaxy, it has done so very carefully and has left a lot intact. It would seem more likely that no colonising wave ever existed.

Meanwhile, Jason Wright's objections to percolation theory are more astrophysical. Stars don't stay still – although on short timescales they appear to, over millions of years stars can move quite a bit, weaving in and out and bobbing up and down through the spiral arms of the Galaxy while on their orbits around the galactic centre. The stars all move at differing rates and in slightly different directions, so if a colony is trapped in a void, eventually it will move out of that void. Similarly, Earth might be in a void now, but in the future it could move out of the void, and in the past it may not have been in a void.

'Active colonies cannot get stuck in big regions of occupied, non-colonising colonies with nowhere to go,' says Wright. 'They'll eventually find themselves back in virgin territory in a few million years.'

Of course, a few million years is an extremely long time to us, and Landis counters the stellar-motion argument by suggesting that civilisations and colonies will have limited lifespans that are much shorter than the time it would take for their colony to move out of a void.

'Stars move but they don't really move over the lifetimes of civilisations that we have had in human history,' he says. 'But now you're getting into the question of, what is a civilisation going to be like when it is tens of thousands or hundreds of thousands of years old? That's a very hard question to answer.'

If civilisations keep changing, then it becomes a very, very hard thing to answer.'

So we return to where we began, by dealing with huge scales of time and distance, of technology and energy far beyond the experience or know-how of the human race, and then trying to say, or guess, something meaningful about civilisations that have conquered these scales. Interstellar colonisation may be how twenty-first-century humanity would go about things, were we suddenly thrust into that scenario, but truly advanced civilisations may very well have a different outlook.

I admit I'm a fan of Christopher Nolan's 2014 film, *Interstellar*. It touched me with a sense of wonder and hope for the future of humanity that few films manage, but it also reminded me of what incredible objects black holes are. In a film that is fundamentally about humanity's transcension into the Universe at large, the scientifically accurate portrayal of a black hole is no coincidence on the part of Nolan and the film's original creator and scientific advisor, Professor Emeritus Kip Thorne of Caltech. They are not the first to speculate that the fates of black holes and the future of life in the Universe could be intertwined.

Black holes have a bad rep with the public. They're dangerous and mysterious objects of doom from which there is no escape, so going anywhere near one is considered a 'Bad Thing'. For scientists, though, black holes are far more exciting, being the exotic remains of dead, collapsed stars that test the laws of physics as we know them to the limit. They come in different sizes, too; the most common are those with masses only a few times greater than the mass of our Sun. They are created from the fires of supernovae, where the explosion of a star blows the exterior layers of the star outwards, while the dense iron core collapses upon itself under the inevitable pull of gravity. If the star's core is massive enough, it crushes down to a single point of near-infinite

density and begins to seriously warp space around it. This is a black hole.

Large black holes, which are thousands, millions or even billions of times more massive than the Sun, are thought to have been born from the mergers of many black holes, or the collapse of giant clouds of gas, a long time ago, shortly after the first generation of stars lit up the Universe a few hundred million years after the Big Bang. These black holes began to attract matter – mostly interstellar gas, but stars too – and swallow it whole, acquiring the mass to grow ever larger. Today, the greatest 'supermassive' black holes are found in the centres of galaxies, including our own Milky Way Galaxy, where a behemoth of a black hole with a mass 4.1 million times greater than that of our Sun lurks (and all this mass is crammed into a volume just 44 million kilometres – 27 million miles – across, small enough to fit inside the orbit of Mercury with room to spare).

Albert Einstein taught us that energy equals the mass multiplied by the square of the speed of light. In other words, if you have a lot of mass, then you also have a lot of energy locked up within that mass. One way to draw energy from a black hole is to allow its gravity to pull in other objects such as asteroids, comets, even whole planets and stars.[*] The gravitational tidal forces from the black hole rip the objects apart until they are rendered little more than a hot gas in a disc spiralling around the black hole. This hot gas radiates energy that could be collected. And if a civilisation does not want to throw things at a black hole in the hope of collecting energy from the resulting gas, on some occasions a star can be found next to a black hole, close enough that the black hole's gravity is slowly unravelling the star, tearing a constant stream of gas from it that flows into the disc around the black hole. This spinning disc of gas steals angular momentum from the

---

[*] Don't think it is possible to move a star? Think again. Russian physicist Leonid Shkadov came up with the idea of using giant mirrors that are gravitationally bound to a star to act as sails that will pull the star in a preferred direction.

rotation of the black hole, slowing it down, and the energy that radiates away from the disc can theoretically be captured. The energy efficiency of such systems is around 10 per cent (so 10 per cent of the mass–energy that you chuck in, you get back out). 'It is the most efficient, sustainable way to convert mass to energy that I'm aware of,' says Jason Wright.

There's another way to draw energy from a black hole, which is by skipping the gas disc stage entirely and going straight for the gravitational energy of the black hole itself. As we know, the gravitational strength of a black hole is incredible; it can trap light, for goodness' sake! In a scenario developed as a thought experiment by Kip Thorne, John Wheeler and Charles Misner for their 1973 textbook *Gravitation*, spacecraft carrying a million tonnes of rubbish each swoop down from a region just outside a rotating black hole's maw called the ergosphere, which is found between two boundaries: the black hole's outermost boundary where gravity is so strong that photons of light are slowed to a standstill, and the event horizon, beyond which not even light can escape. The name ergosphere is derived from the Greek 'ergon', which means 'work' or 'task', and, in theory, it should be possible to extract energy from the ergosphere. Thorne, Wheeler and Misner imagined that their hypothetical dumper trucks would take a trajectory through the ergosphere that enabled them to tip their loads out into the black hole and, since every action incurs an equal and opposite reaction, the trucks would experience a recoil that flung them away from the black hole, stealing some of the black hole's rotational energy in the process. This is what's so clever about this scenario: because the dumped loads increase the mass of the black hole, there is therefore increased rotational energy available to steal and the dumper trucks leave with more energy than they began with. Up to a third of the mass of a black hole can be expressed in terms of its rotational energy and the energy available could power a civilisation like our own for at least a trillion trillion years, long after the stars have exhausted themselves. So why waste time with stars when you can tap directly into a black hole?

Well, black holes are not the perfect solution. A civilisation still has to develop interstellar flight to find a black hole and there are far more stars than black holes. Furthermore, the solar-panel technology for collecting a star's energy is pretty mundane, whereas the notion of collecting energy from a black hole is verging on science fiction at present. Still, it is theoretically possible and so, in that case, who are we to say what a supremely advanced civilisation can and cannot do?

But wait, there's more. Energy generation is not the only feature of black holes that makes them attractive to advanced civilisations. Black holes are potentially the most powerful and efficient natural computers in the Universe. Their computing power is a function of their mass (which the largest black holes have plenty of) and computational efficiency, which requires an ordered environment – a bit like when you de-frag your computer to speed it up. The trouble is, black holes are a jumble of energy and information, so we would need to sort it by using Hawking radiation. First proposed by Stephen Hawking, this radiation is formed of pairs of 'virtual' particles that are generated just on the boundary of the event horizon.

Virtual particles are one of those weird consequences of quantum theory. You'll have heard of Heisenberg's uncertainty principle, which describes how it is impossible to know both the position and the momentum of a particle – you can only know one or the other. This is partly a result of a particle not being a particle as such, but a wave in the quantum field, and the particle has a given probability for appearing anywhere on this wave. This extends further and more profoundly, though: there is always a probability that in every point in space a particle and its anti-particle could appear, briefly, before annihilating each other and disappearing back into the ether. They are said to 'borrow their energy from the Universe', which is a romantic way of looking at it. Such particles are called virtual particles, but around black holes things become real. The creation of a pair of virtual particles close to the black hole's event horizon leads to bizarre occurrences where the virtual becomes the real. A pair of virtual particles created here will gain more than enough energy from their violent

acceleration around the black hole to pay off their energy
debt to the Universe and become real particles. Nor is that the
end of the story. Recall that probability wave along which
a particle can exist. Those virtual-now-real particles that
spontaneously appear on the event horizon sometimes have a
probability wave that extends outside the event horizon and
hence outside the black hole. There's a small probability that
they can exist outside the black hole and inevitably some do –
we call this 'quantum tunnelling', where particles seem to
'tunnel' through space. So black holes are not completely
black – they do radiate some energy – and it was this realisation
that made Stephen Hawking's career.

In Hawking's theory of black holes, one particle remains
inside the black hole while the other is able to 'tunnel'
through the horizon and escape, but the pair are forever
inextricably linked at a quantum level. In other words, what
happens to one affects the other, which could, in principle,
allow black-hole IT experts to program the black hole. If
the loads on the hypothetical dumper trucks are sent into the
black hole in a specific manner, they will interact with the
in-falling Hawking particles in a controlled fashion, in a
sense programming them, which also programs the escaping
Hawking particles, which become the computer's output. Put
like that, it sounds so easy, doesn't it? In truth a thorough
understanding of black holes beyond our current knowledge,
combining quantum mechanics with relativity to produce a
unified theory of quantum gravity, would be essential to
make all these black-hole operations feasible.

Building new universes

There's one extra hypothesis that adds to the black-hole
alternative, which is that they may play a role in the birth of
new universes, under a principle of 'cosmological natural
selection'. It was developed by the theoretical physicist Lee
Smolin and expanded on by the likes of such eminent
physicists as Stephen Hawking, Martin Rees and Alan Guth,
who developed the theory of cosmic inflation that describes

how the Universe expanded exponentially in the first fraction of a second of cosmic history. The idea stems from the observation that our Universe seems eerily fine-tuned for life – alter any of the fundamental constants of nature, such as the charge on an electron or the mass of a proton, and stars, planets and life could not form. However, if there are very many universes, each with slightly different values for these constants, then we would inevitably find ourselves living within the Universe that can support life.

Black holes, says Smolin, could punch through space-time and create new daughter universes. Those new universes with the right characteristics – the suitable values for the fundamental constants that allow stars and hence more black holes to form – would be naturally selected to produce more new universes and so on. In some cases, those universes could be even better than ours; our Universe seems to be fated to die a cold and empty death as the stars fade out and the cosmos continues to expand for ever.

Smolin's theory is not without its critics, not least his fellow theorist Leonard Susskind, but if it is correct and if advanced civilisations do develop technology and an understanding of physics that allow them to manipulate black holes, then one could imagine entire civilisations entering black holes to populate the new universes spawned from them. They may even wish to artificially create their own black holes and hence their own universes, perhaps by sending stars supernovae in a specific way. This leads to one intriguing scenario, speculated upon by Stephen Hsu of the University of Oregon and Anthony Zee of the University of California, Santa Barbara, in which the hypothetical creators of our Universe, should it have been produced by a black hole, may have left a message in the cosmic microwave background (CMB) radiation – the relic heat from the Big Bang, which is now just three degrees above absolute zero – for us to find.* Suffice to say, despite detailed surveys of the CMB by the likes of the

---

* The television science-fiction series *Stargate: Universe* (2009–11) dealt with a plot line about a message discovered in the CMB.

European Space Agency's Planck spacecraft, no inkling of a message has been found so far.

If black holes really are destinations for intelligence, then they would neatly explain the lack of Type III civilisations in the Universe. Intriguingly, the scientific philosopher Clément Vidal points out that astronomers using NASA's orbiting Chandra X-ray Observatory have noted a surprisingly large number of X-ray binaries – systems involving either a black hole or a neutron star stealing matter from a normal companion star, releasing X-rays in the process – within a radius of four light years of the galactic centre, where our own Galaxy's giant black hole lurks. More than 10,000 X-ray binaries have been identified in this small region and their presence probably has a natural, astrophysical explanation in regard to the propensity of the galactic centre to produce massive stars that leave black holes behind when they go supernova. Vidal, though, suggests an outlandish explanation: that there are a large number of advanced civilisations anchored around the black holes within those X-ray binaries, who have migrated to the galactic core with their black hole to the big daddy of black holes that resides there.

There is one other possibility I'm going to mention. At the beginning of this chapter we entered the mindset of building mega-projects, be they 20km (12-mile) towers, Dyson spheres or interstellar spacecraft as progenitors to the million-year quest to build a 'galactic empire'. The inherent assumption behind such thinking, however, is that, as a civilisation progresses, its energy consumption increases at a rate equal to its own expansionist ambitions. Yet suppose optimisation becomes the key word, not expansion? This isn't too different to what is happening on Earth. The climate emergency and environmental damage are forcing us to look at more efficient, optimised ways of doing things. Population growth through births is actually on the decrease in large parts of Europe, Japan and other nations. Nuclear and particle physics – the amazing things that happen at the scale of atoms and smaller – are where all the research money is being driven, while technological advances often come in the form of miniaturisation. Big developments from

large-scale projects tend to stall or never arrive, sidelined by a lack of funding or a lack of motivation. Science-fiction author Neal Stephenson, who has been pushing the Tall Tower project discussed at the beginning of this chapter, has summed this up by suggesting that the type of people who 50 or 60 years ago might have been laying transatlantic telephone cables now work on microchips, IT and nanotechnology.

Which is fine, by the way. Nobody says that we have to do mega-projects or that mega-projects are the only route to a successful future. Stephenson wants us to get back the compulsion for tackling big projects, but advanced extra-terrestrial civilisations could decide that they're quite happy with what they've got and see no need to expand beyond their own planet or their own system. Certainly, that's the idea put forward by Serbian astronomer Milan Ćirković: it was an idea born out of his need to re-examine some of the old assumptions, such as the Kardashev scale, that are embedded within the SETI mindset.

'I think Kardashev's classifications should be regarded as part of what was done in the early days [of SETI], in what I like to call the "time of the founding fathers of SETI",' says Ćirković. 'These founding fathers are people like Kardashev, like Frank Drake, like Philip Morrison, like Iosif Shklovsky and Carl Sagan. We now know the situation is much more complicated and we don't perceive, over astronomical distances, any activities, phenomena or manifestations of advanced technological civilisations.'

He wonders if advanced civilisations are eschewing galactic empires in favour of staying closer to their home in an analogy to the city-states of Ancient Greece. Like the Greeks of Athens or Sparta, extraterrestrial city-states might still send out scouts, launching nano-sized probes to explore space. Indeed, such probes could theoretically already be in the Solar System, silently watching us from afar. Such city-state civilisations would feel no pressure to colonise the stars, particularly if their population growth was close to zero. Their penchant for optimisation would also find a match with the optimised Benford Beacons that we discussed in Chapter 4.

'An optimised society is intrinsically less likely to be observed because most of the things that we observe and tend to associate with advanced technology and advanced societies actually consist of waste energy and the waste of resources,' Ćirković tells me. 'As we strive to increase sustainability in our present-day civilisation, it is only natural to imagine that civilisations further along the curve of progress would actually do much better in this respect and they would be very hard to detect from their minimal emissions.'

The great galactic empire appears to have been a dream never given form. If ET exist, then the evidence is stacking up that, assuming they are technologically intelligent (and admittedly, that is a big 'if', as we saw in Chapter 2), something is steering them onto a path away from the later stages of the Kardashev scale. Maybe they do vanish down black holes, or struggle to penetrate very far into the Galaxy. Perhaps they turn their back on expansion completely and reach a state of balance with the resources of their home system, or choose to live in a virtual-reality world instead. A few paragraphs above, I said that if civilisations choose this direction, then that's fine, but personally, I'm going to take that back. Civilisations that take a step back, that decide not to explore the Universe and adapt to it are the antithesis to the young Freeman Dyson, who was forever climbing trees towards the stars. Instead, those civilisations would climb back down before ever reaching the heavens. Looking back at the wonderful possibilities that we have discussed in this chapter, I cannot help but feel that a future for advanced societies – for our society – that does not include the ambition and curiosity and manifest destiny so finely espoused by the expansionist plans from our best futurists, science-fiction authors and scientists, would be a great shame. As Felix Dennis, poet, publisher and planter of trees, once wrote, whoever plants a tree, winks at immortality.

Two Clocks

Somewhere in west Texas, deep inside a limestone mountain above the scrub and dust of the desert floor, is a clock. It's the last place you might expect to find a timepiece. The remote location is seldom visited and difficult to reach. After a hard day's hike to the mountain, you're forced to climb 460m (1,500ft), scrabbling over rock and desert shrubs, battling against a dusty wind, arid air and a harsh sun, just to reach the front door. After turning the circular handles that unlock the stainless-steel blockade that greets you upon arrival, you encounter a secondary inner door that acts a bit like an airlock, beyond which is a long, dark tunnel, at the end of which is a towering spiral staircase up which you ascend towards a distant point of light, and the clock. Only the most dedicated visitors make it all the way.

It's meant to be that way. After all, you don't think they're going to give eternity to just anyone, do you?

As you may have gathered, this is no ordinary clock. It ticks so slowly that you will never see its hands move. Hours and minutes become but trifling moments of time. Instead, the clock records years, thousands of them, more time than is counted in the rings of the oldest tree. As much time as humanity has existed. It's a clock for the deep future.

The 10,000-Year Clock is the legacy of the Long Now Foundation, based in San Francisco. Founded in 1996 (or 01996 as the Foundation calls it, in keeping with counting to 10,000 years) by a cadre of futurists and technologists, the Foundation's aim is to help build the foundations for a civilisation that can survive for 10,000 years or more. The clock is a symbol, a way to look over the precipice of time and into the future.

As you climb the spiral staircase, your footsteps echoing up the length of the shaft, you come across the first of the

counterweights that hang from the top, each one weighing 4.5 tonnes. The counterweights belong to the clock's drive system and are formed from stacks of giant stone discs, connected to a capstan, which is a rotating machine similar to those used on sailing ships to winch an anchor up out of the depths. It takes several people to pull the counterweights up and wind up the clock face.

Above this winding station is the giant gear system that enables the clock to keep track of tick and tock. A system of rotating cogs, wheels and pins that act as a giant computer, the gear system features 20 'Geneva wheels', each 2.4m (7.9ft) in diameter and weighing 450kg (990lb). Imagine a peg close to the edge of a rotating wheel that latches onto one of a multitude of slots in an adjoining cog and pulls it around, turning the clock's gears ever so slowly to calculate the time and ring a melody on a system of bells each time the clock is wound up by visitors. In 10,000 years, it will never play the same melody twice. Each visit to the clock is unique and special, a moment in time never to be recaptured. As you listen to the haunting chimes reverberating up and down the stairwell, you can feel yourself precariously balanced on the edge of a cliff between the past and the future. Just for that moment, you feel like a part of the next 10,000 years. Then the chimes end, the moment passes, and you fall off the cliff and into the next moment.

Truth be told, the concept is as daunting as it is majestic. If they're lucky, a human being might live to be a century old. Our everyday concerns about the future usually revolve around tomorrow or next week. Next year might seem far off. The next 10,000 years is a vast ocean of time that we may on some level understand, but comprehending it to the extent of being able to manage civilisation's voyage across that expanse is another thing altogether. The 10,000-Year Clock is a step towards at least appreciating deep time.

Back in California, at Long Now's base in San Francisco, Alexander Rose has as deep an appreciation of the future as anyone. As Director of the Foundation and manager of the clock project, he thinks about the future all the time, but

because he trained as an industrial designer, he says his initial attraction to the 10,000-Year Clock was just the engineering challenge.

'I signed on to see if it could be done,' he says. 'But the engineering and the materials science have actually been the easy part, compared to thinking through what aesthetic and experience design would work for people, especially far in the future.'

In other words, the clock isn't just a way to measure deep time. It also has to be relevant for people 1,000, 2,000, 3,000 years or more from now, so understanding how to accomplish that became an exercise in planning for the future. Even if visitors feel the design doesn't work from an aesthetic point of view, says Rose, they've already made that leap to having to think about those long time frames for them to form an opinion about the clock. So either way, you're going to leave the clock thinking about the future.

'It's certainly changed the way I think about making certain decisions in life, as well as the way that we might run the Long Now Foundation, because our intention is to pass the Foundation on through the generations and everything we do is just laying the groundwork for that time,' says Rose. 'One of the main principles that has come out of this has been trying to figure out how to make decisions that open up options for the future, rather than limit them.'

Clearly, creating a longer, better future for humanity is important for civilisation, driven perhaps by the same altruistic forces that sculpt the principles of kin selection and inclusive fitness, but on much larger scales. It also has dramatic repercussions for SETI, in the form of a single factor that we denote by a letter: L.

When formulating an agenda for the first ever SETI conference, held at the Green Bank radio observatory in 1961, Frank Drake developed the equation for which he is best known.* As we have seen in earlier chapters, his eponymous

* See the description in the footnote in Chapter 2, p. 73.

equation is an effort to estimate the number of transmitting civilisations in the Galaxy. It utilises just seven terms, ranging from prosaic astronomical factors such as the rate of star and planet birth, to evolutionary factors and finally social factors. The last factor is L: the average lifetime of a transmitting civilisation.* The longer civilisations survive, the more chance they have of overlapping with the existence of other civilisations, meaning that our chances of detecting them will increase.

In the most optimistic of scenarios, L is very, very big. The Universe is 13.81 billion years old. It's not entirely clear when the first planets with habitable conditions could have arisen, but if intelligent aliens could have developed at any point in cosmic history, then the greater probability is that they did so perhaps billions of years before us. If they're still around, their civilisations must be very old. We hark back to Chapter 1, in which Carl Sagan blew William Proxmire's mind by convincing him that if SETI were to find an extraterrestrial civilisation far older than ourselves, it would be proof that our future does not necessarily lie in the ruins of self-destruction. If they can build a civilisation that can last for so long, it gives us hope that we can too. It's yet another mirror that we can hold up to the stars and see ourselves reflected back.

Building a clock to count 10,000 years into the future doesn't guarantee that civilisation will last that long. Much more is needed. In Chapter 5 we encountered the idea of building megastructures, be they tall towers, space elevators,

---

* Technically, L refers only to the length of time that a civilisation is transmitting a signal that we could detect, and there could be all kinds of reasons why they could be living happily and not transmitting. However, as SETI has progressed to the point where we also search for technosignatures such as Dyson spheres, L has come to represent not the time spent transmitting, which is irrelevant in the search for ET technology, but the lifetime of a civilisation, and that's how we shall approach it in this chapter.

Dyson spheres or a host of other challenging engineering and technology concepts. Other mega-projects might involve curing ageing, fixing human-incurred climate change or ridding the world of disease and starvation. A project to ensure civilisation progresses for thousands of years is the biggest mega-project of them all, incorporating all of these mega-structures and smaller mega-projects. Can a long-lived civilisation develop its longevity just through chance, with its society stumbling along the correct path through luck more than anything else? Or will it require a guiding hand, a collection of people with a long-term plan to drive humanity forward?

Carl Rhodes, a Professor of Management at the University of Leicester, thinks that organisations have the potential to act as those guiding hands. Certainly, he thinks that the goal of building organisations that can last for centuries or millennia is a unique challenge. The best way to overcome the entropy that time inflicts on organisations, he says, is with something that sounds like a paradox: to survive, an organisation must change, but stay the same.

'If you think about organisations that have lasted a long time, is the organisation the same today as it was 100 years ago?' he asks rhetorically. Probably not, is the answer, but for Rhodes the aim must be for organisations 'to reach a sense of balance between change and stability'.

So an organisation might change ownership, or working practices might alter, or the immediate aims of the organisation might shift, but at the heart of it all is the same ethos. A way to maintain this ethos is through story or narrative.

'One can argue that what keeps an organisation together over a long time is the fact that there is a story that you can tell about it that traces its development over time, just like an individual's personal history,' says Rhodes. It doesn't even have to be a story of an individual, but just something that helps define the culture of an organisation and provide the touchstones that form its foundation and its goals. Perhaps that's why religion has been so successful over the centuries – all religions have a built-in story that defines

them. Organisations looking towards the deep future, or a future in space, could use science fiction to provide their story lines and communicate their set of values to the public.

A future for humanity as depicted in science fiction such as *Star Trek*, or Iain M. Banks' *Culture* novels, or Peter F. Hamilton's *Commonwealth* sagas, or many other futuristic tales, is the dream. Yet maybe a dream is all it will ever be. It could quickly turn into a nightmare, because there is another side to L: the possibility that the lifetime of civilisations is short.

The 10,000-Year Clock has a nemesis.

You won't find it hanging on any wall, or fixed atop any tower. As a timekeeper, it's pretty shoddy. It's been telling the time since 1947, yet its hands have only ticked on 23 occasions in all that time. Like the 10,000-Year Clock, this clock also measures humanity's future, but not in millennia, not in years, not even in days or hours, but only in minutes.

Unlike the 10,000-Year Clock, the existence of its nemesis is only metaphorical, but the time it tells is just as profound. As I sit writing this during the uncomfortably hot summer of 2018, the time on the clock currently reads two minutes to midnight. As I look at the time, the sweat I feel around my collar isn't just the summer heat. For should the clock strike midnight, then the bells will toll for all of humanity as a new day dawns: doomsday.

The Doomsday Clock is a figurative device designed to warn those who take heed how close we are to annihilating ourselves through misdemeanour or misadventure. The Doomsday Clock is the invention of artist Martyl Langsdorf and nuclear physicist Eugene Rabinowitch, who edited the *Bulletin of the Atomic Scientists*, and its hands move in reaction to world events that may place the survival of humanity in

greater or lesser jeopardy. Back in 1947, when Langsdorf and Rabinowitch first told the time on the clock, it read seven minutes to midnight. The United States had used the atomic bomb twice and was the only country to wield such destructive power, but in 1949 the Soviet Union tested their first nuclear weapon and the hands of the Doomsday Clock turned to three minutes to midnight. Over the years the clock has been backwards and forwards; in 1991, after the fall of the Berlin Wall was followed by the fall of the Soviet Union itself, the members of the *Bulletin*'s Science and Security Board moved the clock back to 17 minutes to midnight, the clearest distance we've ever had from nuclear war. In the years since, as global politics have become increasingly destabilised and other threats, such as the climate emergency, have begun to loom large, the Doomsday Clock has steadily ticked closer to midnight. It's entirely up to us what happens next, which harks back to something said in Chapter 1: maybe the true sign of intelligence is not that a civilisation is able to invent nuclear weapons, but that it can choose not to use them.

The L-factor and the Doomsday Clock are related. Should Doomsday Clocks across the Galaxy regularly reach midnight, then we should expect L to have a low value, reducing the chances of another civilisation existing for the same short period as we do. If L is a low value, then we would not expect SETI to be successful, since all the aliens would have already become extinct.

It's a dangerous Universe out there and the list of threats is long. Not only do we have nuclear war and climate change to worry about, but we could also be destroyed via a global pandemic, a depletion of natural resources accelerated by overpopulation and overconsumption, or an unforeseen technological accident. Outside of Earth we have the hazards of asteroid and comet impacts, supernovae, interstellar dust clouds that could block the Sun's light and, in the long run, the death of our Sun, all of which will threaten our existence. Those are only the threats that we know about; there are also undoubtedly all the ones we don't know about yet,

and we find ourselves existing at a time when human civilisation has never been more vulnerable. We currently languish in a bottleneck, 7.5 billion people all crammed onto the same blue-white-green globe. One misstep and we're all wiped out.

The Great Filter

This could be what economist and futurist Robin Hanson of George Mason University terms the 'Great Filter', which is an attempt to explain the Fermi Paradox. One of the most popular, if downbeat, explanations of the paradox is that the value of L is small, resulting in humankind simply being alone in the Universe at this current time. Perhaps a small L is the result of Hanson's Great Filter. Let's assume for now that such a filter exists, cutting short life's potential time and again across the Universe, like some great scythe that comes crashing down from the sky at some predetermined point in history. Whatever it could be, it has to be ubiquitous, a pre-determined fate that applies to all life and all potential civilisations, whatever shape they may take, without exception. Otherwise civilisations would inevitably slip through the net and go on to prosper, resulting in there being no paradox. If we're going to take the Fermi Paradox and the Great Filter seriously, then there can be no escape.

If the Great Filter exists, then it could lie somewhere on the various evolutionary mega-trajectories that we mulled over in Chapter 2. Perhaps the filter is the origin of life itself. It would surely explain a great deal if it is. The first living cells on Earth were formed over 3.7 billion years ago[*] from the self-assembly of seemingly random organic (carbon-based) molecules. Yet there were so many molecules, and so

---

[*] This figure of 3.7 billion years comes from the oldest evidence for life on Earth, in the form of sediments called stromatolites, which were laid down by ancient microbes.

many ways that they could combine, that at first glance it seems like pure luck that they happened to assemble into living cells. In their laboratory experiments and computer models, evolutionary biologists search for fundamental rules in biochemistry that could govern how organic molecules formed amino acids, then proteins, RNA, DNA and then cells, in much the same way that the rules of physics allow protons, neutrons and electrons to come together to form the atoms that then ultimately bond to form those molecules. Suppose, though, that it turns out there are no rules, and life on Earth is just a fluke of nature. If that is true, then we wouldn't expect SETI to be successful because the odds of life forming by chance more than once would be just too great. So maybe the Great Filter was at the very beginning, and we were just lucky to sneak through.

Alternatively, maybe the Great Filter was the development of eukaryotes from prokaryotes, or the jump from single-celled organisms to complex, multi-celled life. Possibly it is the development of large brains, or tool use, or complex social structures. Some might say that it's the environmental conditions, with most planets being too unstable over millions of years to permit life to develop down any really interesting avenues. However, we countered this Rare Earth hypothesis in Chapter 3.

If we could find a separate origin of life on another world in the Solar System, such as in the ocean of Jupiter's moon Europa, it would be a big deal. This is because if life on Earth really is a fluke, then the odds would be even greater against it happening a second time on another body orbiting our Sun. Should life be found in, say, the oceans of Europa or Enceladus, it would effectively rule out the proposition that it is hard for life to form. The more complex life is, the later in life's development the Great Filter must fall.

This is the scenario that keeps Nick Bostrom, head of the Future of Humanity Institute at the University of Oxford and whom we first met in Chapter 1, awake at night. Suppose SETI continues to come up empty-handed, but that we find

microbial life elsewhere in the Solar System.* Great! But we shouldn't celebrate, says Bostrom, because it would strongly suggest that all those early steps in life's evolution are not where we will find the Great Filter. Instead, it could mean that the Great Filter is not in the past, but lies in wait for us in the future.

'We would still hope, even if we found bugs on Mars, that the Great Filter is behind us,' he says. 'But the more advanced the independently evolved life we discover, then the fewer places there are in our past where the Great Filter could reside, and so that would shift the probability over to the hypothesis that the Great Filter is waiting for us in our future.'

So again we return to the bottleneck that we're currently in. 'There could be various kinds of "failure modes" that are common to all sufficiently advanced civilisations,' Bostrom muses as he contemplates the downfall of intelligent life on a galactic scale. 'For example, there could be some technology that is bound to be discovered once you become advanced enough, and once you discover that technology then it inevitably destroys you. It could be artificial intelligence or nanotechnology or a technology that we haven't yet thought of.'

In his 2005 book *Collapse*, Jared Diamond investigates the nature of some of these failure modes in the context of societies on Earth that have undergone catastrophic collapse in the past. Startlingly, he finds that a common theme across

---

* Mars and Earth have swapped a lot of material over the past 4.5 billion years, as shards of rock blasted into space by giant impacts on one planet have fallen as meteorites onto the other. It's plausible that this transfer of material may have also transferred biological material, or even life itself. Therefore, if we find microbial life on Mars, it may be impossible to determine if it originated there, or on Earth. Perhaps even life on Earth originated on Mars. For a truly independent origin of life, we'd be better off looking for life in the sealed oceans of Europa and Enceladus.

almost all these failed civilisations was how they exceeded their habitat's 'carrying capacity' – in other words, the total population that an environment's natural resources can sustain. From Easter Island to Greenland, and from the Anasazi to the Mayans, a common theme to all their troubles was overpopulation and consumption in the face of finite resources, leading to ecological disaster.

It doesn't need reiterating that Earth – or rather, the life that inhabits our planet – is headed straight for its own ecological disaster. Climate change, deforestation, over-population and pollution are all affecting our planet's carrying capacity. As long ago as the eighteenth century, with Europe reaping the benefits of the Agricultural Revolution, the cleric Thomas Malthus warned of what he believed to be the tendency for human population to rapidly grow in size in response to increasing abundance, to the point that there would quickly become too many people, exceeding the carrying capacity in terms of food production, causing mass starvation and forcing population numbers to fall drastically.

In the years since, the logic behind this 'Malthusian trap' has been fiercely debated. In 1972 the 'Club of Rome' – a group filled with people from a variety of backgrounds including academicians, diplomats, politicians and scientists – issued their controversial *Limits to Growth* report based on primitive computer models. The outlook, they claimed, was gloomy, with ecological disaster right around the corner based on assumptions of runaway population growth and resource consumption. It was the Malthusian trap again, dressed up for the twentieth century.

Although *Limits to Growth* was immediately met with resistance and criticism, it still has its supporters. A paper published in the journal *Nature Sustainability* in 2018 by researchers at the University of Leeds argues that, in order for all 7.6 billion people on Earth today to live in comfort, we would have to exceed Earth's carrying capacity.

The problem that many critics have with *Limits to Growth* is the pessimistic assumptions upon which its conclusions are based. The data fed into the computer models that formed the

basis of the *Limits to Growth* report assumed that population growth and consumption would continue exponentially, when in reality the opposite is happening. In Europe, the United States, Japan, Taiwan and many other countries, affluence is corresponding with lower birth rates that have declined close to, or even below, death rates. Many predictions expect that the rest of the world will follow suit over the following decades, with the global population reaching a peak of between 8 and 10 billion people and then reducing, naturally, towards the end of the twenty-first century.

The *Limits to Growth*-type predictions assume that the carrying capacity of an environment is a fixed value. This, however, need not necessarily be the case. Through care, good long-term planning, intensive agriculture, the use of alternative energy sources such as nuclear and renewables, and the invention of new technologies, we can increase the carrying capacity of Earth. And why stop there? In Chapter 5 Jason Wright spoke of extraterrestrial civilisations moving their energy production and computing facilities (which can produce a great amount of waste heat) into space. Imagine vast solar arrays in orbit converting the Sun's energy into microwaves that can be beamed down to Earth and converted into electricity to power our homes. We don't have to be limited by the carrying capacity of one planet – long term, we can talk about the carrying capacity of the entire Solar System.

Alas, it isn't going to be easy. The climate emergency is acting to reduce the Earth's carrying capacity and is the biggest danger humanity currently faces. Already it is slowing global yields of major crops, and increasing desertification and drought will only enhance that decline in agricultural productivity. A 2018 study concluded that a 2-degree Celsius (3½ degrees Fahrenheit) average warming across the planet – and we are already halfway towards that – would enhance various feedback effects and cause them to accelerate in unison to create a runaway greenhouse effect and a 'hothouse' Earth. This particular prediction isn't a sure thing – we're still grappling with fully understanding how those feedback effects will

operate – but if we are to allow warming to continue unabated then whatever happens, there will be no rosy outcome.

We do have the tools to fix things, and the understanding of what needs to be done. The biggest problems in combating the climate emergency are our own ignorance, our own greed, our tendency to leave problems for someone else to solve for us. We need an immediate and global reduction in the production of greenhouse gases. Those who know better but still lie about climate change being a hoax, or those who put profits ahead of solving our climate problems, are the biggest traitors to the human species that we have.

So, it seems that our civilisation's path through industrialisation to a more technologically advanced state inevitably must overcome the challenges set out above: carrying capacity, the potential for mass destruction and the climate emergency. You could think of them as coming-of-age rites for civilisations – figure out how to deal with these problems and you can move on to the next phase of your development; fail, and you will stutter and possibly die. The question that SETI needs to ask is, are these coming-of-age rites ubiquitous for all civilisations? The assumption is yes, but a closer examination shows that this is, once again, projecting human experience onto extraterrestrial civilisations.

The course that a civilisation takes depends largely on the socio-cultural origins of that civilisation – after all, that's what anthropologists study in the various civilisations on Earth, from lost tribes to the vast empires of history. Without knowing the socio-cultural origins of an extraterrestrial civilisation and how that may affect their longevity, we can only guess – and as we have seen, that often means using western human experience as a template. But surely, any technologically advanced species must have had to deal with climate change as a result of their industrial emissions, and find a way to live in harmony with their environment's carrying capacity?

Hmm. Okay, try this for size. Imagine an advanced extraterrestrial civilisation that evolved in such a way that it is more reliant on its environment than we humans are in order to survive. Such a civilisation would have adapted to be more in tune with its planetary environment, more receptive to the signs of it becoming overloaded, and so more aware of the need to protect that environment. If they did develop a fossil-fuel-based industrial economy, perhaps they were aware of the potential dangers from the beginning and have been able to mitigate them.* The path taken by their technology need not be the same as ours either, and perhaps they figured out how to split the atom before they developed large-scale global industries based on fossil fuels. Or maybe their environment is more conducive to the use of renewable energy; a planet with constantly strong winds or clear sunny skies might foster a civilisation that uses more wind or solar power, for example. In short, their biology, culture and technology could have developed completely differently so that they didn't go down the same path that we have trodden. What this means for SETI is that it lessens the likelihood that the Great Filter is something that is the fault of life, because life and civilisations will evolve and develop in different ways, taking them down different paths and encountering different obstacles. If the Great Filter is real, and remember whatever it is it must be 100 per cent efficient, then for this reason it is probably not something intrinsic in civilisations. Instead, maybe it's something extrinsic, and that's an even scarier thought because we would have a lot less control over it.

Sixty-five million years ago, the dinosaurs were helped on their way to extinction by the impact of a 10km-wide (6-mile) asteroid. There was nothing the dinosaurs could have done about it. We, however, are different: we can potentially do

---

* An article in the March 1912 edition of *Popular Mechanics* describes how the burning of fossil fuels adds billions of tonnes of carbon dioxide to the atmosphere every year, gradually raising the temperature of the atmosphere. 'This effect may be considerable in a few centuries,' it said. We can't say we were not warned.

something about hazardous asteroids. Blowing up an incoming asteroid with nuclear weapons, à la Sean Connery in *Meteor* or Bruce Willis in *Armageddon*, isn't really an option. Instead, the trick is to subtly alter an asteroid's trajectory so that it misses Earth, and early in the 2020s, NASA will put this theory to the test with its DART (Double Asteroid Redirection Test) mission, which will crash into a small moonlet belonging to an asteroid called Didymos in an attempt not to blow the moonlet to smithereens, but merely give it a nudge so that it alters its orbit. Of course, when confronted with an asteroid that will impact Earth, we have to discover it in enough time to send a mission to deflect it, but several astronomical surveys, such as the Pan-STARRS telescopes in Hawaii, are designed to find these rogue rocks.

If we can defend Earth against asteroid threats, then it would seem fair to assume that any extraterrestrial civilisation with space-faring technology could do so too. There is a window of vulnerability until a civilisation achieves space flight, but the rate of extinction-level impact strikes is low enough that civilisations will have enough time to develop, much as we have. A 1km-wide (0.6-mile) asteroid impacts Earth on average every half a million years, and the impacts of larger objects are even less frequent.

Exploding stars

So, while impacts can be a filter for life, they are not the ultimate Great Filter. What about something from beyond even our Solar System – the death of a star in a supernova event?

When we look into the night sky, we find the closest candidate to us for the next star to go supernova is the red supergiant Betelgeuse, on the shoulder of Orion, the constellation of the Hunter familiar to us through the three stars of its Belt. Stars can 'die' once they have run out of fuel to fire their nuclear reactions in one of two ways, depending on their mass. Lower-mass stars like our Sun expire gently, swelling, cooling and expelling their outer layers to leave

behind an inert core, which we term a 'white dwarf'. Stars with eight times the mass of the Sun, or more, however, go out more violently. When nuclear fusion reactions in their core cease, gravity causes them to collapse. Their core condenses to become a neutron star – a dense ball of concentrated matter just a dozen kilometres (7 miles) across but with the mass of several suns – while their outer layers bounce off the collapsing core, producing a shockwave that rips the star apart as a supernova.

There's no way to tell whether a star has nearly run out of nuclear fuel in its core, so for all we know Betelgeuse might explode in a million years, or we could watch it explode tomorrow. All that we know is that it is sufficiently massive to explode one day. Fortunately, it's too far away from us – 640 light years – for its radiation to cause us any harm. It would put on a great light show, though.

However, there have been stars closer to us that have gone supernova. Exploding stars are alchemists, forging rare isotopes of heavy elements and spreading them across space as they ride the supernova's superheated blast wave. Among these elements is iron-60, which has a half-life of 2.6 million years (meaning half of a given quantity of iron-60 will undergo radioactive decay in that time). Studies have found anomalous amounts of iron-60 in sediments deposited on the floor of the Atlantic, Pacific and Indian oceans, and calculating backwards based on its half-life, the iron-60 was laid down during two time periods: the first between 1.5 and 3.2 million years ago, and the second between 6.5 and 8.7 million years ago. A similar abundance of iron-60 dating to the same time periods has also been identified in Moon rocks. Only nearby supernovae, at distances of 290 and 325 light years, which exploded during these two periods could have flooded Earth with that much iron-60. How did these two supernovae affect Earth?

Investigating the impact of cosmic events upon life on Earth is Adrian Melott, Emeritus Professor at the University of Kansas. Although trained as a cosmologist, he now pioneers the field of 'astrobiophysics'. By his reckoning there have been

19 mass extinctions on Earth in the past 500 million years (the exact number varies depending upon whom you speak to, since there is some debate about how much of the biodiversity has to die off in order for it to be considered a mass extinction), and at best the causes of only two of these are understood to any satisfactory measure. It's a scary thought that our planet repeatedly experiences a vast and sudden loss of life, and we don't know why.

The timing of one of these mass extinctions, which took place 2 million years ago at the boundary between the Pliocene and Pleistocene epochs, coincides with one of the supernovae that deposited the iron-60. So Melott, as part of a team of astronomers led by Brian Thomas of Washburn University in the USA, has built computer models that try to mimic in the digital world the effect that the radiation from the supernova would have had on Earth. What the models found was startling: the supernova produced cosmic rays, which are high-energy particles moving at almost the speed of light, so powerful that they passed straight through Earth's magnetic shield, continued through the stratosphere and into our lower atmosphere, called the troposphere, where they smashed into a number of molecules that make up our atmosphere – molecular nitrogen and oxygen, carbon dioxide and the like. The collisions caused the instantaneous fission of the impacted molecules, producing a shower of 'daughter nuclei' – particle fauna such as protons, neutrons and, in particular, muons – that acted as a wave of ionising radiation that penetrated through to the surface and as deep as a kilometre (over 3,000ft) into the oceans. It meant a 20-fold increase in the radiation dose for life on Earth at the time.

It's tempting to say that the ionising radiation as a result of the supernova definitely caused the mass extinction at the Pliocene–Pleistocene Boundary, but the evidence is still circumstantial – the correlation of the timing of the supernova and the mass extinction does not necessarily mean causation. 'There have been a lot of people who have talked about the effects of nearby supernovae,' says Melott. 'The big difference now is that we have actual evidence of an event at a certain

time, and it's a time that is recent enough that we have a decent fossil record and geological information, so it is possible to do a pretty good check.'

If they're right, then a supernova has to go off only within 300 light years to do some damage to Earth's biosphere. Although there are currently no supernova candidates within that distance of Earth, stars are moving all the time and in the future we will find ourselves once more too close to an exploding star. The rate of supernovae in our Milky Way Galaxy is estimated to be about one per century. Eventually extraterrestrial civilisations on other planets will find themselves in the firing line.

However, like the impact hazard, the danger from super-novae can be abated by colonising space. If a civilisation can embark on interstellar travel and spread colonies across many hundreds of light years, then no one supernova explosion can take out the entirety of that civilisation. Of course, interstellar travel on that kind of scale seems far-fetched to us at the present time, and we may never accomplish it. However, we know that in principle interstellar travel is feasible, so other civilisations could accomplish it, particularly if they evolve to be post-biological, having merged with artificial intelligence. Therefore, supernovae explosions cannot destroy every civili-sation that ever arises. They cannot be the Great Filter.

What's needed to ensure that every civilisation in the Galaxy meets its doom is a galaxy-spanning threat. It turns out that there may be one.

The Universe's biggest explosions

The signing of the 1963 Partial Nuclear Test Ban Treaty forbids all tests of nuclear weapons between the signatories – primarily the USA, UK and the Soviet Union, plus another 120 nations that joined over the years (proving that we can make good choices sometimes). The US, however, was concerned that the Soviet Union might try and get around the treaty by testing nuclear weapons in space, and so during the 1960s the United States launched the top-secret Vela

series of satellites, designed to detect the X-rays and gamma rays from covert nuclear explosions. The usually dreary task of sifting through the Vela data fell to scientists at the Los Alamos National Laboratory in New Mexico, where a team led by Ray Klebesadel noticed something peculiar. The Vela satellites were detecting powerful bursts of gamma rays, but not from nuclear tests. These 'gamma-ray bursts', or GRBs for short, were hailing from random directions in deep space. For almost 25 years nobody knew how far away they were, never mind what they were.

The mystery was solved in 1997, when an afterglow of visible light resulting from a GRB was traced back to a distant galaxy located six billion light years from us. Things became even more complex when it was realised that there are two main types of GRB. One type lasts for several minutes and are hence known as 'long' GRBs, whereas the other type are fleeting blasts, lasting less than two seconds, and hence are known as 'short' GRBs.

The first type are pretty nasty. Our best explanation, Stan Woosley's collapsar model, depicts a fast-spinning massive star that collapses at the end of its life, just like a supernova. The difference is that in an ordinary supernova the core collapses down to form a neutron star. In a collapsar, the runaway gravitational collapse of the core doesn't stop at the neutron-star stage, but keeps going to form a black hole. Much of the rest of the star follows the core collapse, but there's too much matter for this newly born black hole to swallow all at once, so the stellar material forms a spinning accretion disc as it waits its turn to tumble beyond the event horizon. The fast rotation and magnetic fields inherent in this spinning disc funnel some of the stellar matter up into columns that blast away from the black hole at almost the speed of light. All of this, by the way, takes place in mere fractions of a second. As electrons in the beams spiral around the magnetic field lines, they generate gamma rays, which we then see as the GRB flash. The energy released in these beams is tremendous, typically about 10^{44} (that's, gosh, 100 trillion quadrillion quadrillion) joules. The most powerful GRB

ever recorded was observed in September 2008. This beast had an energy equivalent to 9,000 ordinary supernovae.

Observations suggest that long GRBs tend to take place in environments with low abundances of heavy chemical elements, *i.e.* in the early Universe, or in chemically stunted dwarf galaxies. It's not clear whether our Milky Way Galaxy could give birth to a star that could explode in a GRB, but our Galaxy does cannibalise smaller dwarf galaxies and could potentially import one. Should a GRB explode in our Galaxy, the beam would sterilise any planet in its path, right across the Milky Way.

The second type isn't much fun either. The short GRBs are produced when two neutron stars orbiting one another collide and merge tumultuously, quite possibly creating a new black hole. Remember, neutron stars are created by ordinary supernovae, and to have two neutron stars orbiting one another, one just needs a binary star system in which both stars are massive enough to go supernova. There are many such systems identified in our Milky Way Galaxy. Of course, it's the ones that have already exploded that are the more immediate danger, although it can take many millions, even billions, of years for the neutron stars to spiral close enough to merge. It doesn't help that, because neutron stars are small and dark, they are very hard to find. In Stephen Baxter's novel *Space*, published in 2000, an advanced extraterrestrial civilisation attempts to prevent the collision of two neutron stars. They know their efforts will fail and that time will run out for them before they can complete their project, but they hope that their efforts will instead be passed down to the next generation of intelligent civilisations to try and prevent the next short GRB in the Galaxy.

The Vela satellites were designed to detect nuclear explosions and discovered GRBs quite by accident. Today, we have specially dedicated satellites, such as NASA's Swift mission and the Fermi Gamma-Ray Space Telescope, watching for GRBs. On average they see one per day, from somewhere in the Universe. Melott has even suggested that the Ordovician

mass extinction 440 million years ago was the result of a GRB in our Galaxy, its gamma rays having depleted our ozone layer, allowing deadly ultraviolet radiation to pass through the atmosphere.

The thing about GRBs is they are not isotropic (isotropic means unvarying in magnitude in any direction). Instead they concentrate their energy along a narrow beam, albeit one that can wreak devastation across the breadth of the Galaxy. However, in theory, as long as we stay out of that beam, we'll be relatively safe. So again, a civilisation colonising the Galaxy should be immune. Assuming that civilisations can, in the long run, expand across such wide expanses of space, then not even a GRB could be their Great Filter. Remember, all it takes is for one civilisation to accomplish this – and as we saw in Chapter 5, it could be achievable in relatively short timescales, cosmically speaking – and they would render the Fermi Paradox and the Great Filter null and void.

Above the galactic parapet

There could be one more cosmic threat that could potentially affect every star and every planet. Sifting through the fossil records of Earth in his search for mass extinctions and their causes, Melott has identified another controversial correlation, specifically a proposed periodicity of about 62 million years between some mass extinctions. Actually, lest Melott correct me, that's not entirely accurate. Rather, he has found a periodicity in bursts of biodiversity in the fossil record, which are a proxy for extinction events.

'On average, about 10 or 15 million years after a drop in biodiversity [after a mass extinction] there will be a jump in biodiversity,' he says. In other words, mass extinctions are always followed by a period of blooming biodiversity – the dinosaurs, for example, evolved in the aftermath of the ominously named 'Great Dying', the Permian–Triassic mass extinction 252 million years ago, which wiped out over 90 per cent of all species on Earth. Of course, it was another

mass extinction almost 200 million years later that killed the dinosaurs; what comes around goes around.

Back to the cycle of biodiversity. Exploding stars, asteroid impacts and supervolcanoes are all events that are randomly distributed in time and cannot possibly be responsible for regular mass extinctions. Whatever caused these extinctions was something that Earth runs into time and time again. Therefore, Melott started looking at the Sun's – and consequently the Earth's – passage around our Galaxy. It takes 220 million years to orbit our Galaxy, at a distance of about 26,000 light years from the Galactic Centre. But as the Sun orbits, it also bobs up and down out of the plane of the Milky Way. Not by much – no more than 230 light years – but Melott thinks it is significant because it puts our Solar System in harm's way. Checking the fossil record for the falls and rises in biodiversity, Melott noticed that the extinctions occurred when the Solar System was at its highest point above the plane of our Milky Way Galaxy, and that's a dangerous place to be.

Our Galaxy is part of a small family of galaxies called the Local Group; other members include the famous Andromeda and Triangulum galaxies. Together, this little community of galaxies is falling at 200km (125 miles) per second towards a much bigger city of galaxies called the Virgo Cluster,* which is about 50 million light years away, give or take. Yet even this far from it, we find that the Local Group is ploughing through the edges of the intra-cluster medium – a fog of hot, X-ray-emitting gas centred on the Virgo Cluster. Our Galaxy is approaching the Virgo Cluster at a tilt, so that one side of the Milky Way is exposed to this hot gas whereas the other

---

* As far as the hierarchy of galaxy clusters goes, the Virgo Cluster turns out to be fairly middle-of-the-road. In 2014 it was discovered that both the Local Group of galaxies and the Virgo Cluster are just part of a much larger structure called the Laniakea Supercluster, which encompasses 100,000 other galaxies spread across half a billion light years.

side is shielded by all the gas and dust in our Galaxy's spiral arms. On that leading side the hot gas interacts with our Galaxy's magnetic field, and the shockwave resulting from that interaction accelerates particles to high velocities – they become cosmic rays. Every 62 million years the Sun and its attendant planets, including Earth, stick their heads up above the parapets of the plane of the Galaxy and into that maelstrom of cosmic-ray radiation.

The radiation dose that this incurs would be modest compared to a supernova – perhaps tripling the annual average dose – but it's the fact that this would last for several million years that has a cumulative effect, says Melott. The last time Earth was in this position above the plane of the Milky Way was about 55 million years ago, when biodiversity dropped by about 10 per cent.

'If this idea is right, then in less than 10 million years we will be at maximum cosmic-ray exposure,' says Melott. The clock is ticking.

Not everyone agrees with Melott. The alleged periodicity causes the most consternation, with critics pointing out that the periodicity doesn't exactly match when the extinctions took place. However, Melott says that's missing the point that the evidence for the periodicity is from the increase in biodiversity in the aftermath, which isn't going to be on an exact timer. As for the Great Filter, a 10 per cent drop in biodiversity does not sound as though it would be fatal to all life. Could a civilisation survive this cosmic radiation exposure? We'll find out in about another 7 million years' time.

Under the shadow of the magnificent St Paul's Cathedral is a rather more modern cathedral built not in the name of God, but in the name of capitalism: the London Stock Exchange. Here, stocks are bought and traded, driving international commerce and deciding whether we are in a period of economic boom or economic recession. So

complex have the stock markets become that they are increasingly driven not by human intuition, but by algorithmic programs designed to respond quickly to movements in the markets. Yet the decisions performed by these algorithms, which are a form of artificial intelligence, can be perplexing. Some have likened them to black boxes – you provide them with an input of numbers, and they produce an output of stocks bought and sold, but what goes on in between the input and the output, how the algorithm chose to buy or sell those particularly stocks, remains a little murky. It's a genuine concern, considering how markets have a habit of falling like dominoes in response to anything out of the ordinary.

Austin Gerig is the man whose job it is to better understand the high-frequency trading of these algorithms. As the Assistant Director of the Division of Economic and Risk Analysis at the US Securities and Exchange Commission, Gerig models the actions of the algorithms statistically in order to figure out what they are going to do and perhaps help to prevent or mitigate stock-market crashes.

Stock markets are complicated creatures, and working in them can be a stressful, tense job. So how does a man like Gerig, for whom statistics and maths and logic are his thing, unwind? By considering the consequences of parallel universes and the end of civilisation, that's how.

Gerig isn't joking. In his spare time he's found an opportunity to research these heady subjects, applying his statistical rigour to them. Most notably, he's focused on a terrifying theory known forebodingly as the Doomsday Argument.

The disquieting logic behind this argument, which declares that we really are heading towards the twilight of our existence, all comes down to maths and probability. First raised as a fearsome possibility by the Australian theoretical physicist Brandon Carter in 1983, the more common version of the argument goes like this:

Suppose humankind does have a long future ahead of it, perhaps one that sees us expand out and colonise the rest of the Solar System, or indeed the rest of our Galaxy. By the

time the 10,000-Year Clock reaches the year 10,000, humans could number in their trillions. Compare that to today, when it is estimated that some 108 billion people have so far been born and lived on Earth (according to figures from the Population Reference Bureau in Washington, DC) since the advent of *Homo sapiens*. Just comparing these two figures makes it clear that there would be a lot more human lives ahead of us than behind us, and if any of us were inserted into the human race at random, we'd be more likely to find ourselves in the deep future when there are many more people than in the here and now, simply because there should be many more opportunities for an individual to exist then.

Except that we do find ourselves in the here and now. Statistically, that seems unlikely, unless those future humans' lives will never exist and humanity is on the edge of falling off a cliff. And so Carter, and subsequently others, have seen this as a logical argument that humanity does not have a future that we could exist in. Doomsday is coming.

It's fair to say that the Doomsday Argument has caused, well, some arguments. Critics point out that the 7.5 billion human beings alive on Earth right now represent just 7 per cent of the total number of humans that have ever lived up to this date. Therefore, would we not have been more likely to have existed in the past as part of the 93 per cent of other humans to have lived so far? It depends upon how you look at it – next to the trillions of potential lives in the future, 108 billion people are but a tiny amount.

Gerig has another criticism. 'The original Doomsday Argument says that you should consider yourself a random person in our civilisation,' he tells me with the same easy nonchalance that he might use when discussing economics, not extinction. 'But that assumes that you already exist, and so given that you exist you should expect a random birth number.'

However, says Gerig, you are more likely to exist the more people there are, which contradicts the Doomsday Argument that there will be a limited number of human lives. A smaller

total population throughout history would explain your (relatively) low birth number better, but a civilisation with a total population throughout history of trillions, maybe even quadrillions, would better explain your existence. You can't have it both ways; the two would seem to cancel out.

'That's why academics initially thought the Doomsday Argument was incorrect,' says Gerig, but he doesn't think that humanity can relax just yet. Along with his colleagues Ken Olum and Alexander Vilenkin of Tufts University in Massachusetts, Gerig believes that he has fixed that flaw, meaning that the Doomsday Argument is back with a vengeance.

They argue that thinking about our birth number relative to all potential human beings is thinking too small-scale. Instead, we should be considering all individuals across the Universe, and maybe even beyond in the parallel universes of the multiverse.

If there have been lots and lots of civilisations, then we are more likely to find ourselves in a long-lived civilisation, regardless of our birth number within that civilisation.

So, if there are many extremely old and populous extra-terrestrial civilisations out there, then the chances are that the Doomsday Argument will not hold. But we knew that already, in a sense – if other civilisations can survive for far longer than we have, then we surely have the potential to do the same. However, if SETI is unsuccessful and we find an empty Universe containing no other surviving civilisations, then Gerig does not rate our chances.

'It would mean that we're not going to have a civilisation that exists for a very long time,' he says gloomily.

He's not absolutist about it, though. There's a chance, he says, if we can spread out among the stars, limiting our vulnerability should something happen to Earth. You might imagine a GRB taking out Earth and neighbouring colonies, but if we can truly go interstellar then we will possibly render human civilisation immune to total collapse. Something would have to end the entire Galaxy to wipe us all out.

Evolved humans

Interstellar migration might also hint at another explanation for the Doomsday Argument. When we refer to all possible humans, it's under the assumption that what it means to be 'human' – both physiologically and consciously – doesn't change in the future. A million years ago, our *Homo erectus* ancestors were wandering the Earth having just figured out how to control fire. In another million years, who knows how we will have evolved? This is further complicated if humanity spreads out and colonises other planets, perhaps light years apart. Evolution will take its own twists and turns on each world if they are sufficiently isolated, potentially leading to new human species on different planets. Technology will also play its part in influencing, and perhaps even over-riding, Darwinian evolution. The Technological Singularity describes the point when computers are able to match and even exceed the complexity and potential of the human brain. If and when that happens, we may be consumed by such technology, or we may merge with it on an equal footing. Either way, the purely biological evolution of humans that do merge with advanced computers would be over, as the merger would irrevocably change what it is to be human. Self-aware robots would be better suited to interstellar travel, immune to the biological challenges of zero gravity and radiation exposure, and able to survive countless years journeying across vast distances. A few million years spent colonising the Galaxy could seem like a short time to our cyborg descendants. The relevance to the Doomsday Argument is that when considering the range of possible humans that will exist through time and space, could we possibly equally expect to have been born as an advanced or evolved human? What makes them human could be different from what makes us human, so perhaps they are off limits in the random birth game.

'The way that philosophers describe it is that they [future evolved humans] are outside of your "reference class",' says Gerig. 'It may be that you are specified by a very restrictive set of properties and that those properties always tend to

occur in the middle or early parts of civilisations. If that's the case then the Doomsday Argument fails, but then it would require that there is something about you that correlates with your early existence in a civilisation.'

So, maybe the Doomsday Argument isn't telling us anything about doomsday after all; maybe it's telling us about our evolution instead.

It's therefore dispiriting that we currently see no evidence for other civilisations having colonised the Galaxy. Earth has been around for 4.54 billion years, so aliens – be they biological or robotic – have had plenty of time to set up home here. If it is imperative that a civilisation conquers the stars in order to survive into the long term, we should see them. The fact that we do not suggests that the Doomsday Argument might be a problem after all. On the other hand, if they do exist and if they had colonised Earth long ago, maybe we would not even be here, having never had the chance to evolve. Perhaps we have to be alone in the Galaxy in order to exist – how about that for a solution to the Fermi Paradox? Yet being alone in the Galaxy may mean we're doomed – another paradox. It's swings and roundabouts.

Hold on. Maybe we are making too many assumptions, yet again. It's the same mistake we make when assuming that the reason the Universe seems silent (I say 'seems' because it could very well be the case that we just haven't searched for long enough or thoroughly enough to discover their signals) is that other civilisations don't exist. There are no facts on which to base that conclusion. We have no idea what a civilisation millions of years older than ourselves would want to do. Maybe they have no interest in colonising planets, or beaming signals at us to try and get our attention. If alien life does evolve into a post-biological robotic status, then perhaps information processing – essentially the curating of knowledge and data – could be their driving motivation. Is that so different from what our own robotic emissaries are doing right now as they explore the Solar System, gathering data and information? To 'learn all that is learnable' was one of the

goals of V'Ger, the fictional Voyager 6 space probe that was made self-aware by an unknown, advanced extraterrestrial civilisation in *Star Trek: The Motion Picture*. If information processing is important to the vast intellects of technologically advanced civilisations, then in that case thermodynamics will play an important role, because computing produces heat (which is why Jason Wright suggested in Chapter 5 that civilisations may move their computing servers off-planet). The Second Law of Thermodynamics describes how heat energy flows from hot to cold, and the colder the surroundings, the faster the heat flows. If an advanced civilisation wants to achieve the most efficient computing (which, if its members are truly post-biological, essentially translates into thinking), it needs to find the coldest environment possible to act as a heat sink. To that end, Milan Ćirković and Robert Bradbury have suggested that advanced civilisations may migrate to the edge of the Milky Way Galaxy, where temperatures are close to absolute zero as a result of the scarcity of stars and dust grains that can warm space. So, as soon as they become post-biological, civilisations might head out there rather than come here, which would explain why Earth has never been colonised. It would also explain why we can't find them, since SETI spends most of its time looking into the Galaxy and towards the centre of the Milky Way, where there are more stars.

It also hints at how extraterrestrial civilisations may survive not just a few million years, or even a few billion years, but into the deep, deep future, a 100 trillion years or more from now, in a distant era of decay when the stars have all gone out, the expansion of the Universe has carried all the other galaxies away over the cosmic horizon, and the planets themselves are coming apart at the seams. Any advanced life that still lingers will camp around the dark remnants that are left – black holes and neutron stars – deriving energy via the steep gravitational gradients of these objects to power their data processing, which for a post-biological life-form might be the same as gathering energy to power their thoughts.

Life cannot survive in our Universe indefinitely. Neutron stars will disintegrate as protons decay. Black holes will evaporate thanks to Hawking radiation. The Universe will undergo heat death, as the flow of heat energy across the Universe eventually results in the cosmos becoming exactly the same low temperature everywhere. Hotter and colder will no longer exist, there will be no flow of energy and computer processing/thinking will become impossible in over 10^{106} years' time. It will be the ultimate filter to strain out life.

We are beset on all sides. The self-inflicted threats of the climate emergency and nuclear war lurk over everybody's shoulders. A deadly pandemic could hit at any time. Natural disasters wait in line to eradicate us. The failure to find evidence for extraterrestrial life bodes ill. It seems even the logic of probability is against us.

In the face of all this, life still persists, too stubborn to be told when to quit. Mass extinctions litter history, yet they have never been 100 per cent fatal. Life has survived them, clawing its way back. In the same way, human extinction is not inevitable, despite what the Great Filter or the Doomsday Argument might say. That's not to say we're invincible – we don't have Teflon armour or Hollywood heroics to guarantee our survival – but we do have choices. We can choose to remain on Earth and allow the environment to rot, or embark on suicidal war, or become careless about technology. Or we can choose to be aware of the dangers and start planning now, preparing our defences against incoming asteroids and comets, decommissioning our weapons of mass destruction, acting immediately to alleviate the worst of global heating and starting to look towards the stars. Our actions today can have consequences that will echo into future history. Can we safeguard our various cultures, our knowledge, our technology so that our descendants can benefit from them? Don't we have a moral obligation to create a better world for those who

will follow, or at the very least to make sure there is a world left for them?

Catastrophe could still happen, to us or to extraterrestrial civilisations, as the result of some event that we cannot account for or control. However, such catastrophes would be stochastic (random) events, and it is down to sheer chance whether they strike before or after a civilisation has the technology and forethought to deal with them, or before or after a civilisation has spread itself among the stars. The Great Filter can only work if it is 100 per cent efficient at wiping out life on every planet where intelligence and civilisation arises, and so far we have not identified any single thing that can fulfil this role. The likelihood, then, is that some civilisations must be able slip through the net of the Great Filter. The success of SETI relies on it.

Our future is going to be the story of one clock or the other. One story is a grand narrative in which humanity thrives and survives long into the future; the other is a fable in which society burns brightly for a short time, only for the lights to go out. We wait to see which of those two stories will be ours, and all the while the clocks keep ticking.

Tick, tock. Tick, tock.

Messages from Earth

M octezuma stood atop the Great Temple of Tenochtitlán, a stepped pyramid at the heart of the Aztec Empire, and gazed down at the approaching phalanx of Spanish conquistadors. He'd received intelligence reports of these foreign invaders, of course, and knew of their alliances with the troublesome Tlaxcalan and Totocanas peoples, neighbouring tribes who rejected the Aztecs' greatness. He'd also heard of the recent slaughter of the people of the loyal city of Cholula at the hands of the Europeans. It had taken half a year for the Spanish to reach Tenochtitlán, but now they were here, coming down through the pass between the volcanoes and approaching the causeway between lakes that acted as the entrance to the city that would ultimately become Mexico City.

In the 17 years under Moctezuma's rule, the Aztec Empire had flourished, expanding aggressively into new territories as they waged war with their neighbours and won new territories. The Empire had never been stronger. Yet with the approach of Hernán Cortés and his conquistadors, 11 of whom were mounted on the strange beasts that the Spanish called *caballos* (horses), and whom some considered to be deities from lands afar, Moctezuma had never felt weaker. Translated, his name roughly meant 'the noble who frowns'. On this day of 8 November 1519 in the European calendar, as he stroked his short black beard anxiously, Moctezuma was living up to his name, with the frown on his face being that of fear. Gods or not, the Spanish were the greatest threat that the Aztec Empire had ever faced.

History tells us the rest of the story. Moctezuma and 200 of his chieftains met Cortés on the causeway and, despite any fear they may have felt, remained noble, inviting the Spanish to stay at Moctezuma's palace. Cortés was happy to work a

political angle, the bloodlust of the slaughter at Cholula sated, for the time being at least, as he sought to negotiate the opportunity to claim the Aztecs' treasures as his own in the name of the King of Spain, Charles V. Yet tensions grew between the conquistadors and the Aztecs. When Cortés was briefly away from Tenochtitlán, the tensions exploded into violence and Cortés' right-hand man, Pedro de Alvarado, took Moctezuma hostage. When Cortés returned his attempts to defuse the situation failed, and Moctezuma was also unable to quell the righteous anger of his own people. The Aztecs rebelled against both Moctezuma and the Spanish, and Moctezuma was killed, possibly slain by his own people who, it is said, came to see him as a traitor. The Spanish were chased out of Tenochtitlán during what became known as 'La Noche Triste' – the sad night. They returned a year later with their Tlaxcalan allies and more Spanish reinforcements, determined to conquer the city once and for all, only to find it drastically weakened by the ravages of smallpox. And thus 500 years ago the great Aztec Empire, the most powerful native force in the New World, fell.

What befell the Aztecs also afflicted the other native Americans as Europeans came first in their thousands, then in their hundreds of thousands, and then in their millions. Yet, while the conquistadors were certainly in the New World for conquest, riches and new territories, their contact with the indigenous population was more complex than simply massacring the natives. They made political alliances, essentially thrusting themselves into the middle of a civil war between different tribes and the Aztecs, and inter-bred with the indigenous population – Cortés' consort and mother to his child was known as La Malinche, a former slave given to him when he conquered the Tabasco people after arriving on the shores of the Gulf of Mexico, and the wily La Malinche proved vital to Cortés since she spoke the native languages and was able to help form those political alliances.

What really destroyed the Aztecs, though, was the diseases that the Spanish brought with them, and to which the natives had no immunity. The situation with imported diseases – not

just smallpox but also chickenpox, scarlet fever, TB, typhoid, plague, even the common cold – became so dire that in the 50 years following the arrival of the Europeans, Mexico's population dropped by 90 per cent. A similar scenario of rampant disease played out across North America. In total, across all the Americas, there were up to 100 million deaths from diseases imported by European colonists and conquerors.

The fate of the Aztecs is commonly cited as a classic example of what happens when a more technologically advanced civilisation encounters a less technologically advanced society, as a warning to those eager to make contact with extraterrestrial civilisations that are almost inevitably millions, if not billions, of years ahead of us. However, Kathryn Denning, an anthropologist from York University in Toronto, Canada, reminds us that the reality was more complex.

'The case of Europeans in the Americas was not about technology or cultural superiority,' she says. Instead, she reiterates that 'Infectious disease was the key factor.'

Which is why Doug Vakoch isn't worried about making contact with extraterrestrial life. A psychologist by training, and for 15 years the only social scientist at the SETI Institute in California, today Vakoch is the President of METI International, an organisation that he founded. METI stands for Messaging Extraterrestrial Intelligence; during his schooldays Vakoch was enthralled by the possibility of beaming messages into space that could be detected by an extraterrestrial civilisation, and would concoct his own messages based on binary code. Now, Vakoch and METI International beam messages into space for real, with the intention of provoking a response from whomever – or whatever – may be out there.

Vakoch has his own doubts about the usefulness of the Aztec example in understanding a possible future contact event with an extraterrestrial civilisation.

'The analogy of European explorers coming to the New World implies a unilateral contact in which the indigenous people had no choice, and a physical contact that I think, with regards to extraterrestrial contact, is implausible,' he tells me over the telephone from sunny California. In his

scenario, contact would be bilateral – we would be inviting them by either looking for their signals, or by transmitting a message to them – and even if there is a risk we should still be safe because 'the contact that we expect is going to be at a distance'. For Vakoch, that means no alien invasion and no biological diseases.

Nevertheless, opposition to METI is fierce, with critics concerned that beaming messages into space and revealing our existence to other beings in the cosmos is incredibly dangerous, especially given that we do not know anything about who may be out there, what their capabilities might be or whether they are malevolent or benevolent.* To that end, in February 2015, 28 scientists and invested members of the SETI community, including Jim Benford, Denise Herzing, SpaceX's Elon Musk, Dan Werthimer and Shelley Wright, published an open letter denouncing METI.

'Our main objection is not so much against METI in its own right, [but] rather it is the behaviour of a very small, insular community of arrogant individuals who are pursuing an activity that might profoundly alter human destiny, without first bothering to discuss it with their scientific peers or with the public,' says David Brin, a Hugo Award-winning science-fiction author and one of the signatories on the open letter, who outspokenly refers to METI's supporters as 'zealots'. With that kind of language, it's not hard to see how the SETI community has been torn asunder by the arguments about METI that rage during scientific conferences, in the pages of learned journals, in op-eds printed in popular publications and through e-mails flung between the opposing sides.

Those who are anti-METI remain concerned that initiating contact with an advanced civilisation could have dire consequences for us if we are not prepared. They point out that normal SETI – in other words, simply searching for extraterrestrial signals or some other evidence of their

---

* Of course, we could be alone in the Universe and 'they' may not even exist. That's certainly a strong possibility and not one that I'm blind to, but for the purpose of this chapter let's assume that 'they' do exist.

existence – is safe, since if we detect a message, we don't have to reply and confirm that we are here. Meanwhile, METI's supporters, including Vakoch and the Russian radio astronomer Alexander Zaitsev of the Russian Academy of Sciences, both of whom have already transmitted messages into space for ET to hear, argue that we are allowing fear to cloud our judgement about METI.

'Fear is a wonderful thing,' says Vakoch. 'It has helped us survive as a species. The question is, when does fear get in the way of a better understanding of the world? So I think, let's get the greatest fears and concerns out there, and then after we've articulated those, we can analyse them and ask, are they rational?'

So let's take up Vakoch's challenge and do just that. Let's explore the possibilities of contact, an adventure that will encompass everything from historical contact events and cultural diffusion to Earth's visibility and the feasibility of interstellar travel and, underlying them all, the role that altruism has to play in how a technologically advanced alien culture might behave towards us. Everything that we have discussed in the previous chapters has led us to this point and the problem of the great Contact Paradox.

The Spanish didn't just bring violence and disease to Mexico. They also brought horses and bulls, a new religion in Christianity, coffee plants and sugar cane and orange trees, and new trade links. Each of these plays a significant role in Mexico's culture and economy today, and while some modern Mexicans curse the names of Cortés and La Malinche, others praise the conquistadors for bringing horses and Christianity, and coffee and sugar and oranges, the growing and export of which provide jobs and livelihoods.

None of which is to say that these benefits justify the deaths during the conquest; rather, they are just examples of the consequences of contact that echo through the centuries. It's important to remember that when we're discussing contact events, we should not only be concerned with what happens

around the point of contact, but also about its repercussions on societies throughout time, as the diffusion of ideologies and technologies into cultures steadily increases in the aftermath of contact. Even if the original contact is peaceful and mutually beneficial, the longer-term consequences can sometimes go unforeseen.

Carolus Clusius was a sixteenth-century multilingual Frenchman and practised botanist, with training in medicine and law. Such varied and useful talents brought him to the attention of one of the most powerful families in Europe, that of the German merchant Anton Fugger, whose wealth was tied into the mining of precious metals made viable by a mercury mine that they owned near the Spanish town of Almadén (mercury, despite its toxicity, is used to distil gold and silver from the mucky ores that they are found in).

Clusius had two responsibilities while working for the Fuggers. Principally he was to be a tutor to Anton's youngest son, Jacob, and together tutor and pupil headed for Spain, where the younger Fugger would be shown the ropes of the family business by Clusius.

His second role, however, was to use his entrepreneurial eye to spot new business opportunities for the Fuggers. So, amid the hustle and bustle of a Spanish dockside, walking the wooden gangways and keeping out of the way of burly men heaving barrels off the wooden decks of tall-masted galleons that had sailed into port from the far-away lands of the New World, Clusius' botanically trained eye spied something both fascinating and peculiar being hauled off the decks of newly arrived ships: a strange root vegetable. He purchased some samples to show his employer, speculating that the Fugger family could make big money from the distribution and sale of these humble vegetables across Europe. Little did Clusius know what impact the vegetable would have. Today, potatoes are a staple diet in kitchens around the world – they are an example of a successful consequence of contact.

The fame brought to him by the humble potato meant that Clusius' reputation now went before him, and he was quickly hired by the Holy Roman Emperor, Maximilian II, to oversee

the curation of the Imperial Gardens in Vienna. This was a plum job for a botanist, and it was during his time in Vienna that Clusius encountered a remarkable flower: the tulip, which had been imported to the Imperial Gardens during contact with the Ottoman Empire a few years earlier by Clusius' predecessor, who worked under Maximilian's father, Ferdinand I. When Maximilian II died in 1576, Clusius departed Vienna, ultimately ending up at the University of Leiden in the Netherlands, tulip bulbs in tow, and he subsequently successfully established them in the botanical gardens of the Low Countries by the 1590s. They were just flowers; what could possibly go wrong?

Tulip mania

The details of what happened next are highly debated among historians, and some of the extremes described in reports – particularly that of the nineteenth-century Scottish journalist Charles Mackay – are strongly questioned. However, even if parts of the story that follows are exaggerated or apocryphal, they still serve as allegory.

The Dutch became entranced with tulips. The flower's tall, strongly coloured petals, painted with stripes and streaks and flame-like patterns, were quite unlike any other flower in Europe. Owning a tulip quickly became a status symbol, and rare varieties cultivated by botanists changed hands for large sums of money. Early varieties of tulip were given grandiose, self-important names like 'Admiral' or 'General'; later, when new varieties were cultivated, the growers attempted to outdo the earlier types in the naming stakes: 'Admiral of Admirals', 'General of Generals'. The growers who were selling them, especially the rare species, began to receive big money for them. Eventually, so the story goes, speculators got involved, buying the flowers and their bulbs just to sell on. Contracts started being agreed to buy tulips at the end of the growing season in the spring. Tulips flowed into Amsterdam, and flowed out too: with demand coming in from other European countries, tulips became the Netherlands' fourth-biggest export.

Mackay named this economic bubble 'tulip mania', and he describes how, inevitably, the mania did not last. Prices reached a peak when, according to Mackay, tulip bulbs started exchanging hands between speculators up to 10 times per day. Many of these speculators would never see the tulips, or their money. In February 1637 the bubble burst and prices collapsed. Mackay writes of people losing everything except the tulip bulbs that they could not sell because nobody wanted them any more.

Although historian Anne Goldgar of Kings College London, in her book *Tulipmania: Money, Honour and Knowledge in the Dutch Golden Age*, questions whether tulip mania did any real economic harm, she suggests that it did lead to a social and cultural crisis in the Netherlands as the Dutch responded to the mania by questioning their ideas about capitalism and immigration (Amsterdam was quickly becoming the merchant centre of the world) and the value of materialism, particularly of the worth of exotic trinkets from overseas. All because of some 'alien' flower that came from afar.

What tulip mania tells us is that during contact between different societies, the subsequent cultural diffusion – the merging of cultures, or the adoption, sometimes forced or without consent, of ideas or manifest objects – can prove disruptive to those societies, especially if one side does not understand the culture and technology of the other side. Take cargo cults, for example; although the phenomenon had been observed prior to the Second World War, it was most noticeably seen after the US military pulled out of New Guinea following the end of the conflict with Japan. Tribespeople in New Guinea and the surrounding Melanesia islands tried to replicate the activities of US servicemen by building runway strips and speaking into boxes in an effort to summon valuable commodities from thin air, not understanding the relationship between the men on the ground with radios, and the cargo drops from overflying aeroplanes.

Contact with an extraterrestrial civilisation may well take place at a very large distance, but cultural and technological

information can still be shared by way of radio or optical signals, and like the tulip this information or technology could disrupt our societies, or like the cargo cults we might not understand it, and powerful ideas and technology that are not understood can wreak havoc. Just look at modern technology such as motor cars or the Internet. They may not have come from contact with other civilisations, but their presence has been disruptive, bringing good and bad, and the bad was not fully understood until it was too late. Cars have the obvious benefit of providing mobility, which leads to increased commerce and employment opportunities, but car accidents claim over a million lives each year, while the pollution they produce and the destruction to the environment to make way for motorways and car parks were not appreciated sufficiently until the damage had already been done. Similarly, the Internet provides vast amounts of information at the touch of a button and provides interconnectivity between everyone on the planet who is online, but we are only now beginning to get to grips with the changes that social media has brought to sectors of our societies, and the misinformation that can spread faster than facts along the cyber highway. Alien technology that is given to us during contact, but of which we lack a full understanding, could potentially be even more disruptive.

Still, humans are a remarkably adaptive species. 'A grand new technology, especially one of mass communication or transportation, has a great potential to deeply affect a society into which it is introduced, whether that society is capable of developing it or not,' says Yakup Bektas, a historian at the Tokyo Institute of Technology, whom we first met in Chapter Five. Bektas studies the history of science and technology, in particular the arrival of western technology to the rest of the world during the nineteenth century – things like telegraph poles and railways – and the impact these technologies had on less technologically advanced cultures.

'The society on the receiving end learns very quickly how to operate and appropriate [the new technology], but it might not – at least in the short term – radically change the social structure,' he continues. He cites the introduction of railways

into nineteenth-century India under the rule of the British Empire, and how not only did the railways pose no threat to the old caste system, they actually reinforced it through a system of first-class and second-class seats and carriages, while bringing all the benefits of increased mobility. 'Visually, railroads and locomotives were majestic and powerful with all their noise and smoke, and they captured people's imagination as wonders, broadening their horizons and bringing them into contact with other people and places.'

Similarly, one could imagine alien technology being introduced on Earth as a majestic and powerful wonder, helping to broaden our horizons. Goodness knows, society needs something like that right now.

Extraterrestrial influence

Less majestic was the introduction of gunpowder in Japan during the mid-sixteenth century by Portuguese traders, says Bektas. At the time, Japan was in the midst of a century-long civil war, and the appropriation and further development of guns and cannons quickly tipped the scales in the war and brought it to an end, uniting Japan under the central government of the Tokugawa shogunate and bringing about the long, peaceful Edo period that lasted between 1603 and 1867. The Tokugawa shogunate were, however, rather isolationist, targeting European traders and European religions, working to eradicate Christianity from their country after it had been introduced by foreigners. Such distrust of outsiders did not benefit their society in the long run and ultimately they relied upon an offshore colony of rich Dutch traders for news about the outside world, which led to the Japanese being increasingly misinformed about what was going on elsewhere. Isolation ultimately results in stagnation, while interaction can stimulate a society.

The introduction of firearms technology thus helped change the political and social scene in Japan, which is quite a dramatic consequence of contact. A similar thing nearly happened in nineteenth-century China during the Taiping Rebellion, where Christian converts led by Hong Xiuquan, who believed

he was the brother of Jesus Christ, waged a 14-year war with the ruling Qing dynasty in an attempt to bring about societal change. In the end the self-proclaimed 'Taiping Heavenly Kingdom' forces were defeated, but only after the deaths of somewhere between 20 and 100 million people.

Yet the events in Japan and China, and other examples from history, involve the introduction of human-made technologies and ideologies into other human cultures. It's not a stretch to see how various societies could adapt to them, given that they were made for humans by humans. Extraterrestrial contact would bring about a very different dynamic of technologies and ideologies made by non-humans and it's impossible to determine exactly what the consequences of those would be. Imagine how an alien technology could alter the dynamics of current world politics, and just as there are many ways in which it could make things better, there are equally as many ways that it could make things worse. Suppose advanced technology got into the wrong hands? But that begets another question: whose would be the right hands? Should everyone have access to alien technology, regardless of how powerful it is, or should it be locked away in a secret warehouse somewhere reminiscent of the one in *Raiders of the Lost Ark*? These are questions that are best asked now, before contact happens, so that we can debate and plan what our reaction should be.

It's worth pointing out that ordinary SETI is not necessarily safe either. Suppose we detect a message, and we manage to decipher it and find that it is an *Encyclopaedia Galactica*, or contains some form of revolutionary scientific or cultural information that we adapt to our own societies. This could be just as disruptive as if we had solicited the contact in the first place. Science fiction, as usual, runs the gamut of possibilities, and is just as valuable an allegory depicting the consequences of contact as tulip mania. Indeed, few people have spent more time thinking about alien cultures, how they might behave and how we might misunderstand them than science-fiction writers. In John Elliot and Fred Hoyle's 1961 science-fiction television series, *A for Andromeda*, advanced extraterrestrials, detected during a SETI survey, beam to us instructions

for building an advanced computer, which then becomes malevolent and tries to conquer humanity. On the other hand, in Carl Sagan's 1985 novel *Contact* (and the subsequent 1997 film), the aliens send us instructions describing how to build a craft that can take humans (a crew of eight in the novel, just the lead protagonist Ellie Arroway in the film) on a brief journey to visit them, and (without spoiling the plot too much) in such a way that does not disrupt society.

These two scenarios, while initially identical in terms of them involving instructions for technology that we barely understand, are at the extremes of the first-contact scale. The reality, should first contact ever happen, will probably be somewhere in between.

That said, it is quite probable that the language barrier will protect us if we detect a signal from an extraterrestrial civilisation before we contact them and give them our own languages to learn. So far in the debate, there has been an inherent assumption that in an extraterrestrial contact event we would be able to understand each other. Unlike in *Star Trek*, however, we will have no universal translator. Languages are not just about having a different word for something in another language. Rather, languages are complex beasts that each have unique characteristics determined by the evolution and nature of the language speaker, cognitive differences, history, cultural differences, environments and a host of other factors. For example, a biological entity would probably have a very different language compared to a sentient artificial machine. A species that communicates primarily with radar echoes, like bats, would inherently have a different view of the world, and a different language, expressed non-verbally, to represent that. We would find it difficult to translate, never mind understand. It would be like trying to tell someone who has been blind all their life what the colour red looks like. Then there is the issue of more complex communication with much denser information content than our own – remember Chapter 2 and our discussion of information theory, Zipf's Law and Shannon entropy. We could be like Koko the gorilla, trying desperately to discern meaning from an extraterrestrial language that has a

Shannon entropy much higher than human languages. We might convince ourselves that we think we know what they mean, but this could lead to misunderstanding, and in a first-contact encounter so pivotal that it might change the course of human history, misunderstandings would be a huge risk.

First contact

Returning once again to science-fiction allegory, the future history presented in the television science-fiction series *Babylon 5* is strongly influenced by the events of a disastrous first-contact event between humanity and an advanced alien species known as the Minbari. When the Minbari's sleek blue space vessels, sporting large fins like sharks, first encounter humans in the form of an Earth expeditionary fleet, the Minbari approach with their gun ports open – essentially pointing their guns at the Earth ships. In Minbari culture, however, this is not a sign of aggression or even a defensive posture, but rather a sign of respect, the same as approaching open-handed, showing they were not trying to deceive. Naturally the human captain of the expeditionary fleet misreads their actions, assuming that the Minbari's gun ports are open because they are about to attack. The Earth ships launch a pre-emptive strike, killing the Minbari leader who is on board one of the alien vessels. This simple misunderstanding between two different cultures, and its catastrophic consequences, precipitates an interstellar war that brings Earth to its knees.

It's fiction, yes, but it also serves as a lesson that extraterrestrial societies will have different cultural norms to our own, and it could be easy to misunderstand them. However, not everyone thinks that would necessarily be a bad thing.

I reached out to the iconoclastic British-born historian Felipe Fernández-Armesto, of the University of Notre Dame in Indiana, USA, to ask for his thoughts on the nature of contact between civilisations, and he had some surprising things to say.

'One of the biggest assumptions about contact is that misunderstandings are bad,' he tells me. 'Really, they are creative and generate new ideas.'

Fernández-Armesto fleshes out these thoughts by taking us back to examples of contact between native peoples and imperial colonists or conquerors, such as Europeans arriving in the New World. While Fernández-Armesto accepts that these contact events are destructive, he points out that that is only part of the picture.

'They [also] inspire and exact innovation, [such as] adjustments to the new environment on the newcomers' part, new languages, new hybrid ways of life,' he says. Misunderstandings can lead to questions between the involved parties and the desire to learn more about each other, or to integrate more closely. There are seldom misunderstandings during contact events in human history as severe or one-sided as that depicted in *Babylon 5*. Then again, in first contact with an extraterrestrial civilisation, we would literally be dealing with an intelligence beyond human experience, and that is something that neither human history nor the best science fiction can teach us about. As we embark on first contact, we will effectively be in the dark as to what to expect, and as probably the junior party of the contact event, we will be relying heavily on the extraterrestrial civilisation to show us a little patience, and to do the heavy-lifting, nannying us through the early stages of the process.

Whether they are willing to do that depends on what it is they want out of contact, and their motivations will be completely unknown to us, at least to begin with. Again, we're back to the altruism assumption and the hope that ET will have our best interests at heart, yet as we saw in Chapter 1, the dominant altruistic forces in nature are kin altruism and reciprocal altruism. Pure altruism – the kind of altruism where you help a stranger, sometimes at a cost to yourself, just because you can – seems relatively rare, at least on a species-wide basis. That's not to say that a culture could not arise that is based on selflessly helping others – indeed, that's the kind of species many of us hope humanity will aspire to be – but we're clutching at straws if we hope to rely on ET being selflessly altruistic during contact, because all the evidence given to us by nature suggests that this is unlikely.

We cannot be genetic kin with ET, so kin selection would appear to be irrelevant, leaving reciprocal altruism as the most likely option. Which in itself does not need to be a bad thing – human civilisation practically operates on it. Look at how political treaties and economic trade deals are organised; they inevitably rely on the partners doing things for each other. That's possibly why more selfless, bigger-picture treaties, such as the 2015 Paris Agreement that attempts to address the climate emergency by curbing emissions, sometimes run into trouble when one of the parties asks, 'What's in it for me?'

This is one of the reasons why David Brin is so worried about METI. Some of METI's supporters have suggested just beaming everything we have into space in one big transmission. 'If I were broadcasting, I would send the Google servers – why not send it all?' the SETI Institute's Seth Shostak rhetorically suggests. We're reminded of Dan Werthimer's statement in Chapter 4 that it would be possible to transmit the entire content of the Library of the US Congress into space on a high-powered laser beam in just a few minutes. It harks back to the idea of the *Encyclopaedia Galactica*, except that this time we'd be the ones beaming it into space. The prospect of this alarms Brin, because in a Universe where the protocols of contact between civilisations could be based on reciprocal altruism, then the only currency that we would have to trade would be our knowledge, art and culture – the kind of things that can be transmitted across the interstellar air waves. With our METI activities potentially offering everything up front for free, we'd be leaving ourselves with absolutely nothing to trade or bargain with later.

'One can wag a finger all day, reminding people of possible dangers and the need for open, critical discussion [about METI] and not betting our children's future on unproven assumptions, and you can explain that our music and art and culture compose our only supply of interstellar trade goods, and it won't make an iota of difference,' Brin tells me. 'Some eager dopes will assume they know better than all our sages and freely elected tribal elders and will pour all our culture into the sky as a free gift while shouting, "Yoohoo!"'

A little leakage

It has been argued that we are already doing what Brin is so against us doing. Where is our culture more commonly found than on the radio waves of television? For almost a century our television and radio signals have been leaking into space at the speed of light in every direction. Inhabitants on planets orbiting the stars of the Ursa Major Moving Group – a collection of co-moving stars, many of which make up the famous pattern of the Plough/Big Dipper in the constellation of the Great Bear – about 80–83 light years away, should just be receiving the television broadcast of the 1936 Summer Olympics in Germany and watching Jesse Owens win his four gold medals, while also getting their first taste of Nazi propaganda – some of the best and worst that humanity has to offer, all in one package. And all our other analogue television and radio transmissions broadcast since then are similarly racing out towards the stars. Doesn't this all make criticism of METI rather pointless?

Doug Vakoch certainly thinks it does. 'It's an understandable motivation that people would want [Earth] to be quiet, but the reality is that we can't take back the signals that have already leaked out,' he points out. 'I just don't think that it's plausible that we can hide.'

It turns out, though, that the issue of Earth's television and radio leakage isn't quite as straightforward as Vakoch, and others before him, including Frank Drake, suggest it to be. To understand why, we have to consider that electromagnetic radiation of any kind – be it visible light or radio waves – loses power with distance according to the inverse square law. What this means is that if a signal travels twice the distance, its strength will be a quarter of what it was at the source; at four times the distance, the strength will be one-sixteenth; and so on. Our television broadcasts are rather feeble to begin with, since they are intended for consumption on Earth rather than being transmitted across interstellar distances, so they are barely detectable upon leaving the Solar System. Integration times are a problem as well; as Earth rotates, any specific radio signal will disappear from view, preventing the

opportunity to build up a good enough signal-to-noise ratio to detect it. Suffice to say, Seth Shostak has shown that if we had a colony on the planet orbiting the nearest star, namely Proxima Centauri, 4.2 light years away, we would not be able to detect our own television signals from Earth using a telescope the size of, say, Arecibo. So it's really not the case that our television leakage could definitely be detected.

But wait! If our extraterrestrial neighbours really are millions of years older than we are, surely their detector technology has advanced beyond ours, with radio telescopes much larger than Arecibo or even the Square Kilometre Array in South Africa and Australia. Seth Shostak has pointed out that a radio telescope the size of Chicago could detect our radio leakage across several hundred light years. That doesn't sound too bad until you calculate – as Jim Benford has done – that a detector with a surface area of 24,800km² (9,575 square miles), which is roughly the same size as the metropolitan area of Chicago, priced at the same amount as the unit cost for each of the Square Kilometre Array's million antennas, would have a total cost of $70,000,000,000,000,000. That's 70 trillion US dollars (£53 trillion). In 2017, the combined gross national product (GNP) of the entire Earth was 127.5 trillion US dollars (£96.5 trillion), so we're talking more than half the planet's entire GNP – and that's not even including the cost of the energy required to operate it and the cost of processing and analysing the data that it collects. It's not exactly change that you might find down the back of your sofa! It's a similar argument to the Arecibo Myth that we talked about in Chapter 4, and the same rules apply here as they did there. Of course, we don't know what alien economics will be, but building and operating such a telescope would involve a significant chunk of their resources; perhaps disproportionately so, unless they are a Kardashev Type II civilisation or greater.

A long-lived advanced civilisation might instead build their detector a piece at a time over the course of centuries or millennia, but remember our discussion from Chapter 5 about building Dyson spheres and how the Galaxy may be littered with half-built structures because interest or economics could

not be maintained across such a long timescale. The point is that, while a Chicago-sized telescope is not impossible, when we factor in the resources that it requires, it becomes more unlikely, which means it is certainly not a fait accompli that our terrestrial television signals have been detected. Furthermore, as we increasingly transition to digital communications rather than analogue, Earth will effectively grow radio quiet. In the old days analogue radio broadcasts would indiscriminately broadcast in all directions from towering transmitter stations, whereas today low-power digital signals are bounced between satellites before being directed back to Earth in confined beams, meaning much less leakage in the future and a narrow window in time during which we will be detectable as a result of our leakage.

Ultimately, it would take a significant effort from ET to be able to detect our leakage, which begs the question, how great are the resources that ET would be willing to invest to strain their listening devices to be able to hear our feeble radio leakage? This would depend on the resources they have at their disposal. Let's remember as well that the idea that a civilisation moves up the Kardashev scale of increasing energy usage as it gets older is also an assumption based on human consumerist and materialistic tendencies, as we discussed with Milan Ćirković in Chapter 5. If civilisations become increasingly optimised, or are very focused in how they use large amounts of energy, then they might not have invested those resources in a giant antenna to watch our television. In hindsight, the assumption that our radio leakage will inevitably have been detected has been bandied about so recklessly and so often by so many people that most just think it's correct without having heard the complexities of this assumption. Arguing for METI as a result of this assumption seems misleading.

But wait again! Artificial radio signals are not the only signs that there is life on Earth. In Chapter 3 we encountered the concept of biosignatures, which can take a variety of forms. Biosignatures are substances produced by life that provide evidence for the existence of that life. An extraterrestrial

civilisation observing us from light years away might notice certain gases in our atmosphere: methane made from carbon-12 atoms that can only be produced by life, or if they cannot distinguish between isotopes of carbon in the methane in Earth's atmosphere, then the simple combination of methane with oxygen would be a huge giveaway that life is producing these gases, particularly as methane would only survive in our atmosphere for about 10 years if it were not being replenished. Seasonal variations in plant life on the surface result in seasonal variations in the amount of carbon dioxide in our atmosphere, while the green leaves of plants themselves strongly reflect not just green light, but infrared light too, creating a 'red edge' in our planet's spectrum.

If ET were to observe Earth from a distance, they would come to the inevitable conclusion that there is life on our planet. Indeed, many of these biosignatures have been present for hundreds of millions of years (land vegetation developed between 725 and 500 million years ago and modern trees only 130 million years ago), or even billions of years (the widespread oxygenation of Earth's atmosphere began about two and a half billion years ago, and dramatically increased following the Cambrian explosion about 540 million years ago). Yet natural biosignatures reveal nothing about the existence of intelligent life. What about artificial biosignatures, such as the pollution content of our atmosphere? In 2014 Harvard-Smithsonian scientists Avi Loeb and Gonzalo González Abad published research that suggested that to detect a level of CFCs[*] 10 times more abundant than the amount in Earth's atmosphere on a nearby exoplanet would require a space telescope larger than the 6.5m (21ft) mirror on NASA's James Webb Space Telescope, which will be the largest telescope ever launched into space. To detect Earth's

---

[*] Of course, CFCs rose to infamy when it was found that they were eating into our protective ozone layer. If we did find a planet with 10 times more CFCs in its atmosphere than on Earth, it would certainly be evidence that there was life, but the destruction of the planet's ozone layer might mean that life was now dead.

pollution would necessitate an even bigger telescope, which is certainly feasible – there are ambitious proposals for creating a giant telescope on the far side of the Moon, away from the glare of reflected light from the Earth, by filling a crater with reflective liquid mercury.

More problematic than having the optical hardware available is the time frame in which pollution has been evident in the atmosphere of our planet. Detectable pollution in our atmosphere has perhaps been around for a century. That's a relatively short span of time relative to the age of the Earth, or indeed the expected age of extraterrestrial civilisations. Astronomers are discovering that pretty much every star has planets. There are upwards of 100 billion stars in our Galaxy, and therefore even more planets. That's a lot of planets to keep your eye on. For all we know, many of them could also display biosignatures, with worlds dominated by microbes or non-technological life, so Earth's natural biosignatures might not necessarily look out of the ordinary. It's entirely possible that a civilisation that is millions of years old hasn't taken a look at Earth in over a century, and will have missed our polluted atmosphere. Sometimes we forget how short a time we've been here for.

It is not inevitable that our technological biosignatures have been detected or that ET knows that there is intelligent, technological life on Earth. There's a good chance that we have gone undiscovered so far. Our artificial biosignatures, be they radio leakage or pollution, could be easy to miss, which is really the point of METI: to beam into space messages that are much more difficult to miss. Or are they?

When Frank Drake received the angry letter from Sir Martin Ryle, he probably sighed inwardly.

It was 1974, and deep within a giant sinkhole nestled in the jungle-covered mountains of Puerto Rico, the largest telescope in the world at that time was getting a makeover. The wire-mesh surface of the giant 305m (1,000ft)-diameter

bowl of the Arecibo radio telescope was being replaced by 38,788 aluminium panels, dramatically increasing the range of radio frequencies that Arecibo could hear. The upgrade transformed Arecibo into the world's most powerful astrophysical tool of the era, with astronomers using it to study pulsars, quasars and interstellar gas in our Milky Way and the galaxies beyond.

So when it came to the time to throw a party in the jungle to celebrate Arecibo's reopening, a grand gesture was needed to demonstrate the telescope's new powers. It just so happened that the Director of Arecibo was none other than Frank Drake – the man who began modern SETI in 1960 with the first search for extraterrestrial radio signals – and it was his assistant, Jane Allen, who came up with the idea of topping the reopening ceremony by using Arecibo to beam a signal intended for intelligent extraterrestrial life to the stars.

You see, Arecibo no longer just listened to the stars. A radar transmitter had been added as part of the upgrades, meaning that now it could talk to the stars as well. But what should it say?

The idea of transmitting a message into space was not new, and Drake had been playing around with the idea of messages incorporating binary code that, when decoded, displayed a kind of pictogram that carried some kind of fundamental meaning about life on Earth. Adapting this technique, he designed the Arecibo message with a total of 1,679 binary digits[*] which, when arranged in a rectangle of 73 rows by 23 columns, revealed the pictorial message.

Drake's message began with a primer on the binary counting system, from numbers one to ten, with which any

---

[*] The number of bits in the message is the product of the multiplication of two prime numbers, 73 and 23. The hope was that this would automatically highlight the signal as being of intelligent origin. However, there's a more prosaic reason why 1,679 bits was chosen. The time taken to transmit them was just under three minutes, and Drake feared people at the transmission ceremony might start growing bored if they had to wait longer for it to send!

aliens who detected the signal would be able to decode the rest of the message. Drake wanted to provide a little bit of basic knowledge about the biology of human beings, so his message also incorporated the atomic numbers (in binary) of the five elements that make up DNA – hydrogen, carbon, nitrogen, oxygen and phosphorus – as well as the chemical formulae for DNA and its component bases and sugars. A pictorial depiction of a DNA helix is also incorporated in the message. Then, Drake provided some information about our planet and the people who sent the message, including the population of Earth in 1974 (which was about 4.3 billion) next to a pixelated graphic of a stick-figure human being and a human's average height of 1.76m (5ft 9in), again in binary. Below that in the message was a simplified depiction of the 'Sun and the nine planets of the Solar System (Pluto was, of course, still considered a fully fledged planet in 1974), with the third planet – Earth – standing out from the rest to imply that was the planet where the message came from. Finally, the message ended with another pixelated image, this time of Arecibo itself with its diameter also provided in binary.

During the ceremony, 250 invited guests sat in a marquee tent close to the radio telescope as the message was beamed to a globular cluster of stars called Messier 13, which is about 22,000 light years away. The audio beeps and bleeps of the message were played out over loudspeakers as Arecibo's transmitter did its thing. Afterwards, everyone went back to their glasses of wine and the canapés and forgot about it. If anyone living in Messier 13 detects Drake's message, then we're going to be in for a long wait to receive a reply – about 44,000 years.

The Arecibo message was a bit of a publicity stunt, a fun way to commemorate the reopening. The signal was never repeated, and so there would be no way for the inhabitants of Messier 13 to verify the signal. The chances of anyone or anything detecting the Arecibo message are vanishingly small. Yet that didn't assuage Ryle, a former Astronomer Royal and Director of the radio telescopes at Cambridge. Brilliant yet famously volatile, Ryle's combative style got

Figure 4: This crude pictogram is the most powerful transmission ever beamed into space, from the Arecibo Observatory in 1974. The top line indicates the numbers 1 to 10 in binary code, which acts as a key to information contained within the rest of the message. Beneath that is a blocky symbol that is the binary numbers 1, 6, 7, 8 and 15, the atomic numbers of the elements hydrogen, carbon, nitrogen, oxygen and phosphorus. Beneath that are representations of organic molecules called nucleotides, which are built from those five elements and which are the building blocks of DNA and RNA. Below the nucleotides is a simplified image of the DNA helix, and the number of nucleotide pairs within the human genome, which in 1974 was thought to be 4.3 billion (today we know the number to be about a billion fewer). Then there is a stick-person representing a human, with an average height of 1.76m (5ft 9in) on the left, and the total population in 1974, which was also 4.3 billion. Underneath in a line are the Sun and the nine planets (Pluto was included), with Earth raised up to indicate it as the origin of the message, and finally an upside-down picture of what is supposed to be the Arecibo telescope receiving radio waves from space, and the size of its dish, 306.18m. Image credit: Frank Drake (UCSC) et al/Arecibo Observatory (Cornell/NAIC).

straight to the point, arguing that beaming unsolicited messages into the cosmos was 'very hazardous' and that by revealing our presence in the Galaxy we could alert any alien species out there that might be 'malevolent – or hungry'.

Ryle had a history of being concerned about the consequences of contact with an extraterrestrial civilisation. We first met him in the introduction to this book: he was present at Cambridge in 1967 when Jocelyn Bell discovered pulsars – spinning neutron stars that emit jets of radio waves that seem to pulse as they flash in our direction and which at first looked like extraterrestrial beacons – and when an artificial explanation for them was briefly considered, Ryle is reported to have half-jokingly suggested burning all the records of the discovery, lest someone send a signal in reply and provoke an alien invasion. So the news that Drake had sent a signal lit the blue touch-paper within Ryle, resulting in his angry missive to Drake.

In return, Drake humoured Ryle and wrote him a reply making several points that we have already tackled in this chapter, from the detectability of our own radio leakage to whether contact over a distance could still be dangerous. Regardless, it was the first and last radio signal that Drake sent, and it took until 1999 before anyone else became serious about beaming messages into space.

Calling across the cosmos

Using the 70m (230ft) planetary radar dish at Evpatoria in the Crimea, radio astronomer Alexander Zaitsev of the Russian Academy of Sciences in Moscow transmitted a message named 'Cosmic Call' to four stars, the most distant being 70 light years away. Cosmic Call was devised by Charlie Chafer, who was head of a US-based company named Team Encounter, as well as Canadian astrophysicists Yvan Dutil and Stephane Dumas. It not only repeated the content of Drake's earlier Arecibo message, but also incorporated a message based on a language called Lincos, which had been devised in 1960 by the mathematician Hans Freudenthal for

potential use in communicating with an extraterrestrial civilisation. Lincos does not rely on any human syntax, which might be problematic for aliens to understand, but is instead built upon mathematical rules. The idea is to transmit a Lincos 'dictionary' – what Dutil and Dumas call their 'Interstellar Rosetta Stone' – which describes these rules, along with their message. Cosmic Call also had an outreach part to it, incorporating the names of members of the public. Indeed, the thought that has gone into the message construction of not only Cosmic Call but also the Arecibo message highlights one of the traits of METI that is unanimously agreed to be a positive: that by designing our own messages, METI can help us think about what kind of signal a civilisation would send, and therefore better tailor our search strategies to find those signals.

The Cosmic Call message was repeated in 2003, under the name 'Cosmic Call 2', which was beamed to a further five stars. Between the two sets of transmissions, Zaitsev broadcast another message to a further six stars. Named Teen Age Message, the transmission included music from a theremin* concert as well as digital images and text from Earth. Even NASA got in on the act in 2008 by beaming a transmission of The Beatles' song 'Across the Universe' towards the Pole Star, Polaris, using the Deep Space Network's† 70m (230ft) radio dish in Spain, as a publicity stunt.

That same year, Zaitsev was back on the interstellar airwaves. The burgeoning industry of exoplanet discovery was, by now, providing hundreds of targets with planets known to be in orbit, allowing METI's practitioners to start directing transmissions to stars known to have worlds in the

---

* A theremin is an electronic musical instrument, responsible for the eerie, wailing sounds common on the soundtracks of 1950s science-fiction B-movies.
† The Deep Space Network consists of three 70m (230ft) radio dishes, in California, near Madrid in Spain and in Canberra in Australia, which are used by NASA and other space agencies to communicate with spacecraft that are exploring the Solar System.

habitable zone. Zaitsev sent a broadcast named 'A Message from Earth' to the planetary system orbiting the red dwarf star Gliese 581, which is 20.5 light years away and has up to five known orbiting planets (a couple have been strongly hinted at in the data, but not confirmed). At the time of the transmission it was thought that at least one of those planets could be habitable, but doubt has since been cast on that assertion in the subsequent years. More recently, in 2017 and 2018, Doug Vakoch's METI International made a series of transmissions towards a red dwarf known as Luyten's Star, which is 12.4 light years away and which is definitely home to one planet, a super-earth, in the habitable zone. In November 2017 the message was beamed into space, in conjunction with a music concert, by a 32m (105ft) radio dish that repeated the transmission three times each day for three days, to enable anyone who receives the musical gift to verify and perform error correction on the signal. In April 2018 a follow-up message was sent containing instructions for the time and date that METI International will be listening for a reply in 2043.

The choice of Luyten's Star as a target highlights the most tempting thing for METI's supporters. We don't know if the planet orbiting Luyten's Star really is habitable, but with potentially habitable planets starting to be found everywhere, there's no shortage of candidates within a few dozen light years. If a civilisation exists on one of these worlds and detects a signal from Earth, then we could potentially have a reply back before the century is out, if not much sooner. It's all the encouragement METI's practitioners need to ramp up their programme of transmissions.

However, thanks to our discussion of the Arecibo Myth in Chapter 4, we know that even in the most optimistic estimate, Drake's message will be very difficult to detect by the inhabitants of Messier 13, and that logic follows for the other deliberate messages sent from Earth, too. A combination of limited transmission time corresponding to limited integration time at the aliens' detector, targets chosen too far away for the power of the transmitter, and the transmission

rate all conspire to make every deliberate signal sent from Earth so far difficult to detect, at least according to an analysis by James Benford and the former head of NASA's SETI programme, the late John Billingham. Benford should know; unlike many in the METI debate, he builds high-powered radar transmitters for both military and civilian purposes through his company, Microwave Sciences, Inc. His and Billingham's calculations indicate that Cosmic Call would not even be detectable at the nearest star to the Sun, Proxima Centauri, using an Arecibo-sized telescope. The alien equivalent of the Square Kilometre Array of radio telescopes would do better with its much larger collecting area, enough to detect the message content of Cosmic Call out to a distance of 19 light years, but this is still not far enough to reach any of the stars that Cosmic Call was beamed towards. Benford's analysis of METI International's signal to Luyten's Star (which was transmitted with a bit rate of 125 bits per second and a power of two megawatts at a narrowband frequency of 929–930.2 MHz) similarly finds that it is unlikely to be detectable at its destination.

Had the Cosmic Call message been repeated for many hours at a glacial bit rate, allowing extraterrestrial observers the chance to integrate the faint signal (in other words, allowing the energy of the signal to build up over time in their detectors), then an Arecibo-like telescope could detect the raw energy of Cosmic Call as far away as 108 light years, and a Square Kilometre Array equivalent as far as 648 light years. That's a long way, but this would just be the pure radio energy, with none of the detail of the message.

Similarly, the pure energy of powerful interplanetary radar,[*] or military and airport radar, could also cross significant distances in space and be detected. However, these radar

---

[*] For example, both NASA's Deep Space Network and Arecibo use radar beams to search for and to map the size and shape of dark asteroids, or to probe the surfaces of nearby worlds such as Mercury, Venus and the Moon.

beams are not targeted at any particular stars, but instead would be seen from afar to flash in random directions. Military and airport radar are directed more towards the horizon than upwards into space, again limiting their detectability. Furthermore, they rarely shine in the same direction repeatedly, hence they do not form recurrent signals over a prolonged period of time that would allow ET to verify their detection, and of course they contain no information. So radar too can be discounted to a large extent, because while it is possible that an extraterrestrial civilisation could pick up on one of our radar flashes, it would not be seen to repeat to allow them to hone in on its origin, and it would probably remain a mystery to them, in the same way that the Wow! signal is still a mystery to us. Our radio telescopes pick up random bursts of radio waves from unknown sources across the Universe all the time, but there's nothing to single them out as artificial rather than being the result of some high-energy natural phenomena such as accretion onto a black hole or a neutron star.

There are potentially technologies awaiting us in our future that could make human civilisation more visible in the electromagnetic spectrum. The Breakthrough Starshot project, which aims to fire powerful laser beams towards a fleet of nano-sized spacecraft attached to light-sails, will make Earth eminently visible at interstellar distances, at least along the line of sight of the laser beams. The idea is to send the probes to the closest stars – Proxima Centauri and alpha Centauri A and B, Barnard's Star, Wolf 359 and so on – so anyone living on planets around those stars will be able to see us coming.

Unauthorised diplomacy

The various Breakthrough projects – Starshot, Listen and so on – illustrate the power that today's billionaire philanthropists can have. Yuri Milner – the philanthropist behind the Breakthrough Foundation – reportedly has no interest in sending messages, but the worry for those critical of METI is that one

day a billionaire will build a transmitter and send their own messages that are powerful enough to be detected at large distances, without any previous international consultation and without the proper protocols put in place.

There already is one protocol written and agreed upon. 'The Declaration of Principles Concerning Activities Following the Detection of Extraterrestrial Intelligence' is better known in SETI circles as simply the First SETI Protocol. It's a nine-point plan designed to advise scientists what they should do if they happen to detect an extraterrestrial signal, be it a radio or laser signal, or some kind of techno-signature like the detection of Dyson spheres or a probe in our Solar System. Most of the protocol deals with verifying and announcing the discovery, to ensure nobody jumps the gun at a false alarm. Point eight, however, stipulates that 'No response to a signal or other evidence of extraterrestrial intelligence should be sent until appropriate international consultations have taken place.'

The First SETI Protocol was conceived by a working group of SETI researchers and interested parties led by Michael Michaud, on behalf of the International Academy of Astronautics (IAA).

'That process began in the context of the IAA's SETI sessions at the annual International Astronautical Congress,' says Michaud, a former US diplomat who specialised in international scientific and technological concerns, and who drafted the formal text of the Declaration, which was published in 1989. 'The principle of not sending a reply without international consultation was largely my invention. I saw this as an opportunity for getting people to think more responsibly about contact and as a way to promote international consensus-building.'

Alas, as sensible as the nine principles are, and despite being ratified by numerous astronomical organisations, they remain unofficial recommendations rather than the rule of law, and scientists and nations may choose to ignore the Protocol if they wish. In many cases, they probably don't even know of the Protocol's existence.

'Everyone in the SETI community knows about them,' says Alan Penny, Coordinator for the UK SETI Research Network and a scientist at the University of St Andrews. 'But if you talk to a general astronomer, they probably don't.'

The existence of a First SETI Protocol implies that there is also a second, and indeed at one point there was to be a Second SETI Protocol. Again drafted by a committee led by Michaud, this was essentially an upgrade of the First SETI Protocol, but with one important addition: a clause that would have prohibited the beaming into space of deliberate transmissions intended to provoke a response from another civilisation.

A draft of the protocol was written and initially voted on by members of the IAA committee, which led to amendments that ultimately saw the removal of the clause about deliberate transmissions. The fallout from this was a bitter one. Michaud and John Billingham, who was also chair of the IAA's SETI Committee, resigned in protest, and the foundations were laid for a bitter struggle between the two opposing sides of the debate. Each time Zaitsev or Vakoch broadcast a transmission, it was met with disdain and public outcry by METI's dissidents, and each time in reply METI's supporters would try to knock back the critics, with straw-man arguments about invasion, or with assumptions about television leakage or sheer distance protecting us, all of which have been shown to be more complicated than assumed, and all of which dodge the real concerns of the critics, which is that contact is always a messy, unpredictable affair. Furthermore, say the critics, by sending messages without international approval, METI's supporters are showing extraordinary arrogance by claiming to speak for all of us on Earth.

Vakoch has faced this criticism first-hand. Back when he was a member of the SETI Institute, he and Seth Shostak pushed for Institute funding to conduct a small METI programme, but their efforts were stymied by a sceptical Board of Trustees and, in particular, the chair of the board, John Gertz.

Not a scientist himself, Gertz is the philanthropist founder of Zorro Productions, which owns the rights to the character of the masked hero Zorro. He's also not shy about his feelings

regarding METI, being one of the signatories of the 2015 open letter, mentioned earlier in this chapter, which denounced METI activities.

'METI, as far as I am concerned, is unauthorised diplomacy,' he tells me over the phone from his offices in California. 'Doug Vakoch and Seth Shostak make a lot of noise about it, but they are out on a limb. I argued with the two of them and they tried to get funding for METI when I was chair of the SETI Institute, and under no circumstance would I support that.'

Vakoch promptly opted to leave the SETI Institute and found METI International in the belief that fear is holding us back from making the required efforts to establish contact with whoever might be out there. His critics, in particular David Brin, accuse him of impatience, suggesting that because SETI hasn't found anything yet, Vakoch and others want to try and force the issue.

Vakoch is unrepentant. 'It doesn't seem like impatience to me,' he says, suggesting that bringing up the issue of impatience is actually missing the point of transmitting, which is to add another string to SETI's bow. A two-pronged attack at SETI, both listening and messaging, would cover all the bases. 'I think we have only just begun the search, but it's a matter of whether to add other strategies that are based on a different set of assumptions that may get a response back.'

SETI operates on the assumption that ET is willingly transmitting with large beacons that can be heard. Yet if for some reason other civilisations opt not to light up a beacon, SETI's task becomes inordinately difficult, if not impossible. That's where METI comes in, suggests Vakoch.

'My concern is that ET might not be transmitting, so perhaps we could elicit a response by our actions,' he says. 'If I had my way, when Frank Drake did his first SETI search in 1960, he would have also begun transmitting, and if he had we would be looking for responses from civilisations out to a distance of 30 light years by now.'

Taking the risk

It really comes down to one question, which is not 'Whose assumptions are correct?' because we cannot answer that, but rather 'Whose assumptions carry the least risk, and is that risk fairly balanced with the relative benefits to be gained from the decision to transmit or not to transmit?'

In other words, we need to make a risk assessment, and to do so we can take inspiration from another, tangentially related, area of science.

Brent Sherwood, who is Program Manager of Solar System Science Missions Formulation at NASA's Jet Propulsion Laboratory in California, is also concerned about alien invasions – but this time the worlds under threat of invasion are other potentially habitable bodies in the Solar System, such as Mars and Jupiter's moon Europa, and the aliens doing the invading are ourselves, or rather the microbes that live with us on Earth. His concern, shared by many in the planetary science community, is that terrestrial bugs hitching a ride from Earth on space missions could contaminate other worlds, for example potentially wiping out any native Martian microbes, or tricking our life-detection experiments into thinking they've found alien life when instead all they've found is transplanted terrestrial life.

Currently, says Sherwood, there is a level of contamination on our rovers and landers that is acceptable – a probability no greater than 1 in 10,000 that a single microbe carried on board will contaminate another world. This value has been unchanged since the 1960s, and Sherwood is raising the point that we shouldn't just assume that this is an appropriate value. Perhaps it should be even stricter, or maybe it is too strict, either of which would impact the way we design missions and plan for astronauts to visit Mars. The crucial difference between Sherwood's concerns, however, and previous studies of this 1-in-10,000 probability is that he thinks we need to introduce an ethical viewpoint into the debate – what obligations are we under, as a species, to protect other-worldly life?

So Sherwood draws risk-assessment analogies with two examples in science. The first was over the test detonation of

the world's first thermonuclear bomb in 1952. A concern at the time was that the explosion could ignite a runaway chain reaction that could incinerate our atmosphere and all life on Earth. Obviously that did not happen, but top-secret deliberations had taken place beforehand to assess the risk, and the question of whether the experimental explosion should take place was never placed in the wider world's hands.

Another example was some people's fear that the Large Hadron Collider (LHC) – the powerful particle accelerator at CERN on the French–Swiss border, which discovered the Higgs boson – might accidentally create a black hole that could swallow the Earth from the inside out. This time the debate was held in the public domain, ending in the courts when judges ruled, having seen the scientific evidence, that the LHC could be turned on with negligible risk to the Earth.

These are not perfect analogies; neither really came up with a satisfying answer to the question of who should be able to make a decision on behalf of humanity, just as METI has not come up with a good answer yet as to who should be allowed to speak for Earth. The most democratic means would be through international discussion, debate and the drawing-up of a consensus, perhaps by a vote. The United Nations would be the ideal vehicle for this, but so far they have shown negligible interest in SETI or METI.

'I've had personal confirmation that the UN Committee on the Peaceful Uses of Outer Space [is not interested in] SETI,' says Yvan Dutil, who worked with Alexander Zaitsev on the Cosmic Call broadcasts. '[The SETI Institute's] Jill Tarter tried to get the UN interested, but for political reasons nobody wanted to touch it.'

Doug Vakoch points out that the UN Committee has many more issues of more imminent importance to discuss, including preventing the militarisation of space, searching for and exploring technologies to ward off hazardous asteroids, and the growing problem of space junk – bits and pieces of debris in Earth orbit from old space missions, which pose a threat to satellites, spacecraft and indeed the International Space Station.

'The UN Committee on the Peaceful Uses of Outer Space is the committee that, if there is an asteroid coming towards Earth and we can deflect it a little bit, but it will still hit somewhere, will decide where it hits. I think that's a pretty compelling issue, so I understand that when you have limited time on an agenda, asteroid deflection is going to take priority over SETI,' says Vakoch. However, he accepts that 'if we could get this issue [of METI] in front of the United Nations, and the Security Council says, "Sorry folks, there's just too great a risk of this, on behalf of humankind our view is that there should be no intentional transmissions from Earth", then I would go along with that.'

Without interest from governments or the UN, it's going to be left to the rest of us to figure it out, and we can look to Brent Sherwood's proposals for dealing with contamination of other worlds for inspiration. Sherwood suggests that humanity can start to discuss what an acceptable level of contamination would be via a two-pronged process, which we could adapt for the METI debate. First would be to initiate an information campaign that explains for the public what kind of transmissions we can send today and what messages have already been sent, the true detectability of Earth's radio leakage, and input from historians, anthropologists and social scientists – people that David Brin calls 'our great sages' – about the benefits and risks of contact events. With all the relevant information concisely placed in the public domain, the second part of the process would then be an open and inclusive discussion with people from all over the world, weighing up the pros and cons and somehow drawing a conclusion, and only then making the decision whether to transmit or not.

'I think we need to have a global discussion about it, and think very critically about how we would do it, because the more we educate the public and educate the world [about METI], the better it will be for us,' says Shelley Wright of the University of California, San Diego, whom we first met in Chapter 4 with her infrared SETI search. 'I've had a heated discussion with Seth [Shostak] about it, I have pretty strong opinions on if we do it, it should be done properly. That's

where I get nervous about it because I've seen it multiple times or being talked about where people just run off and do things at telescopes.'

Vakoch doesn't buy into this idea of an extended discussion, suggesting that it plays on our natural tendency to search for 'absolutes, for black and white answers, or a global consensus ... but some would say that until you have seven billion people coming to a consensus, it would be too early to go ahead [and transmit].'

Seth Shostak also thinks that extended discussion is ultimately not helpful, because any risk assessment will always come to the same conclusion not to transmit, because risk can never be ruled out. We'd forever constrain our civilisation based on nothing but fear of the unknown. 'It is a straightjacket for our species that would never be taken off,' he says, a little anger, or maybe frustration, evident in his voice.

This is the Contact Paradox. We search the Universe for evidence of extraterrestrial life to make contact with others, for humanity to be able to share the Universe with others. Yet we find ourselves in a position of not being confident about whether we should try and make contact. Everything that we have learned about SETI, from the altruism assumption to the differences in types of intelligence that life could take, and from the potential to colonise the Galaxy to the mystery of the Fermi Paradox, not to mention our own haphazard history of contact, teaches us to be wary. 'If the cosmos has races more advanced than us, and they are hunkering down silently, then should we not ponder that they know something we don't?' asks David Brin. Contact is dangerous, and metaphorically screaming into a silent and possibly dangerous jungle without knowing what lives in that jungle might be unwise.

While history cannot tell us what will happen if and when we make contact with an extraterrestrial civilisation, it can provide some handy signposts for what might happen, and we ignore history at our peril. Although it may have been disease that ultimately did the greatest damage to the Aztec Empire, Cortés' intentions were not benign, and we do not want to be in the position of Moctezuma looking down with fear at the

conquistadors marching on his capital. In the previous chapter we explored different possibilities that could shorten the lifetime of a civilisation, but we left one existential risk out: the consequences of a disastrous contact with an advanced extraterrestrial civilisation. It would be a case of what science-fiction author Iain M. Banks would have described as an 'Outside Context Problem', from his novel *Excession*: an event or technology that no one sees coming and that no one can understand or counteract. Ominously, he suggested that civilisations meet an Outside Context Problem just once, rather as a sentence meets a full stop.

As Brin suggests, maybe the civilisations that last are the ones that keep their heads down and out of trouble. On the other hand, points out Vakoch, 'maybe what other civilisations are looking for as evidence that we are stepping up and becoming a good galactic civilisation is a willingness to reach out, and maybe there are implications if we choose not to.'

This is the dichotomy at the heart of the Contact Paradox. It is a maze of assumptions, cherished beliefs and few facts. In the seven chapters of this book we have explored some of these assumptions and beliefs, and tried to add in a few more facts. METI's supporters ask us to focus on the possible positive outcomes while sweeping the negative possibilities under the rug, while METI's critics highlight the more dangerous scenarios and argue that the risk should override our urge to transmit. The reality will probably lie somewhere in between the most extreme outcomes, because contact events are messy, and they can sometimes be beneficial, but at other times they can be disastrous and deadly. What none of the protagonists in this debate can deny is that we need more information to base a decision on, because with so little hard data, we are limited in the firm conclusions that we can draw. Doug Vakoch has come to one conclusion; David Brin and his cohorts another. I'll describe my own conclusion in the final chapter, but with all the information that is presented here, what will be your conclusion, I wonder?

21st Century SETI

Humanity is standing at a crossroads. The Intergovernmental Panel on Climate Change has warned that failure to act before 2030 will see catastrophic environmental consequences as global temperatures rise by more than 1.5 °C (2.5–3°F). Plastic fills the oceans. As I write this, the news headlines tell of Russia adding a new hypersonic missile – the Avangard, capable of flying at 27 times the speed of sound – to its nuclear arsenal. Lines in the sand have been drawn between those who fight for civil rights and those who fear them. And the perennial problems of poverty and overpopulation, disease and famine show no signs of going away anytime soon. There are so many worries in the world, it's hard not to shudder at the thought of them.

Yet it is not hopeless; the future is not yet lost. Maybe these are just the growing pains that every adolescent civilisation goes through. Discovering an alien civilisation from whom we might learn how they overcame similar difficulties in their past could be quite illuminating, as Carl Sagan implied. Or perhaps our troubles are unique to ourselves. Either way, I'm not ready to throw in the towel, but it is clear that we need to act now to make a wise choice at the crossroads, to instigate a rapid change in our actions and our attitude on a global scale, in order to pull ourselves back from the brink.

The fate of civilisations is ingrained in the fabric of SETI. What happens to civilisations in the long term weighs heavily on the chances of SETI being successful, so it makes sense that our current global concerns are also of interest to SETI; but there's another, deeper link.

SETI is not just a search for aliens. It's also a search for ourselves. We project our hopes and fears, our history and our expectations about the future of humanity onto what we think extraterrestrial civilisations might be like. The stars are a mirror

and, when we gaze up at them, if we look closely enough, we see our reflection staring back. Study that reflection and we may learn something about ourselves. That's the true power of SETI.

SETI and its bastard cousin, METI, prompt us to evaluate ourselves by imagining contact between humanity and an intelligent, technological alien species. Furthermore, we've seen how contact is likely to be a complex affair, one that is impossible to predict and with outcomes ranging from the triumphant to the utterly catastrophic, and including everything in between. The way that we approach contact could help influence what that outcome is, but it seems presumptuous to expect an advanced civilisation to understand our hopes and expectations of contact when we ourselves don't even know yet who we are, what we want or where we are going as a species.

That's the beauty of thinking about extraterrestrial civilisations, even if they are only hypothetical. By searching for life among the stars – by looking into our mirror – we force ourselves to confront these questions, as evidenced by the chapters of this book. In particular, we can learn much about ourselves by debating the METI issue, which tackles topics of history and science, of sociology and human nature, but the rancour that often overpowers the debate has led to people avoiding talking about it. Yet to ignore the debate is shortsighted given the bigger picture. The METI debate is a crucible, an arena into which all these fundamental questions about our existence and our future, and our ability to understand and think and plan on greater, longer scales, all come together, but in a way that avoids the stresses and the politics and conflicts that afflict other, similar, crucibles, such as the battle to mitigate the climate emergency, or social politics, or the sharing of resources.

To foster the METI debate and turn it into something that is both constructive and instructive, one must intend to arrive at a conclusion at the end of the debate. That means keeping an open mind. The issue is more complicated, however, than simply sitting down, talking it over and then voting 'yes' or 'no' to transmitting. As we discovered in the previous chapter,

there are inherent dangers to making contact that could have long-term consequences, a possibility that has too often been swept under the rug by METI's practitioners in their enthusiasm for transmitting messages into space. Yet regardless of the dangers, contact is surely the eventual aim of SETI, so if we assume that we are not alone in the Universe, then someday we are going to have to face that reality. Humans are a community-building species; it's in our nature to try to reach out across space and build new relationships. The key to METI is figuring out how we can integrate the act of transmitting into a framework that can sit alongside the more passive SETI, by using METI responsibly and appropriately at the right time as a tool in our search for life.

This implies that a new strategy for SETI is in order, one that has a long-term plan and encompasses every tool and tactic that we have in our scientific arsenal, and which pushes SETI into the mainstream as a key long-term objective for humanity. A SETI for the twenty-first century needs to take into account concepts such as the altruism assumption, the possibly wide-ranging nature of extraterrestrial intelligence, the acceleration in exoplanet discoveries, the consideration of concerns about how to handle first contact successfully, and the transition from a search dominated by radio communication to a search that treats optical SETI, and technosignatures in general, such as megastructures, on a more equal footing.

'Technosignatures' is the new buzzword among the SETI community. First coined by the SETI Institute's Jill Tarter, a technosignature is anything that could be evidence for a technological civilisation, from Dyson spheres and manipulated black holes to more conventional radio and optical signals. We've spent a lot of time with radio searches since 1960, and optical SETI is slowly growing in prominence, but to find those other technosignatures we'll need to employ even more ingenious and revolutionary tactics, and fundamentally change the way we think about the search for extraterrestrial intelligence. As it happens, that change is already under way.

It was while she was sitting in the audience of an excruciatingly bad concert that the flash of inspiration hit Lucianne Walkowicz.

'I was at this terrible experimental music thing in New York, with still half an hour to go and me wondering how I was going to get through it,' she recalls. Her mind began to wander away from the sounds being played on the concert stage and instead towards a recent call for proposals for a grant from the John Templeton Foundation to continue the search for extraterrestrial intelligence in some new and innovative way. Walkowicz figured it would be fun to do something with SETI. 'So I just sat there and thought about what I could do to look for intelligent life in the Universe, and it sort of popped into my head.'

The John Templeton Foundation – a philanthropic agency interested in projects that exist at what it believes to be the boundaries between science and religion – was requesting proposals for projects considered too speculative for mainstream funding avenues. Proposing a simple radio search wouldn't have sufficed; the proposal had to be of a more speculative nature, and Walkowicz realised that she knew just the thing.

It was 2012 and the way professional astronomy was being conducted was really beginning to change. It was the dawn of the age of the great astronomical surveys and 'big data': telescopes that week after week, month after month, year after year, scan the sky, surveying everything in their sight and watching for anything that might be seen to change, from supernovae and volatile black holes swallowing huge amounts of matter, to transiting exoplanets and variable stars. These surveys, such as those conducted by the Kepler space telescope, the Sloan Digital Sky Survey, the European Space Agency's Gaia astrometric mission, NASA's Transiting Exoplanet Survey Satellite (TESS) and, in the near future, the 8.2m (27ft) Large Synoptic Survey Telescope and the Square Kilometre Array, to name but a few, produce vast amounts of astronomical data – terabytes upon terabytes. Far too much, in fact, for human beings alone to even begin to make a dent in it.

Walkowicz had previously been working with a new technology that would provide a solution: unsupervised machine learning. You program into a computer the search parameters that you'd like it to look for in the data, and then allow algorithms to weave their way through the information and parse out the data relevant to whatever it is that you're looking for. So, if you are looking for potentially habitable planets orbiting red dwarf stars observed by the Kepler space telescope, you can program a 'clustering algorithm' to search for stars that experience periodic dips in light that could be produced by a transiting planet – that is, moves in front of its star, blocking some of its light – with an orbit in the habitable zone.

The algorithms are referred to as 'clustering' because if you program the search parameters to reflect the general characteristics of stars and planetary transits as we understand them, then the data tends to divide into clusters, with each grouping representing a different phenomenon: stars with transiting planets of different orbital periods, stars plagued by star spots, pulsating stars, binary stars eclipsing one another, and so on. However, there are always outliers: strange or weird objects that are set apart from the clusters in the data and which don't really fit in with the established norms. It's these outliers that can often prove to be the most interesting, since they can sometimes represent new types of object that we have never encountered before.

Walkowicz, who is an astronomer at the Adler Planetarium in Chicago and the fifth Baruch S. Blumberg NASA/Library of Congress Chair of Astrobiology, realised that if an advanced extraterrestrial civilisation was able to somehow affect its star, either directly or indirectly, it could show up as an outlier in the data collected by Kepler. The John Templeton Foundation agreed and funded Walkowicz and her students to start using clustering algorithms to sift through all the data collected by Kepler, looking for the outliers.

'In some sense it is a quantitative way of defining weird,' says Walkowicz. But what, exactly, is she looking for in the Kepler data? The beauty of it is that Walkowicz herself doesn't know.

'We have zero idea what another civilisation would choose to do,' she says. However, as we explored in Chapter 5, their capabilities could potentially be quite impressive. Perhaps they are deliberately stimulating the vibrational modes of stars, which were detectable by Kepler[*] as oscillations in brightness, and encoding a message into those vibrations. Or, perhaps, a civilisation exists on a planet orbiting a highly magnetic red dwarf star, and that civilisation might be tapping into the stored energy of the red dwarf's magnetic field, which could possibly create an observable consequence for the star in terms of anomalous brightness fluctuations. The advantage of this kind of search is that it doesn't matter that we do not know exactly how a technologically advanced civilisation might affect its star. All that matters is that if they can do that, then we could detect it.

'The strength of not presupposing what the signal is, is that you don't have to guess, you just have to look,' Walkowicz tells me, before tantalisingly adding, 'At the moment the problem isn't finding outliers – the problem is sifting through them. There are lots of weird things in the data!'

That's not to say that everything that is weird must be aliens. Indeed, to date, Walkowicz has not identified anything that suggests it is alien. Some of the weird things turn out to be nothing but interference in the data or instrument artefacts, such as light bleeding in from bright stars just outside the frame, or unusual astrophysical behaviour.

Walkowicz's daring project is just the start of this kind of SETI, because with more and more surveys coming online, there is going to be no shortage of data to search through. A similar project using unsupervised machine learning is VASCO, the Vanishing and Appearing Sources during a

---

[*] Note the past tense; the Kepler spacecraft was shut down in October 2018 when its fuel became so depleted that it could no longer manoeuvre to point at targets. At the time of its shutdown, Kepler had discovered 2,682 confirmed exoplanets and a further 2,899 unconfirmed exoplanets, while the huge amount of data Kepler collected will keep scientists busy for many years to come.

Century of Observations project. Scrutinising modern all-sky surveys and also comparing them to historical sky surveys, such as the collection of glass-plate negatives that cover the entire sky that are collected at Harvard College Observatory (the plates are in the process of being digitised by the DASCH – Digital Access to a Sky Century at Harvard – project), VASCO's network of researchers, including Beatriz Villarroel and Kristiaan Pelckmans at Uppsala University in Sweden, are searching for stars that have vanished, or perhaps suddenly appeared, by way of interference from an advanced extraterrestrial intelligence.

Now even NASA have shown an interest in searching for technosignatures. In September 2018 NASA hosted a workshop at the Lunar and Planetary Institute in Houston, Texas, centred on ideas about what technosignatures could be and how we could search for them. This was quite a remarkable turn of events. For 25 years there had been no official funding or interest for SETI from NASA.* Indeed, at NASA the term 'SETI' is thrown around like a hand grenade, thanks to the stigma attached to it following Senator Bryan's sabotage of SETI that saw it unceremoniously cut from NASA's budget in 1993. It seems that today the space agency finds the term 'technosignatures' to be far more palatable than 'SETI', perhaps partly because searching for techno-signatures sounds like it goes neatly alongside the search for biosignatures, which plays an integral part in both NASA's astrobiology strategy and in the design of new telescopes and space missions that could potentially detect such biosignatures.

---

* At the Houston Technosignatures workshop, NASA's Deputy Associate Administrator for Research, Michael New, claimed that NASA had always welcomed SETI proposals, at which point all the researchers sitting in the audience politely informed him that was not true at all, and including SETI on a NASA funding proposal was inevitably the kiss of death for that proposal. New promised to make sure that would no longer be the situation in future.

The alien megastructure star

The sudden upsurge of interest in technosignatures didn't come from nowhere. In 2016 a possible technosignature made headlines around the world, and although in the end it turned out to be a natural phenomenon and not evidence for ET, it nevertheless excited the public and assisted in the revitalisation of SETI for the twenty-first century.

Its story began with the discovery of an outlier in the Kepler data, which was a finding made not by Walkowicz, but by a handful of citizen scientists scrutinising light curves from Kepler on planethunters.com, a website set up by scientists to give the public the chance to become involved in the search for exoplanets. Users log on to the website and are presented with a light curve – depicting the brightness of a star over a period of time – and if that light curve has a dip that looks as if it could be a transiting planet blocking

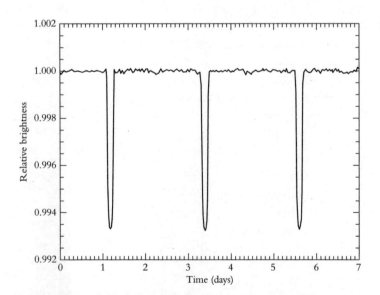

Figure 5: An example of the light curve of a transiting exoplanet, in this case the hot jupiter HAT-P-7b. Note how the star's light remains virtually constant, until a transit takes place, blocking some of the light and causing a dip in the light curve. Because the planet orbits its star every 2.2 days, the dips in light are regular and predictable, and are always the same depth.

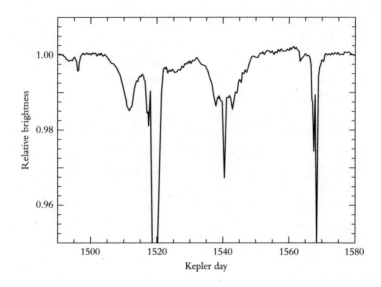

Figure 6: Here is a section of the light curve of Boyajian's Star, KIC 8462852. Notice how the dips in light caused by something transiting it are very different to those of a planet, seen in Figure 5. The dips are of varying magnitude and duration, and there's no obvious periodicity. Clearly, something very unusual is happening around this star!

some of the star's light, the users are asked to flag it up, before moving on to the next light curve, and then the next one, highlighting all the possible planet transits. The website presents just 30-day segments of light curves, and with 150,000 stars in Kepler's original field of view (and now with light curves monitored by the TESS mission also being included), there are plenty of light curves to go around. If enough people (to avoid human error) flag a specific light curve as showing a transit, professional scientists will then follow up on it.

One of these professional scientists is Tabetha Boyajian of Louisiana State University in the United States. Several citizen scientists had referred the star KIC 8462852 (a telephone number of a name if there ever was one; KIC stands for Kepler Input Catalog) to her after they found some really odd dips in the star's light. Since they could only see

month-long segments of the star's light curve, they could not piece together the full picture by themselves, but when Boyajian assembled all the little segments to create a four-year-long light curve, she was astonished. The star was behaving really strangely. In fact, it was so odd that she had never seen anything like it before.

When a planet transits a star it does so with a regular periodicity, with the period being that planet's length of year, which in turn tells us how far away it is from its star. For example, a civilisation observing the Sun would see our planet transit once every 365 days, and because Earth doesn't change size or shape, it would be seen to block the same amount of the Sun's light each time it transited. Of course, if more than one planet is transiting at the same time, more light is blocked, but it's possible to disentangle all those signals and work out what's what. KIC 8462852, on the other hand, seemed to break all the rules.

Its light curve was a mess. Lots of little transits, some bigger ones, and some really huge transits, apparently made by swarms of objects. No periodicity was evident. The size of the transits was really remarkable. On one occasion, 22 per cent of the star's light was blocked, which is extraordinary when you consider that a Jupiter-sized planet would obscure about 1 per cent of the light, and an Earth-sized world would block just 0.008 per cent.

Boyajian describes just how bizarre the light curve was. 'There was a very deep dip in the middle of [the light curve], and then it started really going nuts, which was kind of alarming,' she tells me.

Her best guess was that we were witnessing the transits of a swarm of several hundred comets and their huge tails, the comets being the debris from the break-up of a giant icy body that measured about 100km (62 miles) across. Such an event, however, is to our knowledge unprecedented in our Solar System.

Then the star got even weirder, as evidence came to light from archival photographs currently being digitised by DASCH that the star seemed to have been dimming gradually for more than 100 years, to the point that today there is 20 per cent more

material dimming the star than there was in 1890.[*] If it were comets to blame, then it would take 648,000 comets, each 200km (124 miles) across and with a combined mass of a third of the Earth to account for that much dimming over 100 years. A cometary explanation seemed out of the question.

By this point, Boyajian had shown KIC 8462852's light curve to Jason Wright of Penn State University, whom we met in Chapter 5. As we know, Wright had been specialising in searches for Dyson spheres and other technosignatures, including outliers found by Kepler.

'I contacted [Wright] for something entirely different, but he mentioned a paper that he was writing about weird stuff that Kepler had found that could possibly be signs of megastructures around stars blocking some of their light, so I told him about KIC 8462852,' says Boyajian. Wright added the bizarre star to his paper, journalist Ross Anderson of *The Atlantic* heard about it, and before long the idea of the 'alien megastructure star' – popularly named 'Tabby's Star', although by astronomical convention it should really be called 'Boyajian's Star' – entered the public consciousness.

Wright and Boyajian favoured a natural explanation, although they were at a loss as to what that might be. Nevertheless, as Wright previously pointed out in Chapter 5, every natural explanation must first be considered and ruled out before you can seriously contemplate that a phenomenon such as KIC 8462852 is the work of extraterrestrial intelligence.

As it happens, we didn't have to wait long for a natural explanation for KIC 8462852's unusual behaviour.

---

[*] The claim of the 100-year dimming was made by astronomer Bradley Schaefer of Louisiana State University. However, it was disputed by the independent astronomer Michael Hippke and Daniel Angerhausen of the Blue Marble Space Institute of Science in Seattle, leading to a fierce war of words with Schaefer, whose expertise is photometry and determining the magnitudes of stars on old photographic plates. Schaefer was partly validated when an analysis of Kepler's four years of observations of KIC 8462852 also showed long-term dimming beyond just the dips caused by the transits.

Follow-up observations by Boyajian and Wright, made possible by a crowd-funding effort on Kickstarter, found that the size of the dips in the star's light differ depending on what wavelength of light you are looking at it in. If whatever was passing in front of the star were solid, it would block all the light equally, regardless of the wavelength in which you observed the star. On the other hand, if the dips in light were caused by giant clumps of dust, then you would expect that more blue light would be blocked than red light, since interstellar dust preferentially scatters blue light and transmits red and infrared light. As it so happens, the new observations showed exactly that, with the dips in light shallower towards the red end of the spectrum than in the blue. Therefore, we now conclusively know that it is giant clumps of dust that are blocking the light from KIC 8462852, although the origin and structure of this dust, and even whether it is in orbit around the star or merely somewhere in the 1,480 light years of interstellar space between us, remain uncertain.

NASA's interest in technosignatures is a promising sign for the future of SETI, which has spent most of the last six decades lacking a reliable cash flow. Back in 2010, during the fiftieth anniversary of SETI and around the time I began researching this book, global spending on the search for extraterrestrial intelligence was probably less than $1.5 million (£1.1 million) per year, says Andrew Siemion, who as the Director of the SETI Research Center at the University of California, Berkeley, is one of the leading lights of the field.

'SETI funding, historically, has been very up and down,' he tells me. 'Because there was not a sustained, consistent funding source, it was difficult to attract new people with new ideas into the field because they could not see a career path for studying SETI.'

Everyone needs to pay the bills, and more often than not scientists interested in SETI would go away and do something

else for which they could get funding, but this meant there was little new blood coming into SETI. As those working in the subject grow older and retire, the SETI community is steadily diminished and expertise is lost.

So behind the scenes, leading members of the SETI community began to do something about this. John Gertz set up an organisation called the Foundation for Investing in Research on SETI Science and Technology – FIRSST for short – that included on its advisory board scientists from the world's two leading SETI research groups: the SETI Institute and Siemion's Berkeley SETI Research Center. The intention behind FIRSST was to open up a dialogue with billionaire philanthropists with the aim of getting them to fund SETI for the long term.

'We have to be able to guarantee funding for a cosmic search that could last another six years, or six hundred years, or six thousand years – we do not have the slightest idea how long it may take,' says Gertz.

While FIRSST was courting the hyper-wealthy, machinations were afoot elsewhere. Until 2015 Pete Worden was Director of NASA's Ames Research Center in California, where he was growing bored with the minutiae of managing a large organisational arm of the space agency. Deep down, his fascination was with the 'big questions', including whether life exists beyond Earth. So when Worden heard that the Russian billionaire and philanthropist Yuri Milner was interested in getting his foundation, Breakthrough Initiatives, into the SETI game, he jumped at the chance. Promptly retiring from NASA, Worden signed on with Milner and, in 2016, helped launch a new SETI programme: the aforementioned Breakthrough Listen project, promising funding for SETI worth $100 million over the course of 10 years, with the possibility of more beyond that.

Suddenly SETI was transformed by its newfound riches. Up until 2016, only around a thousand nearby stars had been searched in depth by SETI experiments (and 'in depth' here means observed for 10 minutes at radio wavelengths). Now, Breakthrough Listen's adopted telescopes – primarily Green

Bank radio telescope in the USA and the Parkes radio telescope
in Australia – are listening intently to the nearest million stars
for radio signals, and that's just the beginning. They are also
scanning myriad stars in the plane of the Milky Way, as well as
checking out the nearest 100 galaxies for faint radio messages.
It's an extraordinary increase in coverage, yet such is the
scale of the challenge that the odds remain stacked against
Breakthrough Listen succeeding. Even if there are as many as
10,000 civilisations in the Milky Way Galaxy, and assuming
there are an estimated 200 billion stars in our Galaxy, we will
still have to search 20 million stars on average – that's 20 times
Breakthrough Listen's 10-year coverage – before we can
reasonably expect to find just one civilisation.

Clearly there is still work to be done in financing the
continuation of SETI in the long term, but in the short term
FIRSST has gone into hibernation in response to SETI's
newfound riches, although not everybody has been completely
happy with the situation. Somewhat controversially, Breakthrough Listen decided to funnel its money through Siemion's
Berkeley Research Center, leaving the SETI Institute out in
the cold. There has been a degree of rivalry between the two
groups in the past, further exacerbated by tension over METI,
and now this; it was a slap in the face for the SETI Institute,
which had helped lead NASA's SETI project until it was
cancelled in the 1990s. However, in 2018 Siemion was made
the Bernard M. Oliver Chair of SETI at the SETI Institute,
in one fell swoop unifying the SETI Institute, the Berkeley
SETI Research Center and Breakthrough Listen.

SETI doesn't exist in a vacuum. It impacts on so many areas
of the physical and social sciences, and those areas impact
upon it. Yet it is still seen as the pariah of the sciences, and
for SETI to truly flourish, and for a long-term strategy to
be enacted, it's going to need money from elsewhere. Ideally,
its funding should not come from isolated sources, but be
entwined with all other academic and space exploration
funding, because it is truly integral to science as a whole.

Just consider how much of our fundamental scientific research has, at its core, questions about life. We study the other planets in the Solar System partly because they are there and the urge to explore grips us, but on a more prosaic level we can compare them to Earth and seek to understand why the other worlds are different, and through an understanding of those differences can come a better appreciation of the circumstances here on Earth that made our planet habitable. Then we can ask the question: those circumstances arose here, but could they arise elsewhere? And thus the driving force in the search for exoplanets – a search that gets huge amounts of money spent on it[*] – is the quest to find a second Earth, another habitable planet on which there might be life. In a similar vein, astrophysicists study different types of stars to try to understand what makes them tick, so that we can better understand why our Sun is stable enough to allow life to thrive on Earth. We probe nebulae to watch star systems being born from the firmament, and look for the chemistry of life within their gaseous, dusty confines, where we find life's organic building blocks. We watch galaxies cartwheel gracefully through space, or crash messily into one another, giving birth to waves of stars that could support habitable planets.

Galaxies, nebulae, stars, planets and life – none of this would exist if the Universe had not spawned matter, and so crucial to everything is understanding not only the nucleosynthesis that transformed a Universe with just three-quarters hydrogen and one-quarter helium into a cosmos teeming with different elements and molecules that allow for the complexity of life's biochemical processes, but also the

---

[*] Between them, NASA's Kepler and TESS have cost the best part of a billion dollars, while the European Space Agency's soon-to-launch PLATO and ARIEL missions will cost up to 500 million euros each. Then there are all the ground-based exoplanet detectors and a large amount of research grants, and it quickly becomes apparent how seriously the field of exoplanet research is taken. All that money is spent on finding exoplanets, yet comparatively little is spent looking for life on them.

particle and quantum physics that allow those atoms and molecules to form and decay in the first place, and which govern those aforementioned biochemical processes.

None of which would be possible without the Big Bang, which is the unknown event that produced our Universe. It's not just a matter of figuring out what the Big Bang was; we also have to ask why the Big Bang produced a Universe capable of supporting life, as opposed to producing a Universe that is dead, dreary and deserted. One of the greatest mysteries of science is why the fundamental constants of nature – among them the mass and charge of electrons and protons, the strengths of the strong and weak forces, the speed of light and the gravitational constant – have just the right values to enable atoms to form, nuclear reactions to take place, galaxies and stars and planets to assemble, and for biochemistry to proceed. Dark energy, which is the mysterious force that is driving the accelerating expansion of the cosmos, has a strength 10^{120} times smaller than what theory predicts that it should be. The assumption is that there is some mechanism, or perhaps a 'filter', which reduces dark energy to its observed strength. Yet if such a filter exists, then it must be extremely precise, because if dark energy were instead just 10^{119} times less strong than theory predicts, it would cause the expansion of the Universe to accelerate so hard that it would rip the cosmos apart before it even had the chance to form galaxies, stars and life. It is these suspiciously perfect values of the fundamental forces and particles that create a Goldilocks Universe that seems curiously fine-tuned for life, but nobody knows why. Perhaps we're missing some vital mathematical law, a theory of everything that explains all of this. Or perhaps our Universe is just one of an infinite panoply of universes, each with different values of the intrinsic fundamental constants of nature, and we find ourselves in this Universe because it happens to be the one where everything is set up exactly right.* We just don't know.

---

* The concept of the multiverse is quite a controversial one in scientific circles, because some scientists have argued that since we

The point is, the great questions of astronomy and cosmology, quantum physics and particle physics, nuclear physics and chemistry, and so on – the laws of nature upon which everything that we see in the world around us today is based – are intricately wrapped up in the question of life. SETI and astrobiology are absolutely a part of that. They are the manifestation of all our questions about the Universe, and deserve to be at the forefront of our scientific thinking. If nothing else, they're bound to interest the general public more than some abstract conceptions about the Universe that often have little in common with people's lives.[*]

Towards the beginning of this chapter I alluded to the case for a new, over-arching strategy for SETI that goes well beyond searching for radio signals and which better prepares us for contact. If, as a society, we can recognise the importance of SETI, then we can make the resources available for it. The biggest enemy in any first-contact situation is a lack of information, so a new SETI strategy has to address this. Let's look out into the cosmos, do some reconnaissance and learn about what is out there before we attempt to transmit any deliberate messages. As it happens, we're already in the process of doing this. The Kepler space telescope found thousands of planets, but most are over a thousand light years away. Its successor, TESS, is searching for planets orbiting much closer

---

know of no way to test the theory, then we cannot call it science. In some ways, belief in the multiverse concept comes down to faith, but to say it is no more scientific than religion is grossly inaccurate, since the multiverse has scientific and mathematical foundations, whereas God does not come from any equations that we know of. The multiverse could well be real but we might never be able to directly test for its existence; if that is the case, it would be an incredibly frustrating brick wall for science to hit.

[*] Not that some of these abstract concepts are not compelling – far from it, I love blue-sky thinking and examining really deep cosmological concepts – but experience tells us that many of the public are not tuned into thinking about the Universe in that way. This is why SETI could be a great gateway into those fundamental issues for the public.

stars, and the European Space Agency's PLATO (PLAnetary
Transits and Oscillations of stars) mission will join it in 2026.
Yet already, numerous potentially habitable worlds close
enough for us to study have been identified: Proxima Centauri
b, the TRAPPIST-1 system, Ross 128b, LHS 1140b, Luyten b
and so on. NASA's James Webb Space Telescope (JWST),
Europe's forthcoming ARIEL (Atmospheric Remote-sensing
Exoplanet Large-survey) mission, and both the ground-based
Thirty Meter Telescope being built in Hawaii and the 39.3m
(129ft) Extremely Large Telescope under construction in
Chile, will be able to follow up on the closest of these worlds,
particularly if they are seen to transit, and perform spectroscopic
analysis of their atmospheres. This will tell us more about the
true conditions on these planets and possibly even reveal
biosignature gases or even industrial pollutants such CFCs
including CF_4 (tetrafluromethane) and CCl_3F (trichloro-
fluoromethane), both of which could potentially be detectable
by the JWST. These giant telescopes could perhaps even
directly image some of these worlds. The resolution won't be
enough to show distinct oceans and continents, but overall
colour and brightness changes as the planet rotates and traverses
through its seasons could provide hints of oceans or vegetation.

Suppose that we find a planet that displays promising biosignatures and isn't too far away, maybe a handful of light years.
Yuri Milner's other speculative project is the aforementioned
Breakthrough Starshot. This is aiming to send fleets of small
spacecraft called 'StarChips', which will be just a few centime-
tres across and have masses of just a few grams, to the nearest
stars. Each StarChip will be a marvel of miniaturisation,
carrying 2-megapixel digital cameras, navigation computers,
radioisotope-powered batteries, and most importantly a light-
sail, perhaps 4m (13ft) square and made of an ultra-thin material
such as graphene but with a reflective coating on it, which will
catch a 'wind' of laser light beamed from Earth by an array of
powerful lasers. The momentum of the photons in the laser
beams will push the light-sail onwards to its destination. The
intention is to accelerate the StarChips and their sails to a fifth
of the speed of light, reaching alpha Centauri in a little over
20 years' time, or arriving at Luyten's Star – to which Doug

Vakoch and METI International beamed messages – which is 12.4 light years away, in 62 years. The StarChips, perhaps numbering in their hundreds, will sail through their target system, their trajectories designed to take them close to any interesting planets, and the data they collect will be transmitted back to Earth, giving us our first close-up views of other stars and exoplanets. Admittedly there are still technological hurdles to overcome, not least generating and focusing the laser power, and figuring out how to transmit scientific data collected by the probes back to Earth, but the overall feasibility of the concept seems promising.

Meanwhile, our grand astronomical surveys will continue to produce truly enormous quantities of information for machine-learning algorithms of the type developed by Lucianne Walkowicz to hack away at. Vast amounts of radio-wavelength data will be produced by the Square Kilometre Array (and when I say vast, I mean vast: a minimum of three terabytes per second, and overall ten times more data than the entire global daily traffic on the Internet, amounting to 3,000 petabytes – 10^{15} – per year). SETI experiments are already planned for this giant radio telescope. And, of course, other radio telescopes will also continue their own SETI experiments, bolstered by ever-improving back-end multichannel detectors that are more sensitive and ever more 'frequency nimble', as Seth Shostak likes to say, all thanks to the (so far) reliable Moore's Law.

Closer to home, astrobiologists will continue to look for life on other worlds in the Solar System, in particular on Mars and in the oceans of icy moons such as Europa and Enceladus. NASA has already got a plan for exploring Europa, beginning with the Europa Clipper mission that will blast off for the Jovian system in the early 2020s, with the intention of following it up in the coming decades with a lander and then an ambitious mission to enter and explore its subsurface ocean. Meanwhile, Yuri Milner also has his sights set on Saturn's moon Enceladus, with Breakthrough Initiatives collaborating with NASA on putting tentative plans together for a new mission to fly through the geysers that spew from cracks in Enceladus' icy surface and into space, and which could be laden with biological material from the ocean below the ice.

The discovery of extant life in the Solar System would be a big deal. I've not really dealt with the origin of life in these pages, mainly because it's a topic worthy of an entire book in its own right, but the discovery of even simple life on, say, Europa or Enceladus, would tell us that life on Earth is not a fluke. If microbial life can develop and evolve completely independently on at least two occasions in the same planetary system, it would suggest that microbial life, at least, will be commonplace throughout the Universe. Of course, that doesn't mean life will necessarily be particularly complex or of human-equivalent intelligence, and it certainly does not mean that it will be technological, but on the face of it such a discovery would make us feel more buoyant about our chances of discovering extraterrestrial civilisations. That said, remember Nick Bostrom's words of warning from Chapter 6: the discovery that simple life could be widespread in the Universe, while evidence for more complex life seems absent, could imply that the Great Filter and our own extinction still lie ahead of us. Maybe we've just been lucky to make it this far.

Either way, when all is said and done, our new telescopes and surveys and space missions will mean that by the end of the twenty-first century we will be in a far better position to say whether there is life in any nearby planetary systems. In fact, I'm willing to make a bet with you that if life exists on a planet orbiting a star within 50 light years of the Sun, we will have found it by the year 2100. That's not discounting searches further afield, since it is entirely possible that SETI could have picked up a signal from further away by then, while telescope technology may improve over the next 80 years in a way that allows astronomers to study stars and planets in detail at greater distances.

A plan of contact

Suppose we do find intelligent life in a star system next door. This is where integrating METI into our new SETI strategy will have merit. We must first resist the temptation to immediately send them a message. Before we do, we can observe them carefully from afar by directing our largest

optical and radio telescopes towards them and listening to their leakage. Let's face it, if we find an extraterrestrial civilisation then there will be no shortage of funding made available for studying them. As we observe them, do we see any evidence that they are violent, or do they appear peaceful? How much more technologically advanced than us do they seem to be? For their technology that we could observe the effects of, do we understand what it does and the basic principles of how it works? Is it even possible to understand them? Our knowledge about who is out there will increase by leaps and bounds, and while contact will never be entirely risk-free, we will be in a much better position to then initiate METI and open hailing frequencies so that specially trained diplomats and envoys can make contact on behalf of Earth.

On the other hand, if we do not find any life, intelligent or otherwise, then that is useful information too. It provides more constraints on both the upper limits on the number of intelligent civilisations in our Galaxy and on our subsequent expectations for finding them. We will just have to broaden our search, but METI supporters should not feel that they are missing out on much – if other civilisations are so far away that we would not receive a reply in our lifetimes, then there really should be no rush to transmit on behalf of our descendants, who might not be too happy that we were presumptuous enough to do so.

So when Doug Vakoch suggests that it is pointless to wait to transmit until we know more because we can always try to find out a little bit more, to be on the safe side, that avoids the fact that we can define, right now, what information we will need to know and, more importantly, how we are going to discover that information. No moving the goalposts, no never-ending quest. We search, we find, we observe and then we contact. It's a unified, scientific and responsible strategy for both SETI and METI.

This is my solution to the Contact Paradox. It will require a great deal of patience, but also a determination from ourselves as a species to see it through and learn of our place

in the Universe. Either we are alone in the Universe or we are not. Nobody knows which is the case. If we find that we share the Universe with other life of some form or, even better, with other civilisations, then we would encounter tremendous possibilities, but also greater responsibility to act on the interstellar stage in a way that we hope a more technologically advanced civilisation would act towards us. If other civilisations exist, then they are very likely much older than we are. Their mere presence will encourage us to grow and develop, and to transform our approach by eschewing short-term gains for longer-term thinking, which could ultimately save our planet as we learn to better understand how the consequences of our actions today can ripple through time to what lies ahead. By making the right choices now, we can maintain our civilisation into the future, using the other civilisations that we find in the cosmos as inspiration, just as Carl Sagan suggested to William Proxmire. Whether our deep future will resemble what we imagine technologically advanced societies to look like, with Dyson spheres, interstellar travel and Kardashev civilisations, or whether we shall find ourselves growing into a new and fertile yet unimagined landscape, remains to be seen.

On the other hand, we could be alone in the Universe, the sole spark of consciousness anywhere in the cosmos. If that is true, then it will be a tremendous burden to bear, and a great responsibility. We would be forced into viewing Earth, and all the different types of life living on it, in a very different way. Earth and all its life would have to be protected from existential catastrophe at any cost, otherwise we would face snuffing out the Universe's only experiment of life. Should we succeed and survive, we would stand to inherit the entire Universe.

By doing SETI, by looking into the mirror, we will learn about ourselves and who and what we want our species to be. By appreciating who we are and how we fit into the greater cosmic context, we will ultimately be better placed to face whatever the future has to either throw at us, or offer to us. Regardless of whether that future is a lonely one or not, our adventure is just beginning.

Glossary

Arecibo telescope The second largest single-dish radio telescope in the world, with a diameter of 305m (1,000ft), often used for SETI experiments.

Biosignature Typically a naturally occurring molecule, or the relative abundance of different molecules, which are produced by biological processes and which could potentially be observed from a distance in a planet's atmosphere.

Carbon–silicate cycle The recycling of carbon dioxide from the atmosphere, into the oceans and then the mantle, and then back into the atmosphere via volcanic processes. As a greenhouse gas, the recycling of carbon dioxide acts as a thermostat for Earth's climate over millennia.

Contingent evolution The idea that natural selection results in a wide variety of evolutionary solutions that are never, or rarely, repeated.

Convergent evolution Another view of evolution by natural selection, which posits that evolution repeatedly converges on the same common solutions.

Dispersion As broadband radio signals propagate through interstellar space, collisions with electrons in the interstellar medium slow longer-wavelength radio waves, causing the overall signal to disperse.

Doppler shift The compression and stretching of waves – either light (including radio) or sound – caused by the emitting object moving towards or away from us.

Drake equation A calculation that attempts to estimate the number of technological, communicative civilisations in the Galaxy.

Dyson sphere/swarm A hypothetical megastructure, consisting of a spherically distributed swarm of solar-energy collectors around a star.

Electromagnetic spectrum The entire range of wavelengths (and frequencies) of electromagnetic radiation (i.e. photons of light). The spectrum ranges from radio and microwaves, through infrared and the colours of visible light, and then the shorter wavelengths of ultraviolet, X-rays and gamma rays.

Encephalisation quotient (EQ) A way of comparing relative brain size between species, by comparing the ratio of brain mass to total body mass to their predicted values based on a specific mathematical relation.

Exoplanet A planet outside of our Solar System, orbiting around another star.

Extremophile A microbial life-form capable of surviving and thriving in extreme conditions, be they extreme temperatures, extreme pH, extreme radiation, extreme lack of water and so on.

Fermi Paradox A rhetorical question reputed to have been asked by the physicist Enrico Fermi, along the lines of 'If interstellar travel is possible, why have aliens not already colonised Earth?' The paradox has since been expanded to include the apparent radio silence in the Universe.

Galactic habitable zone The region within a galaxy where conditions – in terms of the right amount of materials and not too many supernovae – are conducive to life developing in planetary systems.

Great filter The idea that somewhere along the various evolutionary trajectories of life, there is some kind of evolutionary obstacle that most life-forms are not able to overcome.

Habitable zone The region encircling a star at a given distance, where the temperature is just right for liquid water to exist on the surface of a world with an atmosphere that is able to maintain that temperature.

Information theory A means of analysing the complexity of the content of a message in a signal.

Kardashev scale A measure of a civilisation's energy use. A Kardashev Type I civilisation uses all the energy available to it on a planet; a Type II civilisation uses all the energy available to it from its star; and a Type III civilisation uses all the energy in a galaxy.

Kin selection A theory of altruism that proposes that life-forms are most altruistic to those with whom they share genes – siblings, children, grandchildren *etc.* – as a way of ensuring their genes are passed on.

Light curve The change in brightness of a star over time, with dips and rises caused by transiting objects, star spots or stellar flares.

METI Messaging Extraterrestrial Intelligence; the act of transmitting messages into space for other civilisations to detect and respond to. Sometimes called 'active SETI'.

Milankovitch cycles Regular cycles in Earth's climate over tens of thousands of years, determined by the Earth's axial tilt, polar wander and the eccentricity and precession of its orbit around the Sun.

Optical SETI The search for laser communication, rather than radio messages, from extraterrestrial civilisations.

Plate tectonics The movement of continental plates in the lithosphere (a planet's outermost shell), which results in volcanic activity that releases heat and, most crucially, carbon dioxide into the atmosphere as part of the carbon–silicate cycle.

Radio waves The radio regime spans frequencies between 300 GHz and 30 Hz (wavelengths of 1mm and 10,000km respectively) on the electromagnetic spectrum. One hertz is one cycle per second; a gigahertz (GHz) is a billion hertz.

Rare Earth The name given to the controversial theory that habitable planets such as Earth are incredibly rare in the cosmos because of what some scientists see as the huge coincidences required to create those habitable conditions.

Reciprocal altruism A form of altruism in which favours are granted based on a quid pro quo basis – you scratch my back and I'll scratch yours.

Red dwarf The most common type of star in the Universe, the smallest and coolest of all stars. Their low temperature means that their habitable zones are very close to them.

Shannon entropy A measure of disorder within the message content of a signal; the greater the disorder, the greater the complexity of the message and the higher the Shannon entropy.

Super-earth A rocky (or icy) exoplanet larger than Earth and with up to ten times the mass of our planet.

Technosignature Some evidence of artificiality or technology, such as a megastructure, pollution in an atmosphere, a radio or optical signal, or even city lights, which reveals the existence of technologically intelligent life.

Transit The passage of an object in front of a star, causing a dip in that star's light curve. Transits are our main method of discovering exoplanets.

Von Neumann probe A hypothetical robotic space probe, quite possibly armed with a sophisticated artificial intelligence, that is able to self-repair and replicate itself by building daughter probes from raw materials found in, for example, asteroids.

Water hole The region in the electromagnetic spectrum between 1,420MHz and 1,666MHz, which are the frequencies of radio waves emitted by neutral hydrogen atoms and hydroxyl molecules respectively. It gets its name because one hydrogen atom coupled with one hydroxyl molecule forms a water molecule.

Zipf's Law Another way to measure complexity in language, by plotting all the components of a language (*i.e.* letters, words, sounds) against their frequency of use; complex communication results in a slope with a gradient of −1.

Further Reading

Introduction: Little Green Men

The story of how Jocelyn Bell's discovery of pulsars was initially thought to be aliens has been expertly told by Alan Penny in his article 'The SETI Episode in the 1967 Discovery of Pulsars' in *The European Physical Journal H* (vol. 38, no. 4, February 2013).

Chapter 1: The Altruism Assumption

Stephen Pinker's somewhat controversial book about increasing altruism in human society is *The Better Angels of Our Nature: The Decline of Violence in History and its Causes* (Allen Lane, 2010).

For a detailed explanation of why human cooperation is relatively unusual in nature, check out Martin Nowak's article 'Why We Help' in *Scientific American* (vol. 307, no. 1, July 2012).

You can learn more about the COMT gene and its possible role in human altruism in M. Reuter et al., 'Investigating the Genetic Basis of Altruism: The Role of the COMT Val158Met Polymorphism', in *Social Cognitive and Affective Neuroscience* (vol. 6, no. 5, 2011, pp. 662–8).

The evolutionary biologist William Hamilton's theory of kin selection is presented in *Innate Social Aptitudes of Man: An Approach from Evolutionary Genetics, Biosocial Anthropology* (Malaby Press, 1975, pp. 133–53).

Raymond Firth described his experiences in Tikopia in his 1936 book *We The Tikopia: A Sociological Study of Kinship in Primitive Polynesia* (reprinted in 2004 by Routledge).

Chapter 2: Intelligence

Andrew Knoll and Richard Bambach talk about evolutionary mega-trajectories in their research paper 'Directionality in the History of Life: Diffusion From the Left Wall or Repeated Scaling of the Right?', published in *Paleobiology* (26 (sp. 4), 2000, pp. 1–14).

Stephen Jay Gould's remarkable analysis of the Burgess Shale is his book, *Wonderful Life: The Burgess Shale and the Nature of History* (W. W. Norton and Co, 1989).

There's a helpful description of the encephalisation quotient in Douglas Fox's *Scientific American* article, 'The Limits of Intelligence' (vol. 305, no. 1, July 2011).

Robin Dunbar's explanation of how sociological problems helped drive the development of intelligence is 'The Social Brain Hypothesis', published in *Evolutionary Anthropology* (1998).

Were dolphins really recorded talking to each other about how to open a container? It's a controversial matter, but the original research into this event is by Holli Eskelinen et al.: 'Acoustic Behaviour Associated with Cooperative Task Success in Bottlenose Dolphins', *Animal Cognition* (vol. 19, no. 4, July 2016, pp. 789–97).

Justin Gregg has written a book about dolphin intelligence and communication, called *Are Dolphins Really Smart?* (Oxford University Press, 2013).

Laurance Doyle's research into the role that information theory might play in SETI is 'Information Theory, Animal Communication and the Search for Extraterrestrial Intelligence', published in *Acta Astronautica* (vol. 68, February–March 2011).

Will machine intelligence supersede biological intelligence? Ray Kurzweil's gigantic book *The Singularity is Near* (Gerald Duckworth and Co, 2005) provides an optimistic view.

Chapter 3: Homeworld

Peter Ward and Donald Brownlee's seminal book *Rare Earth* (Copernicus, 2000) is sceptical about the existence of other habitable planets in the Galaxy.

Following Ward and Brownlee's lead, Dave Waltham's book *Lucky Planet* (Icon Books, 2014) is another sceptical look at planetary habitability.

Jim Kasting's book *How to Find a Habitable Planet* (Princeton University Press, 2010) takes a far more optimistic view of habitability.

To really learn how a habitable planet like Earth is assembled, Charles Langmuir and Wally Broecker's enormous tome *How to Build a Habitable Planet: The Story of Earth from the Big Bang to Humankind* (Princeton University Press, 2012) is essential.

Could life exist on a frozen world like Saturn's moon Titan? Chris McKay and Heather Smith explore this possibility in 'Possibilities for Methanogenic Life in Liquid Methane on the Surface of Titan', *Icarus* (vol. 178, no. 1, 2005, pp. 274–6).

Chapter 4: Interstellar Twitter

The first scientific paper written about optical SETI was by Charles Townes: 'Interstellar and Interplanetary Communication by Optical Masers', *Nature* (vol. 190, no. 4772, 1961, pp.205–8).

Learn more about Shelley Wright's NIROSETI project in her research
    paper, 'A Near-Infrared SETI Experiment: Instrument Overview',
    Proceedings of the SPIE (9147–18, Astronomical Instrumentation, 2014).
Giuseppe Cocconi and Philip Morrison's seminal paper introducing the
    concept of radio SETI was 'Searching for Interstellar Communication',
    Nature (vol. 184, no. 4690, 1959, pp. 844–6).
The concept of Benford Beacons was described by Jim, Greg and Dominic
    Benford in 'Searching for Cost Optimised Interstellar Beacons',
    Astrobiology (vol. 10, no. 5, 2010).
The full story of the Wow! signal and the continued search for it to
    reappear is covered in Robert Gray's book *The Elusive Wow* (Palmer
    Square Press, 2012).

Chapter 5: Galactic Empire

The bible of orbiting space colonies and solar collectors is
    Gerard O'Neill's, *The High Frontier* (Corgi Books, 1978). You might
    also want to check out W. Patrick McCray's truly excellent book *The
    Visioneers* (Princeton University Press, 2013), which details the story
    of O'Neill and his disciples.
Freeman Dyson introduced the concept of Dyson spheres in his paper
    'Search for Artificial Stellar Sources of Infrared Radiation', *Science*
    (vol. 131, 1960, pp. 1667–8).
Neal Stephenson introduces his 'Tall Tower' concept in his short story
    'Atmosphaera Incognita', published in the anthology *Starship Century:
    Toward the Grandest Horizon* (Lucky Bat Books, 2013). Freeman
    Dyson also wrote an essay entitled 'Noah's Ark Eggs and Viviparous
    Plants' about his comet trees idea, for the same collection.
A wonderful book about interstellar migration and its human analogues
    is *Interstellar Migration and the Human Experience*, edited by Ben Finney
    and Eric Jones (University of California Press, 1985).
Could we detect evidence of extraterrestrial asteroid mining? Duncan
    Forgan and Martin Elvis weigh up the possibilities in 'Extrasolar
    Asteroid Mining as Forensic Evidence for Extraterrestrial
    Intelligence', *International Journal of Astrobiology* (vol. 10, no. 4, 2011,
    pp. 307–13).
To blow my own trumpet just a bit: I wrote about colonising, self-
    replicating probes in 'The Interstellar Ethics of Self-Replicating
    Probes', published in the *Journal of the British Interplanetary Society*
    (vol. 67, 2014, pp. 258–60).
Three estimates for how long it would take to colonise the Milky Way
    Galaxy: Michael Hart's timescale of 650,000 years comes from his
    paper 'Explanation for the Absence of the Extraterrestrials on
    Earth', *Quarterly Journal of the Royal Astronomical Society* (vol. 16,

1975, pp. 128–35); Frank Tipler countered Hart's assertions with his
own estimated timescale of 300 million years in 'Extraterrestrial
Intelligent Beings Do Not Exist', *Quarterly Journal of the Royal
Astronomical Society* (vol. 21, 1980, pp. 267–81); and Ian Crawford's
own estimate was 5 million years, as described in 'Where Are They?
Maybe We Are Alone In The Galaxy After All?', *Scientific American*
(2000).

Geoffrey Landis' percolation theory is explained in 'The Fermi Paradox:
An Approach Based on Percolation Theory', *Journal of the British
Interplanetary Society* (vol. 51, 1998, pp. 163–6). Recently, Jonathan
Carroll-Nellenback et al. (including Jason Wright) have attempted
to refute Landis' approach in their paper 'The Fermi Paradox and the
Aurora Effect: Exo-civilisation Settlement, Expansion and Steady
States' (https://arxiv.org/abs/1902.04450).

Chapter 6: Two Clocks

The Clock of the Long Now: Time and Responsibility by Stewart Brand
(Weidenfeld and Nicolson, 1999) describes the motivations behind
the 10,000-Year Clock.

Martin Rees asks whether our time might soon be up in his book *Our
Final Century?* (Arrow, 2004).

Jared Diamond's book *Collapse: How Societies Choose to Fail or Survive*
(Penguin, 2005) is an epic look at the downfall of civilisations from
Greenland to Easter Island.

Did a nearby supernova cause a mass extinction on Earth? Adrian Melott
has explored the consequences that radiation from a supernova that
exploded 2 million years ago may have had on Earth's biosphere in
several papers, but principally in 'Muon Radiation Dose and Marine
Megafaunal Extinction at the End-Pliocene Supernova', *Astrobiology*
(2018).

The Doomsday Argument first found a voice in Australian astrophysicist
Brandon Carter's paper 'The Anthropic Principle and its Implications
for Biological Evolution' (*Philosophical Transactions of the Royal Society
of London* (vol. A310 (1512), 1983, pp. 347–63).

Chapter 7: Messages from Earth

An even-handed look at the challenges of trying to frame the METI
dilemma in a manner in which it can be debated sensibly is
Kathryn Denning's 'Unpacking the Great Transmission Debate' *Acta
Astronautica* (vol. 67, issue 11–12, December 2010, pp. 1,399–1,405).

The specific *Babylon 5* episodes dealing with the misunderstanding at first
contact that led to the Earth–Minbari War are Season One's *Legacies*,

Season Three's *A Late Delivery from Avalon*, Season Four's *Atonement* and the TV movie *In the Beginning*. But just go and watch the whole show – it's a masterpiece of SF storytelling.

Brent Sherwood's paper describing risk assessment in scientific endeavours that potentially harbour ethical consequences is 'Forward Contamination of Ocean Worlds: A Stakeholder Conversation', *Space Policy* (July 2018).

Chapter 8: 21st Century SETI

Tabetha Boyajian's paper about the star KIC 8462852, which caused such a stir with talk of alien megastructures, is 'Planet Hunters X: KIC 8462852 – Where's the Flux?', in *Monthly Notices of the Royal Astronomical Society* (vol. 457, no. 4, 21 April 2016).

General reading

Seth Shostak's book *Confessions of an Alien Hunter* (National Geographic, 2009) is an excellently entertaining look at what it's like to be a SETI scientist.

Although slightly on the dry, technical side, and quite pricey too, *Searching for Extraterrestrial Intelligence: SETI Past, Present and Future* (Springer-Praxis, 2011), edited by H. Paul Shuch, is an indispensable collection of articles written by the field's foremost thinkers.

Michael Michaud's rather thorough tome *Contact With Alien Civilisations* (Copernicus, 2007) was one of the first books I read that really talked at great length about the possible societal consequences of contact.

If you're fascinated by the Fermi Paradox, Stephen Webb's brilliant *Where is Everybody? Fifty Solutions to the Fermi Paradox and the Problem of Extraterrestrial Life* (Copernicus, 2002) provides plenty of ideas to chew over.

Stephen Baxter's *Manifold* series of novels published by Voyager – *Time* (1999), *Space* (2000), *Origin* (2001) and the short-story compilation *Phase Space* (2002) – revolves around many of the themes and ideas that I've discussed in this book. These ideas include the future of life in the Universe, astrophysical hazards to life such as colliding neutron stars, intelligence in other Earth species, the Doomsday Argument and the Fermi Paradox.

Acknowledgments

For Fox, who proves that you don't have to be the same species to be best friends.

The author would like to thank the following people: Gemma Lavender, Stephen Baxter, Paul Gilster, Anna MacDiarmid, Catherine Best, Jim Martin, Jim Benford, Michael Michaud, Marc Dando and all the scientists, academics and researchers who the author spoke to during the writing of this book.

Index

Page numbers in italics refer to 'Further Reading' entries. Page numbers in bold refer to glossary entries.